THE
QUEEN'S
DOG

AN EMPIRE AT TWILIGHT NOVEL

N.L. HOLMES

WayBack Press
P.O.Box 16066
Tampa, FL
⚱

The Queen's Dog
Copyright © 2020 by N. L. Holmes

Empire at Sunset™ 2020

Cover art and map by Streetlight Graphics. Author photo by Kipp Baker.
Quotes from the Ba'al Cycle by Theodore Lewis, found in *Ugaritic Narrative Poetry*, ed. Simon B. Parker, SBL, Scholars Press, 1997.

Quotes from Hittite decrees, tr. Gary Beckman, in *Hittite Diplomatic Texts*, SBL, Scholars Press, 1995

Ugarit

TO KIZZUWATNA

MUKESH

TO ALASHIYA

TO NUHAŠE
AND AŠTATA

APPU   MA'HADU

RAHBANU RIVER

NORTH

THE
CITY

KM 100
CYPRUS

SOUTH

TO SHIYANNU
AND AMURRU

Dedicated to my cousin.

HISTORICAL NOTES

OUR STORY TAKES PLACE ON the northern coast of Syria around 1230 BCE, toward the end of the period we know as the Late Bronze Age. Ugarit, like Amurru, was one of the small but rich kingdoms that managed to stay alive by leveraging their usefulness to the great powers that surrounded them. Despite its importance in its day, Ugarit was something of a "lost civilization", not even known to us moderns until its rediscovery in 1928, resulting in the excavation of the site by French teams. The most important find there was the royal archive, its clay tablets fired and preserved by the conflagration that ended the city. It is this discovery, with its copies of diplomatic letters exchanged with other powers, that has enabled historians to reconstruct so much of the history of the Late Bronze Age and has provided the historical core of our story.

Enviably wealthy by virtue of their overland and especially maritime trade and their manufacture of luxury goods, the Ugarites were over the centuries allied with Egypt, with the inland Syrian empire of Mitanni, and with

Hatti. They had their own Western Semitic (more or less Canaanite) language, and an alphabet of thirty character pressed into wet clay tablets, borrowed from the more ancient Akkadian cuneiform system still used at that time by the Assyrians and Babylonians. Ugarit's relationship to Hatti was that of vassal—semi-independent but owing their imperial overlords obedience, trade privileges, and military assistance. The foreign policy of the day made it advisable for the great powers to avoid direct confrontation, and so they often used their vassals as pawns to attack and weaken one another. Thus the small kingdoms might bargain with the empires for favorable conditions of vassalage by threatening to go over to the enemy.

At just our period, the Assyrians, based in northern Iraq, were rising as rivals to the Hittite empire (Hatti). It was important to their economy to gain a foothold on the Mediterranean coast, and so they began a policy of wooing or even attacking the Syrian vassals of Hatti. Assyria would become the last of the powers left standing in the area in the early Iron Age, after the mysterious collapse that would destroy Hatti and Ugarit and many of its neighbors soon after 1200 BCE, bringing an end to the Late Bronze Age.

The Hittites inhabited a small, barren homeland in northern Anatolia (modern Turkey) but for many centuries, against all odds, administered a widespread empire, thanks to regional viceroys like Ini-tesshub. The origin of the Hittites is unknown, but it was probably somewhere in the Caucasus or north of the Black Sea. Thus they spoke an Indo-European language called Neshite, more closely related to Greek or Latin than to the Semitic languages of their neighbors. Their king, known as the Great King (as distinct from his royal vassals), was considered to be the vicar on earth of the thousand gods of Hatti, and he was expected to rule with justice and clemency, going to war only when unavoidable. Hatti was the only kingdom that represented any real threat to gigantic Egypt in the Late Bronze Age. Unfortunately, strife within the royal family was common, and civil wars and Hatti's dependence on its vassals helped eventually to destabilize it.

Precise dating is almost impossible for this time and place, but by at least some chronologies, all the events of our story may have taken place in the year 1230—although we have no reason to think Ammishtamru was assassinated rather than dying of natural causes. The revolutionary brothers, Ahat-milki's curse, and the divorce—resulting in near-war with Amurru, extradition, Shaushga-muwa's remark about "throwing her in the sea", and the probable execution of the queen—are real events, and Ibi-ranu will really abandon his vassalage to the Hittites for a closer walk with Assyria. Except for the faked correspondence, the letters and decrees read by characters in the story are real. I have adapted the translations of Gary Beckman (*Hittite Diplomatic Texts*, 2nd ed., SBL, Scholars Press, 1995).

All the royal characters are historical. Takhulinu was really the vizier of Ammishtamru. Ili-milku, too, was a real person, and in later life he would finish his poem, which we know still today as the Ba'al Cycle, one of the peaks of Ugaritic literature. In fact, there is no meter in Near Eastern poetry, but I have made use of this western convention to give the characters some way to discuss poetics. Taddu is real, but the documents never name her; she is simply called the daughter of the Great Lady or the daughter of Benteshina.

The figure known as the queen in Ugarit, as in Hatti, held office until death, independent of the death of her royal husband, so that the wife of the king might simply be called the Great Princess until her mother-in-law's death, but I have used the more familiar English terms of queen and dowager queen or queen mother. These women were very powerful, and often served as councilors and regents for their absent son even in his adulthood.

Nahish-shulmanu's Assyrian name and his nickname of Naheshi were indeed found as a scribal signature in the archives of Ugarit, but I have given him a persona. Eunuchs were very common in the ancient Near East, "manufactured" not only for their singing voices, but also to populate the courts of kings and supervise their harems. They were thought to be more loyal than men because they had no progeny to provide for. The disturbance of their hormones before puberty resulted in a range of physical alterations (for example, a kind of gigantism) and health problems, including acute anemia, from which Naheshi suffers in the later chapters. No matter how admired their talents might be, eunuchs were held in contempt as individuals, seen as a third gender between men and women. Theirs was a lonely life.

At one point, Naheshi debates asking for an omen through the practice known as extispicy, that is, the reading of the lobes of the liver of a sacrificed animal, according to a manual of shapes and their meaning. This was an important way to consult the gods' will, both in Assyria and in the Canaanite world.

One might finally mention, in Naheshi's defense, that vengeance was considered a virtuous act in his society.

A GENEALOGY
OF THE ROYAL
CHARACTERS

THE HITTITES

Tudhaliya IV, Great King of Hatti. Son of Hattushili III and Puduhepa, the Great Queen.

Gasshulawiya, queen mother of Amurru, known as the Great Lady, is his older sister.

Ini-tesshub, king of Karkemish and viceroy of Syria. His grandfather and that of Tudhaliya were brothers.

THE AMURRITES

Benteshina son of Tuppi-tesshub, the elderly king of Amurru, dies as our story begins. His widow is Gasshulawiya.

Ahat-milki, the queen mother of Ugarit, is his sister.

Shaushga-muwa is his son and successor, and

Taduhepa (known as **Taddu**) is his daughter. Two older sisters of hers are married into the Hittite royal family.

THE UGARITES

Ammishtamru II, son of Niqmepa of Ugarit and Ahat-milki of Amurru, is king of Ugarit. He is married to Taddu, but also to

Pizidku* of Shiyannu.

Heshmi-sharrumma is his elder brother.

Abdi-sharrumma is his younger brother.

Ibi-ranu is his son by Pizidku. Ibi-ranu will succeed his father on the throne. His sisters are **Dalaptum** and **Apapu**. His brother Niqmaddu has no role in the story.

Utri-sharrumma is Ammishtamru's son by Taddu. His sister is **Batashiya**.

THE ALASHIYITES

Pukanu son of Kushmeshushu is king of the island kingdom of Alashiya (Cyprus). His daughter is married to Heshmi-sharrumma.

GLOSSARY OF NAMES AND TERMS

Ahhiyawa: one or another of the city-states in the area we now call Greece, perhaps Thebes or Mycenae. In Homer, whose *Iliad* probably describes the same period as our story, the Greeks (or part of them) are known collectively as the Achaians (Akhaiwoi).

Alashiya: an island kingdom just off the coast of Ugarit today known as Cyprus. They were nominally allies of Hatti, but never very loyal.

Amurru: a small coastal kingdom of Syria lying somewhat south of Ugarit. Its capital was probably Tsumur, modern Tel Kazel. The kingdom was artificially formed in the fourteenth century BCE by two generation of bandit-kings, who conquered enough legitimate cities that Egypt was forced either to put them down (which it was unable to do) or to recognize them as a vassal. Over time, it became attached to the Hittite Empire.

Anat: the sister of Ba'al; in mythology she is a warlike virgin princess who goes to battle for her brother.

Appu: a coastal headland near the city of Ugarit where the summer palace was located.

Asherah: the consort of Ilu and mother of the gods.

Assyria: a kingdom of northern Mesopotamia (modern Iraq). It began life as a peaceful trading nation, but after its humiliating conquest by Mitanni in the fifteenth century BCE, it began to expand aggressively. At the time of our story, it had just absorbed the last pieces of Mitanni and was considering further westward expansion. The Assyrians spoke a Semitic language known as Akkadian, which was also the diplomatic language in formal exchanges between nations.

Athtar: god of the evening star. He was a male avatar of Athtart, the morning star. Together they represented a deity resembling the Assyrian Ishtar. In mythology, Athtar attempted to usurp the throne of Ba'al and ended up as a kind of vassal to the latter.

Ba'al ("The Lord"): a title of and commonly an alternative name for the god **Haddad** or **Haddu**, deity of storm and rain. He was the king among the younger generation of gods and hence a figure of the earthly king. He resembles the Mitannian storm-god **Tesshub**, whose name occurs in that of Ini-tesshub.

Dagan: the god of wheat and agricultural fertility, in some myths the father of Ba'al. One of the special patrons of the city of Ugarit.

The Gracious Gods: Dawn and Dusk, whose birth is described in a famous poem. (Translation used in the text is by Theodore Lewis, found in *Ugaritic Narrative Poetry*, ed. Simon B. Parker, SBL, Scholars Press, 1997.)

Hatti, or the **Hittite Empire**: a powerful but precarious agglomerate of small vassal states centered in Anatolia (modern Turkey) and including Syria. The Hittites spoke an Indo-European language and had a distinctive culture, but borrowed freely from their neighbors, especially Mitanni.

Hepat: a Mitannian mother goddess, consort of the storm god Tesshub and mother of Sharrumma. Her name appears in that of Puduhepa, Taduhepa, and Niqmepa.

Ilu, which means simply "God" (the Biblical cognate is El). The king of the older generation of gods and father of many of the gods, he was considered one of the special protectors of the king.

Ishtar: Mesopotamian (including Assyrian) goddess of love, sex and war. She is also known by the Mitannian name **Shaushga**—which occurs in the name of King Shaushga-muwa, "Shaushga is mighty"—and at least regionally in Ninuwa as **Nina**. Ninuwa (better known from the Bible as Nineveh) is thus the City of Nina. Although she was worshipped in Ugarit under these names, she also translates into the Western goddess Athtart, or Astarte.

Karkemish: a kingdom of northern inland Syria which was the patrimony of the viceroys of Hatti in Syria. These loyal cousins of the Great King were the immediate superiors of Hatti's small vassals in the area, including Ugarit.

karubu (pl. *karubuma*): the Ugaritic form of a supernatural being shared by the Assyrians and other Semitic-speaking cultures of the time, as well as the Hittites. Karubuma occur in the Bible as *cherubim*. They were winged lions with androgynous human faces, thought to be messengers of the gods.

Kinnaru: the Assyrian god of music. With a lower-case *k*, it is the name for a kind of harp.

Mahadu: the port of Ugarit, modern Minet el-Beidah.

maryannu (pl. *maryannuma*): a Mitannian title that originally referred to the chariot-driving nobility of that kingdom, but which spread throughout the Semitic-speaking West and became synonymous with the ruling class. It seems to be Indo-European in origin, although which branch is disputed, and may mean "warrior."

marz'ikhu: this Canaanite custom, only partially understood, seems to refer to the worship of distinguished ancestors, primarily royal—dead kings were considered to become minor gods— but also, more broadly, aristocratic. The rites were carried out in the context of banquets or drinking parties.

Mitanni: a kingdom of inland Syria and Turkey, which at one point administered an empire extending throughout today's Kurdistan. Although it had just ceased to be an independent state by the time of our story, its cultural and especially religious influence was still strong. The people of Mitanni spoke a language called Hurrian.

Motu: the god of death. His name means simply that, death.

Mukesh: a small coastal Syrian kingdom directly to the north of Ugarit. Conquered by the Hittites some years before our story, it was ruled directly by the Great King's viceroy.

Nergal: an Assyrian god of the underworld.

Ninuwa, or Nineveh: an Assyrian city on the Tigris—not especially large or powerful at the time of our story—that would become one of the empire's capitals in the Iron Age.

qinah: a type of Ugaritic verse. In fact, it does not refer to poetic meter as it does in the story, since Near Eastern poetry did not and does not make use of meter, but it seemed worthwhile to alter its meaning a little to make it more comprehensible to modern readers.

Rahbanu: the largest river in Ugarit.

Rapi'uma: the divinized dead. The earliest, semi-mythical generations of the kings of Ugarit were thought to be Rapi'uma, whose ranks subsequent kings joined upon death.

(Mount) Sapunu or Zaphon: the mountain north of Ugarit where Ba'al was thought to dwell in the clouds.

senet: a board game played by two people, using pieces like checkers; originally from Egypt.

Shapshu: the Ugaritic goddess of the sun and of justice. Her Assyrian cognate was **Shamash**, considered to be a male.

Shulmanu: an Assyrian god who presided over the underworld, fertility, and war. His name occurs in that of Nahish-shulmanu. The same word, presumably with no reference to the god, could mean a diplomatic gift, such as those regularly exchanged among rulers of the Late Bronze Age.

Shiyannu: another small coastal kingdom, directly to the south of Ugarit, between that country and Amurru. Its fate was identical to that of Mukesh. The whereabouts of its capital, **Shubanu**, is still unknown.

Tiamat: In the mythology of Mesopotamia, Mitanni, and the Canaanite cities, Tiamat was the monstrous representation of the primal waters. At creation, she was split (cf. "and God parted the waters" in the Bible) and the land came forth.

Tsaduq: an Ugaritic god personifying justice.

Ugarit (modern Ras-shamra): The setting of most of our story, Ugarit was the name both of a small Syrian kingdom and of its capital city. Its language and culture were part of the larger matrix we would call Canaanite. With a population of about 25,000, it was a heavily maritime state, specializing in trade and the manufacturing of luxury goods, including the purple dye made from murex shells, so dear that its use was limited to kings and their elite. Ugarit provided most of the navy of the Hittite Empire, which gave it a certain power disproportionate to its size.

Yammu: the god of the sea. In mythology, he was defeated by Ba'al, which symbolized the conquest of the waves by man.

Yarikh: the Ugaritic god of the moon.

zaluzi: a kind of song. The term is Mitannian but so were many musical terms of the Near East in the Late Bronze Age, much as Italian dominates the musical vocabulary today.

ziggurat: a high "man-made mountain" built of earth and mudbrick, which supported many temples in Mesopotamia, including Assyria. The Biblical "Tower of Babel" was such a ziggurat in Babylon.

CHAPTER 1

NAHESHI STOOD ON THE PLATFORM of a temple at twilight—whether at daybreak or sunset, he could not say. It was a temple such as he had known in his childhood—a *ziggurat*, a man-made mountain where the goddess might be pleased to dwell on earth—but taller than any building he had ever seen before. Far below him, a bird floated lazily past. Even below that was a market square filled with tiny worshipers, their remote, doll-like faces raised to the platform in expectation. Over his head was only the sky. An unearthly, luminous golden-rose around the horizon shifted to green then to indigo at the height of the heavens. The gods were above that sky, and their ears were bent toward him.

He stood poised for a minute, as if to catch the note struck by an invisible string. He could see himself from the outside—a skinny eight-year-old boy—and yet he was inside himself as well. A note was making its way up his throat, swelling—a sunrise, a life that was more than his own, the song of the gods themselves, the song that created the heavens and the earth. And then the moment came, and he opened his mouth, and the music poured out like that made by the stars as they passed: a celestial, throbbing, melancholy arc of song that was at the same time supremely joyous. His lungs swelled and his throat pulsed with the physicality of the music, yet the sound seemed not to be his own but, rather, descended from above and wrapped around him like an embrace. The voice was not a mere child's but held within it all the sorrow of conquered peoples, fallen cities, and abandoned altars. Nonetheless, it was a song of joy. Tears starred his lashes, yet his heart was bursting with unbearable ecstasy.

The dream faded, and Naheshi's eyelids fluttered reluctantly open.

His mouth was pasty and his face slick with sweat. He slitted his eyes against the glare from the outside. The bumping of the wagon had lulled him to sleep. Under the tented cover, held up into a long half cylinder by wooden hoops, the air was breathlessly hot, but there was a beautiful golden light sifting through the linen canvas. The maids were drowsing, too, their pretty heads lolling. No stream of girlish chatter broke the quiet.

Naheshi grasped in vain at the fleeting shreds of music that echoed in his ears as the dream faded. He could not quite reach it, could not quite make that melody come back to life in his waking mind. Ever since he had left home, which had to have been thirty years before—*Dear gods, can I really be thirty-eight years old?*—the dream had haunted him, unutterably sweet in its promise yet somehow bitter, because he always awoke before it finished. It left him feeling as if he were on the edge of something wonderful and important, a deep and marvelous revelation that would make him truly happy, as he had not ever been. He would willingly have plunged into this dream and never returned... which was far from true for most of his dreams, troubling as they were. The priests said the gods sometimes sent dreams to instruct men. He didn't know, after all these years, whether kindly gods or cruel had sent this one. The disappointment of its abrupt ending made waking life almost physically painful.

Naheshi consoled himself with a dried date slipped from the small bag in his purse. As he chewed and savored the syrupy fruit, he ran over lists in his mind. He had double-checked everything. Nothing was missing, no one left behind. No one hurt, no fights, no illnesses. The one exception was his manservant, Pilsiya, who had disappeared—run away, no doubt, or killed in a brawl in the port. He'd been a decent servant, but though Naheshi was embarrassed to admit it, he hadn't liked the fellow very well. Pilsiya had been silent and efficient, keeping the apartment and his master's clothes immaculate. He had produced excellent meals. He'd been, in short, irreproachable... except that everything he did had seemed sauced with a sort of veiled insolence. Naheshi still smarted from the aggrieved sigh Pilsiya had heaved the night before his disappearance, when Naheshi—the master—had dared to ask his servant's opinion on something quite harmless.

Well, good riddance. The feeling that he constantly had to impress his slave had been tiring. On the other hand, he had to fend for himself until he could find a replacement. As the queen's chamberlain, he could hardly be expected to take his linen down to the washerwomen and do his own shopping forever. Even if he was a slave, he had a certain amount of dignity to maintain. His pauper's style of living did not reflect well on the queen.

The court of King Ammishtamru of Ugarit had spent only a few weeks at the coast this year. Ammishtamru was expected to make the long annual journey to Hattusha to pay his respects to the Great King, whose vassal he was, and he had to be back before the fall rains started. So there they were, in the stifling weather of late spring, a great multicolored procession of wagons and chariots and men and horses, reversing their usual seasonal itinerary. They streamed up the road from the summer palace at Appu, heading northeast back to the city of Ugarit itself. A seagull patrolling the skies along the shore would have seen them shaken out along the dusty white road like a bolt of the finest brightly dyed wool.

Perhaps the queen would go back to the summer palace later if the king's other women chose not to. She didn't like to share the coastal residence any more than she liked to share the king. That would mean a lot of extra work for Naheshi, who was not a bit fond of the sea in any case. He preferred the hot city to the airy summer palace within hearing distance of the surf. In fact, it would be a relief to get back to his snug apartment and his tablets. But the choice was his lady's. It was his greatest pleasure to make himself useful to her.

He must have drifted off to sleep again, because he woke suddenly to the clatter of galloping hooves. One of the mounted couriers who kept watch alongside the royal caravan had pulled up his frothing horse beside the wagon.

"Chamberlain, the queen wants to see you."

"Tell her I'm coming." A sparkle of anxiety raised the

hairs on Naheshi's neck. *Have I forgotten something? Is the queen displeased?*

The soldier galloped away.

"Stop for a moment, driver," Naheshi called through the open front flap of the tent. The man hauled back on the reins, and the long-suffering mules slowed to a halt. Naheshi stumbled up to the driver's bench, groped for a spoke of the wheel with his foot, then slid awkwardly over the edge of the wagon and jumped to the earth with a thud. He heard the crack of the man's whip almost before he'd teetered to a balance, and the wagon rumbled forward again, catching up with the rest of the caravan.

Naheshi hurried through the dust toward the front of the line, avoiding the rumps of pungently sweating animals. At its head were the chariots of King Ammishtamru and his older sons, moving at the slow pace of the foot soldiers who surrounded them. Behind them followed the queen's mule-drawn litter—a long cushioned palanquin of gilded cedarwood, its carrying poles tipped with stylized lilies, its sides veiled with gauzy Egyptian linen. The little bronze bells suspended from the bottom tinkled to the rhythm of the ambling animals. Directly behind came the litter of the king's second wife, Lady Pizidku, and her daughters, followed by that of Prince Ibi-ranu's wife and, finally, the litter bearing the royal concubines. A small face peeked out through the crack in the Lady Pizidku's curtains, and Naheshi nodded respectfully at the girl. Princess Apapu stared back at him, solemn and unsmiling, as he trudged past. He heard over his shoulder her childish voice announcing to her mother, "It's that eunuch of *hers.*"

Naheshi was breathless and his hair was sticking to his

temples by the time he reached his mistress's litter. "My lady," he called several times before the curtain drew back.

Taddu was stretched out on the cushions with her two children, who were sleeping like a pair of puppies, curled up together. The queen took after her father's side of the family: small and slim, with broad cheekbones and a little pointed chin that gave her a foxy aspect.

Her golden-brown eyes narrowed with exasperation. "Shhh, Naheshi," she hissed. The young queen was hot and testy and made no effort to be charming. "Don't wake them up. It's taken me all this time to get them to sleep. Bring me that game board we packed, and tell Ishtar-ummiya to come up here with me. I'm dying of boredom."

"Immediately, my lady." He bowed low to the curtain, which she had let fall again, and retraced his steps to the wagon at the back of the line from which he'd just come. The return didn't take as long as the going, since the train was moving forward slowly, but he barely had the energy to climb back up over the side of the driver's seat. He would never get used to the humidity in coastal Ugarit. He was a mountain boy.

The maids were sprawled over the contents of the wagon, half-asleep in the suffocating heat of afternoon. The one with a single dark brow opened an eye as Naheshi stumbled over the their legs.

"Ishtar-ummiya," he ordered, mopping his face on his sleeve, "up, my beauty. Your mistress wishes to see you right now. Where is that game board?"

"Did we pack the game board?" She shrugged. "I thought it was still on the clothes chest."

Naheshi lifted his eyes heavenward. *These slaves are*

impossible. "Look for it, featherbrain dear. Open some of those boxes you're sitting on. And hurry. The queen is waiting for you. In fact, go on up to her litter. I'll find the board."

Again, the driver hauled back on the reins. The handmaid slid out of the wagon with considerably more grace than her overseer had, and she swished off into the white dust. The driver followed her swaying silhouette admiringly with his eyes.

No grumbling this time. Funny how much appearance counts in the way people treat you, Naheshi thought.

The board, the board—where was it? Surely, he hadn't left it in the apartment. He'd looked around, and he would have sworn he'd forgotten nothing. The queen, already uncomfortable and out of sorts, would be very disappointed in him. Pulling out his penknife, he cut the sealing string on one chest after another and rummaged around, but it was nowhere. The girls exerted only a desultory effort to help. Finally, he gave a reluctant prod to Agipsharri, who was drowsing on the other side of the wagon. Even the thought of touching the disgusting old thing made him shudder, and he knew a scene would follow.

The older eunuch opened one eye and considered Naheshi with bleary distaste. "What is it?"

"The queen wants her *senet* board. It's in one of the other wagons. Go find it, and take it up to her."

"Why should *I* do it, eh? There are plenty of younger people here—"

"You should do it because I, your supervisor, tell you to, you insubordinate dog. Now, move." *And I tell you to go*

25

*because I want you out of the wagon; I don't want you near
me. You reek of pee, and you're always judging me.*

"Oooh!" Agipsharri fluttered his eyes at the maids. "To
find the *sssenet* board, he tells me, our sssupervisor. Will he
ssspank me if I don't, think you, girlsss?"

Naheshi felt the heat rise to his cheeks as if his face had
been suspended over coals. The piece of dog shit was doing
his rankest imitation of an Assyrian accent. Naheshi knew
his Ugaritic was impeccable; everyone told him so. He had
a gift for languages—that was one of the very few things
he could say in his own favor—and he knew he'd never
sounded like that, or at least not for a long time. His tenuous
control over the other servants would be undermined if they
started laughing at him. With his youthful face and natural
timidity, he had no automatic dignity and had to work hard
at looking and sounding authoritative. Agipsharri never let
pass an opportunity to make him appear a fool.

The old reprobate was grinning and looking around
to see what impact his performance had had on the maids.
They were whispering and giggling. "Ssspank you? Yesss!
We want to ssee it!"

Naheshi drew up to his full height and armed himself
with his most imperious expression. If he backed down at
this point, he would never be able to control the vile fellow.
"I'm warning you, Agipsharri. Now."

"Would you care to make me do it, *karubu*-face?"

He always calls me that, curse him. Naheshi ground his
teeth. The *karubuma* were sexless—and well-fed—divine
messengers with the winged bodies of lions.

Agipsharri continued, reveling in his superior's chagrin.
"We all know how you Assyrians just take over whatever you

want. Care to employ a little aggression, eh? Just because I'm old and have brittle bones—"

"Up and out of this wagon, Agipsharri." Naheshi heard his own voice shooting skyward.

"Ooh, catfight!" squealed the maids, fully awake.

By the gods, Naheshi hated such squabbles. They played into everyone's most ridiculous expectations: two silly eunuchs screeching at each other. *Agipsharri has no sense of dignity.*

"I know you don't recognize our mistress as the rightful queen, Agipsharri, but your opinions don't matter. Lady Pizidku herself has accepted in good grace the king's marriage, and I think you—who are, after all, nothing but a slave—should, too. Believe me, it was none of my doing that got you switched to the Lady Taduhepa's household."

Agipsharri had not been the only member of the former queen's entourage to be transferred, but most of them had eventually come around. Naheshi had labored tirelessly to make everyone happy, and for once, his mild temperament had worked to his advantage. He was not so sure that they actually respected him, but they seemed to like him well enough. Still, all it took was one insolent spark for him to lose control of the whole household. The queen would be disappointed in him and angry. He couldn't bear the thought of it. He sat back and tried to breathe calmly while he thought about what to do.

From out of the shriveled old puffball of his face, Agipsharri's small eyes were watching him, a sneer curling up his lip.

Naheshi fretted. *He thinks he has me.* Then with a dull

pang, he added to himself, *Dear gods, is that what I'll look like in a few years?*

Aloud, he said haughtily, "You are the queen's slave. Perhaps I should go see if she would like to have you whipped for insubordination. Or maybe the king would like to hear about how a slave has dishonored his wife's service."

"And you are what, Nahish-shulmanu, eh? Are you not a slave, too? Or are you her pretty little lapdog? Is that it, eh? Are—"

The slap exploded like a thunderclap in the enclosed space of the wagon tent. Naheshi drew back, staring at his hand as if it had acted of its own accord. Agipsharri was too dumbstruck to react. The maids were agog. In the five years he had supervised the queen's household, Naheshi had never laid hands on anyone. He was not a violent person. He was, quite frankly, afraid of Agipsharri and his poisonous tongue. The old bastard probably had the gift of the evil eye. But no one could speak that way about his queen, his dear Lady Taddu, let alone this toad.

"Out! And if I ever hear any words disrespectful of my lady from you again, you'll be cleaning latrines for the rest of your life."

Muttering maledictions, Agipsharri stumbled to the front of the wagon and snarled at the driver to stop. He lowered his vast bulk over the side, rocking the whole wagon as he relieved it of his weight, and stumped off to the vehicle behind theirs, making sure everyone heard his groans and complaints. Naheshi watched him uneasily through the back flap of the tent cloth to convince himself that Agipsharri was really making an effort to find the board. The gods only knew what tale he would carry up to the queen when he found it. She would be angry that he'd taken so long to fulfill her command.

Naheshi opened his purse, pulled out a few dates, and stuffed them nervously into his cheek to chew. He needed a taste of sweet. His good mood had curdled. Just when he felt he had taken care of his duties well, he made a bad decision or did not measure up in one way or another.

Despite his efforts to relax his eyebrows, his anxiety must have shown on his face, because one of the maids said with unexpected sympathy, "Don't mind him. He's just a hateful old prune."

Naheshi managed a smile, spat the pits into his hand, then straightened up and put on his chamberlain expression. "Let's get these boxes tied back up, girls. We'll be back at the palace before much longer, and someone's going to have to carry them."

Moments later, as they passed the quarries that pocked the rocky coast between the road and the breakers, they heard Agipsharri's shrill voice again outside the wagon, demanding that the driver stop. The old eunuch crawled up the spokes of the wheel and heaved himself back into the wagon, tilting everyone momentarily. He stumbled, wheezing like a blown horse, to his spot among the bales.

"*Karubu* face, the queen you wantsss." He grinned insolently at Naheshi. A bright-pink imprint of four fingers shone on his puffy cheek. Naheshi, his heart pounding, braved the driver's annoyance and climbed out of the wagon again, trudging up through the dust and heat to the queen's litter.

"My lady, it's Naheshi," he called in a loud whisper as

he walked along at her side. The curtains flipped open, and the queen confronted him, her eyes blazing and her pretty mouth a downward sickle.

"What's going on between you and Agipsharri? He said you hit him."

"It's true, my lady. I... I slapped him. He was impertinent and insubordinate. Forgive me. I lost control of myself. He defiles your name even to take it in his mouth." Naheshi bowed his head meekly, ready for her wrath, but instead, she burst out laughing.

"Why are you apologizing? He's just a slave; you should have him flogged if he's insubordinate. You know he reports everything to *her*, the evil old spy."

Naheshi realized she meant the former queen. "Lady Pizidku seems to be an honorable person, my lady. I can't imagine she would do any harm, no matter what he reports."

"Stop defending the Old Cow. I think she's put a charm on the king to win him back, even though she's old enough to be my mother." She thrust a silver ewer at him, dangling it by its handle. "Refill this while you're running around; it's so hot, and we're all parched."

"I—"

"Don't wake the children!" The queen pulled shut the curtains in his face.

He bobbed his head. The litter continued to move forward, its bells tinkling, but Naheshi halted and let it pass him by. He trudged back to his own wagon and climbed in again, picking his way unsteadily over the sprawled legs of the drowsing maids to where the tall clay jar of water was wedged among the chests and bales of textiles and pieces of furniture. Naheshi ladled out enough to fill the ewer, splashing his shoes. Then he stopped the wagon, climbed out, and plodded forward again, nearly staggering. With a bow, he proffered the icy ewer to the queen, who took it without a word of thanks—without even interrupting her conversation with Ishtar-ummiya, who was crowing appreciatively at her mistress's story.

As he dragged himself rearward yet again, the king's chariot circled back as well and positioned itself alongside the lady Pizidku's litter. He heard Ammishtamru's growly laughter over the clatter of harness and saw him throw back his head in hilarity, his red beard pointed upward. Naheshi shook his head, saddened for his mistress. It should have been her litter the king sought.

Naheshi called once more for the wagon driver to stop, and the man actually extended a hand to pull him up, grinning with malicious humor. "All your pretty clothes are a mess, eunuch. I hope she smiled at you at least."

Naheshi glared at the fellow, but the driver was freeborn. There was nothing the chamberlain could do to curb his insolence. Naheshi settled himself, hot and exhausted, among the bundles. His stamina was meager; such days drained him. The maids, between sleep and wakefulness, watched him, boredom plain on their faces.

"Abdi-rama." He smiled wearily at the little servant with the long hair in her eyes, who was drowsing beside him. "Do you remember the palace at Amurru? You must have been just a child when we left."

"Of course I do, silly." She flicked his arm pertly with the back of her fingertips. "I'm the same age as my lady the queen. I had just been assigned to serve the king's daughter, as she was then. What a time we all had. Oh-ho! You can't imagine. She was always getting all of us into trouble, the mistress. Oh, there was never a dull moment around her!" She clapped her hands at the delightful memory of their mischief.

"Do you remember the Great Lady? I was her personal secretary."

"Yes, Nahish-shulmanu. You've told us that ten thousand times." She rolled her eyes, but her smile was warm. "I liked her. Everybody did. There was nothing high-and-mighty about her, for all that she's the sister of the Great King. Everybody said she ran the kingdom. Well, she really will soon, I guess, when King Benteshina dies."

"She was like a mother to me." He sighed, remembering her quiet solicitude that had been balm for his lacerated young soul. The good Queen Gasshulawiya, his dear Great Lady. He thought of her as an older woman, although she was probably not that much older than he.

Abdi-rama hooted with laughter. "You sure didn't take after your 'mother'! What a towering bag of bones you were. We used to laugh like anything to see you trailing after her, as tall as the city wall and as big around as a stylus. We called you the Pine Tree."

Naheshi winced. How could she laugh about such a thing? His memories of life in the palace of Amurru, in the service of the Great Lady, were sacred to him. "I was just a boy when I came to Amurru. I was growing into my height. I could never get enough food or sleep—"

"And your bones hurt. Yes, you've told us. And the Great Lady entrusted her daughter to you when she got married. You've told us that, too."

He dropped his eyes, ashamed of his lack of discipline.

The girl patted his hand. "Hoi, Nahish-shulmanu; you're not so bad. A little young to be repeating your stories, but you're a nice supervisor." She rearranged the folded tapestry beneath her head and rolled over onto her side, away from him.

That probably means I'm not hard enough on the girls. I shouldn't let them be so familiar.

The other maids were sprawled over every folded-up cushion and carpet, their skirts pulled up over their knees with no pretense of modesty. Naheshi was too exhausted to rebuke them. He felt he would collapse if he so much as had to wave a hand. Even Agipsharri was spread out on his back, snoring, a toad-like mound of fat. An unsavory sight, but at least Naheshi was spared his mockery for a few hours. He did not understand what attracted people to power. It took too much energy.

Again, the sound of hooves clattered alongside the wagon.

"Chamberlain," came the rider's raised voice. "I have the prince and princess here.

Our lady the queen wants you to take them for a while. She said to tell you she wants to sleep."

The royal children were sitting, one in front of the other, before the soldier, their tunics hiked up and their chubby bare legs sticking out. They reached for Naheshi as he extended his long arms across the driver's seat and lifted Prince Utri-sharrumma, still drowsy and red-faced, under the armpits.

"Here you go, my little prince. Come sit with Naheshi while your lady mama takes a nap."

He set the boy down in the wagon then ferried the

little princess Batashiya over. They were too sleepy even to complain. Batashiya whined a bit and repositioned her thumb in her mouth, but then she and her brother snuggled up next to Naheshi as he settled himself among the bales. They sank back into sleep, the four-year-old prince's little fist clutching a handful of the eunuch's skirts. He watched them tenderly. Their dark curly heads were damp with the heat, their plump faces flushed. They looked so much like his Taddu and her brother when they were babies that it took him back to those happy days in Amurru, serving the Great Lady. He stroked the prince's ringlets. Maybe he himself had looked like that once. Even sweaty, the children smelled sweet, like small animals. They were as hot as braziers against his hip, but he didn't care. His mistress needed a little space in her narrow litter.

Abdi-rama opened one eye, saw the royal children, and smiled before falling back to sleep. Before much longer, Naheshi himself had drifted off, and he didn't even smell the dye works as they passed the port and headed inland up the steep road to the city.

CHAPTER 2

NAHESHI ENTERED THE WRITING ROOM of the chancery and made his way to the long table, where the scribes sat bent over their work. The queen wanted to send a letter to her mother, and he needed to make a good copy from the hastily dictated version. He pulled the reusable wax tablet, in its little wooden frame, from the bag at his waist and unfolded it on the table. There was his rough copy, if he could read his own pigeon tracks; the young queen had changed her mind so many times he had no longer even been able to erase between corrections. He drew a reed stylus from his pen case. Now he just needed to select a blank tablet—or rather, a few. He also had to send orders to several suppliers in the port of Mahadu. Naheshi reached across to the pile of roughly shaped patties of damp clay the scribal servants had prepared for the day's work.

They knew him in the king's chancery both from his signature, which they'd often witnessed during his days as the Great Lady's secretary, and from his frequent appearance as a chamberlain in search of tablets. There were only a handful of scribes at work that morning, but among them was his friend Ili-milku, who waved from across the room and sidled around the long table. They exchanged an embrace, Naheshi stooping to match the height of his stubby friend.

"Well, if it isn't the Tall One! I haven't seen you since last spring. How goes life in the queen's household?" Ili-milku's small brown eyes creased with delight.

"Superbly well, my friend. The queen keeps me busy; she really couldn't get on without me, you know. How are things in the chancery?"

"Oh, same as always. Busy. I've been copying legal documents for the archives until little wedges dance before my eyes at night. You remember what it's like! And I'm not complaining; believe me. I've got a family to feed. But it hasn't left me much time to work on my poem."

The two settled themselves side by side upon their stools and scooted closer to the table with a squawk of wood on tile. Naheshi smiled. "You'll be working on that poem until the day you die, Ili-milku. I swear you must have been rewriting the same few lines ever since I've known you. How far have you actually even gotten?"

The scribe laughed, his whole face crinkling with good humor. Although he was some ten years younger than Naheshi, he could have been the elder of the two by as many years. He was a merry-looking, rounded stump of a man, thick without being exactly fat. His forehead was already rising, foreshadowing a bald middle age.

"Not nearly as far as I wish. I guess I'm a perfectionist. It's such a stirring tale—no credit to me there—that I just get excited working on it. And then it's back to divorce cases. It would be great to be independently wealthy and be able to set my own pace, like"—he lowered his voice and cut his eyes around at the few busy scribes in the room to be sure no one was listening—"well, naming no names."

"There are people who don't work?" Naheshi found something sublimely attractive about the idea of scribal leisure.

"No, no. They work hard enough. But they're always getting pulled out for important duties. You know, diplomatic missions and things like that, not just making copies of documents. Those people own half the country, unlike some of us, whose fathers were just low-level pen pokers." Ili-milku waggled his eyebrows significantly.

"At least you're a free man, Ili-milku," Naheshi murmured.

Ili-milku's forehead crinkled with apologetic chagrin. "Sorry, old man. I didn't mean to be..."

"It's all right. So where are you in the poem?"

The young scribe's eyes brightened as he pounced on the subject he really wanted to broach. "Let's see. I'm to the place where Ba'al Haddu defeats the sea. It's a big scene, and I want it to stand out. I thought of changing meter at this point, putting it into something surging and full of repetition, like the waves. This is a really important story for Ugarites, you know, because we rule the sea."

Ah, yes, the sea. The realm of the god Yammu. The mere thought sent cold, wet fish undulating up Naheshi's spine. He had only sailed once, when the queen had come to Ugarit to be married, but the voyage had left a dreadful memory. His sensitive stomach and the heaving waves made an unfortunate combination.

"Well, I'm an inland boy. I don't know much about the sea."

"True. But you've certainly seen it, here and at Amurru. If you wanted to capture the sound of the sea, what would you use?"

Naheshi pursed his lips in thought. "Maybe a *qinah*?"

"There you are! Why didn't I think of that?" Ili-milku chortled with such glee that several of the scribes looked up at him in disapproval. He made a guilty moue and added more quietly, "That's what I like about you, Naheshi. You have a great sense of the music of things. A *qinah*—of course! Ba-da-da-da-DUM, just like the waves."

There was a moment of stiff silence. Then the poet said enthusiastically, "I want to do it in the general tradition of Akkadian narrative hymns without really copying them. The language is different, of course. You put your verbs at the end and all."

Naheshi remained expressionless, remembering Agipsharri's mocking imitation Akkadian accent.

"I'm thinking this poem might make a terrific hymn—I mean a real sung hymn. Maybe I can present it to the priests of the big Ba'al temple for use on some of Lord Haddu's festivals. Can you imagine—with a whole choir and a boy soprano or two for the heartbreaking parts? It will sweep us all away on a flood of tears!"

"Would they pay you for it?"

"I don't know. But even if they only accept it as an offering, it would be great exposure. Other people, maybe even the king, might hear it and like it and think to commission something from me. The only thing is…" He bit his lip hesitantly. "I need someone to compose a melody for it, a really superior melody full of emotional colors, something that would absolutely reduce the listener to tears. I don't know much about composition myself, just play a little *kinnaru*—a rank amateur."

Ili-milku glanced hopefully up out of the corner of his eye.

Naheshi dropped his gaze and toyed with a tablet, fighting back an urge to change the subject. He said blandly, "Maybe the priests will have a composer."

"No doubt. But I figure it would have more of an impact if I could give them a finished product from the beginning. I was thinking maybe you could... you know, put it to a tune. I'd be willing to pay you."

"What?" Naheshi's head jerked up. "Me? Why do you think I know anything about music?"

"Well, I thought... your kind... sometimes were—"

"'My kind' who? Ninevites? I'm a scribe, Ili-milku. A scribe, like you." He set down the damp tablet he'd been fingering—a movement so abrupt that it flattened the clay. Naheshi sat staring ahead of himself rigidly for a moment then pushed back his stool and stood up. "Look, Ili-milku, I'm sorry. We've had this conversation before. I can't help you."

"Sorry, sorry, Naheshi, old thing. Sorry." Ili-milku's face crumpled apologetically. "You know I meant no harm. It was insensitive, a thoughtless stereotype. I just... by all the gods, how I want this hymn to be a success. You can't imagine how important it is to me. I have a wife and three little children to support on a low-level scribe's pay, and this thing has my whole heart in it. It will show everybody what

39

I'm capable of, you know? It's not that I'm not grateful to work in the palace, but this poem will make me."

Ili-milku laid a pleading hand on the arm of his friend then took it away when he saw Naheshi's frosty expression. The scribe added, half-defensive, half-guilty, "I... I just have seen you copying music tablets, that's all. Maybe they were for the queen."

"You're watching what I write now? Honestly!" Naheshi drew himself up to bluster but then let his pretense of indignation deflate. He managed a wobbly smile of contrition. "I'm sorry, Ili-milku. I didn't mean to snap at you like that. It's just that I don't care to have my private life spied on." *As if*, he told himself morosely, *a slave has any private life.*

"It's fine, it's fine. I'll never mention it again. Still friends?"

"Still friends. I'm honored by your friendship, Ili-milku. I really am."

After a moment of awkward silence, Ili-milku said hesitantly, "Would you like to read my latest draft? Don't feel obliged, if you—"

"Of course, of course. Give it to me when you get a chance. Now, if you don't mind, I do have some letters to write."

"Back to the divorce cases, then. It's enough to make a man hate women!" Ili-milku slapped the chamberlain amicably on the shoulder and sidled away around the table to his place.

With a pale smile, Naheshi watched him go. Then sinking back down onto his stool, he lowered his head over the tablet. He would use this one for an order so the text didn't have to wrap around the misshapen back.

You touchy idiot. That man is your only friend. He drew another tablet toward him and cleaned up the edges with a wetted finger.

⁂

Naheshi made his way down the corridor back toward the queen's apartments, letter in hand, sunk in recrimination over his foolish sensibility. How like him to insult the one person who seemed to care about him. He was nothing but trouble, a walking disaster.

Angrily raised female voices suddenly interrupted his silent monologue. An adult figure and two young girls erupted from the queen's doorway and took a few quick steps away then paused. It was the former queen, the king's second wife, Lady Pizidku, accompanied by her daughters. This was the woman Taddu called "the Old Cow." She was not especially old, but there was something cowlike about her, in the best sense of the word—her movements were slow and graceful, her manner tranquil, her eyes serene, dark, and heavily lashed. Everything about her had a softness to it, from her mouth to her comfortably broad-hipped silhouette. Pizidku bent toward one of the girls. Naheshi could hear her calm voice consoling her younger child, who clung to her waist.

"Dalaptum, darling, she didn't mean to be unkind. You have to remember that her father is dying, and she can't go to be with him. Think how sad you would be if Mama or Papa were sick."

"She didn't have to yell." The little one sniffled.

Her big sister added, "She just isn't very nice, Mama. I think she hates us."

Lady Pizidku didn't answer. She looked up as if in prayer for a moment. As Naheshi bore down on them with his long, ungainly stride, her eyes turned toward him.

"My ladies." He greeted them with a bow. "Can I help you?"

The royal wife smiled her grave smile and stroked her daughter's hair. "No, no. We're fine. We just wanted to express our sorrow about King Benteshina's illness." Her eyes, Naheshi saw, were troubled. His mistress must have said something thoughtless and hurt her feelings. Taddu was a spirited girl; sometimes she spoke without thinking.

"My lady is too kind. I'm sure the queen is grateful, although grief may have made her short." He squatted down beside the girls and fished a bag of pistachios out of his purse. "Perhaps the lady princesses would like some nuts?"

"I don't want anything from *her*..." mumbled little Dalaptum against her mother's hip. Her sister, Apapu, glared at Naheshi as if he were a leper.

"But these are not from the queen. They're from me. And I'll tell you a secret: these are magic pistachios. No bird can resist them. They're guaranteed to bring any bird right to your hand if you're quiet and patient."

"Of course, we would love to have them," said Pizidku. The king's wife caressed her daughters' hair. "My dears, you know we never refuse someone's gift if it comes from a generous heart. A great lady must be willing to receive as well as give." She caught Naheshi's eye with a complicit little smile.

Apapu looked up at her mother then reached out a hand, still thunder browed. Naheshi laid the bag in her palm and closed her fingers over it.

"What do you say, my lamb?" her mother urged.

"Thank you."

Naheshi hoisted himself to his feet and beamed at the three. "Just see if the birds don't come. And I will assure my lady the queen of your good wishes, my lady." He bowed, and the royal wife and her daughters moved away, Pizidku mouthing, "Thank you," silently across the girls' heads.

Naheshi turned to the queen's door. From behind him, he heard Apapu's sullen, "But he's just a slave, Mama."

Her mother murmured, "Slaves are human beings, my dear."

The guard, who had been standing like a log of wood at the queen's door through the entire conversation, avoided Naheshi's eye, his mouth twitching.

＊

Naheshi sailed into stormy weather in the queen's apartment. Her maids were clustered uneasily around the walls, as far away from her as they could get, which probably meant she had been screaming at them. Old Agipsharri watched from the safety of the loggia door.

"Naheshi, here you are at last. How long does it take to find a tablet? I want to add some things to the letter, too." Her face was red and her eyes swollen from tears, her voice raw with anger.

She's just a child herself, far from home, Naheshi thought, his heart melting. He knew what that was like. He could remember only too well the nights he had cried himself to sleep alone as a boy. The queen was the pampered daughter of her father's old age, and now he was dying, and she was far away. Her mother, the Great Lady, who gave strength to all those around her, was by her husband's side every minute, as Naheshi knew from her letters, which he read to the queen. How Lady Taddu had to miss her mother, too. Why, she was nearly an orphan. He felt his own eyes prickling with sorrow for her and for himself all those years ago.

"Forgive me, my lady," he replied. "I am at your disposal now."

"I needed you, Naheshi!" She burst into tears and threw herself into his arms, clinging to his waist. "These stupid girls are no use at all." He swayed there awkwardly for a moment, his flesh tingling, not sure what he dared do with his hands, while she sobbed against him. The maids watched with indecipherable expressions that bordered on amusement. The plump one mimed wiping tearful eyes and elbowed her neighbor. Agipsharri bared his yellow teeth in a sneer.

Naheshi gently disengaged the queen and bent to address her as one might a child.

"Has there been more news from Amurru, my lady?"

"Papa is going to die, and I can't even be there with him," Taddu said, her hands clenching and unclenching in rage. "The Old Dragon says I can't go. She's a cruel monster, Naheshi. All those stories they tell about mothers-in-law are true. I hate her; I hate her! Never ever trust her! She's a demon. It's she who has turned Ammi against me. She twists everything I do or say. If she loved her brother, wouldn't she want me to go to him?" She threw herself onto her bed, pounding the mattress with her fist. A paroxysm of sobbing shook her whole body.

Naheshi glared around at the maids. "You three, make yourselves useful, by the gods. Bring our lady a basin of fresh water to wash her face; bring her some sweetmeats. Go on, shoo. Agipsharri, go do something. Bring a fan."

Having dispersed the servants to their tasks, Naheshi balanced himself carefully on the edge of the bed and patted his mistress's hand. "My sweet lady, the gods have given you a heavy burden to bear," he reassured her, his voice breaking. "The whole court suffers with you. I'm sure the queen mother has her reasons for keeping you here. Perhaps my lord the king needs you to show strength to the country while he is away—"

"Shut up, Naheshi; you're always defending people. She's evil, and you know it." Taddu buried her face in the pillows.

Naheshi hung his head then started again. "Lady Pizidku sends her prayers and wishes—"

"Wishes that I'd drop dead! That old cow! And those daughters of hers—I bet they just came to put some kind of curse on me. Have you seen those eyebrows? No one is going to want to marry them! They're jealous of little Batashiya. She's already prettier than they'll ever be."

Naheshi sought again to change the subject. "Would my lady like me to pay for a sacrifice for the Lord Benteshina's health up at the temple?"

"Yes, yes. Make the gods spare my father, Naheshi. Don't let them take him." Her rage dissolved into tears, slicking her cheeks and blurring her kohl-rimmed lids into dark slices of plum. Taddu did not often find herself powerless, but death did not heed even a princess's orders.

Naheshi lifted her hand to his lips and kissed it respectfully. "I go to do my best, my lady. Be brave. You come from a race of great kings. Are you hungry? Can I bring you something to eat?"

"Gods, no. All you think about is food. Just go to the temple for me. Beg Ilu, protector of kings, to have mercy on my papa."

Naheshi bowed his way out. As he descended the stairs, he realized that in fact he *was* thinking about food. He fumbled in his purse for his little bag of pistachios, but then he remembered they were no longer there. He crossed the street and set off to the temple of Ilu, still savoring the perfume of the queen's childlike hand beneath his nose.

⚜

That evening, Naheshi dismissed the day-shift servants and sent a page down to order the queen's dinner as usual. The night maids came, but the queen, deeply subdued by her grief, ordered them all out into the garden for the evening.

"You stay with me, Naheshi. I don't want those stupid girls around, laughing and acting silly." Taddu was sitting in bed with her linen night shift on and her hair loose, propped against a profusion of brightly colored cushions.

"Of course, my lady." *There's nothing to go home to anyway.* If he wanted a proper dinner, he would have to go down to the kitchen himself.

Silence filled the room, broken only by the whistling wings of a dove settling for the night in the garden outside. The curtains at the long windows of the loggia fluttered briefly in a moment's breeze then lay still with a sigh, while between them, the evening light pooled on the floor, as thick and golden as honey.

When the queen spoke, her voice was small and pensive. "Have you ever lost a loved one, Naheshi?"

Me, he thought. *I am lost.* But he replied gently, "No, my lady. I can only guess at your pain."

"Everyone says I'm just like Papa. We've always understood each other very well. We're lively and adventurous. We used to go riding and hunting together, just me and Papa and all those men, and sometimes the two of us would ride off together in his chariot and leave the others behind. It used to make his servants furious, but what could they do? He was the king, after all. He used to put on funny clothes, with things over his head, and burst into the nursery, roaring like a lion. Even when I was tiny, it didn't scare me at all like it did my sisters. I would scream with laughter."

There was another long silence. She gave a secretive little smile, sinking into her memories. "I can't imagine the world without him in it somewhere," she murmured. Then her lip thrust out. "I think Mama despairs of me ever becoming proper and boring like her."

"My sweet lady, your mother is a great statesman. Both your parents were needed to rule Amurru according to the gods' will."

She patted the bed beside her, and he sat down, careful not to touch her. "Rule, yes," she said. "But by all the gods, Naheshi, isn't there more to life than ruling? Does a person have to be so serious all the time? Can't there be a little excitement to life, too? I feel like I'm drying up and blowing away here in Ugarit. My revered mother-in-law won't let me do anything fun. Work, work, work; that's all she wants me to do, the Old Dragon. She just wants me to be old and boring like her." The queen's mouth drew downward in a crescent of resentment. "Naheshi, I think she's jealous of me because *she* wants to control her son. Ammi used to love me; he'd come to my apartments all the time, remember? Then he stopped. Why? It's not as if I've suddenly gotten old and fat, or pockmarked. Don't tell me he's not seeing *someone*. I'll bet it's that cow Pizidku. She's as old as my mother, for love of the Lady Shaushga. I'll bet the Old Dragon told him not to visit me anymore." Her amber eyes flashed. "How dare she! He's my husband, for Shaushga's sake."

"My lady is a beautiful and desirable woman," Naheshi said. "I'm sure that if the king doesn't come anymore, it's not because she doesn't please him."

Taddu leaned forward with a deep sigh and hugged her knees. Her small heart-shaped face tilted toward his. "Am I? What good is being beautiful if there's no one to… respond to that beauty? Maybe you don't know what it's like to be lonely, Naheshi. Everybody here hates me. I'm all alone. It's not just that I want more babies from the king—I want him to look at me with love, to talk to me, to… touch me. I want him to be a husband to me. How's a woman supposed to live with no one to love her? How is she supposed to know if she is desirable if no one desires her?"

"My lady's children—"

"It's not the same." She gazed at him, eyes bright with sudden curiosity. "Poor Naheshi. I guess you have no idea, do you?" An embarrassed silence settled upon them. "What's it like, Naheshi?"

"Like?" He shifted on the edge of the bed in a rush of acute discomfort.

"Being a eunuch."

Naheshi managed a strangling swallow and, after several efforts, answered with a forced smile, "I couldn't say, my lady, because I don't know what it's like *not* to be one."

"What do you mean? Weren't you a man once? How did it all happen, Naheshi? Tell me what happened."

Naheshi felt as cold as if a north wind had suddenly swept up under the skirts of his tunic. This was not a place he wanted to go; it was a room he kept scrupulously sealed against anyone's prying. But then the queen had never, in the five years of his devoted service, showed the slightest interest in hearing about his life. No one had, not even the Great Lady—although perhaps she was driven by discretion and respect for the fragile state he'd been in when he'd come to her. He felt sure Lady Taddu had been curious before—she clearly valued him—but he was a slave. Who ever asked about a slave's life story? His dear, dear mistress. Did she really care about his past and the burden of misery he carried? The very thought filled him with such a boiling mixture of emotions that he felt he might choke.

"My lady, surely you are not interested in these things. They… they happened so long ago, and I am just a slave."

"No, no. I want to know. You've been part of my life as long as I can remember. Where are you from? How did you get to be a slave?" She took his hand and clasped it warmly in her small ones, smoothing the knuckles, playing with his rings.

Naheshi shivered with a visceral thrill that lay somewhere between anguish and delight.

"Tell me, Naheshi."

"Well, my lady, I was born in Ninuwa, in Assyria. My parents were poor servants of the temple of Nina—Ishtar, that is, or Shaushga, as you would call her here."

"The goddess of love! You see how romantic your story already is?" She wriggled with excitement, inching closer.

"I... I could sing. I had a beautiful voice as a child. Everyone said it was like something that came down from the gods." He closed his eyes for a moment, struggling to go on, but it was worse with his eyes shut because then he saw himself, a skinny child with enormous eyes, his mouth open wide, and he could almost hear the music, the music...

He continued in an increasingly small, unsteady voice. "My parents were very poor, and when a great lord offered to buy me and train me to sing for the king in Asshur, they were delighted to get so much money. That would be the end of their debts. And of course, to think that I would be famous and have the king's favor—"

"That was nice, wasn't it?"

He was forced to pull a hand free to wipe his face, which had begun to trickle with icy sweat. "But to keep my beautiful voice, I had to be... cut, or else I would lose it when I grew up."

"I see." She grimaced. "That's not so nice. So they did it. How—no, don't answer that."

"They did. But... it didn't work. I lost my voice anyway."

"What do you mean? What happened?"

"I... I don't know. I guess I was never really as good as they thought I would be. Or maybe I couldn't stand up to the training, which was intense. But whatever the reason, within a few years, it was clear that I would never be a great singer after all. I got worse and worse. My voice was barely even ordinary; I could hardly croak. Everyone else had passed me right by. I buried my little statue of Kinnaru, the god of music, facedown in the courtyard so I'd never have to see him again, and... I never sang another note." Something dark and sharp edged pushed its way up inside his chest, lacerating him as it came. He had so wanted to please, but he just hadn't had it in him—he wasn't good enough; he had disappointed everyone; he was a failure—and Naheshi prayed that he would not break down completely in front of his queen. She was peering into his face very closely, and he dropped his head so that his hair covered his trembling lips from her sight.

"Poor Naheshi. How old were you?"

"Nine. Thirteen when it all ended." His master's words still echoed in his memory like the discordant clash of a fallen harp: *What do you mean, "he can't sing"? What about my investment?*

"And then what?"

"My master had me taught to be a scribe. I served him for five years, and then he gave me as a diplomatic gift to your mother, the Great Lady, to be her secretary. He was an ambassador and had come to your court."

The queen leaned toward him across her knees and lifted his chin with the tip of a hennaed nail. Her eyes were curious but not unkind. She swept his face with her gaze. "I

51

wonder what you would have looked like as a man. I think you would have been very handsome."

Naheshi felt a tear escape from his eyelid. He managed a smile. "But if I were a man, I would not be in my lady's service."

Taddu reached up and wiped off the tear with the side of her finger. She put the finger into her mouth and sucked it, her eyes sweeping Naheshi's face with feline curiosity. She swung her legs aside and slowly put her arms around him, her head barely coming up to his breast.

"Poor Naheshi. So you do know what it's like to be sad."

He nodded, unable to speak, his hands hanging at his sides.

"Haven't you ever wondered what it's like to touch a woman, Naheshi?" she murmured into his chest.

"I... I..." *You,* he thought; *only you have I dreamed about, my dearest lady—what it would be like to touch you.* He was gasping like a beached fish, terrified of misinterpreting her intentions and inflicting upon himself a mortal humiliation. He scarcely dared to believe what seemed to be happening.

She pushed him down on his side next to her and snuggled against him, her eyes burning into his. His skin seemed to catch fire; her body was like a furnace, an incense burner, releasing her fragrance, compounded of styrax, flowers, and her own salty animal odor. Naheshi could barely swallow. He lay against her, stiff and fearful, his nipples tingling. He was aware of how his increasingly ample belly sagged sideways when he lay on one shoulder.

She would find him slack, unmanly, and disgusting. He would die of shame if she recoiled.

Finally, the queen picked up his hand and pulled it around to her back—his virgin hand that had only ever held a stylus. "We're both alone, Naheshi. We're both far away from home."

"Yes, my lady," he whispered. "Should we be doing this? I... I—"

"I just want someone to touch me!" Taddu cried. "My father is dying, and people sneer at me. I want someone to love me. I don't want to be alone."

Fear burst inside him like a boil, and relief too powerful to bear flooded through him. Naheshi clutched her to his chest with all his strength, his shoulders shaking with silent sobs; he couldn't help himself. She wanted him to touch her! Through how many lonely nights had he dreamed of being able to lay a hand on those shining tresses.

He buried his face in her long, wavy locks, kissed them tenderly as one might a child's, sniffing their perfume, then tipped her face up to his and kissed her forehead. Oh, the ecstasy of it—the touch of a human body, the smooth, living ivory of her brow beneath his lips. He reveled at the nearness of her—those eyelids edged with kohl, and the flutter of those perfect lashes against his love-starved cheek.

She grabbed his curls and forced his mouth hungrily to hers. He could have eaten and drunk her. He could hardly breathe; he was starving, suffocating. She was his food; she was his air. Her small hands raked his back, and he wept for joy. He felt her breasts through the thin linen of her shift; she was pressing her body urgently to his. Her leg was over his hip, locking them together. There was no revulsion on her face; she understood the cruel parody of a man that he was, and she still wanted him. There was music in him again. His very flesh sang. He was remade; his body soared, all at once a blessing and not a curse. She licked his face of its tears, and he buried it against her throat, down between her hair and her shoulder, breathing in the warm, perfumed skin, thrilling at the pounding of her pulse, the percussion of his new beatitude. He rolled over on her, oblivious to the lumps of his tablets and seals between them. He felt he could consume her, devour her. He could never be close enough to her. His lips followed the delicate arc of her clavicle, moving into the warmth and softness below, the secret cleft of her armpit. Oh, to be an infant again and really to drink her in. His being and hers had to merge to end the terrible loneliness.

Her arms encircled him; her face was upturned to his, her lips parted. He followed them with his own, like a fledgling receiving life from its mother. It *was* life: this was his birth from the cold darkness of all that had gone before. He kissed her lips, her cheeks, and her brow again and again as if he might consume her, his own cheeks slick with tears. She burrowed her face into his hair and licked his ear, and Naheshi's heart ignited at the intimacy of her touch. She loved him. He willingly gave over to her his most secret core, for once in his cowardly life fearless, because she was his safety. In all the tragic universe of broken human beings, there was no paradise so sweet and safe as her soft and perfect little body, her love. *Yes, yes!* She wanted him. He felt as if he would simply burst into flame with the ecstasy of being loved.

A knock sounded at the outer door of the apartment.

The queen pushed him back with an oath and swung her legs under the covers. Naheshi jumped up from her body, from the bed, from his bliss, his thoughts in total disarray as if he'd been awakened suddenly from a dream. He tugged at his disheveled clothes, ran his shaking fingers through his hair, dusted the queen's bedcovers where he had kicked with his shod feet. Without daring to look at Taddu, he rushed to the door, breathing raggedly, his heart pounding, his face aflame. He put on his best imperious expression as he loped across the antechamber and swung open the heavy leaf of the outer door. There stood the page with the queen's dinner.

"I'll see to it that my lady the queen gets it." Naheshi took the tray and shut the door, waiting while his heart slowed down. He took a deep breath then another, trying to control the grin that split his face.

He bore the tray back to the bedchamber, where Taddu had set herself into a semblance of order and was modestly sitting up under the bedcovers, her hair spread out over the cushions. She was smiling, but he couldn't meet her eyes.

"Your dinner, my lady."

"Thank you, Naheshi."

"My lady... forgive me. I... forgot myself..."

"You have to obey me, Naheshi." Her little-girl voice was faintly sly. "And now, since I'm in so much better a mood, bring the girls back in, won't you?"

He bowed, turned to the balcony door, and called to the maids, whose laughter and shrieks from the dusky garden proclaimed their whereabouts.

"Will that be all, my lady?"

"Yes, Naheshi. Good night."

He was almost to the door when she stopped him. "You know what, Naheshi?" The queen looked up at him from under her lashes, a sly little curl at the corner of her lips. "You have dimples when you smile."

"Yes, my lady." He bowed and left, still grinning.

⬥

Naheshi floated back to his apartment without seeing a thing around him. His heart was filled with dulcet song— the refrain from "The Birth of the Gracious Gods." *He bows down to kiss their lips. Ah, their lips are sweet! They are succulent fruit!* The glorious verses washed over him like the light at dawn, suddenly full of meaning. Succulent, yes—sweet, satisfying, nourishing. Her lips were like the rich juice of a fig, dribbling comfort into his famished soul. Oh, how had he not known! He had never in his pitiful, truncated life kissed anyone since he was taken from his mother at the age of eight.

He unbarred his door with unsteady hands and let himself into the emptiness of the apartment. Oblivious to his surroundings, he stood for a moment at his long window, grinning, tingling with the golden memory of the last few minutes. He closed his eyes and felt again the queen's perfumed hair with its heavy, silken weight; he felt her hands on his face, her warm little body against his chest, and the intimate heat of her tongue in the shell of his ear.

He knew it was hopeless to think this evening's taste of paradise would ever be repeated. There were laws against it, in fact. But they hadn't meant anything improper; it was just a realization of how they shared the loneliness of foreigners in a strange place. Life was so short, and everyone was so alone. This had to be why people made babies—to perpetuate themselves in the face of death. And he, who had no hope of progeny—was love completely forbidden to him as well? When he died, there would be nothing at all left of him, just an empty place left behind, a missing piece of the world in his odd, elongated shape. There would be no family tomb, no children and grandchildren sacrificing in his honor. He would be gone, gone. If there were to be any joy for him at all, it had to be here on this earth; the gods couldn't be so cruel as to forbid those few moments of innocent pleasure. No, pleasure wasn't even the word. A good meal was pleasure; an evening on the breezy roof after twilight was pleasure. This was... life? Truth? Affirmation that he wasn't a bad, useless, failed, cursed monstrosity after all? Salvation?

Something so beautiful could not be wrong.

He needed to get some dinner but couldn't make himself go down to the kitchen and break the spell of happiness that hovered over him. He could still smell the queen's perfume on him and feel her tongue on his face, her fingers in his hair. She had not been repulsed by his appearance or disgusted by the story of his shame. She... he dared not say it even to himself, lest the gods take it away. And so he said instead—silently, in his heart, which had become her altar—*I love you.*

CHAPTER 3

T HE NEXT DAY'S COURIER BROUGHT word that, against all expectations, King Benteshina was still hanging on to life. Taddu was morose; nothing seemed to hold her attention for long. The servants all walked softly, never knowing when she would flare up against them. Vases had been hurled, their flowers strewn around the floor, and lunch pushed unceremoniously off the tray with a sweep of the royal hand.

"Naheshi, I want some distraction until we find out if the Old Dragon will let me go back to Appu. Find me something to do." There was misery in her knotted brow.

"Perhaps my lady would like to sit in the garden. Can I bring some dancers for my lady?"

"I want a singer, that boy from Qode. I can forget myself in his voice."

A boy singer? Naheshi stiffened and bowed, hoping his unease didn't show. A boy singer? Was she testing him, or had she forgotten everything he'd revealed to her in that moment of sublime weakness?

"Yes, my lady." He left the apartment and headed

toward the king's apartments with the intention of talking to Ammishtamru's chamberlain about the young performer. Then he remembered that the official was with the king in Hattusha. Well, Ammu-rapi, the head of the royal musicians, could tell him where the lad holed up. Naheshi would also need a harpist, anyway. He wondered what songs were appropriate for the queen's present mood. Melancholy songs about the brevity of life, or something livelier to distract her?

"You there, eunuch. Where are the queen's apartments?"

He looked up, surprised. Two foreigners, dark-skinned and richly dressed, stood before him. One had a patch over his eye. The elder, a somewhat-fierce-looking white-bearded old fellow, blocked the corridor. Behind him, the one-eyed man bore an armful of luxurious boxes.

Merchants. Naheshi drew himself up and crossed his arms, putting on his most intransigent guardian face. "Why do you gentlemen have no escort? You shouldn't be in the private area, wandering around."

"Our soldier got called away and left us standing here," said the elder of the two. "We want an escort, believe me. This place is a labyrinth. No one who wasn't raised here could possibly find his way."

"We came to present our king's gifts to the queen mother, and she suggested that the young queen might be interested as well." The younger man flashed a brilliant smile.

Or maybe diplomats. It was never clear where trade goods left off and royal gifts began in Ugarit's mercantile court. But surely, this sort of exchange belonged in public, not in the queen's private quarters. Or maybe not. Naheshi realized he didn't know as much about protocol as he should. Once again, he felt out of his depth. He did not want to offend them or their king. He eyed them uncertainly, trying to decide what to do. They spoke flawless Ugaritic with an upper-class accent.

"Where are you from?" Naheshi demanded.

"Alashiya. King Pukanu son of Kushmeshushu is an old friend of your royal family. We're relatives of his."

"Very well. But I will escort you. I'm the queen's chamberlain." It occurred to Naheshi that this might actually be just the distraction his lady craved. She was fond of beautiful things.

He turned around and led the way back to the queen's apartments. In the antechamber, he bade them wait while he spoke to his mistress.

"You have the singer, Naheshi?" she demanded as soon as he entered.

"No, my lady." He hurried to add, "But I happened to encounter some Alashiyite diplomats in the hall who were seeking you at the queen mother's instructions. They have gifts from their king."

"Ah, that sounds entertaining," she said, brightening. "Send them in."

Naheshi admitted the two with a nod, gracious but chilly. They entered and bowed low before the queen.

"We come from Pukanu of Alashiya with gifts for the ladies of King Ammishtamru's household—" began the elder.

"Fame of your beauty has reached even our distant island, my lady." The younger diplomat stepped forward with his caskets and ranged them neatly upon her table. His dark eye crinkled with a winsome smile. There was something irresistibly charming about him, Naheshi had to admit—a kind of instant intimacy that made one feel compelled to admire his goods for fear of hurting his feelings. Naheshi found he disliked the man's easy, ingratiating manner right away. The queen, on the other hand, simpered adorably.

The Alashiyite opened a small ivory-inlaid box and exposed within a necklace made of gold and amber beads. The amber, imported from who knew how far away, was cut into the shape of little transparent golden leaves, alternating with images of Ishtar, the goddess of love, sex, and war, her naked body confronting the world without shame. It was exquisite. Naheshi heard the queen draw in her breath. He drew in his as well, remembering his sublime epiphany of Ishtar.

The young diplomat leaned toward the queen, the necklace in his outstretched hands. "Permit me to place it around my lady's neck—"

"Permit *me*, my lord." Naheshi interposed himself, snapping out of his delicious memories. "We have standards of propriety at this court." The irony of that statement did not escape him.

"As you will, my loyal fellow," said the diplomat, drawing back with a grin.

Naheshi reverently laid the queen's veil and braids in front of her shoulder and clasped the collar behind the slender column of her neck, careful not to dislodge her cylindrical cap. Delicate hairs uncaught by the braids curled downward over the almond skin and made a point over her vertebrae. The smell of her perfume drifted upward from her warm flesh. He offered his mistress her polished-bronze mirror to admire herself, and she turned back and forth to enjoy the full impact of the subtly colored jewels.

"I love it! Have you anything else?" She gazed at the other boxes. The elder diplomat opened a small cedarwood casket and unfolded a length of fine linen. Within was a pair of eardrops in the form of palm trees with tiny dates made of lapis lazuli. The queen gasped greedily. The gold and blue of the jewels were stunning; the detail of the miniature trees, which were no bigger than the joint of a man's thumb, was superhumanly fine in its execution. The younger diplomat lifted one eardrop between his fingers and offered it to her. The queen unhooked her own earring. Her eyes met the diplomat's, and his fingertips brushed hers as he laid the jewel on her palm.

Naheshi felt ice stealing over his face like frost. Did he dare to feel possessive of the queen? She had never met this insolent foreigner before, but there was an unmistakable spark: they were tinder and fire stick. Naheshi's heart shriveled.

"Naheshi," purred Taddu, "do go fetch that singing boy. It would be wonderful to see these jewels to the sound of beautiful music."

"Ah! One beauty capping another!" cried the younger diplomat, his white teeth sparkling in an enthusiastic smile. "Such sophistication!"

The queen laughed archly. Naheshi bowed, scarcely able to control the scowl contracting his brows. He couldn't prevent himself from saying, "If my lady thinks it appropriate to be left alone in the company of strangers..."

Her voice grew sharp. "You don't own me, Naheshi. I am an adult, and I will do what I like. Is that clear? Fetch the singer. I told you to get him a long time ago, and where is he?" She turned back to the diplomats with a conspiratorial little shake of the head as if to say, *These slaves.*

Naheshi retreated, his face aflame.

Nearly an hour later, he returned, the musicians in tow. The diplomats had departed. The young queen was still preening before her mirror, new jewels at her throat. Her face was dreamy and excited. All the languor and gloom of the past few weeks had fled. She was on fire, transfigured. Naheshi, on the other hand, was sweaty and out of breath and very much out of sorts. He set the musicians up on the loggia so they could be heard and not seen, and then he left for other tasks. He did not want to listen.

Ahat-milki, the dowager queen of Ugarit, was acting as her son's regent in his absence, as she had since the beginning of his reign and, indeed, during that of his father. At the moment, she paced up and down her office with the tense fury of a lioness, and the prey she wanted to savage was her daughter-in-law and niece, Queen Taduhepa. The court had only just returned from the summer palace at Appu, and Taddu already wanted to return.

Is she unaware of all the duties a queen has to perform, even—especially—when her husband's out of the country? Ahat-milki huffed, shaking her head until her earrings clacked. *She seems fond enough of the perquisites of queenship but not so interested in the duties. By the Lady Anat, protector of royalty, the damned girl was brought up a princess. How can she be so irresponsible? She would do well to show a little more interest in the welfare of the kingdom.*

The dowager pivoted on her toe and stalked down the length of the room again. *She seems to think she has discharged her duty to her adopted country by producing three children in five years and is now free to fritter away her days in laughing and playing and gossiping about the court. What if the other two should die the way the last little girl did? Take away her children, and she has nothing to show for herself.*

Ahat-milki took a deep breath and tried to calm herself, without success. "How did my brother raise such a feckless, immature child?" she barked. Had Gasshulawiya, the very image of hardworking probity, conveyed nothing about the responsibilities of queenship to her daughter? The girl was no longer a child. She was twenty, by the Gracious Gods. Ahat-milki looked down at her clenched hands, knobby and veined. She herself was an old woman. When she died, could Ammishtamru count on his young queen to rule the country in his absence as he now counted on his mother? Her beloved husband, Niqmepa—*may he rejoice among the Rapi'uma*—had also counted on her. That lovely Pizidku, Ammishtamru's first wife—a mature and gracious woman with grown children all ready to take over when their father died—had been pushed to the side. What a regent she could have made, always so prudent and thoughtful. Ahat-milki had been delighted when Ammi married that wonderful woman, but of course, Pizidku was no longer the queen and her handsome, well-bred son no longer the heir. That was the price of being from a kingdom that had ceased to have an independent existence. No matter how much Pizidku's husband might love her, she was of no political advantage to him anymore—or to the Great King.

Ahat-milki sighed with the force of a small whirlwind.

That meddling boy in Hattusha, their Lord and Sun the Great King of Hatti, was to blame. He was the overlord of the two small kingdoms of Ugarit and Amurru, her own homeland. Like every ruler, his objectives were selfish. It was in his own interest to bind Ugarit and Amurru again in this generation, even as her own marriage with Niqmepa had bound them in a former. But not being there with her, he took no account of what his actions did to her adopted country, her Ugarit, her family. Luckily for everyone, Pizidku was the perfection of self-effacing obedience. Otherwise, they might have had a revolution—another one—on their hands when the Great King decreed that Ammishtamru should marry an Amurrite princess and make her queen in Pizidku's stead and her Amurrite son his heir.

And that, of course, was what silenced her anger. If it had not been for the meddling boy in Hattusha, her son would be king no longer. He would be dead, sitting among the Rapi'uma with Niqmepa and his ancestors. That was what it meant to be a vassal. You gave and gave, and then every so often, you got a little something back.

Just put Taddu out of your mind. You're on edge because the news from Amurru isn't good.

Indeed, reports of her brother's failing health had taken a turn for the grim. The messengers kept the southern road hot, galloping back and forth as each day brought a change… but always a change for the worse. She cast her eyes out the window automatically as if she could spy a horseman already clattering up to the palace gate. But of course, all she could see was the paved courtyard below and the square white roofs of the city, like crystals of salt, clustered down the hillside and, beyond them, the glittering black sea.

Once, a very long time ago, she'd been a little girl in Amurru, and her brother, Benteshina, had been a handsome, laughing adolescent who teased her and pulled her braids. Even then, she'd been an imperious little thing, she remembered with a twitch of the lips. She had known how to bend people to her will, using every wile of the glib tongue and striking face, the calculated pout, and the reward of the smile. But in time, Benteshina had become king, and she had been married off to Niqmepa son of Niqmaddu, the ruler of neighboring Ugarit. The whole of her loyalties had gone with her; that was the way it was. She'd sat beside her husband on his throne and set all her strength of will to the good of his kingdom. He had been a just and able ruler, but she'd been the one with the vision. How could a little nation like Ugarit, with a small army, achieve power and keep its independence among the colliding giants? Careful diplomacy, careful marriage alliances, careful treaty terms, and careful leveraging of trade rights. Nothing could be left to chance.

Now Benteshina was dying, and she was old. Soon young Shaushga-muwa would replace his father on the throne of Amurru, and Benteshina's daughter was queen in Ugarit. *Taddu again.* Ahat-milki could not keep her anxious thoughts from that girl, because everything depended on her. Taddu would need to maintain those oh-so-careful relationships with the local nobility and with the rulers of other nations that Ahat-milki herself had labored a lifetime to construct. After five years of marriage, the immature creature had yet to write a single letter to the Great Queen of Hatti—her own grandmother—or to her counterpart in Egypt. She had no idea of the power that would be hers if she just had the will to use it.

Ammishtamru was off in Hattusha, paying his annual visit of respect to the Great King, a man five years younger than him. Ahat-milki sighed. It was up to her, yet again, to run the kingdom in his absence, to oversee the port, to judge law cases, and to mediate between his feuding wives. Sometimes she felt too old for all this, but she had to keep going because there was no one else.

Ah, dear Pizidku, if only you were still queen...

In a few minutes, she would call her litter bearers to take her to the palace, where she would spend the morning going over the petitions and letters brought to her by Takhulinu—the vizier—and Urtenu, her devoted chief scribe. When she was acting as regent, Urtenu was almost a second vizier; he was a solid, intelligent, discreet man who managed not to make Takhulinu feel threatened. *Now, that's a talent. These men and their touchy egos.* So many of the men in the government were *maryannuma* nobles, wielders of great wealth and power, holding seats on the council and growing rich off royal concessions. She sometimes wondered if they were really the king's servants or if he were theirs.

There was a knock at the door of her apartment.

"Come in," the old queen said in the deep, gravelly voice that had commanded respect and a little fear in Ugarit for fifty years.

The heavy panel cracked open with a grating of the hardware, and the face of her housekeeper appeared. "The

Lady Pizidku to see you, my lady. I can tell her to come later if you need to leave—"

"No, no! Show her in, show her in."

Ahat-milki rose and swept her tiny body toward the door as a larger and younger woman entered and sank to her knee with a murmured, "My mother."

"Ah, dear daughter! No formalities, please." She lifted Pizidku and embraced her, pecking her on both cheeks with her dry rouged lips. "How are you? How are my darling grandchildren?"

The king's secondary wife was a lovely woman, only a little past her prime, tall and amply built, with a long, generous mouth and a serene gaze. A gentleness touched by sorrow radiated from her face. Like nearly every mother alive, she had lost children, and more recently, she'd watched her son be pushed out of line for the throne. Ahat-milki loved this woman dearly. Her daughter-in-law's every thought was for the welfare of the realm.

Pizidku smiled her sweet smile and gestured behind her to the nearly adolescent girls who trailed in her wake. "Here are two of them to greet you."

The young princesses enveloped their grandmother in a flurry of colorful sleeves and flying braids, giggling and twittering like songbirds. Ahat-milki laughed for sheer joy. Here was the reward for her long years of hard work: this lovely little family. "And where are my grandsons?" she asked in mock severity. "Where are those brave lads? Afraid of a little old lady?"

"They're hunting in the mountains, my mother. The beautiful day was too much temptation, but they send their love and the promise that you will have the finest piece of game they bring back."

My mother. Yes, dear Pizidku was the daughter the dowager had never had. *She deserves better than to be shoved aside.* To his credit, Ammishtamru knew that. He had to obey the boy in Hattusha, but his heart still and always belonged to Pizidku. Ibi-ranu was the son he would have liked to see on the throne after him. Instead, Taddu's four-year-old child, Utri-sharrumma, was the heir. Ahat-milki worried about the unfairness of this succession. No one knew better than she the bitterness such a decree could breed in an older son, a legitimate heir. Ibi-ranu might one day decide he wanted his rightful inheritance back. Gods forbid that he should become another Heshmi-sharrumma.

She pushed aside thoughts of her firstborn. "You girls are getting big. It won't be long before you are married away to help your country make peace. Has your mother told you all about your duties?"

"Yes, Grandma," the girls chorused.

Of course she has.

"Apapu wants to marry the Great King!" Little Dalaptum giggled.

Her elder sister squealed in blushing protest, but the two women laughed.

Ahat-milki smoothed back the older princess's curling fringe. "And why shouldn't you? Ugarit is a rich kingdom, and the Great King himself should be proud to wed you. Although," she added mischievously, "I have heard his mother is a dreadful old virago who makes life terrible for his wives. Much like your mama's evil old mother-in-law!" They all giggled.

I am, in fact, a terrible old woman but not to these dears—only to those who mean ill to my son and his kingdom. "Now, go along, my pretty lambs. Your tapestry pieces are in the usual place. Why don't you work on them while your mother and I talk grown-up talk?"

The two princesses bobbed curtsies and bounced away, still giggling and chattering, so full of life and fresh-faced beauty that it melted her heart. Ahat-milki watched them go, smiling, until the heavy door thudded shut behind them.

As soon as the girls had departed, Pizidku's face grew sober. "My mother, what's the news from Amurru? How is your brother?"

"The will of the gods be done." The old queen sighed. "He's sinking lower and lower with every message. Poor Benteshina, always so eccentric and full of life. He's never been able to sit still. How he must hate lying helpless in bed, if he's even conscious anymore. Gasshulawiya is watching at his bedside and notifies me whenever there is the slightest change. She's preparing Shaushga-muwa for his coronation. It won't be long, I fear. But then, my brother is an old man, my dear. He has ruled Amurru for nearly sixty years." She shrugged. "We are all old."

Pizidku took her mother-in-law's little clawlike hands and squeezed them, her serene brow creased with compassion. "I think our queen Taduhepa is taking her father's illness very hard, the poor thing."

Ahat-milki's expression hardened. "Who knows? She is enjoying the sympathy it earns her; that's all I can say. Do you think she has come to see me once since we got the news? Do you think it has crossed her selfish little mind that Benteshina is my brother, too? No doubt—if she cares at all—she is wallowing in self-pity with those awful handmaids of hers all telling her how deserving she is of everyone's attention. Is this what Amurru has come to? It was not so in my youth, believe me."

"Perhaps you're a little hard on her, my mother. She is very young—"

Ahat-milki interrupted her angrily. "She's damned well twenty years old and the mother of children. I was younger than she when I came to Ugarit. You weren't much older yourself. But we weren't spoiled brats; that's the difference. She refuses—and I choose my words carefully—she refuses to do her duties and then complains that she's bored. She claims her husband pays no attention to her." She *harrumph*ed in disgust. "As if he had nothing else to do, by the Lord Ba'al! He's a king! He has a country to rule, and she expects him to sit around cooing to her! He's given her three children, and two of them have lived. Can't she ever be satisfied? I've never seen such a thing. She's driven him away from her herself by being so demanding. No one can relax in her presence."

Ahat-milki hissed through her teeth and shook her head, earrings tinkling. "May the gods forgive Benteshina for this girl's upbringing when he stands before his ancestors. Shallow. Selfish. And all her handmaids are exactly the same."

Pizidku said mildly, "You know, my mother, not all her people are so unworthy. Her chamberlain, that eunuch, is kind. He just made a point of being nice to me." She smiled at the recollection. "And I've seen him with the children. He seems genuinely tender. I like him very much."

Ahat-milki stroked the younger woman's cheek affectionately. "You never have an unkind word for anyone, Pizidku. I'm sure I couldn't find a nice thing to say about that whole brood, even though they are my countrymen. Who is this eunuch? Do I know him? He might be someone we could use for our purposes, if he's not just pretending to be nice in case the wind changes."

"What do you mean, my mother? What purposes?"

"Trying to turn that stupid girl's heart." The old queen pounded a fist into the other palm with the vehemence of her frustration. "Taddu, that brainless niece of mine. Maybe someone solid, even a servant, could have some influence on her." Suddenly thoughtful, she pursed her lips, eyes distant. "Perhaps I should talk to him."

Perhaps, indeed, I should talk to him. If he is sensible and intelligent, he might be just the person we need to keep an eye on her. He's her chamberlain... he must see her letters. I wonder, does she trust him?

"My dear daughter, I hate to chase you out, but I need to do some work this morning. The viziers will be chewing their fingernails if I'm any later."

Lady Pizidku opened her mouth to say something, but the old queen interrupted, "No, no. Don't apologize. It's always my very great pleasure to see you and the babies. Well, they aren't babies anymore, are they?" She laughed and kissed her daughter-in-law warmly on the cheek. "Go join the girls in their parlor. You can stay there as long as you want if they're busy on their tapestries. You know that you're always welcome at Grandma's house."

CHAPTER 4

AHAT-MILKI HAD JUST SEEN HER daughter-in-law out and turned back to her desk when a hasty knock sounded at the door, and her housekeeper appeared once more, bowing deeply.

"My lady queen, there are some diplomats in the antechamber who are insistent about getting in. I tried to tell them you had business to see to, but they were extremely pushy. They said they had come all the way from Alashiya to talk to you about something important. I didn't—"

"Who are these diplomats?" The old queen stiffened, her heart pounding with a sudden presentiment. "How many are there?"

"There are two, my lady. They wouldn't give their names. They swore you'd know them and be glad to see them."

Oh, great gods of heaven, can it be? Ahat-milki gnawed her knuckles to keep from making some noise that would give her emotions away. *Would those boys be so stupid, so proud, so fearless?* It could only be they. A mother's heart could not be deceived.

"Send them in. And clear the antechamber. I want no one around."

The woman backed out with an obeisance, and Ahat-milki was left alone. It couldn't be. It had to be. After five years, her sons had come back.

The door opened again. Two men, their faces muffled in cloaks despite the muggy spring weather, bowed their way in, ornate jewel cases under their arms, then stood there before her, grinning. The taller pushed back his hood and swept the conical Alashiyite cap from his head. He was very dark with a long gray beard and grizzled hair combed down low over the eyes, but she knew him: Heshmi-sharrumma, her firstborn. His black eyes glittered at her moment of nonrecognition as she made sense of the disguise and pierced it. By that time, the second man had bared his head. He, too, was dark-skinned and graying, but his face was young and impudent beneath the eye patch and fake length of beard. Abdi-sharrumma.

"'Welcome, my sons. It's been too long since I've seen you.' Isn't that what you say at this point, Mother?" Heshmi laughed with the familiar dry, ironic edge to his voice. They strode forward together and swept her into their arms without waiting to see if she would call the guards on them. They were that sure of her love.

Tenderness and rage warred in Ahat-milki's heart, and her voice came out in a growl. "What are you doing here? Are you mad? You'll be put to death if you're seen. You're not supposed to leave Alashiya. You idiots, this is insanity. Look at these ridiculous disguises. There are too many people here who know you. Someone will recognize you."

But she was kissing them, her dear boys, as only a

mother who had not embraced her children in five years could.

"No one will see us. We were very discreet. Just another pair of diplomats coming from abroad to offer gifts to the queen mother." Heshmi-sharrumma grinned, spreading his arms to display the foreign cut of his short-sleeved tunic. "Where is our august brother, the king?"

"He's in Hattusha, paying his visit of vassalage."

Heshmi snorted, his face hardening. "Licking the Great King's boots, you mean? That's why Tudhaliya wanted *him* on the throne. Ammi can be counted on to bow and scrape."

"That's unfair," the queen said sternly. "He has a treaty; he must honor it."

"Do you people never grow tired of being the loyal hounds of the Great King? This treaty is all about giving him what he needs. What about Ugarit?" Heshmi's voice was rising, his face growing scarlet with the pressure of his intensity. "What does Ugarit get out of it? Protection? Hatti looks to our navy for protection. Food? They can't even feed themselves. We fight their wars for them, we ship their grain for them, we bow and truckle and let them walk all over us, but what do we get out of it at the end?"

"You keep saying 'we,' my son," said Ahat-milki dryly. "Let me remind you, you don't live here anymore, nor will you ever again if the Great King has his way. Have you risked your lives to come to my house just to rant against Tudhaliya? He spared your lives, you know. His father would never have been so lenient. An attempt to kill a rightfully enthroned king is sacrilege. And Ammi is your own brother. Remember, when I gave you your inheritance from my dowry, they made me put a conditional curse on you if you ever came back. How can you even be sure I don't hate you myself?"

"We see that in your expression, Mother," said Abdi-sharrumma with a grin, tipping her face up to his own. "Look at all that hostility!" He kissed her forcefully on the nose.

Damn him. He's the charming one, without his eldest brother's hard edge. Charming and handsome and... as false as a plated ingot. Those sons of hers. They were each so different but every one of them ambitious, like their father. Like their mother.

She searched their darkened faces and false beards for their own features, wondering how much they had aged in five years. Heshmi had to be nearly fifty, Abishu perhaps in his late thirties. Ammi was in the middle. In some ways, he seemed older than the others, cynical and a little stodgy, thicker in body and in soul. Perhaps that was what having a real kingdom to rule did to a man—it took the stars out of his eyes. There was nothing extraordinary about Ammishtamru except his red beard, at odds with his dark hair, but he was steady and prudent if not terribly perceptive. Like many in the merchant kingdom he ruled, he had always been fond of gold. Lacking his brothers' charisma, he found that wealth bought him the influence he wanted. Those were her three boys: the one who wanted power, the one who wanted gold, and the one who wanted to be the center of everyone's hearts.

"I do love you," she said, crossing her arms, "but I can never forgive what you did. There is no excuse for an attempt on a crowned king. I'm sorry." She held up a warning hand as Abdi-sharrumma opened his mouth, his spread hands and reasonable expression signaling that he was about to utter something ingratiating. "Nothing justifies it. If anyone could come along and put whomever he wanted on the throne, the world would sink into savagery."

"Put whomever he wanted on the throne?" Heshmi cried, his face suffused with passion. "Does it not matter to you that I'm the firstborn, mother? I'm the legitimate heir. We're not talking here about a usurpation but a restoration of the right. Ammi is not the choice of the gods. Ugarit will never be prosperous until the gods' will is done and the true king is on the throne."

"Oh, yes, he is legitimate. The firstborn is not always the heir; you know that. Your own father was a second son, and Hattushili actually set him on the throne to replace his elder brother. The choice belongs to the Great King, and he chose Ammi, who was formally consecrated. And that, my son, is that. I certainly see signs of prosperity if—"

"We didn't come here to argue politics, Mother."

"What, then? You just had to see your old mother one more time—is that it?" Her voice grew quieter. "You've heard, I guess, that your uncle Benteshina is dying?"

Of course they would have heard. Even in distant Alashiya, such things were known.

After a moment of pained silence, Ahat-milki asked, "How are my grandchildren?"

"They're well." Heshmi fixed her with his dark almond-shaped gaze. There was something sly about his mouth. "No doubt, you'd like to watch them grow up. Can you say to my face that my son should not take his rightful place in the world?"

She sneered at his trap and refused to answer. "So why are you here?"

"The world is about to change, Mother," said Abdi-sharrumma earnestly. "New powers are rising, and old ones are falling. Ugarit has to be on the right side when things come apart, or she will be swept under."

"What exactly does that mean, my son? Is it really as treasonable as it sounds? We have a treaty with Hatti. We have sworn before all the gods to support them."

Heshmi snorted, and his lips took on a contemptuous curl, an expression that she had never liked. "For forty years, yes. But before that, my mother? Before that, we were the good and loyal friends of Egypt, remember? And before that, not even the powers of darkness could separate us from Mitanni. I tell you there is nothing divine about a piece of clay with marks on it, and that's all a treaty is. A wise king seeks his country's best interests at the moment. And at this moment, Hatti is not a good investment for us. They're going down before our eyes."

Ahat-milki whirled on him. "Is that a threat?"

"No, Mother, it's a statement borne out by evidence. Tudhaliya is like a man riding four horses at once. What's going to happen when they decide to go their own directions? He'll be pulled in pieces. Look, it's already happening. Hatti would starve to death without Egyptian grain shipped in our ships." Heshmi held up a hand and began to enumerate on his fingers. "What if Alashiya or somebody else decided to break that line of ships? What if Tudhaliya's precious cousin in Tarhuntassha decided he wanted his rightful throne back and refused to pass the grain along to Hattusha? What if Mira or Sheha River Land decided to be friends with the king of Ahhiyawa instead of with Hatti? What could the Great King do? He has no ships of his own to go after them. What about the king that Hattushili deposed? He's still lurking around somewhere." He finished with an explosive clap of his hands. "I tell you, Hatti is a walking corpse."

Ahat-milki felt her anger rise. All that was true. The Hittite empire was overextended, vulnerable. Its homeland of Hatti was small and rocky; by itself, it was nothing. It relied too heavily upon its vassals to feed and protect the empire, and it was no secret that many of those vassals, especially in the west, were actively looking for new masters. On top of that, the usurpation of the throne thirty years earlier by Hattushili, Tudhaliya's father, had left his nephews, the real heirs to the empire, stewing. It was no fault of Tudhaliya's, but he was forced to deal with the consequences. The Great King would have to be a magician to keep all these wolves at bay. The relationship of Ugarit and their overlords was essentially a one-sided alliance, and yet... unless people honored their word, what kind of world would it become?

"So where would you go if you were king, my wise son? We're too small to defy the Great King alone. Egypt is an ally of Hatti these days. Mitanni no longer exists as an independent state."

"Assyria. Assyria is our future."

The queen scoffed. "Those blustering barbarians?"

"Barbarians? They are older than Hatti and far stronger. They want to trade with us, but Tudhaliya forbids it." Heshmi was getting frenetic, as he so frequently did, his voice rising. "Do you know how much profit this is costing us? And why? Because Hatti is afraid of them, afraid that if they once reach the sea, they'll find their way to Ahhiyawa and its willing mercenaries and then split the Hittite empire in two, like Tiamat in the days of creation. That's bad for Hatti, of course, but it's golden for us! We would become the key to their wildest dreams. We could charge whatever we wanted to transport them! They would buy our products, they would hire our ships, they—"

"They would roll us flat and strip us bare, you innocent. What makes you think they would treat us better than the Great King? From what I've heard, they are far less squeamish about shedding blood."

She turned her back and strode away from him, but Abdi-sharrumma followed and took her gently by the shoulder, turning her thunderous face to his. He put on his most winsome smile. "Mother, my brother is right. It's simple self-interest. Ally yourself to the strongest, right? And now Assyria is becoming stronger than Hatti."

"They're farther away, too, and the viceroy at Karkemish is between us," she spat. "Do you think Ammi would ever betray the Great King? He owes him his throne. And his life."

"No, he probably wouldn't." Heshmi advanced on her. "Further proof of his lack of daring and imagination, say I. And it will become a fatal lack; mark my words. What this country needs is a better ruler."

Ahat-milki glared up into at her firstborn's dark, intense eyes. *No revolution.* She willed him to hear her thoughts. *No regicide. No brother killing brother. Please, I'm too old for all this. Take your anger and your ambition and your righteousness away from here. You're not so young yourself anymore, son of my adolescence. Leave this to the next generation.*

"I will not be a part of your plans," she said. "Don't expect me to lift a hand."

"Of course not, my mother. It will all be a total surprise to you when it happens. We have other contacts here"—the brothers exchanged glances—"who will keep us apprised of Ammishtamru's comings and goings, and we don't want to compromise you unnecessarily. For example, we know that the Great King is trying to work out some kind of treaty with the Assyrians right at this moment, but they will have none of it. And why should they? They know quite well they're stronger than Hatti now, especially if it can't count on its vassals. Perhaps the Assyrians will even manage to pick a fight before long, and Tudhaliya may just find himself alone."

Ahat-milki felt the blaze of wrath mounting her cheeks. "This is all outrageous treason. Out of here, before someone hears you. If the guards came, I wouldn't stop them."

They kissed her, the one darkly, the other blithely, and bowed their way out, lifting their hoods as they passed, once more plunged into their disguises. They were just two diplomats from abroad. Only the affectionate wink from the younger man's unmasked eye might have suggested anything different. She could hear their footsteps growing fainter across the tiled floor of the antechamber until silence swallowed them up.

Ahat-milki spun on her heel and stalked to the window, seething with anger and fear for those insane boys. The worst of it all was that she knew they were right. But nothing was worth another revolt. She couldn't bear to see her whole family exterminated in a bloody civil war. Dear gods, couldn't they wait until she was dead? They had tried revolution once, and the Great King's viceroy had put it down in no time. They simply didn't have the support they needed among the *maryannuma*, whose sole interest lay in protecting their businesses. The curse she had been made to lay on her sons at their exiling haunted her.

And who are their "other contacts"? They must have some spy right in the palace if they claim to be aware of the king's movements. She needed to look into that right away.

"Tatasshe," she cried to her housekeeper. "Tatasshe! Call my litter bearers immediately. I'm late. I need to get to the palace."

As she turned to go, her eyes fell upon the jeweled casket her sons had left on the table. With her thumb, she flicked up the latch. Inside was a bronze dagger with a hilt of Alashiyite work: a palm tree cast in gold, flanked by two smooth-faced cherubim, *karubuma*, face to face, their wings spread upright. *A dagger.* She dropped it on the table, suddenly chilled.

Only when the princes had passed through the guard post that separated the palace complex from the city at large did Heshmi-sharrumma speak under his breath. "Our mother was right about one thing: that was incredibly foolhardy. Let's have no more bravado of this sort, shall we, brother? It would be ridiculous to jeopardize our entire movement just to cut a swashbuckling figure. Prudence and bravery are not mutually exclusive."

An eyebrow cocked, Abishu replied tartly, "Why are

you telling me this, Heshmi? You were as eager as I to talk to Mother about our plans. And I've got to admit, I half expected her to say, 'Well, then, I'll come along with you, since your arguments are so compelling.'"

Heshmi emitted a snort and shot his brother a sardonic sidelong glance. "I won't deny she probably approved the argument, but she'll never stand up to Ammi, and you're naive if you think so. Her whole adult life has been shaped by the fact of the Hittite suzerainty, and she's too old to change now. I wanted to tell her just so she can get herself out of harm's way. I don't fancy her manning the ramparts in Ammi's absence and getting shot. I know there's a pretty good chance she's reported us, but that's not all bad. Fear can work in our favor. Let them get nervous, never knowing whom to trust. The main thing is, we stay out of sight and don't give them any clue of where to start searching."

Abishu said nothing. Their synchronized steps on the flagstones were the only sounds until they emerged from the shadow of the north wall of the palace and turned into the more-frequented High Street.

Heshmi glanced at his brother again and saw a beatific grin under the false beard. "What's so funny?"

"Funny? Nothing. I'm just remembering that melting look on Queen Taduhepa's face. What a woman, eh, Heshmi!" Abishu's eyes grew dreamy. "She's like a half-broken horse, all fire and blood. Ishtar in person! What a woman. Did you see that amber around her neck? It was an inspiration to bring that piece. Her eyes are almost that color."

Heshmi made a noise of disgust. "Dog eyes. And speaking of dogs, listen, Abishu, you need to keep yourself on a tight leash around her. Her participation is useful to our movement, and she may even bring us legitimation from Amurru, but she's Ammi's wife. I think you're playing with fire and blood, all right; I just hope it isn't *our* blood. Keep the relationship businesslike, will you?"

"Well, you wanted me to win her confidence," said Abdi-sharrumma with a shrug.

"Yes, brother dear, but we're supposed to be the ones in control. I have a feeling she's already cracking the whip over you. I'm not pleading. I'm in charge, and I'm *ordering* you to be careful. We don't need unnecessary complications. I'd rather drop her altogether than risk you getting sloppy. How discreet do you think she is?"

Abdi-sharrumma laughed happily. "How discreet is any woman, Heshmi? The more in love with me she is, the less likely she is to let something slip to one of her maids."

Heshmi barely suppressed his annoyance. His brother could be remarkably obtuse. The elder prince said with great precision, as if to a child, "The point I'm making is we don't really need her. We have that old lard ball of a eunuch who can sneak around the palace, attracting much less notice than the queen."

Abishu pursed his lips, unimpressed. "To what extent does he really have her ear?"

"You're still missing my point." Heshmi's voice was sharp edged with frustration. *Incorrigible.* "He doesn't need her ear. We can use him to bypass her. She's just a name that adds luster. The less she knows, the better. The idea of you repeatedly making contact with her at the palace, as you so imprudently improvised in her presence, is absolute ass shit. I know Commandant Kili'anu is with us, but this is asking for discovery. Somebody will figure out what's going on and trail you back. Then the whole movement will be exposed."

They reached the door of the house they were renting in an unsavory part of the Lower Town. Heshmi-sharrumma knocked discreetly, and the hobnailed panel swung open a crack. Seeing who stood before him, the doorkeeper pushed it aside for them to enter. As soon as they were safe within the vestibule, the two brothers began to strip themselves of their false beards and brightly patterned Alashiyite cloaks.

Abishu peeled off his eye patch with a whistle of relief. The servant filled a basin at the well and presented it, along with a towel, and the younger prince plunged his face in and began to scrub off the stain. "Oh, the irony! I meet the woman of my dreams, and I'm disguised as some ancient black merchant."

"Yes, and who ever heard of a black Alashiyite?" said Heshmi caustically. "I think you got carried away with the game of let's pretend, Abishu. Gods be merciful, an eye patch! Extremes attract attention, brother. You'll stick in the memory of anyone who saw you. I'm sure her little guard dog didn't fall for your disguise."

"Who, the eunuch?" Abdi-sharrumma laughed. "He's jealous, that's all. Those fellows get very possessive. I've seen it before."

"Well, don't underestimate him. That's just the sort of inattention to detail that spells danger." Heshmi toweled his face and beard and turned away from his brother, who had taken off his bracelets and was rinsing his wrists.

"Tala'abi! Are you here?" Heshmi called into the salon.

A muscular young man with the easy grace of a born

maryannu emerged. His little bow was respectful, but his broad grin spoke of a less formal relationship. He clasped Heshmi-sharrumma by the forearms. "My prince. You have returned safely. We were a bit worried. That foray seemed rather like sticking your heads into the lion's mouth. Was the queen mother open to anything you told her?"

"*Open* is not a word that can be said in the same breath as *queen mother*," said Heshmi with a humorless laugh. "But she heard us, and she's no fool. The palace is warned. Let them begin stewing now. We need to start looking at our allies and what they will bring to us. We need to begin talking about dates and specific duties. If we want this to happen before Ammi returns, we don't have that much time. And we need to act while he's gone, because he has a lot of the most loyal troops with him. Have you been sounding out your young peers?"

"I have, and more of the great houses than you might think support us. It won't be like it was before; fear not. Even some of the graybeards are coming over, although they may watch cautiously for a while rather than jumping in. I don't think they'll make a very active objection, however."

"Good. We just need to take action while everyone is in readiness. If this drags on too long, we'll lose support." Heshmi finished drying his face and threw down the towel.

"Did the young queen seem like a promising contact?" Tala'abi asked.

Heshmi rolled his eyes. "Let my brother describe that part of the day's work."

Abishu turned a rapturous smile upon the *maryannu*. "Ah, good friend Tala'abi, if you could have seen her! What a woman! Those lips!" He kissed his fingertips suggestively.

"I don't think that's what he wants to know, you idiot," Heshmi retorted with a sneer of annoyance. He turned to the *maryannu*. "Abdi-sharrumma is now head over heels in love with the queen after less than an hour in her presence. The issue here is, how much use is her presence to us? If the answer is none, we need to jettison her."

Abishu, his white smile extinguished, thrust his face close to his brother's, looking suddenly minatory. "That's not going to happen, Heshmi. Get that straight. She's in with us. She's mine, and when we take over, she will be sitting at my side on the throne of Shiyannu, which you promised me."

"I didn't—" Heshmi began irritably then pinched his lips. "Whatever makes you happy, little brother. But first, we have to succeed. My father-in-law has ships sitting offshore. He can't commit many men, but he may at least be able to distract Ammi if our august sibling gets wind of this and tries to send his troops back. What I'm really counting on is the help of Assyria. An emissary of the King of Kings is supposedly on the way. Let's hope he comes in time and has something substantial to offer."

Abishu grinned, appeased; he had made his little point. "I'm going upstairs to get out of these togs." He fingered the neck of his tunic with distaste. "See you gentlemen shortly."

Heshmi waved him on. After his brother had disappeared up the stairs with a clatter of footsteps, he ushered Tala'abi into the salon and poured them each a cup of wine from the ceramic ewer that waited on the table. The prince seated himself on a stool while the younger man crossed his ankles and lowered himself to a cushion.

"Sooo…" Tala'abi began uncertainly.

"So we have yet another of my brother's enthusiasms to contend with, and this one could be dangerous. Once his heart is involved, his head gets left behind. You should have seen the queen's chamberlain giving us the evil eye. But of course, Abishu was oblivious. We have to be extremely careful what we let that woman hear, or she or one of her people will blab it all over the coast." The prince savored his wine for a moment. "In the worst case we could envision, Abishu would be the one jettisoned."

Tala'abi eyed the contents of his cup thoughtfully. "That has crossed the mind of more than one of the *maryannuma* I've spoken to, my lord. He's seen as a weak link, full of enthusiasm and charm but easily distracted. Shall I have someone keep an eye on him?"

"I think our ears at the palace may be able to arrange something. But I don't want to harm my brother unless it's necessary; I'd just like to make him aware of the danger he's courting with this infatuation. Scare him away, you might say. See what you can do, eh, Tala'abi?"

"Understood, my lord."

Abruptly, the prince froze, holding out a hand to still the *maryannu*. Heshmi listened intently then turned to his companion, his face grim. "Did you hear something?"

"I did, my lord," said the younger man, equally serious. He strode to the door, slipped out into the vestibule, and a moment later returned, his eyes flashing.

The prince awaited him, scarcely daring to breathe. "What was it? One of the servants?"

Tala'abi said in a low voice, "Your brother, my lord. He was just entering the room on the landing upstairs."

Lords of the Underworld take the devious puppy, thought Heshmi, grinding his teeth. "Do you think he heard us?"

The young man nodded, his mouth hard. "No question about it. He heard us."

※

Lords Urtenu and Takhulinu were waiting in the chancery when the dowager queen arrived. She ushered them behind her into the private chamber that served as the vizier's office.

"I was detained, my lords, and the reason for my delay may be of interest to you." She gestured for them to be seated, and she herself took a seat at the table in the center of the windowless room.

The two men leaned forward attentively—grave, gray-bearded men older than she, who had labored in the service of Ugarit for nearly their entire lives. Urtenu was small and wiry with an aquiline nose, his head a polished globe above unruly eyebrows. His family had held positions of power on the council for generations, and Ahat-milki knew his middle-aged son was highly placed in the chancery as well. Urtenu had served Niqmepa when they were both young, and he'd been rewarded with coveted royal trade concessions abroad. He was exceedingly rich, not a simple secretary by any means.

The other man, Takhulinu, the royal vizier, was of the purest *maryannu* blood as well, although he'd been born in Mukesh. Despite his broad, genial face and wry humor, he was an astute diplomat and ruthless enforcer of the king's will. Five years before, her sons' revolution had been swiftly stifled thanks to his quick thinking. Takhulinu had managed to get word to the viceroy while he was still en route to the fall festival, and his soldiers had met the fleeing conspirators at the gate. Ahat-milki might have viewed him as a rival for her royal son's trust, but she did not. Takhulinu was an experienced and loyal man who had done his job to save the king, and he had her respect.

She said, "Gentlemen, I have credible reason to believe that another coup is in the making."

"Led by the king's brothers again, my lady?" asked Takhulinu.

"None other. I tell you this with a heavy heart, believe me, in the hopes that it can be deflected before it begins. As you may imagine, I have no desire to see any of my sons die. It grieves me that this fratricidal impulse has not been laid to rest, but such is the legacy of our Hittite overlords." She let them interpret that statement. They would understand what was left unsaid. Everybody knew about the career of Tudhaliya's usurping father, but was the Great King not also responsible for the troubled succession in her own family?

"There is a political content to the movement, as well as a simple desire for the throne on the part of my firstborn." She looked at the two men intently, letting the silence grow pregnant. "They want to break our vassal treaty with Hatti and have us ally ourselves with Assyria."

There was no eruption of surprise or outrage. These pragmatic men knew the power structure of the world. Takhulinu said simply, "The king will never agree to that."

"Precisely why the conspirators think a new king is needed. I believe they would prefer to strike while Ammishtamru is out of the country—"

"Now?" cried the vizier, finally surprised. "They're here?"

"But I don't believe they would scruple to assassinate him. They claim to have at least one fellow conspirator within the palace who keeps them apprised of his movements. And I think I can tell you who that is."

They stared at her expectantly but were too discreet to demand an answer.

"The queen," Ahat-milki said.

Urtenu drew back with a sharp and thoughtful expression, smoothing his mustache with his fingertips. Takhulinu spluttered an expletive.

"I have no proof yet," the old woman assured them, holding up a warning hand, "but I think we should put someone in her retinue who can watch her coming and going. I have been told that her chamberlain might be willing to be our eyes and ears."

"Didn't he come from Amurru with her? He may be more loyal to the queen than to her husband," said Takhulinu.

"I came from Amurru, too, my lord, but I dare say I'm as loyal to my adopted city as any," the queen reminded him with a dry smile. "I suggest it's worth a try. If he refuses or fails to do the job, we can always find someone else. But he would be in a position to know all about her movements and read her correspondence. I think you would agree with me that we cannot let her continue to scheme, if that's what she's doing. She has far too intimate contact with the king, and the scandal would be appalling. It would destroy the alliance between our two countries, which is so strongly desired by the Great King."

"What's she after?" Takhulinu shook his big head. "I think we are all aware that the queen lacks a certain maturity, a certain gravity, and her actions don't always express very good sense. But why would she ally herself with conspirators? It seems she has everything to lose. Her son is the heir to the throne now, but if my lady's elder son were to replace our lord Ammishtamru, then *his* sons would inherit. It seems self-defeating."

Urtenu, who had been sitting in thoughtful silence, spoke up. "Who knows what promises the conspirators have made her? Perhaps she has been told that Prince Utri-sharrumma will still succeed his uncle. As you observe, Lord Takhulinu, her actions haven't always seemed to be guided by clear thinking."

"Then I propose, gentlemen, that as soon as this morning's work is concluded, I summon the chamberlain for a little talk," said Ahat-milki. "If the queen is innocent, we need waste no more time at this. But if she's part of something, then perhaps she can unwittingly lead us to the kind of information we need to forestall any more bloodshed. We lost enough lives in that brief revolution five years ago."

The two men nodded. Then Takhulinu shook his head again, clucking his tongue. "The king will certainly not be happy about this."

"Nor perhaps altogether surprised, my lord," the queen suggested darkly. "I say no more. We will resume our meeting this afternoon to deal with the rest of the issues that face us."

The viziers, perceiving themselves dismissed, rose and bowed, and Takhulinu unbarred the door and passed through. Before he followed, Urtenu turned to Ahat-milki and said in a low voice, "My lady, may I speak frankly?"

She favored him with her carnivorous smile. "Of course, old friend."

"I understand you have your own reasons for not supplying us with the evidence for the queen's complicity. But it is also well known that my lady and Queen Taduhepa are not on... the friendliest terms. Is it possible that you suspect the queen because you dislike her?"

These words from anyone else's mouth might have offended Ahat-milki, but she had not ruled a kingdom for fifty years without learning that self-awareness was the difference between a mediocre statesman and an exceptional one. Urtenu was nobody's fool.

Side by side, they passed through the door. Her smile broadened. "Let's say rather that I dislike her because I suspect her."

CHAPTER 5

A HAT-MILKI HAD BEEN THE FEMININE power behind the throne for longer than many people's lifetimes. Not much escaped her. If her son's wife was up to no good, she would find out. There was always a way to get at the truth, always some servant who would sell his master's secrets. Slaves were desperate folk by definition, and she knew how to be liberal to those who served her and the king. She also knew how to be ruthless to those who did not.

The heavy doors of her office in the palace swung open, and her housekeeper swept into a reverence. "My lady, the queen's chamberlain is here as you commanded."

"Send him in," Ahat-milki said.

Bowing out, the housekeeper returned a moment later with the eunuch behind her. "The queen's chamberlain," she announced then disappeared discreetly. The doors swung shut.

The eunuch doubled over in a deep bow then stood upright, hands folded at his waist, wearing the mask of bland complaisance that all subordinates assumed when summoned. He was grotesquely tall, gangling, and effeminate. Though youngish, he was going fat around the hips, as his kind seemed so often to do. He had the lank, etiolated look of a weed that had sprouted in a sunless space. Ahat-milki didn't care for eunuchs. Horrible creatures, neither man nor woman but with the vices of both. She refused to employ them in her personal household, although there were plenty of them in the chancery, and her son seemed not to mind having them in his bedchamber. This one was carefully groomed, dressed tastefully in dark colors with only an appropriate hint of gold at the ears and on his fingers. His purse, tablet, pen case, and several seals hung at his waist. To all appearances, he was the ideal servant. He might not be easy to crack, but then, everyone had something they wanted. Or something they feared.

"What is your name, eunuch?" the queen demanded in her gravelly voice.

"Nahish-shulmanu, my lady."

"What's that? Not an Ugaritic name, I think."

"No, my lady. Assyrian." His voice broke nervously.

"An Assyrian name? Are you an Assyrian, then, Nahish-shulmanu?" The queen's smile began to widen in satisfaction.

"Y-Yes, my lady."

Well, this is a gift from the gods! A perfect point of vulnerability. She pursed her lips thoughtfully and approached the fellow, eyeing him up and down. His lids were respectfully lowered in his pale lunar face, but she caught the gleam of his whites as he tracked her under his lashes.

"And how did an Assyrian come to be a member of the queen's household, if I may ask?"

"I was a gift from an Assyrian diplomat to Queen Gasshulawiya, the Great Lady of Amurru, my lady. I served as her personal secretary until the time of my lady Queen Taduhepa's marriage, when her mother gave me to her to run her household." He licked his lips nervously.

"And this diplomatic gift to Gasshulawiya was when?"

"More than twenty years ago, my lady. I was barely eighteen, but I wrote and spoke several languages."

That explained the slightness of the accent, then. What a risky appointment that had been. Assyria and Amurru had not been at war twenty years ago—her sister-in-law would never have accepted a present from a hostile state— but such a "gift" might well turn out to be a spy. Of course, diplomats were always bringing gifts of horses, dogs, and slaves. In fact, a skilled or attractive slave was a prize worth a great deal. No doubt this fellow, with his fine, androgynous features and gazelle eyes, had been a pretty little boy, and if he was multilingual, he would have been a real asset to the Great Lady's correspondence.

"Most slaves are captives, Nahish-shulmanu. How is it you belonged to one of your own countrymen? Or did he give you an Assyrian name?"

The eunuch began to look uneasy at the turn of conversation. He cleared his throat and swallowed. His knuckles were white. "I was not a captive, my lady. I was... I was sold to be a singer. This is my real name."

She sauntered around him, watching his fingers start to twitch. The eunuch stood facing forward as if frozen into position, unaware that she was no longer standing in front of him. He began to swallow with greater frequency.

"You are aware, Nahish-shulmanu, that we are presently all but at war with Assyria? Assyrians have been forbidden access to all the lands of Ugarit. Their merchants are under embargo in our ports. Does it seem to you appropriate that one of the enemy should occupy a position of trust in the household of the queen?"

The eunuch broke from his position of frozen attention to face her, eyes round with horror. "My lady, I assure you the king has no more loyal subject! I have served the queen of Amurru and the queen of Ugarit for twenty years, and no one has ever had reason to complain of my loyalty! Indeed I have many reasons not to love Assyria. Just ask my mistress. Ask the Great Lady. She will certainly speak for me; I—"

"Yes, well"—Ahat-milki had to talk over him to stop the babble of protestations—"just keep in mind how very precarious your position might be as an enemy in the palace. Who is the first person the king might suspect if secrets get leaked? What frightful punishments might he not mete out to a foreign spy in his court? I fear you will probably be held to higher standards of loyalty than others. It would certainly serve your case well if you should demonstrate your fidelity in some measurable way, don't you think?"

"Absolutely, my lady. I am the king's true servant. Let him ask what he will," he said, white faced, bobbing in acquiescence. But his brows contracted a little. He was terrified, of course. He could be killed, mutilated, sold abroad, or set to degrading manual work, and his soft, long-fingered hands, now clenching spasmodically, made it quite clear that he'd never had to deal with such a fate, even in his servitude. But she perceived that he was intelligent, along with being justifiably fearful, and was probably asking himself what this was all about. He could not have been called into the dowager queen's presence because he was an Assyrian, because Ahat-milki hadn't even known about that until this moment.

She smiled that vulpine smile that had once been seductive as well as dangerous. "You are asking yourself why I have summoned you, are you not, Nahish-shulmanu? Let me be frank with you. The king has reason to think that his queen is not wholly faithful."

The slave, blood draining from his face, made a little noise between a gasp and a moan and clapped his hands to his mouth. Then, as if to prevent any more such revealing gestures, he locked them together again. "Oh, no, my lady! The queen is completely loyal. She—"

"The king," Ahat-milki repeated emphatically in her darkest voice, "has reason to think that his queen is not wholly faithful. It seems to me that as the manager of her household, in charge of her slaves, her possessions, and her comings and goings, you are well placed to observe any irregular activities. Have you really noticed nothing? Consider whether it serves you well to turn a blind eye to behavior the king might consider unfaithful. Even though my niece brought you here from Amurru, you are above all the king's servant, Nahish-shulmanu, as is everyone in this palace. You can imagine how unhappy he would be to discover that the person who is supposed to guard his wife has in fact colluded with her in deceiving him. Men take that very hard."

She walked round to the front again, and the eunuch

swiveled to follow her lead. His aplomb was shaken to bits. Staring eyes starting to tear up, trembling mouth, shaking hands—if Taddu was up to no good, this foreigner was only too aware of it, and he was terrified. *Perfect.*

"Perhaps you can convince my lord the king to be merciful by offering him a token of your goodwill, Nahish-shulmanu. Otherwise, he might think you were party to the queen's misdeeds. And I believe the penalty for cuckolding the king is impalement."

"Cu... oh, gods in heaven. I never... I don't think I could even... oh, my lady, I..." He buried his face in his hands and emitted a broken sob. "Whatever the king wants. I am his loyal subject. Oh, please, what can I do to convince him?"

He fell heavily at Ahat-milki's feet and began kissing her shoes, shaken with sobs. She let him work himself up to a sufficient degree of terror and then stepped away, leaving him folded on the floor, his curly hair trailing the tiles.

"Spy on her," she spat. "Tell me everything she does. Is she meeting anyone? Is she going to a certain shop again and again? Where do her women go when they're off duty? Who does she talk to? You're a smart fellow. Use your imagination. And report back to me immediately if you see anything that might be interpreted as arranging assignations. If she should ask you to carry a message, report to me. If she tells you to turn a blind eye, report to me. Do you understand?"

"I understand, my lady. You're too kind. I promise I won't let her out of my sight. But I'm sure there is some innocent explanation for all her actions. The queen—"

"The queen is the king's wife and high priestess of the

gods of Ugarit, Nahish-shulmanu. Innocent explanations are not enough. She must be above all reproach in appearance as well as in fact. Do I make myself clear?'

"Yes, my lady."

The eunuch struggled to keep his mouth shut. Finally, he blurted, "But what will happen to her? Will… will she be punished?"

"Is this any of your business, slave? I think not. She will certainly not be punished if she is as innocent as you seem to indicate. Do I make myself clear, Nahish-shulmanu?"

"Yes, my lady. Perfectly clear. I will report everything, as you order."

"Then you're dismissed. Notify my secretary Urtenu when you have something to tell us. In fact, plan on checking in with him weekly. We'll make this worth your while." Ahat-milki tapped suggestively the bag of gold that lay upon her desk. It would be good to keep him interested. Eunuchs were supposedly above such considerations since they lacked progeny to pass a fortune down to, but she'd found they were as greedy as the next person.

She turned her profile to him and stood at her table with crossed arms, staring out the window, while the fellow struggled awkwardly to his feet and bowed his way backward to the door. She heard him bump into it then scrabble at the handle. It opened, then it clashed shut.

Ahat-milki remained for a moment, eyes unfocused, her thoughts settling. That had been easy, and she'd found herself changing tactics as she went. Her intention had been to have him try to influence the queen into more prudent ways, but the eunuch had a guilty conscience. He knew something. Or else he'd been mistreated and was quick to be afraid for his skin. Castration took away their spirits anyway. That was one reason people did it: to make compliant cowards. In any case, it didn't matter why he cracked so quickly. He would serve the king's purposes equally well in either case. Now she needed to brief Urtenu on his role in all this.

Outside the balcony, the treetops rustled in a mild breeze. It was early summer, and the fresh scents of new growth perfumed the garden. She sighed, her reverie broken, and turned away from the window.

What is that wretched niece of mine up to? Ahat-milki's instinct, honed by a lifetime of diplomacy, whispered that it had something to do with her rebel sons. Was Taddu indeed their link to the news of the palace, as the dowager queen suspected and had intimated to the viziers? Had they contacted her niece and attempted to enlist her in their plots?

There were times she wished she had never borne children or that they had all been girls. *If only the previous Great King had let Heshmi-sharrumma take the throne in the normal order of things and not meddled, the old usurper. You'd think his own family turmoil, which spilled out into civil war in Hatti, would have enlightened him.*

Now Ammi was so thoroughly indebted to the Hittites that he would blindly follow their orders, no matter how dangerous for Ugarit. And the other boys were legitimately disgruntled. Well, even if she agreed with their politics, she couldn't excuse them. They had attempted to kill their own flesh and blood. What did Abdi-sharrumma think he was going to get out of it if his eldest brother took the throne? Heshmi had male children; they would ascend the throne after him, not Abishu. As charming as Abishu was, her youngest son was always a follower—the perfect courtier. He wasn't the kind to fight his way to power over his nephews as that old warlord Hattushili had done. And now Hattushili's son was on the Great Throne, and the rightful heirs were fuming in exile and awaiting their day. Hatti was indeed living on borrowed time, as Heshmi had foreseen.

She paced the room, twisting her ringed fingers. *But to change allegiance now, after so many years?* Was Assyria going to be a better master than Hatti? The viceroy at Karkemish was not so very far away. He controlled both Mukesh, to the north of Ugarit, and Shiyannu, directly to the south. If Ugarit attempted to break away, his armies would crush it like crab claws. Those boys were engaged in dangerous business, very dangerous indeed. She was not sure Heshmi had thought through all the consequences to the end. His disinheritance had made him too bitter and impatient to see straight. Perhaps the young queen—Ahat-milki couldn't restrain a smile—was what Abishu hoped to get out of his plotting. His mother would know soon enough.

Naheshi tottered in a daze from the dowager queen's office, through the antechamber, and out into the corridor. His knees were shaking so badly he had to lean against the wall for a moment, mopping the tears from his face with a sleeve. Someone must have seen him and the queen. Who had been so malicious as to twist an innocent, girlish embrace into something treasonable? He'd been part of her life since she was born. It wasn't as if he were a danger to anyone.

Cuckolding the king? He let out a barely suppressed

moan. Oh, yes, there was a death penalty for a eunuch getting too close to the king's women—he knew the law—but what did "too close" even mean? Was just touching her a crime—and if so, what would kissing her be? *Yet it was an innocent kiss, surely.* He was no threat to anyone.

But, oh, he had done wrong. He realized it too late. The queen wasn't always prudent. The Great Lady relied on him to recall her daughter to the ways of caution; that was why she'd appointed him the girl's chamberlain. Instead, he had lost control of himself and gotten them both into something terribly dangerous. Could they put him to death for that one moment of bliss?

Worst of all, he might have implicated Queen Taduhepa in something that would cost *her* her position or even her life as well. He could never live with himself if somehow he'd hurt her, if his lack of self-control or his vanity or his hunger for her approval had brought shame to her in the king's eyes.

Grief and desperation sat like twin vultures on his chest, a cold, ominous weight that was almost physical pain. What could he do? He had promised to spy on his precious Taddu, his queen, his mistress. Fear for his own skin had made him agree to betray her. *How could I be such a coward?*

He made his way unsteadily down the corridor past the queen's quarters. He tried to draw himself up and look normal in case he passed anyone, but he felt as if his shame were stamped on his face in letters of fire for all to see: coward.

Coward. Coward. Coward. Every slap of his shoes on the stone tiles seemed to whisper the judgment. At last, he arrived at the door of his apartment, and after reaching above the panel for the concealed cord, he levered open the bar and lurched in, barring the door behind him with shaking fingers. Naheshi half fell into his salon, groping for a stool. He sank down, buried his face in his hands, and rocking back and forth, let loose the sobs that had been choking him.

The rest of the afternoon had vanished before he could stop crying, but exhaustion finally overcame him, and the sobs ended in gulping and gasping. He mopped his face and looked up, his swollen eyes burning. He could hardly breathe. The sun had almost gone down; the room was darkening. There was no one to talk to, no one to bring his dinner, no one to light the lamps. Where was his slave Pilsiya when Naheshi needed him most? Naheshi considered going up to the roof terrace but lacked the energy. He wanted to hide in the dark and nurse his shame, but he needed, with a terrible desperation, to talk to someone.

Aloud, just to hear the sound of a human voice, he addressed the absent servant: "Your master has sold his soul. He's a gutless coward with no honor at all."

Eventually, Naheshi grew almost calm in his self-contempt. That was the beauty of exhaustion: one could take only so much anguish before one became numb. He heaved himself up and went into his kitchen storeroom. There were a big jug of wine, some olives, and a stale half loaf of bread. He poured a cup of wine, splashing it all over his sleeve, and crammed the bread into his mouth then washed it down with the wine, all in one draft. He refilled his cup, took a bowl of olives and the cup of wine, and tottered into the salon, where he sank clumsily to the floor and onto his pallet, left unmade from the night before. As he scraped the olives off their pits with his teeth and chewed them mechanically, he ran over and over in his mind his every action with the queen. Could there seriously have been anything less than innocent there?

Dear Lady Nina, innocent? He'd been in bed with the king's wife. Was that what they called having sex? But he had never even taken off his clothes—heaven forbid...

No normal person would ever believe the profundity of his ignorance, he realized in shame. Still, whatever the law held about his action, in his own heart, it was a joyful and beautiful thing. Its memory was like a warm, glowing lamp of human solidarity in the aching darkness of his life. How could people say it was wrong? The gods themselves had given him that moment of reprieve from his loneliness...

But in any case, how could the dowager queen have known about it? He couldn't imagine a single person who might have seen him that evening, nor indeed could he conceive of anyone who hated him enough to report what they might have seen. Only slaves of the lowest class—pages or maids—had even been near the apartment. He'd always been a just overseer. Abdi-rama had said he was nice. Did anyone really loathe him so much as to spread such grave tales? They made fun of him, yes, but could those brainless girls be so conniving and malicious? What did they hope to gain?

All these were unanswerable questions, tipping upon that imponderable fulcrum, human ambition. Perhaps one of them had been threatened as he had been. They all lived at the fickle good pleasure of the powerful. The Old Dragon could have offered them gold or even freedom in exchange for information. Or, dear gods, had that bloated toad Agipsharri somehow crept around to spy? He was one who might well wish Naheshi ill. But why would Agipsharri have been there after the day shift?

He had to stop these thoughts. His mind was spinning in pointless circles, like the wheels of an overturned wagon. Anxiety was poisoning the most wonderful memory of his life. Naheshi stood up painfully, as if he'd been physically beaten, only to find he was none too steady on his feet. The wine had set to work, but he needed more of it. The numbness was not yet complete. He plopped back down on his pallet.

Naheshi ached to pour his sorrows into a human ear, despite the ignominy. Ili-milku would perhaps tell him reassuringly that he had done no wrong and that everyone in the palace was doing the same thing—spying and reporting all to the king's ear. Perhaps any seasoned courtier would laugh at him and his old-fashioned scruples. And in fact, he had no reason to think the queen was engaged in anything at all disloyal. He would have nothing to report to Urtenu; there would be no repercussions. Week after week, he would tell the Old Dragon, "The queen is his majesty's most loyal subject. She cares only for her children and her husband's kingdom." The king would forget about Naheshi's foolish indiscretion. He would be praised for his loyalty, and so would Taddu. Everything would be fine.

Naheshi tried to bury the memory of her glowing face as it turned to that of the younger diplomat. His thoughts strayed hungrily toward dinner. There would be a roasted pigeon in gravy, and cracked wheat with raisins and pine nuts. He could almost smell it. Perhaps he really did smell someone else's meal from down the hall, although he doubted that his nose could have picked up any scent—he could barely breathe. Weeping was a terrible physical ordeal. He looked longingly at the bowl of olives he'd set on the floor, but it was too far away to reach without getting up, and he had nowhere to spit the pits except his bedclothes. The second cup of wine was empty, and there were stains on the sheets. He could never make it down to the kitchen for food; he would simply have to do without.

Two things troubled Naheshi as he slumped against the wall, feeling control of his hands and head ebbing. One was his utter cowardice. It shocked and disgusted him that fear of punishment could reduce him to abandon his conscience in a matter of minutes. But why should he be surprised? Had he ever at any point in his life shown any courage— or any other virtue, for that matter? No, he had failed in everything, disappointed everyone. This was simply the sad truth about himself. He was a worthless failure. And a coward, a creature—he could not even say a man—without any nobility of character.

All these years, he had been so hurt by his father for selling him. The night he'd overheard, "This will solve our problem," Naheshi had thought, with a child's understanding, that *he* was the problem and that his parents simply wanted to be rid of him. With time, he realized "the problem" had been financial, but it was still a painful splinter in his insecure little heart. It had seemed like a cruel rejection—to sell one's child for money, like a sack of flour. To lay the whole weight of a family's hardship on the frail shoulders of a boy had been doubly cruel.

Yet would he have made any other choice if he had

been the penniless father of a child whose lucrative career promised to erase the family's debt? In fact, the poor sold their children all the time. Self-interest was a powerful—perhaps an all-powerful—motivation. Heroes like the god Ninurta might act against it, brave and selfless and loyal to their principles, but worthless dogs like him rarely did.

Dear gods, had he not just sold out the very sunshine of his life?

He felt a kind of weariness, not just the result of approaching drunkenness but a moral weariness. He'd pretended to be a good person who thought first and only of the queen, talking to himself smugly about loyalty and his high duties as a palace functionary—when in fact he was nothing but a piece of shit who would sell his soul to avoid a blow. He didn't deserve to serve the queen. She was too good to wipe her feet on him.

But then there was the second thing that troubled him. Where *did* his allegiance really lie? The Old Dragon was right: he did, in fact, serve the king, like everyone else in Ugarit. He couldn't imagine that Taddu would do anything disloyal, but if she did, would he not owe it to the king, and indeed the whole kingdom, to make that known?

No, it was unthinkable. His fidelity to the queen was of another order altogether. He had known her since she was born, the Great Lady's precious youngest child. He'd watched her grow up and become a beautiful young woman, a treasured bride. He'd been given to her to be her own servant, her link to her homeland. More important still, he had bared his soul to her, handed her that quivering little core of himself that he'd never revealed to anyone else. He had her... her affection, her trust. She needed him. He could never betray her, no matter what he had promised in a moment of weakness. This was a loyalty so primal it was almost outside his control. No matter how unworthy he was as a person, his love for her was pure and noble; it was the only thing good about him. It was as high above his other fidelities as the gods were above mankind. He could not sully it without somehow ceasing to be. He existed only to protect her.

He fell asleep still sitting upright, dreaming of a soft cheek against his own.

CHAPTER 6

NEWS OF THE DEATH OF King Benteshina son of Tuppi-tesshub of Amurru reached Ugarit by exhausted courier that very evening. The horseman had ridden at top speed, making use of the royal relay stations set up by the viceroy across Shiyannu, and had actually overtaken the Great Lady's previous rider. In Ammishtamru's absence, the message was taken first to the regent, his mother. Ahat-milki tore her clothes and clawed at her face as one should, but in her heart of hearts, she felt relief. The days of suffering and helplessness were over, and Benteshina had joined his royal ancestors in a happier land. Her dear big brother hadn't been that much older than she.

Gods preserve me *from such a lingering death,* she prayed.

She remembered her brother in his youth: funny, impetuous, and full of zest for life. So many times, he'd escaped from the consequences of his ill-considered actions as if by a miracle. But from Motu, there was no escaping in the end. Not even the devotion of a prudent and well-connected wife could shield him from death.

Ahat-milki would have liked to retreat into her

memories, but duty demanded that she tell the late king's daughter, Queen Taduhepa. And afterward, there would be sacrifices to make for Benteshina's smooth passage to the Rapi'uma, and the court would be told to wear mourning for a period. She needed to write a long letter to Gasshulawiya, her sister-in-law, who was suddenly a dowager queen like herself at the age of forty-two. Ahat-milki's work never ended. Given the hour, however, she indulged herself a little and decided to meet with her niece in the morning. She was too tired and felt too vulnerable at the moment to confront that irritating child.

Naheshi was present when the queen mother summoned his mistress to her palace the next morning. He had just come on duty, thick of tongue, his eyelids as swollen and translucent as boiled onions. Ahat-milki was the last person he wanted to see, but Taddu ordered him to accompany her.

They both had a fair idea of what the audience was about; everyone had been expecting the worst for days. The young queen snapped at her handmaids, twitching so much that they could scarcely apply her cosmetics or dress her hair. She set aside her breakfast uneaten and paced up and down, wringing her hands, while Naheshi found some suitably subdued garments for her to wear until the formal declaration of mourning. He walked beside her litter across the royal plaza, surreptitiously stuffing into his mouth the bread and dates she had refused, and trailed her into the queen's vestibule.

"My lady Queen Taduhepa to see the queen mother,"

he announced to the housekeeper, who met them at the door. They followed her up the stairs and were received in her salon, with its windows along one side, overlooking the roof of the royal chapel and the ceremonial plaza. As they entered and bowed, the old woman rose. The heavy Egyptian-style wig she always wore, a relic of the fashions of her youth, dwarfed her gaunt face.

"What's he doing here?" she demanded, eyeing Naheshi at the girl's heels.

"I told him to come," said Taddu in a small voice. "I didn't think I could face this alone. I know what you're going to say…"

With a last chilly stare at the chamberlain, Ahat-milki turned to the young queen. She began in her gravelly tone, even lower than usual with emotion. "Indeed, my niece, my news for you is sad."

There was a moment of gathering tension, like the instant before a storm breaks. Then Taddu sobbed, "Papa! Papa!" Falling to her knees, she threw back her head and began to wail, tearing at her hair and garments.

His eyes blurry with tears, Naheshi hovered uselessly behind her, face crumpling. The old queen stood erect before them for a moment, fighting back her own sorrow. Then she stepped forward and wrapped her arms around her niece's shoulders, laying her cheek against the cylindrical cap on the girl's head.

"Your mother sent a messenger last night, my dear," she said softly. "Benteshina passed away peacefully yesterday afternoon, may the Rapi'uma receive his soul. She said she would write to you as soon as she was able."

Taddu clung to Ahat-milki, animosity forgotten.

Naheshi's nose prickled, and he bit his knuckles to hold back a sob. He, too, had known and respected the old king of Amurru. Benteshina had been a strange, unpredictable little man, capable of outrageously imprudent behavior but not a bad king for all that. Naheshi suspected it was the levelheaded influence of the Great Lady that had made him as successful as he was in his later years. *If only I had someone to save me from* my *folly,* he thought.

"I wanted to be there with him." Taddu wept into her aunt's arms. "Why couldn't I go? Why couldn't I go to him?"

"My dear, all of us who loved him would have liked to be at his side, but our first duty is to our adopted country. Neither of your sisters was able to go, either. But your mother and brother reminded him of your love for him, hoping he was still able to hear. He is finally free of pain." She gently lifted Taddu, whose face was twisted with distress, her lips trembling. "We have things to do for him now. We must notify Ammi, send an envoy to the funeral, and prepare the court to go into mourning. I hope I can count on your assistance."

Taddu nodded, unable to speak. After a moment, she managed to plead, "Why can't I be the envoy to the funeral, Aunt? I'm his favorite. There's no one he'd rather have there than me. And I want to see my mother—"

"My dear, I have just explained that that cannot be, especially as long as Ammi is out of the country. Perhaps Prince Ibi-ranu can go."

"Ibi-ranu?" the queen shrieked, her cheeks flaming. She surged to her feet. "Why him? He's nothing to my father! He's *her* son. He's probably glad Papa is dead."

The sympathy that shared sorrow had wrought

between Ahat-milki and her niece was broken abruptly. The dowager's voice was razor edged with rising irritation. "He would represent the kingdom of Ugarit, Taddu. He has sufficient rank to honor your father. I can't imagine he would feel pleasure in any king's death, and Benteshina *was* his great-uncle, you know. Need I remind you that your own son is only four, hardly up to the intricacies of a state funeral."

But Taddu was unappeased. She spun and stalked a few steps away, her hands clenching convulsively. "It isn't fair. No one here cares anything about me, not even my aunt. You're all against me. Not even my own mother wrote to me first. You're all against me, I say! Motu devour you all!"

Naheshi's jaw dropped in horror. He understood his mistress's anguish, but cursing was dangerous business. He spat surreptitiously over his shoulder. Ahat-milki's face had hardened into stone. She caught his eye and raised a brow as if to say *Do something with her*.

He touched Taddu's arm hesitantly. "C-Come, my lady. You must be exhausted."

"Yes, no doubt," her aunt agreed in a voice entirely devoid of warmth. "I hope you will be in better control of yourself before you are required to make a public appearance."

The young queen shook off her chamberlain's hand and dropped a freezing curtsy. "I take my leave, my aunt."

They departed without ceremony, Naheshi trailing anxiously along, matching his long, ungainly stride to her short one. In her chamber once more, Taddu let fly a stream of furious and very unladylike expletives. Naheshi quaked before her temper, scuttling to catch the bowls and cushions she hurled before they hit the floor. The maids huddled nervously around the walls until he dismissed them. When the queen's squall of anger died out, she threw herself on the bed facedown, sobbing. He hung, uncertain, at her side, not daring to touch her, not knowing what to say.

At last, she snuffled, "Get me my new jewels, Naheshi."

He obeyed, laying them on the bed beside her: the palm-tree earrings, the amber necklace, the broad crescent-shaped collar with embossed lions in a sinuous flying gallop. She drew them to her with a musical tinkle and clasped them to her heart, bending her head over them.

"I won't get to wear them now for ages," she murmured.

"It won't be so long, my lady," Naheshi assured her, feeling a little queasy as he remembered her eyes locking with the Alashiyite diplomat's one good eye, the man's white grin in his dark face.

"No one seems to realize how a woman needs to be loved," she said softly. Naheshi bit his lip, hoping and dreading. But she did not turn to him. Instead, she rested her cheek against the glittering jewels.

Naheshi, as tall as he was, had no trouble seeing over the crowd, but pushing through it was another story. His expensive clothes encouraged a certain sort of people to back off, but others seemed to take a perverse pleasure in obstructing a personage of means, especially one of "his kind." The sheer effort of moving forward with the unwieldy bundle of linens under his arm, along with the shouts and smells and noises of the market, had exhausted him. His nerves were not in good shape lately. He needed someone to do this sort of thing for him, but since his manservant had disappeared more than a month ago, he'd found himself reduced to carrying out such menial tasks on his own behalf. Fortunately, his kind mistress understood; she had not only permitted him to take the morning off from her service but had actually urged it as well.

He finally struggled through the densest part of the market-day crowd and threaded his way among the mule-drawn wagons and laden donkeys that clogged the streets around the square. Naheshi moved carefully, avoiding their droppings and dodging their dangerous hindquarters.

All at once, a hunched gray head rose tall above the crowd, its coarse, grizzled hair standing out like wings as the breeze pushed it back. *Dear gods, it can only be Agipsharri.* Naheshi felt his day grow cold as if a cloud had passed over the sun. He slowed his pace so he would not overtake his fellow eunuch, the very last person he ever wanted to see.

Naheshi drifted to a stop at the intersection of a steep street that led off to the southeast and followed Agipsharri with uneasy eyes as the slave turned the corner. When the crowds thinned for a moment, Naheshi could see the old eunuch's broad, swaying posterior disappear down the street. Agipsharri was moving about as fast as he ever moved, looking around in a downright furtive way.

What's so urgent? Surely, he's not on the queen's business. She has many young pages and maids available for jaunts into the city. Why would she have sent that slow old creature to run an errand? And if he's not running an errand, then why is he off duty in the middle of the day?

Suddenly, there was an explosive crash of pottery, and

a shout rang out behind him. Naheshi spun about, heart pounding, to see several jars in wobbling fragments on the paving stones of the street, olives rolling everywhere in a sluice of muddy brine. A tethered donkey skittered sideways away from the noise, nostrils round with alarm, its packsaddle empty, straps dangling, revealing the nature of the accident.

A merchant—some proprietor of a market stall, from the cheaply dressed look of him—had hold of a cowering man by the ear and was berating him furiously. "You clumsy oaf! Look at what you've done! There's ten silver shekels' worth of olives down in the dirt. You idiot! Can't you even tie a strap?" He cuffed the unfortunate slave across the face and pushed him to the ground. "I've had it with you. You're more trouble than you're worth. Pick'em up. Pick'em up!" he bellowed.

The slave slipped around on his knees on the rolling fruits as he tried to collect them, until he fell flat on his stomach, a comical expression of dismay widening his eyes. Several of the bystanders struggled to contain their amusement. Someone finally snickered and said, "Yes, those are sure the olives *I*'m going to buy!" The crowd roared with laughter.

The merchant glared around. His face grew crimson and seemed to swell, inflated by his wrath. He pulled a stick out of the donkey's pack and beat the slave furiously, flattening him to the ground even as the fellow tried to gather the runaway olives. The servant's cheek struck the street and came up bloodied and dripping with mud. He turned fearful eyes on his master, who rained down ever more ferocious blows on his back and head.

In one long stride, Naheshi thrust himself between the master and his servant and, before he had time to weigh the consequences, grabbed the man's arm. "Look here, I don't think that's necessary, do you?"

The merchant whirled on him, stick still raised and eyes blazing. Naheshi drew back uncertainly, overcome with second thoughts. *Don't let him hit me, dear gods. Oh, why did I say anything?*

"He's my slave, and I'll do whatever I want to him. Get out of my way, gelding!" In his anger, the merchant failed to notice the fine clothes, the tablet case, and the seals at Naheshi's belt. Naheshi in turn ignored the insult. The man made a move as if to draw back his stick, but the chamberlain pulled out his purse, and the gleam of metal distracted the merchant from his rage.

"See here, my... my good man," Naheshi said, his voice as disdainful as he could make it over the terrified hammering of his heart. "How much do you want for him?"

The merchant *humph*ed, his eyes greedy. "I ought to pay *you* to take the oaf," he muttered. His shrewd gaze ran Naheshi up and down, then he said more loudly, "Ten gold shekels, and he's yours."

It was an exorbitant price, but the man had clearly seen the gleaming contents of the purse and finally recognized the quality of his interlocutor's clothing. Naheshi, who hated haggling and was in fact genuinely fearful of the fellow, agreed without arguing. He composed his face into its imperious-chamberlain look and tried to still the trembling of his hands. "Get out your scales, and make it quick."

The merchant, shaking his head, set up his scales on

the level threshold of the nearest doorway and watched, sneering, while Naheshi poured out enough gold to balance the weights.

"You've just been robbed," the merchant snickered, biting a piece of the gold with a satisfied click of his teeth. "Enjoy your new purchase, *sir.*"

Naheshi, eager to get away, pretended not to catch the man's contemptuous tone. He pulled the slave up from the pavement by one arm. The fellow's face was purple and raw; blood, mud, and snot ran into his beard. Blood seeped through the back of his tunic in a crimson constellation. He grinned gratefully up at his savior and spat out a tooth.

"Let's get out of here. Can you walk?" Naheshi asked.

"Yes, master. Oh, thank you, master!" The man hobbled along quickly, managing to keep up with the eunuch's long legs. They walked as fast as possible for a block or so until Naheshi thought it was safe to slow down. He turned to the injured slave and gave him a corner of a towel he had just bought to wipe his face.

"Master paid too much for me," said the slave after a moment's dabbing. "I'm not worth half that much. He was makin' you pay for the olives, and maybe the donkey, too."

"Well, we'll try to make you useful, then. Do you need a doctor, do you think?"

The slave looked up. "A doctor? Is master makin' fun of me? Ah, no. Master is just kind. The gods've given me to a good master!"

"What's your name?" demanded Naheshi, eager to end the panegyric.

"Anani, master. Master is rich and good, a great lord!"

Naheshi rolled his eyes, his cheeks reddening. "Hardly. Master is a slave, too."

"But a rich slave!" insisted Anani. "He works hard and pleases his master. P'raps he even works at the palace, a slave of the king?"

"The queen, yes. I'm actually her chamberlain."

Anani gazed up at Naheshi, his good eye wide and adoring. He was a small, wiry fellow, undernourished and bowlegged, with many of his teeth already gone—whether the result of bad hygiene or brutality, Naheshi could not say. Under the swelling of Anani's face and the blood, it was hard to tell what his age might have been, but he seemed spry enough. His unruly mop of hair was still untouched by gray. Perhaps he was not a terrible investment, although Naheshi feared his impulsive purchase was foolish in the extreme. He suspected that the bystanders were all shaking their heads at his naiveté.

But then, he did need a servant, didn't he? That very thought had just passed through his mind, and immediately, he had found Anani. Perhaps it was a sign from the gods.

"So what kind of experience do you have? Could you be a valet? Can you cook?"

"I can do anythin' master wants me to do," Anani declared enthusiastically, wiping the dribbling blood from his mouth with the back of his hand. "I may not be able to read an' write, but I'm pretty quick. I can take care of master's beautiful clothes, I can clean his house, I can—"

"Well, let's get back, shall we? I think we're making something of a spectacle of ourselves." Naheshi drew the slave after him through the crowd. He saw grinning faces as the unlikely pair passed. No doubt, people thought he had beaten the man or indulged in whatever vices they imagined eunuchs getting up to. The guards at the southeast gate of the palace precinct recognized him even before he showed his seals, and they, too, elbowed each other and smirked. As they passed the massive whitewashed walls of the royal residence, Anani gaped unashamedly at them, craning his neck.

Naheshi led the way up the back stairs and crossed through the chancery corridor, which was mercifully empty, although voices came from within the writing room. He was puffing hard from his determined pace by the time the two had moved down the long corridor past the luxurious quarters of the royal women to the smaller apartments of senior staff, but Anani trotted along with spirit, his head swiveling back and forth to take in everything: the painted walls, the tile floors, the high clerestories under the beamed ceiling. At last, they stopped, and Naheshi released the bar of his door. He herded his new slave in ahead of him and shut and barred the door behind them.

"All right, Anani. Here is your new home."

The little man stared about him in awe. Naheshi could see that the idea of living under the same roof with the king impressed him mightily. The apartment was not large, but it was certainly adequate for a bachelor and his servant. The three rooms were plastered in bright colors and pleasantly full of light, thanks to the tall windows that opened onto a court. There were some well-crafted pieces of furniture and rich cushions and a pair of nicely made bronze bowls starting to turn a little greenish from a month of neglect. It was the lair of a person of taste and someone who liked his comforts, although things were far from neat at the moment.

Anani spied the shelves of tablets and held out a tremulous forefinger as if he wanted to touch them but did not dare. "Books!" he whispered. "Master has all those books!"

"Yes, music mostly, but you don't have to do anything with them. Over here is a bucket of water, and that's the slop jar. There's a drain in the other room, so you can give me a shower in there. There's a well downstairs and latrines; I'll have someone show you tomorrow. Here's a brazier for heat and a bit of cooking. If you want to roast or bake something, you can use the ovens downstairs. I'm not sure how that works, but the kitchen staff can tell you. Let's clean you up now, shall we, and we can eat a quick bite of something before I go tend to some duties. No, wait, you can't reach your back. Peel down your tunic."

Anani started to protest then meekly folded his clothes down to the belt and leaned over. The skin of his torso was white against the leathery brown of his neck and forearms. Naheshi wadded up one of his new towels and gingerly sponged the raw welts and broken skin where the merchant's stick had laid open the slave's back. There was a dense mesh of hard pink scars across the ribs and spine. This had not been his first beating. Naheshi could hardly keep a grimace of revulsion off his face. His stomach wanted to come unsettled, yet simultaneously, he experienced a guilty fascination with the sight of the muscular, hairy, masculine back. At length, the blood was cleaned away. He dropped the gory towel into the bucket and dried his hands fastidiously.

"I'm sorry, I have no bandages, but it seems to have stopped bleeding. You may have to sleep on your side. I'll see to it you get some better clothes, too."

Naheshi felt he needed cleaning up as well. His face was fiery and his hair wet around the edges. He lifted the curls off his shoulders and tried to fan himself with them.

As if that was Anani's signal, the man wriggled his arms back into his tunic sleeves, unmindful of the dried blood and mud, and set to work being a servant. He pulled up a chair for Naheshi and took off his shoes then proceeded to wash his master's feet, face, hands, and neck with cold, clean water from the drinking-water jar, as if he'd done that task every day of his life. Naheshi, accustomed to managing without help for the last few weeks, was at first a little surprised to find himself served again, but he was pleased—more than pleased—by the zeal of his new purchase. He liked to be taken care of. Although he had scarcely been sick a day in his life, he thought of himself as a little delicate and in need of pampering.

His new slave seemed oblivious to what had to have been considerable pain of his own. His eye had swollen shut, and his face was still a bloody mask. "Lemme get master settled first. Where would the food be, master?" He bustled off in the direction Naheshi indicated. Sounds of rummaging came from the adjacent room, and in a moment, Anani returned with a cup of wine and a bowl of dates, which he presented to the eunuch with a ceremonious little bow. Naheshi was almost amused—the fellow seemed to think he was the king's own steward—but the chamberlain was also touched by his slave's gratitude. Anani's life with the hot-tempered merchant must have been grim.

While Naheshi nibbled the dates and sipped his wine, Anani plunged his head into the water bucket and scrubbed his battered face cautiously with his palms, not toweling himself until he'd asked permission to use the cloth. Then he came and stood before his master with folded hands, waiting for a command.

Naheshi, sucking his fingertips, gestured for the servant to have a seat on the floor and pushed the bowl toward him. "Have some dates, why don't you. You must need a little reinforcing after that beating."

"Oh no, master; I can eat later. I want to be sure master has everythin' he needs, before."

"I'm not sure you understand that I am a slave, too, Anani. I may be paid well, but I am no more a free man than you." *And rather less of a man,* he thought with bitter humor. "You need not be quite so obsequious."

"So *what*, master? Obs... obs...?"

"Perhaps my accent confuses you." Naheshi smiled, not wanting to shame the fellow. "Not quite so... humble and obliging, let's say."

"Ah. May I ask where master is from with his beautiful accent?"

"Ninuwa."

"Ah." He looked blank. "And is that a long ways away?"

Naheshi sighed. "Yes, a very long way away. To the east."

"Is it beautiful there, master?"

Is it beautiful? He had once thought so. "I suppose. A smallish city. It's on a kind of cliff. There are mountains. And a river, much bigger than the Rahbanu—an enormous river. It's hot in the summer and very cold in the winter. But dry."

"Are all the people of Ninuwa as kind as you, master?"

"No, I'm afraid there are some rather bad people there, too. How about you, Anani? Where are you from? A captive?"

"From Mukesh, I guess you could say, master. My gran'parents was taken captive in the war by the present Great King's gran'father. I've never actually been there 'cept on buyin' trips with my old master."

So he was almost an Ugarite. Mukesh was just north of the border, and its people spoke the same language. *Was it painful or thrilling to return to the land where your family was once free?* They could have been farmers or craftsmen; maybe they'd even been rich. Everybody suffered the same fate in a war. Those who had once been free and prosperous became slaves to the victors. The Hittites had conquered Mukesh and put it under the viceroy at Karkemish, just as they had done at Shiyannu, where the king's first wife was from—and Ili-milku, if he remembered correctly. No one had conquered Ninuwa since the days of the Mitannian empire, but there were still those there who made slaves, turned people into property. He could not imagine returning there, even on a buying trip, and having to face his mother and father and his brother, Puzuh-asshur, looking as he did. His father had never lacked for a critical comment. He would have a thing or two to say about his son's appearance. He would be downright cruel. Naheshi's mother would weep and blame herself for letting it happen. Better that their last memory of him should be as a child.

"Here, Anani." Naheshi thrust his empty bowl into the servant's hands. "I need to go. I'll be back around sundown. I'm sorry to leave you like this without any more instructions, but I've spent rather a lot of time this morning on personal matters. I have duties to attend to, or my lady the queen will be unhappy with me."

Naheshi reached toward his shoes, but Anani intercepted him and knelt before him to slip them back on his master's long feet. The servant looked up, his good eye shining, as his master rose. "The queen herself, master? You'll talk to her an' everythin'? What a honor to serve such a master!"

Naheshi's throat constricted. He patted the fellow on the shoulder and unbarred the door. "I'll be back around sundown for dinner, Anani. If you don't want to attempt cooking yet, you can tell them in the kitchen that I'll take some food away."

"And what is master's name, please?"

"How silly of me. Nahish-shulmanu." His father had often made it clear how laughable it was for a knobby-kneed ragamuffin to swan along under such a fine, aristocratic-sounding name as Nahish-shulmanu. That was why he never thought of himself by his full name, he realized, but only by his childhood nickname, Naheshi. *Naheshi* was a bungling failure, bowed down with abject apologies. *Nahish-shulmanu* was the queen's supercilious chamberlain.

Naheshi dodged out the door, heard Anani bar it behind him, and started down the corridor. What a touchingly innocent, good heart his new slave had. *He must have suffered under that rascally olive merchant.* Naheshi felt that he needed to deserve Anani's admiration—and then he admonished himself. The slave needed to earn the master's confidence, not the other way around. And Naheshi had virtually apologized to him as if he owed his servant any apologies. After five years, he still wore authority with the greatest discomfort.

CHAPTER 7

L UNCHTIME WAS OVER, AND NAHESHI was on his way back to the queen's apartments. He'd missed his meal, what with his errands and all the business with Anani. He hoped there would at least be a moment for a siesta. Sometimes Taddu wanted to play or talk all afternoon, but more frequently, there would be several hours of inactivity, and he might lean a stool against the wall of the shady loggia and doze in the delightful cool of a sea breeze until the royal household came to life again. There might even be some food left from the queen's repast. His stomach growled. Those dates had only whetted his appetite.

In his mind, Naheshi rehearsed with a sort of half-embarrassed delight the praises of his new servant: "rich," "good," "hardworking," "favored by his master." If Anani only knew. But it felt remarkably comforting to have someone's esteem, even if it was based on complete falsehood. He would try to behave in the manner of a rich, good, hardworking person favored by his master, even though it was an act. Those traits were all praiseworthy goals. It had nothing to do with pleasing his slave.

He sailed down the hall, wearing his mask of competence, and entered the queen's antechamber. He was vaguely aware that the guard post at the doorway seemed uninhabited, but he was too preoccupied with his thoughts to give it much attention. It was all he could do not to laugh aloud. His life was like a game of make-believe. *Here, Naheshi, you be the chamberlain today. Come in, and we'll all pretend to respect you.* The maids on duty jumped to their feet at his entrance and tried to look as if he had interrupted some important activity, but he knew very well they had been sitting around gossiping, and they knew that he knew.

"Well, my beauties. Why are we not with the queen?" He cocked a severe eyebrow at the three girls, who pouted and avoided his gaze.

"She told us to leave. She wanted to rest," Abdi-rama said defensively. She was the one with the straight fringe of hair down to her eyelids. He'd had trouble with her before. But then again, she had said he was nice.

"We can hear her from here if she calls," added the black-browed Ishtar-ummiya, swinging her shoulders like an admonished child.

"How long have you been out here doing nothing, you three?"

"Since just before lunch," said Abdi-rama. "She made us go out. We told her you'd be mad, but she said she'd answer for it."

The little plump one chimed in, "We haven't had anything to eat yet."

Naheshi shook his head, disgusted. It was a shame there were not more slaves of the caliber of zealous, faithful Anani. These girls had no loyalty to their mistress. Perhaps they had been poisoned by palace gossip—started, no doubt, by the Old Dragon, who did everything she could to undermine the authority of her daughter-in-law. It was too bad when even servants felt free to pass judgment on their betters. He knocked on the door of the royal bedchamber and waited, but there was no answer. The queen was undoubtedly taking her siesta. He pushed gently, called "My lady?" and stepped inside. No one was in the bed or anywhere else in the room.

"My lady? It's Naheshi. Is everything well?"

No answer. He walked about, looked under the carved bed frame, behind tapestries, inside the clothes press. No one. He stuck his head out the door leading to the queen's loggia, overlooking the garden. Perhaps she'd gone into the garden to get away from the heat, but that would have meant crossing the antechamber to reach the stairs. *Did the maids fall asleep or leave their post?* He leaned over the rail in an effort to see inside the garden pavilion to his left, but its tented covering made that impossible.

"My lady?" he called hoarsely, trying not to awaken the sleeping household. Outside the windows, the garden shimmered within its white walls, empty and silent except for the pulse of the cicadas and the whistling wings of a dove that rose, startled, from a palm tree. His heart began to drum uneasily. Gods above, could something have happened to her on the one morning he had leave to run errands?

Naheshi composed his face and reentered the

antechamber, where the three maids looked up expectantly. "At ease for now, my beauties," he murmured. "My lady has an assignment for me at the moment."

He swept past the girls and pushed out the door in an increasing state of agitation. He heard the plump maid call out behind him, "Can't we finally get some lunch?"

Where was the queen? Where was the guard, for that matter? He walked as quickly as possible, not wanting to be seen running through the corridor, and clattered down the stairs. It was the siesta hour, of course, and the palace seemed to be a house of ghosts. The garden blazed in the brilliant glare of early afternoon. Sure enough, the pavilion was empty. He stepped between the columns of the open banquet hall, shaded by the loggia above, paused until his pupils could adjust to the darkness, and stared around, nearly desperate. No one. No one. The cicadas were deafening. A headache began to throb behind his eyes.

"My lady? Please answer!" Naheshi's voice was reedy with fear. There were ten thousand places Taddu could be without ever having exited the palace. The building was enormous, some ninety rooms, not to mention the vast underground vaults of the dynastic tombs. But why would she have wandered off alone? And then, of course, there was the even more horrific alternative: perhaps she had left the palace altogether and scarpered off into the city.

Why? Why? Why? The king would have him flayed alive, or something even worse, if any harm had come to her, and he would deserve it. The queen was like a little girl who wanted to shake off her queenly obligations and amuse herself, which to her often meant flouting everyone else's sense of propriety. Maybe she'd carried out some escapade and was just waiting until he, Naheshi, was absent so he couldn't scold her.

He covered his face with trembling hands. Had his severity pushed her to some folly—or conversely, had his willingness to turn a blind eye to some of her larks encouraged this foolish adventure? Naheshi's heart was hammering. What if she had been kidnapped? He couldn't live with himself if any harm had befallen his precious Taddu.

Naheshi stumbled from doorway to doorway, moving through sheds and magazines and the kitchens, unoccupied but for a slumbering scullion propped against the jamb. He could wake the lad and ask if he had seen the queen. No, it was better to tell no one. Asking questions would only cause unnecessary panic, and he might find her at any moment. The service corridor, a kind of porch around the outside of the garden wall, was shady and cool from the overhang of the apartments above, but Naheshi was sweating like a jug of cold well water on a hot day. He could scarcely breathe. Panic rose inside him in a yeasty ferment. He could hardly search the entire palace without raising people's suspicions. There would be guards around, and they would not be asleep.

In fact, there were no guards in sight. Naheshi supposed they were on the street side, trying to keep people out, not in. He jumped as he heard the click of a lock and the grating of hinges beside him. The delivery door into the street creaked open a few inches. He heard whispered voices and a familiar giggle, and then, all at once, the queen was slipping into the passage, her face red and merry, her shoes in her hand. She turned and quietly pulled the door shut behind her and locked it. Naheshi froze. The queen's eye turned toward him, and she started, suppressing a cry with a small hand, as she saw him looming in the shadow beside her.

"Oh, sweet Anat, have mercy!" she whispered. "It's you, Naheshi. You frightened me half to death." She laughed then quickly changed tone, becoming severe. "What are you doing down here at this hour? I thought you were out running errands of some kind."

He was almost tearful with relief. "Oh, my lady, thank the gods you're safe. I was so worried when I couldn't find you, I—"

But she cut him off, her tone as outraged as a whisper could make it. "Keep your voice down. I'm not a piece of lost property, Naheshi. *I* knew very well where I was, and there was no need for you to know. You are not my jailer, if you please. I don't owe you any explanations." She dropped her shoes and prepared to slip her feet into them, but Naheshi knelt hurriedly to put the shoes on for her. Stung, he was grateful to have an excuse to avoid her eyes. He saw wadded under her arm a net—a ladder?—of fine cord. She jerked it away from his gaze and set off around the corridor at a brisk pace, moving quietly. Her back was stiff and angry.

Why is she mad at me? He felt like a rebuked child, even though he realized her tone was to some extent the bravado of the guilty. He followed her meekly up the stairs and down the second-floor corridor through the chancery. Scribes were starting to return to work. They bowed like the wheat in the wind as they realized it was the queen passing, her chamberlain in her wake. *Click-click-click* went her rapid little steps down the corridor past the king's empty apartments.

Naheshi, his mind in turmoil, tried to make sense of what he had just seen: the queen, alone—but not alone; there had been someone with her, to whom she had spoken, with whom she had laughed—in the streets of the city, sneaking back into the palace through a delivery door in broad daylight, a ladder under her arm. This would look very bad indeed if anyone should find out about it. He should report it to the queen mother. But how might she twist it?

The important thing was that Taddu was back safe. Whatever imprudent adventure she'd carried out was over. She was safely home, and no one had seen her in a compromising action but himself. No need to say anything just yet. Now that she was back inside the palace, who could complain? She had every right to be in the service corridor or the throne room or wherever she chose. Taddu was right—that was her business. He was not her jailer; he only managed her household.

They were at her door. The guard was in place. Naheshi realized that the soldier's absence was what had seemed amiss earlier. The man drew to attention, and Naheshi pushed the heavy leaf open for his mistress, who sailed back into her apartments, head high. The three slave girls jumped to their feet and bowed, but she sent them away with a curt command, her voice still rigid with anger. The queen proceeded into her bedroom, while Naheshi hesitated at the door.

She hurled the cord ladder to the bed. "Come in here," she ordered.

133

He followed with trailing steps, as if it had been he who had committed a terrible breach of protocol. Once they were securely alone and the inner door bolted, Queen Taduhepa whirled and stared at him for an excruciating moment with blazing eyes, her mouth working as if she were trying to decide what to say.

Finally, she stepped close to him and laid a hand on his arm. Her voice was suddenly gentle, as if she were addressing a child. "Naheshi, I know you meant well, but you can't be spying on me. I'm not answerable to you."

"No, my lady, of course not. I just—"

"Stop right there. You can't judge me. Do you understand? You run my household; that's all. If I wanted to swim in the sea naked by moonlight, you would have absolutely nothing to say about it. I am answerable only to the king, my husband. Is that clear?"

"Yes, my lady."

"It displeases me when you overstep your bounds like that. I know you're loyal and affectionate and all of that, but if you run around the palace, hunting me, every time I'm not right under your nose, people will think that something is wrong. It will make people suspicious. They'll think I'm doing something wrong when I'm not. Do you understand? You're acting possessive, and I won't have it."

"Yes, my lady, I…"

Suddenly conciliatory, she drew closer, leaning against him, and turned her big eyes trustingly up into his. Naheshi held his breath, his flesh melting.

"In fact, Naheshi, my dear old friend, what would really please me would be for you to make yourself more helpful. If I should want to, well, swim in the sea naked by moonlight, shouldn't I be able to trust you to help me? Isn't it your job to see to it that I have everything I need to make my life pleasant?"

"Y-Yes, my lady."

"Well, then, think about it. I should be able to trust you not to complicate things for me but to make my life easier, right? Wouldn't the king want that?"

"Uh…"

"Of course he would. I know you want me to be happy, Naheshi." She grasped his long hands in her small ones and squeezed them conspiratorially. "And all I did was visit the market anyway."

"Alone? In the middle of siesta?" His anxiety burst forth. He couldn't help himself, although he could see from her hardened face that his implied criticism displeased her. "At least," he amended, "take me with you next time, my lady. It's so much more seemly. And anything could have happened to you alone. You could have been knocked down by the crowd, or worse. I couldn't bear to think of anything happening to you."

She stared him in the eye, as if considering a choice, then in her most winsome little-girl voice said, "That would be lovely, Naheshi. See how much better that would be? You're so loyal and discreet; I know you would see to it that nobody would see anything or say anything bad about me, wouldn't you?"

He wanted to say, *But you mustn't do this again, for all the gods' sake! It's dangerous physically and, even more, politically. You have enemies who are watching you all the time, looking for you to make one misstep. You can't do this again!*

Instead, he said, "You can count on me, my lady."

"I knew it!" the queen cried in triumph. "Dear old Naheshi!" She threw her arms around him and hugged him. "It's our little secret!"

She turned away, fanned herself with her hand, and said breezily, "Now, call the girls, Naheshi. I want a bath."

He bowed and moved to the task, his troubled thoughts a thousand miles away. How could he warn her without openly saying what was afoot? How could he alert her that he, her own trusted Naheshi, was spying on her? Perhaps if he seemed to abet her folly, she would put down her defenses, and he could exercise some sort of calming influence. Maybe little by little, he could help her see how utterly inappropriate this sort of unaccompanied foray was. At the very least, his presence could provide some protection, although he wasn't certain he would be much help in a pitched battle. The only time he'd ever so much as hit someone was that slap at Agipsharri.

Why didn't she take a few soldiers? Why not a well-guarded litter? But he realized, in her defense, that Ugarit was a bigger and more sophisticated place than Amurru. Her childhood in the palace had been informal, bohemian even. She just didn't understand how inappropriate this was.

And he had to admit that she had a taste for danger.

"You three, the mistress requires your presence. She wants her bath." He clapped his hands, and the maids jumped up and ran into the queen's bedchamber as if nothing could have delighted them more.

He considered seeking out Urtenu. He needed to make some kind of a report, but if the man asked him point-blank, "Has the queen's behavior seemed strange in any way?" would he have to tell him that she'd climbed over the balcony on a rope ladder and left the palace? It was not easy for an honest person to tell a baldfaced lie.

At least, he'd thought of himself as an honest person, but in fact, his life had become more and more of a lie lately. Or maybe it had always been. Now that he considered it, honesty was not a virtue a slave could afford. *What would have happened if those girls had said, "Leave us alone. We're lazy, and we don't want to be troubled to draw you a bath"?* He thought with a rueful smile of his own unflappably admiring Anani, wondering how much of that admiration was sincere and how much was just the complaisance of the vulnerable.

But Naheshi's dishonesty went even deeper. It came from a profound cowardice.

Not that his life was worse than many another slave's. He tried to picture what it would be like to be part of a conquered population, dragged out from the ruins of his city, seeing his father killed, no doubt, and his mother... well, one could imagine. The children would all be sold into slavery, like Anani's grandfather. Was that what had happened to the three maids? They had to have a few dark places of their own to protect.

As for himself, he was just a coward. Every time Ili-milku brought up the subject of his poem and setting it to a tune, Naheshi compounded the lie and swore he knew nothing about music. It was ridiculous. It had almost become a ritual. He remembered how he'd felt as if he would faint when the Old Dragon had asked about his past. *Why should I have to admit to her what a failure I have always been? But then, why not? Because it hurts. That's why.* The very thought of pain reduced him to quivering porridge. He was a liar *and* a coward. And so he would go to Urtenu... and tell him nothing.

Naheshi was standing in the antechamber, staring into space, when there was a knock at the outer door. He snapped out of his reverie and pushed open the heavy leaf.

The guard stood there, and behind him waited a page with a leather bag over his shoulder. "A message for the queen."

"The queen is occupied," Naheshi said in his most officious voice. "I can take it for her."

The page pulled from the bag a bulky clay envelope, still not fully dry, and handed it to Naheshi in silence. The eunuch tipped him a bronze piece and demanded, "Who gave you this, boy?"

"I don't know, sir. The soldier at the main gate told me a servant gave it to him and said there was a message for the queen—that's all."

"Thank you. I'll see that she gets it." He pulled shut the door and barred it, as if the stout beam could keep away the dangers that seemed to be gathering over his head like storms from the sea. Or was that just his headache bearing down? He gnawed his lip.

Naheshi set the pillow-shaped envelope on the table. There was no writing on the outside and no seal. Someone had scratched a few marks across the opening to serve as evidence in case of tampering. *Who could be sending the queen a message like this? Certainly not her family.*

The letter had not come from the chancery in Amurru or from any other court. Perhaps a tradesman had sent it as a discreet reminder for purchases made on credit on her little jaunt to the market. But any merchant—any real merchant—would have marked it with his seal. A worm of unease slithered through Naheshi's stomach. If there had been a surreptitious way to slip the letter out, read it, and slip it back in again, he might have succumbed to curiosity.

The inner door opened, and the queen floated out on a cloud of soap and scent, her maids fluttering about like the handmaidens to a goddess, some playful daughter of Ba'al—Talliya, goddess of the dew, perhaps, fresh and young and divinely lovely. Behind the queen, the maids had pulled the gauzy curtain across her window, and the fierce afternoon sun was filtered into a diffuse cloud of brightness from which the queen and her girls emerged in silhouette. Naheshi caught his breath at the beauty of it.

"A message, my lady. It was just delivered. No name." He held it out to her, and Taddu snatched it from his hands, suddenly eager. He inhaled the perfume of her soap and her body.

"Occupy the girls somehow, Naheshi." She retreated back into her bedchamber, and before Naheshi could follow her in, she had pulled the door shut behind her. She didn't need the talents of a multilingual scribe to read a letter, but he'd hoped she would confide its contents to him now that he seemed to have committed himself to complicity.

He turned to the maids to find them grinning at him knowingly.

"Spinning, my beauties. I see the wool over there, waiting for you, and it says it wants to be spun. Show the queen that you know how to put your time to good use. Come on." He clapped. "Busy hands. I'll have a page bring you up something to eat while you work."

He stood over them, pretending to watch them as they

pulled out their wool baskets, but his attention was on the queen's door. She never called him. At sundown, he dismissed the three girls. They wound up their spindles and distaffs full of wool and put them away in the spinning baskets, giggling and chattering now that they were finally free from their taskmaster. They stretched elaborately and cranked their necks around to be sure he realized they had worked to exhaustion.

The night maids came in. Naheshi gave them their orders and knocked gently on the queen's door to tell her that the shift had changed. He took her order for dinner, which she wanted in the garden pavilion, but she did not invite him into her chamber or indicate any desire to talk. When the page came to tell him dinner was laid below, he notified the queen and then bowed out for the evening.

CHAPTER 8

NAHESHI COULDN'T TEAR THE LETTER from his mind. He drifted back toward his apartment as if in a trance, his thoughts running in circles. He had intended to wash his hands of the queen's mysterious correspondence, which was none of his business, but something about that tablet, coming so close on the heels of her strange adventure, knotted his stomach with dread.

Taddu had been gone such a brief time, a few hours at most. She'd returned unharmed—happy, even—and there was certainly nothing inherently sinister about a letter. Still...

On a sudden impulse, Naheshi turned around and quickly retraced his steps to the queen's apartments. The guard was used to him and let him pass without a remark. Naheshi entered and called aloud, but no one answered. After a moment's silent listening, he gently pushed open the bedroom door. Below, he heard the queen's distinctive, girlish voice and those of her maidens talking and laughing in the garden, where the shadows were already long and cool. There was a rhythmic *pof-pof*, the sound of a ball as it flew from hand to hand. They were playing while they waited for dinner. There would be some time before they ate, then, and it would take them a good while to work their way through the repast. Taddu liked to laugh and converse during her meals, even though the court was still in mourning for her father. Naheshi had enough time for what he needed to do. He began to look around for the letter, but it was nowhere to be seen. The soles of his feet tingled with nerves. What would he say if someone intruded on him? Desperately, Naheshi looked under cushions, under the queen's sheets, in cosmetic boxes, and behind chairs and stools in a weird repetition of his search for the queen herself only that afternoon. Then he saw the tall jar of water from the bath sitting on the floor of the loggia—not a very likely hiding place, but he had exhausted every other spot. He peeked inside, only to see in the bottom a finger's depth of water and, below that, a mass of red clay slurry. It took him a moment to realize he was looking at the dissolved remains of an unfired clay tablet. Someone had destroyed a letter.

This was serious. He had to say something to Urtenu. Naheshi carefully rearranged everything he'd touched and fairly ran to the door. He composed himself, nodded to the guard in a relaxed manner, and walked down the corridor at as natural a pace as he could command, his heart pounding in his ears. As soon as he reached his own door, he hammered on it. From within came sounds of unbarring, then Anani swung it open cheerfully, his face purpled and lumpy but clean.

"Good evenin', master. Welcome home. I have dinner

all ready for you. A nice skewer of pork that I had 'em make up for you in the kitchen."

"Later, Anani." His nostrils flared in spite of himself. He could smell the savory aroma, smoky, rich, and spiked with rosemary, and his stomach spoke up in arousal, but the pork would have to be patient. "I'll be back. No, wait. You come with me and bring a torch. It's getting dark."

"Where we goin', master?"

Ah, there is the question. Was Lord Urtenu still at the queen mother's residence, or had he already gone home to his own palatial dwelling in the city? Naheshi realized in shame what a naive conspirator he was. It would certainly be conspicuous if he went running all over Ugarit at this hour, asking for Urtenu, with whom he might normally have no dealings whatever. The Old Dragon would chastise him for his indiscretion.

"Perhaps it will have to wait until tomorrow after all," he murmured. His stomach was so tight he wasn't sure he could eat. The queen had destroyed her letter immediately, as though she suspected him of prowling and couldn't risk him seeing its sensitive contents. He usually read the queen's letters to her and prepared the response from dictation. What was so very private that she would conceal it from her Naheshi? His imagination could answer that question in many ways, each more horripilating than the last.

Anani sat him down and went through the ritual of removing shoes and washing him up. Naheshi let himself be manipulated, his thoughts far away. But when the magnificent roast pork served on bitter lettuce and the pilaf of cracked wheat with vegetables came steaming to the table, he found his appetite. For a few minutes, he put aside all thinking and answered his animal needs, letting the hot, rich meat melt into his gullet, bringing with it comfort and satiety. He ate rather more than he needed to—well, perhaps a great deal more—so sublime was the comfort of the dripping, herb-sprinkled fat, but at last, he could not hold another mouthful, even though there were still a few pieces calling to him from the plate. He leaned against the back of his chair and untied his belt, which dropped with a clatter of seals to the floor. Normally, he would go up onto the flat roof terrace and enjoy the evening cool for a while before bed, but he was too sluggish and fatigued to manage the stairs. The combination of mental exhaustion and more physical effort than he usually generated in a week had completely drained him.

Anani lit the lamps. The room, back in order, grew cozy with the warm glow of lamplight against its red-painted walls. Naheshi had built a safe and comfortable little world for himself here, and now everything was in terrible danger if he made the wrong decision. Perhaps this forced delay in submitting his report was a sign that he should keep the queen's secret to himself. But Urtenu could have found out about her escapade through some other source—someone who'd seen her in the street—and was waiting to hear Naheshi, the one most likely to be aware of the queen's every move, corroborate the story.

He groaned.

"Ha ha! Did master eat too much? It was good enough for master?" Anani's face split in a proud, gap-toothed grin. "They knew his name in the kitchen, and I had 'em make somethin' really nice for him."

"It was fine. It was delicious. It really was delicious,

Anani. I hope you saved some out for yourself. I'm just tired, that's all. It's been a long and trying day." *Tired is not the word,* he thought. Naheshi felt as if his flesh were settling to the bottom, too weary to stay in place on his bones. He was immobilized with inertia.

"Master works very hard," Anani commiserated. "I put master's bedding in the chest over there. Shall I get things ready for you so the bed's made up whenever you want it?"

"Yes, thanks. I'm sorry about leaving everything strewn around. Things aren't usually in that kind of mess, but my old slave ran away, or something happened to the poor fellow." He eyed with longing the cozy pallet Anani was constructing on the floor. His eyelids felt weighted with lead. He yawned in spite of himself. "Normally, I'd read a little before bed, but not tonight. I may go to bed early this evening."

In fact, it was not really so very early. The sun didn't set until late at this point of the summer. He had to be back at the queen's apartments by sunup to put the morning shift to work. And Lady Taddu had been talking vaguely about wanting to pack and head down to the coast. She often spent a few days at a time at Appu when the king was away. He needed to see Urtenu before they left.

Or perhaps not. He crawled to the comfortable nest of bedding Anani had dragged over and arranged in front of the window to catch the land breeze when the wind turned. Naheshi eased between the cool sheets and stretched out his legs. His body grew limp with the voluptuous pleasure of being prone.

"Good night, Anani. Welcome to your new home."

"Thank you for everythin', my good new master. I'm happy to be here."

It occurred to Naheshi as he drifted off to sleep that he hadn't even told the slave where he should make his own bed.

❖

The next evening, Lord Urtenu received Naheshi at his residence. The doorkeeper announced the chamberlain's presence and opened the heavy panels of the *maryannu*'s study to admit him. Naheshi entered, bowing, his hands clasped together to prevent them from trembling. The queen mother's secretary was seated behind a massive table, shelves of tablets at his back. There were rich carpets on the floor, and a stool waited in front of the table, but Urtenu did not invite him to sit on the floor or the stool. Naheshi stood awkwardly, conscious of his exaggerated height and unmanly shape.

"Yes?" Urtenu demanded, looking up from under his woolly brows. His voice was surprisingly melodious in that hawk-nosed old face.

I'll bet he can sing, thought Naheshi.

"My lord, I... I have observed the queen, as our lady the queen mother asked. I have only the slightest... event, er, well, circumstance to report. And I'm sure it's nothing at all sinister. It doesn't even directly involve the queen."

"The queen mother will be the judge of whether it's sinister or not, Nahish-shulmanu. What happened?"

"Yesterday, during siesta, my lady the queen went shopping in the market alone.

She was—"

"What? She left the palace unaccompanied?"

"Oh, no, no, I was with her, of course. By 'alone' I just mean there were no other guards."

Urtenu stared at Naheshi with a mild gaze of dispassionate curiosity, waiting for him to elaborate. "And?"

"Well, there were no guards anywhere. Not at my lady's door, not at the gate, nowhere. It just seemed oddish, so I thought I should say something. It really doesn't involve the queen, you see, but—"

"Yes, actually, that is odd. What time was this?"

"Siesta time, admittedly. But I would have thought the guards would still be on duty."

Urtenu pressed some letters into his wax writing tablet, leaving Naheshi to gaze down on the bald crown of his head. Then the secretary looked up again. "Thank you, Nahish-shulmanu. I've made a note of this and will pass it along to the regent. Please continue to keep your eyes open. Report to me again next week, or even sooner if anything comes up."

Naheshi trudged up the steep High Street, which was broad enough to be exposed to the sun even at that late hour. He tried to stay on the shady side, but it was full of people and pack animals, wagons and handcarts, leading as it did directly from the South Gate and the bridge over the reservoir. Sellers called out; wagons full of jars forced their way through the crowd behind patient oxen. Shoppers and travelers jostled one another, seeking shelter before nightfall—the outlandishly dressed foreigners, the rich merchants in their fringed shawls and gold jewelry, and the ordinary people with tools or sacks over their shoulders. It was a large and cosmopolitan city.

Naheshi infrequently found himself outside in the streets, and in truth, he didn't care much for crowds—he always felt people were staring at him—but he had to admit that under happier circumstances, he would have enjoyed hearing these many languages and accents, seeing the brilliant swirl of colors and the heaped-up products that traveled through Ugarit from the corners of the earth and made her queen of the seas. The ideal would be to view it all from the rooftop.

But these were not happy circumstances.

All these people, and they have no idea what is transpiring at the palace. They're simply going about their little lives, buying and selling, cheerful or sad, thinking of how soon they can be home for dinner and what will be on the table. Some of them probably could not expect much—so many memories of his own childhood were marked by hunger—while others would feast sumptuously. He wondered how many of them were anxious, how many were cuckolded, or sick. Were their businesses failing? Did they beat their slaves?

Did they have a terrible burden of conscience to bear?

Ahead, the hill continued to climb, and above the houses, he could see the towers of the temples of Ba'al and Dagan set ablaze by the sinking sun. Naheshi hoped the divine protectors of Ugarit and its king were keeping their eyes open. With a weary exhalation, he turned left at the temple plaza and made his way into the quieter streets around the royal quarter. By that point, he was almost completely alone in the deep-twilight shade of the high walls. Not until he passed a cross street did even his long, spidery shadow dance across the wall ahead of him. His footsteps seemed to be the only human sound. He suddenly had the feeling that he was the last person on earth and that everyone else had slipped away in his absence, abandoning the palace and the city, leaving only the pigeons and seagulls. But no, there stood a guard at the service gate of the palace. *Where was he the night before?*

The man recognized Naheshi's seals and, bored and expressionless, let him in. No doubt, his relief was coming soon. Naheshi fervently hoped that by alerting the Old Dragon to the absence of guards, she would see to it that they were replaced with more reliable soldiers and that Taddu would thus find it impossible to repeat her escapade. He told himself he might have saved her life.

Slaves were already lighting torches in the corridor as he passed the kitchens and storerooms. Something savory was cooking. He heard feminine laughter from the other side of the garden wall and wondered if the queen and her maidens were dining in the pavilion. Had he left sufficiently clear instructions for her dinner, or had she called for him and wondered where he had gone so early in the evening? *Perhaps I should take a look and see if she needs anything.* No doubt he could see over the wall if he stretched his neck only a little. But then he recognized the voice of the dowager queen, as low and gravelly as a man's, and the calm, musical tones of Lady Pizidku as well as the giggling of her daughters. He would certainly be unwelcome among them.

Naheshi clumped up the stairs. There was a light in the chancery. Someone was working late. He wondered if it was Ili-milku but doubted it; the young scribe had a home and family to return to. He would be one of those sitting down to a cozy meal, playing with his children, fondling his wife, maybe asking her what she thought of his latest lines of poetry.

There was a guard at the queen's apartment door. Again, Naheshi wondered where the fellow had been the previous day. *Perhaps I should take a look-see.*

He was admitted to the queen's antechamber, which was empty, no lamps lit. He stood there in the darkness, sniffing the faint perfume of the queen's recent presence. But suddenly one of the night maids opened the interior door, running in as if in hasty search of something.

She came upon Naheshi in the shadows and let out a little scream then laid her hand to her breast in relief as she recognized him. "Oh, it's you, Nahish-shulmanu. Why are you just standing there in the dark?"

"I thought I'd see if the queen needs anything before I leave for the evening." He hoped Taddu would invite him to enter the bedchamber to exchange a few amicable words before she retired. Maybe she would even have him sit on the edge of the bed and take sweetmeats from her dainty hands, their almond-shaped nails alluringly reddened with henna. He hoped she would tell him in hushed confidence where she had gone the day before and what the letter said. He hoped she would say she was happy he had come to see her and wish him a pleasant night, cocking her head at him with the grace of a small bright-eyed bird. And he would tell her in a low and earnest voice that she really needed to be more careful. Something terrible could happen to her out in the city—but she could count on his discretion.

"I'll ask her." The maid flitted out as hastily as she had

appeared. In a moment, she was back. "No, there's nothing else she needs that we can't do for her."

"The dinner was satisfactory?"

"I'll ask her." She disappeared then returned after a minute. "Yes, she says it was fine." The girl narrowed her eyes and grinned, as if she was not sure what game he was playing with her.

He bade her and her mistress good night and clumped off to his own door. But just around the corner, he heard someone hailing him from behind. He turned to see Ili-milku scuttling toward him, waving something palm-sized and reddish. He had a basket over the other arm. "Naheshi! Hold up!"

Naheshi smiled with genuine pleasure as the scribe caught up to him. "What are you doing around so late in the day, my friend?"

"I wanted to let you have these tablets to look at, but then, you weren't at the queen's quarters. I was just about to go home when I saw you taking off in the other direction. The gods are good! Here is the new part of the poem I promised you." Ili-milku held out the tablet but also indicated the straw-filled basket with a nod.

"All of this?" Naheshi raised an eyebrow at the basket, which was full of tablets.

"Well, no, but I wanted to give you the full effect of the change of meter, so this is the part before and the part after. So don't drop the basket, eh? That would be many nights' work smashed to bits!" The scribe chuckled. "Don't worry: the tablets are numbered. That business of changing to a *qinah* was a brilliant stroke, Naheshi. I can't thank you enough for the idea. See what you think. Notice the words

151

I've used to accentuate that *shush-BAM* of the waves!" Ili-milku beamed up at his friend. "You know, I've had trouble with one part or another, but this seemed to write itself. Sometimes, you just know when you've hit it."

Released for an instant from his anxious obsessions by the magic of friendship, Naheshi laughed at the poet's enthusiasm. Ili-milku joined in, shaking his head.

"Gods forgive me. This would sound absolutely crazy to anybody but you and me, I guess." They gazed fondly at one another for a moment, then Ili-milku commented, "You know, Naheshi, I don't think I've ever actually heard you laugh before. Am I really, really honored to have pulled a guffaw out of you?"

"I guess I just don't like my laugh," Naheshi admitted, shamefaced. "It sounds like a girl's." His father had always told him so as a child, and it was certainly true now.

"No, no, not at all. You should do it more often. If my solemn epic makes you laugh, so be it!" Ili-milku winked. "I know you're busy. Read it when you get a chance, will you? And look at the part where Anat comes in to rescue Lord Ba'al from death. I just put something down there last night, and I don't know if I'm off on the wrong foot. See what you think. Does she act like a believable woman, or is she too bloodthirsty? Looking at divorce cases day after day does something to a fellow!"

"I'm sure it will be wonderful, Ili-milku."

"None of that, now. I want serious criticism. Don't be afraid to tell me what's wrong. Otherwise, I'd just have my wife look at it." He clapped Naheshi on the arm. "Thanks for this, my friend. Gods grant you a good night."

He turned to go, but Naheshi stood staring after him, his thoughts heaving. "Ili-milku..."

"Yes, my friend?"

"I, uh, wonder if I could ask you something."

"But of course! What can I do for you, Tall One?"

"What if"—he swallowed hard—"what if... how... I mean, if a person were to..." Naheshi found it difficult to breathe, impossible to get the words out. "I... I... oh, never mind."

Ili-milku's brow wrinkled in concern. The scribe's voice dropped discreetly. "Something's wrong? Tell me, Naheshi, old man; don't be shy. If I can help, I want to."

But shame had sealed Naheshi's lips. He shook his head. "It's... it's nothing, Ili-milku. I don't want to involve you."

"Are you sure? I know some law. If it's that kind of thing, maybe I can help."

"No one can help. But thank you." Naheshi turned and walked away, feeling Ili-milku's stare upon him. He was painfully conscious of the breadth of his backside.

※

Naheshi was in a stew of self-recrimination by the time he reached the staff quarters. *Fool, fool, and thrice fool. There was your chance to get good, solid moral advice. Ili-milku is an honorable man, and educated besides. He would know immediately what to do.* The chamberlain was approaching his door, absorbed in debate with himself, when someone stepped in front of him. To his horror, it was Agipsharri. Naheshi recoiled, sure the awful toad meant him no good.

"What do you want, Agipsharri?" he demanded, his eyes narrowing.

"Ah, if the Asssyrian it'sss not!" The old eunuch sneered.

Naheshi's voice shot up with weary aggravation. "Stop it right there. We're both off duty, and I refuse to engage with you and your warped sense of humor. If you have nothing to say to me in plain Ugaritic, just pass by and keep going."

"My, my, so hostile, eh. Is this the way we treat a brother eunuch who has come to offer us a friendly warning?"

Naheshi said haughtily, "You're no brother of mine, Agipsharri. Just go away. Go eat your dinner."

"Mmm. You really do think you're better than everyone else, don't you, Assyrian?" Agipsharri's lip curled in derision. He put on a mincing voice. "'Oh, we're so well educated. Oh, we're so pretty and young. Oh, the queen is so very fond of us.' *Why*, though? That's the question. It's not that you do such a great job of managing her household." His expression became a downright leer, and he waggled a fat finger under Naheshi's nose. "Maybe you and she share a few... secrets, eh."

Naheshi felt an icy-cold wind fluttering about in his chest. He tried to draw a calming breath. "What are you talking about, you lying turd?" He hardly dared meet the other's gaze, which was fixed malevolently upon him. His heart was beating raggedly, and his stomach clenched. Naheshi knew that the frozen pallor that washed over his face would be visible to Agipsharri even without dark powers. He spat over his shoulder just in case.

The old eunuch emitted a wheezing, malicious chuckle that set his rolls of fat bouncing. "Ah, I think we're afraid! I think we have a guilty conscience!"

"So what is it you want of me?" said Naheshi in an unsteady voice. "Do you expect me to pay you to keep quiet about some imagined crime? If you think I'm guilty of something, tell our mistress."

"Oh, no. She's not the one to tell. We both know she has no use for me. She knows I'm loyal to the real queen, Lady Pizidku. Besides"—he bared his yellow teeth—"maybe she's not so innocent either, eh."

"I'm warning you, Agipsharri. I will hear nothing against Lady Taduhepa." The hammering of Naheshi's heart surely had to be audible outside his chest. *Dear Lady Nina, what does he know?*

"Go ahead and hit me again, then, why don't you, eh? That must mean you're right—because you can knock down a poor old eunuch who can't fight back."

"I didn't knock you down, you old fraud. You're disgusting. You're worse than disgusting. If you have nothing to say to me, just go away." Naheshi turned to his door, hoping Agipsharri could not see his face.

"Ah, are you afraid to look at me, Nahish-shulmanu? This is how *you*'ll look in a few years. Will she find you so attractive then, eh?"

"If you're saying that the sight of you is enough to give a person nightmares, then I agree. Go away, shoo." Naheshi hated that his voice was quivering.

Agipsharri patted the tips of his fingers together. "Well, if you don't even want to hear what I know, perhaps I'll tell it to someone else."

"I don't think you know your head from your asshole, Agipsharri. Gods grant you a good night."

Naheshi hammered on the door, his back obdurately turned to the old eunuch. The panel opened at last, and Anani's eyes grew round as his master almost fell across the threshold into the salon.

CHAPTER 9

NAHESHI RETREATED TO THE ROOFTOP after dinner. He was brooding painfully on his dilemma, and—gods help him—on the mysterious threat of Agipsharri. What did that vile old toad know?

Usually, a full stomach helped steady Naheshi's nerves, but he felt as hollow and vulnerable as before he'd eaten. Had Agipsharri witnessed the queen's moment of lonely weakness, in which she had turned to her Naheshi as the only available human comfort, or were his innuendos just the envy of the old and ruinous for the young and still reasonably presentable?

Perhaps, even worse, he knew about the mysterious noonday jaunt of the queen and that Naheshi had not reported it accurately. Suddenly, that glimpse of the old eunuch in the town took on a more sinister meaning.

He heaved a tremulous sigh. Perhaps he should tell Lord Urtenu that Agipsharri was spying on him and that their mission might be compromised. But then Agipsharri would be hauled in and made to explain what he had seen. Either way, Naheshi would look like a disloyal villain. *And in all fairness, am I not?* No matter how low the deed Agipsharri might accuse him of, he had really committed it, after all.

His body ached with tension. He needed a chair for his spot up on the terrace and maybe even a shady grape arbor such as he saw on the roofs below him here and there in the city. But it was not his house. One could hardly plant vines on the king's roof. He sat instead on the roof roller, that large stone cylinder the palace staff used to keep the packed-clay roof tight and waterproof. He leaned back in exhaustion against the wall of the penthouse, glad that at least it shielded him from the gaze of other residents, although it limited his view to the west and north. Sometimes, when there was none of the usual haze on the horizon, he could see Mount Sapunu, where the Lord Ba'al made his home. But it was late, and the long summer twilight was drawing to an end. Perhaps everything was drawing to an end.

The penthouse door creaked open, and Anani stuck out his head. "Ain't it gettin' cold up here for master? Can I bring you a blanket?" He emerged from the door and approached Naheshi.

"No, no. Thank you, Anani. I'm coming down." Naheshi swallowed with effort and added in a lower voice, as if someone might overhear him, "Listen, Anani, let me ask you something."

"Anythin', master. I'm not very smart, but I'll do my best."

"Sit here, won't you?"

The little man folded his legs and sank to the ground beside his master, who was a cubit or so above him. Naheshi was unable to look Anani in the eye, so he spoke to the air, watching the shadow of the penthouse lengthen across the rooftop.

"I have this friend whose master is doing something very strange—maybe nothing immoral but definitely strange. And at the same time, my friend and the master were doing something that could be construed as wrong. It wasn't. It was perfectly innocent. But if someone malicious saw them, he might think it was wrong. And then this other person tries to threaten my friend because he says he's seen something, but the friend doesn't know what it is he's seen, so he doesn't know whether to tell anyone or not. What should he do, Anani?"

There was a moment of silence. Then Anani said, "Forgive me, master, for bein' so stupid, but I don't think I'm followin' you."

"No, of course not. I'm not being at all clear." Naheshi ran his hands through his hair. "Let me try again. I left a lot out." He turned anguished eyes to his slave. "My friend has been told to spy on his beloved master, you see. The master then did something strange, so my friend reported on it—in part. He didn't tell everything for fear he would get his master in trouble. Then later—or was it before?—he and the master... not made love, exactly, but showed their affection in a... a physical way. It was perfectly innocuous, but someone malicious might twist it to make it look bad, you see. Following so far?"

"Yes, master." Anani looked dubious and scratched his head.

"But then, after all that, a third person comes along and says, 'I saw you and your master, and I'm going to get you in trouble.' Now, if he saw the strange deed, it's one thing, but if he saw the innocuous affection, it's something else. My friend doesn't know which. So he doesn't know if he should tell those who told him to spy or not. If it's the strange deed, then it will be clear to them that he didn't tell them everything the first time. If it's the innocuous affection, then that might get his master into fresh trouble. And my friend would be in very bad trouble indeed."

"Ah. Did this third person ask your friend for gold?"

"Well, no," Naheshi admitted. "Perhaps he was going to, and I didn't give him time—I mean my friend didn't. He must want something, though, I suppose, mustn't he?"

"If he wants gold or somethin' else, it's all the same—then he's just a lowdown blackmailer, master. You can't never give in to 'em. My old master had a few in his day, and he said you never gives in to 'em, or else there's no end to it. Just let 'im do his worst. Usually, people hates blackmailers so bad they hardly believes 'em when they do go tell."

"Ah," murmured Naheshi, brightening. "That's probably true."

"So tell your friend to stan' firm, master. You said neither thing he did was so bad, really. So let the ol' blackmailer do 'is worst. Nobody'll believe him anyway."

Naheshi felt as if an enormous burden of ice-cold stone had been lifted from his chest. He rubbed his breastbone, as if he could feel the relief physically. "Anani, you're a marvel. You cut right through to the truth of things. Thank you, thank you. My friend will be immensely relieved to have your perspective. He feels better already."

"At your service, master. Didn'tcha want to go in now?

It's plenty nippy out here after dark, and the mosquiters are comin' out."

＊

About a week later, Queen Taduhepa decided on another of her escapades. Naheshi would never have known about it if he'd been able to sleep. Perhaps he had eaten too much or too late. He'd tossed on his pallet for hours, uneasy and uncomfortable, Anani snoring in the kitchen to wake the Rapi'uma. At last the chamberlain had risen, gotten dressed, and put on his shoes quietly, not knowing exactly what time it was, though the profound stillness suggested the wee hours before the palace bakers began their work. He had no idea what he intended to do; he just felt the need for fresh air or movement. The worst sort of memories always haunted the night hours. Increasingly, his conscience gnawed at him, and it was getting harder and harder to get a restful night's sleep. Anani's homespun wisdom had reassured him momentarily, but the sense of impending doom had come back.

Naheshi found himself outside the queen's door, gazing at it with a pulsing brew of emotions he was unable to identify. Then it struck him that, yet again, there was no guard. Perhaps that was usual at this late hour. Perhaps the fact that the king was not in the palace meant that security was less tight. He could not honestly say that he'd ever come to Taddu's apartment at this hour before, so maybe there was nothing to be alarmed about. But then he heard a faint grating as the massive door swung out on its well-oiled hinges. His heart leaped to his throat—there was no place for him to hide. He couldn't tiptoe away fast enough to get around a corner before whoever was emerging saw him. By some inspiration of the gods, he froze, and the door swung back in his face very gently, bumping against his belly. He was hidden. He heard the lightest of steps shuffle. The door swung away from him, but the person emerging had her back to him as she concentrated on easing the lock shut without a sound.

It was the queen. She was alone, her shawl over her head and wrapped tight around her shoulders. It covered the lower part of her face and hung almost to her eyes, but he knew her slight figure and quick movements, her slim ankles, even her embroidered red shoes. Naheshi held his breath, expecting at any moment to be discovered, but instead, the queen crept quietly in the other direction, treading on the balls of her feet. She carried no light but made her way in perfect silence past the dark chancery and down the stairs.

Naheshi stared after her, jaw dropped. Where was the guard? Where were the night maids? Not sure what to do, he remained frozen until she'd disappeared into the darkness. Then he roused himself. If she was leaving the palace, she needed his protection. He was unarmed except for the tiny penknife on his belt, but perhaps the mere presence of a second person—a very tall person, at that—would discourage footpads. At any rate, he could call for help if she needed it. He could not let her wander into the streets alone. This was insanity. What was she up to?

He debated turning back for a lamp but realized he would never catch up to her if he delayed. He disengaged himself from the wall and set off after her as quietly as he could. When he reached the bottom of the stairs, he had no idea which way she'd gone. It was pitch-black under the overhang of the royal balconies. Not even starshine broke the darkness. He hovered somewhere near the kitchens, feeling his way blindly, hoping he would not crash into a jar or step on a sleeping scullion. But then he detected ahead a sliver of amber light. The service gate had opened, and someone held a torch on the other side.

Naheshi saw the girlish silhouette of the queen, dark against the torchlight, then the gate swung shut with the merest scratch of noise. He groped toward it, orienting himself by the whispered voices. They grew fainter and fell silent. He gingerly pulled back the heavy door and slid out into the street, closing the panel carefully behind him as the queen had done. *Again, no guard. Is this normal?* The street was dark. Not a window was lit anywhere, but the flickering orange glow of the torch bobbed ahead of him. He could make out two figures, one tall and one short: the queen and a man. Their shadows stretched and danced in the torchlight like distorted ghosts, and his heart plunged into his belly. Who was with her? What could she be doing? *The king will have both our heads if this is what it looks like.*

The two figures moved at a rapid pace, their footsteps thumping on the paving stones, but no one was abroad to hear except Naheshi, trailing unseen in their wake. They turned one corner after another into ever narrower streets, until there scarcely seemed room for two to walk abreast. They were moving downhill, sometimes even down steps, but that was all he could tell about their direction. He was completely lost.

He prayed they would not turn around and see him, but they appeared to have no fear of being followed. He stayed as close as he dared without emerging from the darkness, close enough to see that the man had wrapped his arm around the queen's shoulders to propel her along. She leaned toward him and put her face up to his as if whispering.

Then suddenly, they turned a corner and disappeared. Naheshi hastened after them to the intersection, but he could see their torch nowhere. It was as if they had been swallowed up by the jaws of Motu himself. Had they slipped into an open doorway? In the absence of their footsteps, the quiet was so profound he could hear crickets. Again, he had the sensation of being the only person left on earth. He stood there, frozen with apprehension, while the silence surrounded and clung to him like a fog. He could smell it, taste it. From very far away, a woman's shrill laughter rose drunkenly and was cut off. It was not the queen's voice.

"My lady!" he called in an urgent whisper. "Where are you?" But clearly, she could not hear—or would not. He considered calling more loudly, but trepidation sat upon him, forbidding him to make a noise. He could hear his own nervous breathing, the pulse in his temple. The silence outside his body seemed to work its way into his nostrils and suffocate him.

What do I do now? he thought, quivering. *I've lost her. She could be in terrible danger, and I haven't the slightest idea where she is… or where I am, for that matter.*

Naheshi could only assume they were still in the city. The gates would be sealed for the night, after all. The alley seemed to be dirty, slippery underfoot, and rutted; the houses were very close together, the whitewash peeling off on his fingertips. The masonry exhaled dampness, even in midsummer. They had gone a long distance. This was no longer near the palace but somewhere near the bottom of the Lower City.

He felt his way along a little farther, but soon, the alley ended in a wall. Along the edges of the street, malodorous piles of a deeper darkness squashed beneath his shoes. Naheshi dared not think of what it might be.

He lurched back, fearing he'd missed the intersection, and realized he no longer even knew where he had last seen the queen. Something moved in the blackness not far away—or maybe it was just the jumping of his own straining eyes.

"My lady?" he called again, but with a sudden rush of heavy footsteps, two large figures closed in upon him, and they were definitely not the queen and her companion. The men, roughly dressed and unwashed—they reeked of sweat and wine—pressed to either side of him and pinned him hard against the wall.

"Hey, what have we here?" one of them snarled, fingering Naheshi's chin. "Is it a Hittite, or is it one of those ball-less beauties from the palace?" The two laughed, and Naheshi could feel his innards liquefying. He froze like a rabbit in the talons of a hawk; his heart seemed to dribble out of his chest like the dregs of a tallow candle.

One of the ruffians felt the wool of Naheshi's sleeve between forefinger and thumb. "Mmm, nice. I smell gold, don't you?"

The other man emitted a crude laugh. "Is that what it is? I thought he shat himself." The two of them brayed, and a wave of sickening wine fumes enveloped Naheshi.

He felt faint, quivering, nearly paralyzed. He could not

so much as speak. The first man's face thrust close to his own in a frightening parody of intimacy.

There was a hiss and gleam of metal as one of them slid out a knife. "Got any gold on you, eunuch?"

"Earrings!" crowed the other, and a sudden blaze of pain seared Naheshi's earlobe as one of the men pulled out the earring, unopened. The chamberlain cried and tried to put up his hand to protect himself, but his assailant's accomplice pinned his arms.

"Wait! I'll take it out!" he whimpered.

But a second stab of agony told him they had pulled out the other ring. He felt his ears pulsing, the blood dripping down his neck.

"Take my purse; just don't hurt me!" he begged, his voice shooting skyward with fear.

While one of the men held him, the other fumbled around until he found Naheshi's belt knot. Naheshi felt the weight disappear suddenly as the knot was sliced through. One of them snatched up the purse as it fell, and it landed in his hand with a dull *chink*. Naheshi's tablet case and penknife clattered to the ground.

But then he realized in horror that he'd also had the queen's seals on his belt, tied on with a leather thong. He shook himself loose and dived to find them. The men groped for him in the dark. One kneed him in the nose, and he recoiled with a shriek of pain, his eyes filling with tears. But he dived again, scrabbling desperately for the seals, while the men began to punch and shake him. A fist caught him in the stomach and knocked the wind out of him. He doubled up with a squeak, stunned, but by some miracle, his fingers closed on the thong of the seal. He tried to tighten his fist over it, but the men were wrestling his arm back, smashing his hand against the wall.

He dropped the seals, and he and the robbers plunged to the ground at the same time, scrambling for them. The knife flipped away into the street with a clatter. Naheshi grabbed the thong, feeling it break. Someone stepped on his fingers. He screamed again but managed to throw the first seal into his mouth and choke it down. A moment of panic overwhelmed him when he feared it was going in sideways and would strangle him, but he swallowed it, gagging.

The men grabbed his throat and began to throttle him. They slammed him against the wall again and again; his hair flopped back and forth. They were enraged. He heard them snarling, "Kill the cur!"

He writhed like a demon, trying to step on the second seal and kick it away where they couldn't find it. Somehow, his feet came out from under him, and he fell flat on his back with a cry. The two footpads were on top of him, someone's knee in his gut. A longer knife flashed, and he knew he was as good as dead, when suddenly, a man's voice shouted angrily from very nearby, "Hey, you dogs, back off, or I call the guard!"

A torch blazed. Someone swung a sword—Naheshi heard it cut the air. As if they'd been sucked out by the tide, his two assailants pulled themselves off him and disappeared into the darkness. He lay there panting and whimpering with pain, nursing his hand, listening to his heart thunder, his breath rattling in his half-throttled windpipe. A man was looking down at him. Quick footsteps approached.

"Abishushu, what's going on?" Someone bent over him in the torchlight.

It was the queen.

Naheshi felt his eyes bug, although one of them was swelling shut. The pain from his nose seemed to fill his whole face. The queen looked as shocked as he felt. Her little-girl voice rose in horror. "Naheshi! Lady Anat be merciful! What are you doing here?"

"You know him?" demanded the man with the sword incredulously. His voice seemed familiar. At first Naheshi thought it was the king, but the king was in Hattusha, and this man was younger. Naheshi felt he might be hallucinating. Everything seemed strangely sparkling and unreal. He tried to lift his head, to speak, but nothing came out.

"It's my chamberlain! I can't believe this." Taddu knelt beside him and gently pushed his hair back. "Oh no! What's happened to you, poor Naheshi? Look at you…"

She cast her eyes around for something to wipe his bloody face and started to use her cloak, but the man held her back with an imperative gesture. "No, don't get blood on you. How will you be able to explain it?"

"But he's hurt. Oh, Naheshi, your hand, your ears…"

Naheshi tried to say, "I saved your seals," but it came out an unintelligible groan and sent pain slicing through his ribs. He was conscious of having soiled himself in his fear.

"What in the name of all that's holy is your chamberlain doing here?" The man stared at Naheshi as if the eunuch were some dire revenant. He slid his sword back into its scabbard and grabbed his head with both hands, moaning, "This is disastrous."

Taddu leaned close to Naheshi and murmured, "Naheshi, did you follow me?"

Naheshi managed to nod and croak out, "I... I was afraid for you." He doubted she could tell what he was saying.

The man with the sword groaned. "Oh, gods of the heavens. This is all we need."

"We have to get him back to the palace," the queen said, standing up.

"No, no, no, my love," cried the man. "*You* need to get back to the palace, and quicker than quick. How can the two of us carry him? You'd be covered in blood. And I need to get out of sight before the watch comes. Someone has probably heard the noise."

"But we can't just leave him here," objected the queen, near tears. "He could die. What if more thieves come around?"

"It'll be morning soon. He'll be all right. They don't actually seem to have stabbed him anywhere. Someone will find him. Let's get going." The man tugged at her arm.

"But he's all... hurt. Naheshi, you were trying to protect me, weren't you? I can't leave him, Abishu."

The man's eyes cut around, the whites glittering like a frightened horse's. He took the queen's hands and hissed urgently, "It's as much as our lives are worth to try to get him back, my lamb. We can't carry or drag him. What are we supposed to do—borrow a wheelbarrow? How could you possibly explain this? You have to get back before someone spots you. A new guard will be going on duty. Don't ruin everything."

He drew her away. Hands clasped to her mouth, she continued to gaze after Naheshi with brimming eyes as they departed into the night. He heard the man mutter, "We should probably just finish him off. Fewer complications." And the queen's horrified, "No! He's loyal! He won't talk."

Don't leave me, Naheshi wanted to cry, but he did not have the strength.

Every part of him hurt. It was all he could do to breathe. He felt the blood running sideways down his face, like worms crawling. He started to shiver uncontrollably. He had no cloak; his tunic was all rucked up to the knees. He was wet and stinking. He tried to sit up, but the pain in his ribs overwhelmed him. His head felt weightless, and stars began to flash in his eyes. Even the sound of the crickets disappeared into a black well of silence as he slipped into unconsciousness.

CHAPTER 10

A S SOON AS HIS WORKDAY in the chancery was finished, Ili-milku made his way down the long corridor to the staff quarters of the palace. Even with the clerestory windows, the air was heavy here in the interior of the second floor. The day had already sunk into twilight deep within the vast building, despite the brightness of the summer-evening sky framed in each high window.

There was scarcely anyone around, except for a few servants heading through the twilit corridor to their dormitory after a day's service. Mostly, Ili-milku was conscious of the ringing of his own footsteps on the tiles. He felt a little lost. The slave Anani had sought him out to tell him what had happened and had given him rough directions to Naheshi's apartment, but the staff quarters were a maze of side halls and doors that all looked alike. He finally stopped a man hurrying past to ask directions.

Ili-milku had never been to his friend's apartment before. In fact, their friendship consisted mostly of brief and superficial conversations over the writing table, when the eunuch came to the chancery for a blank tablet so he could take care of the queen's correspondence or order supplies for her household.

To Ili-milku, that constituted friendship. He and Nahish-shulmanu shared an interest in poetry, they enjoyed one another's company, and he cared about the eunuch's fate. That seemed to be enough.

Would he risk his life for Naheshi? He wasn't certain, but maybe that was more than a mere friend needed to do. A man contracted sacred bonds with those who shared a meal or lodged under his roof, but in fact, Naheshi had never been to the scribe's home. Ili-milku lived near the temple district in a pleasant house that belonged to his wife's family, and he wasn't altogether sure that his wife would like the idea of inviting a slave, even a wealthy one, to sit down at table with her husband.

He had reached the door pointed out to him—heavy, featureless, and secured with iron nails. The comparative rarity of doors along this narrow corridor suggested that the apartments were larger than those he'd already passed. Ili-milku was glad he did not live in the palace, under someone else's roof, although most of the unmarried young scribes did. *Funny, I've never even asked Naheshi where he lived before.*

But as the bowlegged little servant opened the door and let him in, Ili-milku found a small but charming nest. It was cozy, tasteful, and rather expensively decorated. Hangings were drawn over the windows to keep out the strongest of the evening sunlight. He noticed the shelves of tablets and peeked at them. Ili-milku shook his head affectionately. *Music, the lying bastard.* There was his own basket full of tablets—the poem he had given Naheshi to read. He was both surprised and not surprised to see this world his friend had created for himself and hoped he was not an unwelcome invader of Naheshi's carefully guarded private life.

"Master?" the manservant knelt to address Naheshi, who was stretched out on his pallet with a light coverlet drawn over him. "Your friend Lord Ili-milku is here to see you."

He loves him; see how tenderly he looks at him. Old Naheshi must be a kind master.

Ili-milku crossed his ankles, sank down next to the eunuch, and touched his surprisingly thin shoulder. Naheshi opened his good eye and managed a wan smile.

Gods in heaven, thought the scribe, his stomach sinking. Naheshi looked appalling. His round, boyish face was swollen and purple, his lips split. One eye and cheekbone were bandaged with cloth strips that wound around his head from chin to crown. His teeth were tinged with fresh blood, as if some of them were still wobbling.

"Ili-milku," Naheshi croaked. His visible eyebrow was rippled in pain. There were bloody slits in his ears and bruises on his throat.

"By the gods, old man, they didn't leave anything unmangled," Ili-milku cried in spite of himself. "A robbery, eh? You won't believe this, but it was a couple of the young scribes who found you at daybreak as they were coming home from a night on the town. Thank the Lord Ba'al for whatever depraved habits took them down to that end of the city. Otherwise, it would have been some anonymous workman from the Lower Town who found you. But these lads recognized you right away and got servants from the palace to come and get you. The queen was beside herself, they say." He laughed a little, trying to keep the mood light despite the sorrow that wrenched his soul. "What were you doing down there, Tall One? Got some vices we didn't know about, have you?"

He regretted his words immediately when Naheshi's mouth began to quiver. The eunuch closed his eye and expelled a weary breath. Ili-milku contritely took his friend's good hand, the one not wrapped in bandages. The fingers were long and thin, as delicate as a girl's. They closed weakly around the scribe's stubby ones.

Ili-milku felt a surge of anger on Naheshi's behalf. Who would do something so barbaric to this goodhearted soul? It occurred to him that this was not the first barbarism people had inflicted on Naheshi. Ili-milku knew practically nothing about the Assyrian's past, but clearly, he had been enslaved and castrated, a fate not all that unusual for the sons of captured populations. The fact of that servitude stood between the two friends all the time.

Should I have asked about his story? the scribe wondered guiltily. But any such questions ruffled Naheshi's feathers pretty fast. Ili-milku smiled at the image of a large outraged bird. There was always a slight whiff of the ridiculous about Naheshi, poor fellow. There were things back there that he didn't want to remember... and who could be surprised by that? The world was a damned cruel place. All these execrable wars—they weren't just games of *senet*.

He wished he could somehow put all of this anguish into his poem: the very gods had to suffer, too, and on a divine scale. Didn't Ba'al feel fear in the face of death?

Ili-milku wondered what he himself feared. No mystery there. The thing that chilled his blood was imagining some harm befalling his wife or children. Who he was, his most intimate self, was the man who cherished and protected his family. He was that man even before he was a scholar or a poet or a servant of the king.

And you, Naheshi; who are you really, my friend? What do you fear? What do you love? Do you feel the need of a woman?

Naheshi didn't even seem to be comrades with any of the other eunuchs, perhaps because, on top of everything, he was a foreigner—an enemy, as things stood now. Ili-milku sighed quietly and squeezed his friend's hand. *What an irony. The dread Assyrians, the epitome of swaggering manliness.* He had seen a few around, arrogant and ingratiating at the same time, before the embargo had sealed them off from Ugarit. He could not picture Naheshi belonging to this people, although no doubt they, too, had their poets and scholars—and musicians.

Naheshi's eye opened, and he whispered something. Ili-milku put his head close to his friend's swollen lips.

"Seal?" the eunuch murmured.

"Seal? What about a seal, Naheshi?"

"Lost." The patient coughed painfully and licked his lips, shifting about on his pallet. "Tried to swallow them, keep them from being stolen. Swallowed one. One lost. Got to find it…" He looked up, tense and distressed, breathing hard. "Queen's…"

Ili-milku nodded reassuringly. "The palace servants who picked up your tablet and belt must not have seen it. I'll go search for it. Don't worry, old man. What does it look like?"

The eunuch described it haltingly: brown jasper, as long as the joint of his thumb, the queen's name on it—Taduhepa—and the goddess Hepat, her divine patroness. Ili-milku made a little joke about the fate of the swallowed seal, but Naheshi was past the point of humor.

Ili-milku sat for a while, silently holding his friend's hand, until he realized the eunuch had fallen asleep. He rose carefully and whispered to the servant, who stood hovering nearby, that he would be back the next day. The fellow thanked him with tears in his eyes and let him out.

As Ili-milku returned to the chancery, he decided he would take his slave with him and maybe one of the young scribes who had found Naheshi when he went to look for the queen's seal. Even by daylight, he wasn't sure he wanted to be alone in that part of town. What had Naheshi been up to down there in the middle of the night? *Maybe he does have vices, poor fellow. Damn it, he deserves a few.*

"Well, that's all I can do for you," said the royal physician. "The rest just has to heal naturally. You're lucky they didn't get a knife into you." He lifted his bushy eyebrows meaningfully. "The broken fingers are the worst. I've splinted those. Everything else, just scrapes and bruises. Loose teeth will be all right. Just don't eat anything solid for a while. Painful, I daresay, but not life-threatening; your nose isn't even broken. I popped it back in place while you were unconscious."

He got stiffly to his feet and dusted off his skirts. The queen had sent him promptly the morning after Naheshi's misadventure, and he'd checked back in the next days as well.

"You took some hard punches, boy. Fortunately, you're pretty well padded around the middle, or you might have had some broken ribs." He turned to Anani. "Let me know if any cuts start to look puffy and red or if you see pus. I'll be back to check on him in a few days. He can get up and go back to work whenever he feels like it."

But Naheshi did not even attempt to get out of bed for three more days. He found himself strangely averse to taking up his responsibilities again, because that meant seeing the queen. As long as he was being taken care of, he didn't have to make any decisions, whereas whenever he took up his ordinary grown-up life again, he would have to decide what to do about the queen's nocturnal jaunt, and that was simply more than he could face. Lord Urtenu could not be angry with him for not reporting—he was still in bed. It seemed to take more energy than he could muster just to make it to the chamber pot, where Anani had already found the swallowed seal.

The queen did not come to visit him, although Ili-milku did several times and assured him that Taddu was concerned for his recovery. *How would he know?* Naheshi wondered dully. *Is he just saying that to make me feel better?* Ili-milku also brought back the missing seal, which had rolled a good way down the street and had somehow escaped being stolen by a passerby.

But eventually, Naheshi did return to his duties. The maids fawned over him, begging him to describe the attack—which he declined to do, as much as he longed to; he feared to say too much. They marveled at his slit earlobes, the greenish-purple blotches all over his face and wrists, and the splinted fingers.

Naheshi took the queen her seals, hoping that he might describe for her ears alone what he had suffered to defend her property. She was sitting by the window of her bedchamber with her tapestry frame in her lap.

"Here they both are, my lady." He bowed low before her, wincing at the pain in his ribs. "I apologize for not returning them sooner."

She eyed the proffered seals, a little nonplussed. "But you carry them, Naheshi. Why give them to me?"

"Well, I, uh, wanted you to know they'd been recovered, my lady. I didn't want you to worry about them being found by someone who might falsify documents in your name or something of that sort."

"Well, then, thank you, but keep them." The queen smiled vaguely then murmured, "You poor thing. You guarded them with your life, didn't you? Those ruffians could have killed you." She lowered her voice and began to play with the corner of her needlework, suddenly determined not to look him in the eye. "Um... Naheshi... what exactly *were* you doing following me? I know you said you were afraid I was in danger, but how did you even know I left the palace? Were you spying on me again? I don't know whether to be touched or angry. This is not your duty, Naheshi. I've said all this before. You can't be so possessive. I don't want to seem ungrateful..."

But she is, isn't she? he realized with a stab no less painful than that of the blows he had recently received. He hadn't earned her thanks but, instead, had angered her.

He'd complicated her life, caused her embarrassment, and perhaps even endangered her.

She raised her eyes just as his were starting to mist up, and she quickly looked back down at her threads. She seemed conflicted and ill at ease. "Listen, Naheshi. Perhaps I should talk to you more frankly, and I will if I can be absolutely sure of your loyalty."

She beckoned him to sit beside her, and he lowered himself stiffly to the edge of the bed, holding his side. She whispered up almost into his ear. "You know how unhappy I am here, my dear old friend. The king rarely visits me; he openly prefers the Old Cow and her children. He really wants Ibi-ranu to succeed him, not my little Utri-sharrumma. If Ammi should die, do you think Ibi-ranu will just let Utrishu have the throne without a fight? Do you?"

He saw real anguish in her eyes—his dearest Taddu. Her motherly heart was wrung at the thought of a civil war that would no doubt end in her baby's death. Naheshi himself could hardly bear the thought of little chubby Utrishu coming to harm, his big brown eyes falling closed, his busy little legs stilled, lying in his innocent blood.

He gulped. "N-No, my lady. I think he wants the throne, all right... although he seems like an honorable young man. Perhaps—"

"Oh, Naheshi," she interrupted impatiently, "you're so innocent! Can you still not believe anybody is bad, even after what happened to you? He'll kill him; you know that. That's what happens in wars, for god's sake." Her voice dropped again, and she took hold of the breast of his tunic as if to draw him toward her in confidence. "Fortunately, there's a way to avoid that. There are those who are willing to fight now so that blood need not be shed later; don't you see? They are willing to set the kingdom on the right path, establish the right succession. Anyway, Ammi isn't really supposed to be on the throne at all, you know. It was only Tudhaliya's father who made that happen, and we all are paying for it."

Naheshi was certainly familiar with the story. Who knew why kings did what they did? Perhaps Hattushili had felt Ammishtamru was a better ruler or more likely to be loyal. And then five years ago, just before the young queen had come to Ugarit, there had been that rebellion on the part of the disgruntled firstborn, which the intervention of the Great King's viceroy had throttled. After being given the throne a second time by his overlord, could anyone pretend Ammishtamru was not the legitimate king?

Naheshi, who was no fool, caught the whiff of treason. He could hardly imagine that any speech coming from the queen's mouth could be as wholly treasonable as this smelled, but try as he might, there seemed to be no way to interpret her words as innocuous. He goggled at her, not knowing what to say. She looked equally alarmed at his shock, and Naheshi could imagine her thinking she had made a mistake in saying these things to him, but he could not control his face.

"You know that's true." She seized his arms and shook him urgently, unmindful of his bruises. "Heshmi-sharrumma is the rightful king. There are plenty of people—and important people, too—who think so, and they're tired of Ammi's truckling to the Great King."

"My lady's uncle," he reminded her.

"Yes, but so what? I've never even met him. Don't you,

of all people, talk to me about family loyalty—you don't know what it's like to have children. My son comes before everyone else to me, Naheshi. You love him, too, don't you? Little Utrishu? Don't you want to see him on the throne? My baby?"

"Of... of course, my lady... but if Prince Heshmi-sharrumma takes the throne—"

"Then Utrishu would succeed him, and Ibi-ranu and his mother, that drab cow, would be out. Abishu and I would be his regents. Heshmi-sharrumma is older than the king, you know. How long will he live?"

Prince Heshmi-sharrumma had sons of his own, from what Naheshi had heard. Her argument sounded ill thought out. "Why would he turn over the kingdom to his brother's son when he has more than one of his own?"

"Stop being such a naysayer, Naheshi. His sons are off in Alashiya. Things can be taken care of before they ever have a chance to come back. How long will Heshmi live, eh?"

She grinned at him with a meaningful glint in her eye, but Naheshi was not at all sure what it was meant to convey. The hair rose on the back of his neck. What sort of regicidal plot was afoot here? She seemed to be turning away from the Great King, too. And now he had heard about it. He was implicated.

Oh, Lord Ilu, protector of kings, what awful, awful thing am I party to?

"Don't look so scared, Naheshi. I tell you, some very important people are involved, and they know how to do things. They want to get this under way before Ammi gets back from Hattusha. That way, there's no more bloodshed than necessary. He's my husband, after all; I don't want him to get hurt. By the time he even hears about it, it's all over."

"But the viceroy? I mean, the last time—"

"Ini-tesshub's far away. Trust Heshmi-sharrumma. He knows what he's doing!"

I don't trust him, Naheshi thought dully. *I've never even met him, but I don't trust him, and this whole thing sounds foolish in the extreme. He tried this five years ago and failed.*

Yet as a slave, he was accustomed to being guided by others without questioning. He swallowed his foreboding and smiled weakly at the queen. "Whatever my lady says. I am your faithful servant."

"My dear old Naheshi, I knew I could count on you. You can be really useful to me. And you'll be absolutely discreet, right? No matter what you see or hear? Because now you know how high the stakes are. I'm putting my life in your hands, Naheshi."

Those words echoed in Naheshi's memory throughout the day. At one point, having recited that horrible conversation to himself for the ten thousandth time, he'd felt so overcome with nerves that he'd had to sit down and put his head in his trembling hands, and when he managed to get back to work, he felt like a sleepwalker going through his tasks. He saw the slaves watching him when they thought his back was turned. He hoped they believed his stupor was the result of pain. He was conscious of old Agipsharri eyeing him malevolently, but Naheshi hadn't the energy to freeze the old toad with a stare or say, "Get to work." Facing the queen again, even to ask what she wanted for dinner, was agony. He was ready to collapse by the time he tottered away for the evening.

✦

"My lord, there's someone here asking for you," said Tala'abi to Heshmi-sharrumma. "An old eunuch. Says he's from the queen's household and that you'll want to talk to him."

"Well, that may be a little strong," the prince said, with his unpleasant smile. He straightened the wax tablets on the table, more to vent his own tension than out of any lack of order. Time was running out, and things were not going as smoothly as he had hoped. He felt as twitchy as a strung bow. "If it's who I think it is, he's not a person anybody really *wants* to talk to. Gray hair? Obscenely fat?"

"Yes, my lord." The young man laughed. "Although that could be any old eunuch."

"Send him in."

Tala'abi bowed respectfully and a moment later ushered the visitor into his prince's room.

Heshmi-sharrumma wrinkled his nose. "Agipsharri," he said, tapping his stylus on the table in a rhythmic demonstration of his impatience. "You have something to report, I take it? Otherwise, showing up here in broad daylight is risky, and I want no risks taken. I thought I had made that clear."

Agipsharri bowed obsequiously. "I do indeed, my lord. I have had the men my lord so generously financed following my lord your brother, as you directed, eh. They found, as you suspected, that he has begun to meet with some of your allies on his own. I also won the support of some of those gentlemen's servants and have had them listen to certain conversations."

Heshmi-sharrumma drew back his lip in contempt. He threw down the stylus and crossed his arms over his chest to hide the nervousness of his fingers. "The wretched puppy. It's that woman. He has no ambition of his own, but ever since she got her hooks into him, he's constantly demanding things for himself. I had once let drop something about Shiyannu—no reason it couldn't be administered independently again, and it would make a nice little reward for him—but at this point, I'm sure he'd like nothing better than to replace me on the throne of Ugarit."

"That is exactly the case, as my lord so astutely foresees. He has in fact approached me about assuring that outcome. The queen has convinced herself that her son will succeed you and that she and Prince Abdi-sharrumma will rule together as his regents."

Heshmi-sharrumma rose to his feet and began to pace a little. "Well, that makes all the more urgent the need for some misfortune to befall my brother, and immediately. If we are to get this coup off the ground before Ammi returns with his loyal troops, it needs to happen right away, understand?"

The eunuch's eyes grew shifty, as if he knew that what he was about to say would not be well received. "Actually, my lord, the perfect opportunity for an accident occurred in a certain dark alley a few nights ago. Unfortunately, the prince and his... lady friend... were not alone, eh. They were followed by a certain official of her household, the eunuch Nahish-shulmanu. I had our hounds lying in wait in the Lower Town, but instead of attacking your young, strong, and well-armed brother, their natural greed led them to attack the unarmed, lone, and not particularly formidable Nahish-shulmanu, who had the misfortune to be wearing expensive jewelry in a very bad part of town."

The prince stopped pacing and faced the eunuch. His voice grew sheeny with scorn. "What nonsense are you talking? Damn it, Agipsharri, will you keep these brigands of yours under control? If you can't trust them, get someone more professional. What if the watch had come upon them? They would have implicated us, I don't doubt."

"Yes, my lord. The point I want to make here is this: Nahish-shulmanu is following the queen around. He has seen your brother. He knows they're up to something."

Heshmi-sharrumma ground his teeth. "Oh, beautiful," he spat. "I knew that idiot would get us into trouble with his royal darling. I suppose the eunuch will promptly go tell the regent now, won't he?"

Agipsharri pursed his thin lips. "I'm not so sure, my lord. First, he may well not have recognized my lord Abdi-sharrumma, since it was night—and of course you had both left the city before the new queen and her retinue arrived, thanks to our esteemed suzerain in Hattusha."

"Fair enough," Heshmi said. How well he remembered. Everything had been so carefully thought out. They had struck during the New Year celebration, when the whole court was packed into the narrow royal plaza, the king—unarmed—acting as high priest. The suborned soldiers easily surrounded the royal family, and victory seemed assured. But then the damned viceroy had shown up from Karkemish. The one piece of information Heshmi had not possessed was that the old buzzard was almost to the city gate, on his way to take part in the festivities. Ini-tesshub's men had turned the tide against the conspirators, and Heshmi had been dragged inside, manacled, and forced to kneel to Ammi. The memory of the supreme bitterness of that moment tightened Heshmi's jaw. Fortunately, Tudhaliya had been determined to display the clemency that the hypocritical Great Kings so liked to flaunt. Instead of being put to death, Heshmi and his brother had been condemned to the humiliation of perpetual exile over the sea. His mother had given Abishu and him their portion of her personal estate, but the Great King had made her lay a conditional curse on them if they ever returned.

Yet after all, things had not turned out so badly. He had married King Pukanu's daughter and gained an ally in his bid for his rightful heritage.

To the eunuch, he said, "Go on. Second?"

"Second... well, our little friend Nahish-shulmanu is smitten with his mistress, very smitten indeed, eh. I think he's not so likely to say anything if it risks getting her into trouble."

Heshmi-sharrumma shook his head in disgust. "This woman seems to exercise an uncanny power over everyone. I understand my brother has a pronounced weakness where the female sex is concerned, but a eunuch?" He turned back to the table, his thoughts galloping, then faced his interlocutor once more. "All right, Agipsharri. You're in charge of assassinations, and you know this chamberlain of the queen's. What do you, as a professional, recommend as our next step? And make it fast. My brother will be returning soon."

"If I may be so bold, there are two steps, my lord. For the

first step, we have some choices, eh. The first possibility is to draw Nahish-shulmanu into the conspiracy and thereby so compromise him that he would not dare to tell tales. He's Assyrian, you know. Everyone will be quick to believe he has betrayed Ugarit. Or we could simply obliterate him, which I personally recommend, and I would be delighted to carry it out. The second step is to make another, better-orchestrated effort to remove the prince your brother... and the queen, of course, eh."

"Well, I'll give some thought to the eunuch. He might be useful to us in some way. As for Abishu, you have my permission to take care of him. But do it right away. The king will be coming home soon."

Agipsharri bowed deeply and waited, raising one long, puffy hand, palm up. "I will have to offer the hounds a bone or two, my lord."

The prince pulled some gold pieces out of his purse and slapped them into his cupped fingers. "Now, get out, before Abishu comes back."

Heshmi-sharrumma turned away from the eunuch, who backed out of the room and shut the door behind him.

The people one has to deal with, Heshmi thought, blowing through his lips as if he were spitting. *If there was ever a picture of human corruption, it's that awful wreck, Agipsharri.* The eunuch seemed to know everyone in the underworld of the city and was none too squeamish, so he had his uses, even beyond being the conspirators' eyes in the palace, but Heshmi knew it would be foolish to trust him. In fact, the prince had asked his advice mostly in order to see how he was thinking. Heshmi would give him one more chance with Abishu. If the old eunuch botched this try, he needed to go, too.

Heshmi-sharrumma's fingers recommenced their rhythmic tapping on his crossed forearms.

He and his brother were running out of time.

CHAPTER 11

NAHESHI HAULED HIMSELF UP TO the roof, as worn out by his constant internal harangue as by a day's hard labor. He sank heavily onto the stone roof roller and loosened his stiff new belt. It had rubbed his skin red around the waist. He probably needed to tie it looser, what with the spectacular meals Anani had been serving.

There was a breeze coming from the coast, as there always was at this hour. Before long, it would shift and blow from the other direction and, blocked by the penthouse, be lost to him. The sun was getting low in the west over the sea, leaving an almost blinding path of golden light upon the water. A gull winged away from the coast, its mocking laughter trailing. From somewhere, the scent of roasting meat floated.

He wanted to pray, but he'd felt such shame over the buried statue of Kinnaru in his childhood that for years he'd feared the gods had turned their backs on him. In his heart, he tried to call out to Shamash, the great sun god, who saw all things and made justice prevail. Here they called him Shapshu, and he was a she. Who knew about the gods, anyway? Were they male or female? Did they really have wives and children and palaces and wars? Maybe they were all eunuchs.

Naheshi leaned back against the wall and tipped his face up to catch the breeze. Looking back upon them with the eyes of an adult, he was not much impressed by the intelligence—or the honesty—of the priests who had served Ishtar at home. *Nina*, they called her there. They had claimed all sorts of things as the goddess's will, but who really knew?

He laughed bleakly to himself. He could pay the priests to take an oracle for him up at the temple of Ba'al. What would he ask? *"Tell me, Lord Haddu, should I betray my mistress, or should I take part in a plot against the king?"* Was any sheep liver going to give him an answer to a question like that? *"The gods say to Nahish-shulmanu, 'To the underworld with you, boy.'"*

A sense of guilt made him cower a little, as if the gods might have heard his blasphemy. He fought back the urge to weep and instead called in his hoarse voice, "Anani!"

A moment later, the slave stuck his head through the penthouse door. "Yes, master?"

"Bring me a cup of wine, will you?"

With a brisk "Yes, master," the fellow dodged out of sight, and in a minute, the stairs creaked again under his approach. "Here y'are, master. Good red wine of Mukesh and some pistachios. Thought you might like 'em."

"Good man."

Anani turned to go, but Naheshi stopped him. "Wait, stay. Let me"—he split a pistachio shell pensively with his

189

nail as he spoke, as if just entertaining a passing curiosity—
"let me ask you something."

"Yes, master?"

"What do you know about… loyalty, Anani?"

The slave's eyes grew round, and he seemed uneasy, even fearful, suddenly. "Have I not been loyal to my master somehow?"

Naheshi watched this change in mien. He knew only too well the constant fear of displeasing that haunted every slave. "I'm not talking about you. This is for… for Ili-milku. He's writing a poem, and we were trying to work out what people owe to whom. So what do you think? Who is one's first loyalty to?"

"Well, the gods?"

"Yes. And then?"

"One's master?"

As the servant cut his eyes about uneasily, the idea suddenly passed through Naheshi's mind that perhaps Anani was not simply afraid of displeasing. Could he have a guilty conscience?

"Yes, but what if our character's mistr… master is in turn someone else's subject? What if his master's master asked him to do something that went against what his master told him? What then?" *Does it make any difference if you love her?* he added silently, addressing the thought more to Shamash than to Anani. But perhaps Shamash had no ears for the likes of him. Naheshi scarcely dared to raise his guilty eyes to the golden visage of the sun.

Anani screwed up his face in anguish, either with the effort of judgment or the pain of admitting what he thought. Naheshi found himself seeing his servant as if for the first time. *He can't be any older than I am,* Naheshi reflected sadly, *and he hardly has any teeth left. He's as illiterate as a stone, he only comes up to my armpit, and here I am, looking to him for advice. What does that say about me?*

"I… I'd have to say your character oughta obey the master of his master, I guess, master. That's the way it is, ain't it? We slaves obeys our masters, they obeys the king, our king obeys the Great King off in Hattusha. He obeys the gods. But we all still have to obey the gods, too. Ain't that the way it is?"

"Yes," said Naheshi pensively. "I suppose it is. It sounds easy enough like that."

"Will that be everythin', master?" Anani asked, a look of relief on his face. He had delivered the desired answer.

Naheshi nodded, preoccupied with formulating his thoughts, and Anani was scuttling for the door when the former called out again. "What if obeying your master's master should bring harm to your master, though? What if she's actually doing something… well, not good, and by doing what you were told, you get your master into terrible trouble?"

The day was beginning to sink into twilight, and he couldn't see Anani's face as clearly as he'd have liked. Here was the heart of Naheshi's horrid conundrum. His soul was consumed with the terrible knowledge that obedience to the king could bring dire harm to his dearly loved mistress. *Dearly loved.* That had to count for something. Couldn't it release him from what seemed like a simple case of hierarchical loyalties?

Anani, perhaps thinking his master was talking to himself, made a tentative little motion as if to go, looking to Naheshi for confirmation, but the latter desperately wanted his servant to stay. Naheshi hoped that somehow his culpability and anguish could manifest themselves to the slave without words and that Anani would stop looking like a cornered animal and realize that this was neither about him nor about some character in a poem but about Naheshi. He hoped that Anani would give his usual dispassionate, solid advice, untroubled by complications or nuances—that the slave would tell Naheshi, the master, what to do.

But instead, Anani seemed increasingly ill at ease, almost angry—as angry as he dared be. "Why is master askin' *me* this? I don't know anythin' about the law or theolomogy or such things. Doesn't my lord Ili-milku know these things?"

Naheshi hung his head, defeated. Anani was right. No one could tell him what he should do. Life was not that simple. He sighed, lifted his chin, and inserted the last nut into his mouth. "Of course, Anani. Go on about your work. I'll eat at the usual hour. Thank you."

The door closed—rather loudly—and footsteps clattered down the stairs.

Naheshi remained, gazing out to sea. He'd never liked the sea. It was wild and strange and frightening in its immensity, sometimes smiling and glittery but then changing to a malevolent darkness in no time, as it had now. What ship-devouring monsters lurked beneath its sparkling waves? The sun had disappeared, leaving a diffuse, pale light in its wake. A bird cried from somewhere. Athtar, the evening star, had opened his mocking eye. Naheshi remembered Ili-milku's poem. Athtar was a subaltern, a god with power but not independence, who owed allegiance to his overlord Ba'al. Had Athtar ever wondered where his loyalty lay, or did even lesser gods know everything? The gods could be fearful. They could die...

Naheshi glanced at the bowl of empty pistachios shells. All comfort was gone. The stone roof roller was growing icy beneath his buttocks. Even a summer night could be chilly, but he felt sweat soaked under the arms. It had suddenly dawned on him why Anani was so uneasy about the question he'd put to him: his slave was spying on him.

But how could that be? Naheshi asked himself endlessly as he folded his mistress's garments the next morning. Anani had no access to the queen's quarters. He probably didn't even know where they were. His path took him from the kitchen to the staff apartments and certainly to the storerooms or latrine; once or twice, he'd been sent to the chancery on an errand. But when could he have prowled the vast labyrinth of the palace? Where could he have concealed himself... and why?

Anani seemed happy to belong to Naheshi. His gratitude was, in fact, so effusive it was almost cloying, leaving Naheshi ready to declare, "Look, you don't know me. I'm really a dreadful person. Here's what I'm doing: while you are loyal to me, I'm betraying my own mistress."

Naheshi eased down the lid of the queen's clothes chest. He gritted his teeth against the pain in his ribs, but what hurt him even more deeply was to think that his gap-toothed little servant, with his seemingly cloudless sense of morality, was a liar, and all that admiration was just an act. Yet how easy it would be to bribe him—or even threaten him, just as Naheshi himself had been threatened. Fear made the most upright crumble, and slaves lived with fear every day. He needed to be very careful about what he said in Anani's presence.

Then another suspicion insinuated itself into his mind: his attackers might not have been random robbers after all. What if, on the contrary, they had been sent to follow him? What if the Old Dragon mistrusted him and had decided to remove him from the game—or at least follow him to catch the queen? What if the thugs had been sent precisely to take the queen's seals as compromising evidence? Maybe the regent did not trust him enough to report on her niece honestly... and in fact, she was right to be suspicious, because he had no intention of telling Lord Urtenu what he'd seen five nights earlier. In light of what the queen had confessed to him, it was altogether too compromising. If her life was in his hands, he was certainly not going to drop it into Urtenu's palm. There was nothing in the world that would make him reveal the full measure of Taddu's disloyalty.

He regretted with all his heart that he had ever said a word. He'd piqued the Old Dragon's suspicions of her daughter-in-law with that revelation about the guards. But he hadn't realized then how truly grave the young queen's guilt was. And also... he'd been afraid.

Ah, Taddu, little one. She was riding a wild horse, hoping to exploit the royal brothers' hatred out of ambition for her own child, but it seemed so foolishly misdirected. He thought ruefully how he was something of an expert on the folly of parents' misdirected ambitions for their children. And if growing up in a clan of poor people was emotionally perilous, what a viper's nest life in the royal family had to be.

He remembered his own brother, ten years his senior. They'd never been exactly close; there was too much difference in age—he could only dimly recall ever playing in the temple courtyard with Puzuh-asshur, but they certainly would not have wished one another any harm. He wondered suddenly, for the first time after all these years, if he had not done ill to Puzuh-asshur without even intending to. It was always Naheshi, the baby, who had the attention, the singing lessons, and everyone's admiration for his celestial voice—well, almost everyone's. He was going to make the family's fortune. Puzuzi would just be a temple servant like their father—a poor, unskilled sod pushing a broom. Maybe he'd hated his little brother with the voice from the gods. Maybe he'd burned with envy... but he'd never acted envious or hateful. He'd seemed as proud as anyone. Naheshi remembered Puzuzi pulling him against his side once after a performance and ruffling his hair; warm, comforting happiness had flooded Naheshi till he thought he would burst. *No, he loved me, and how did I repay him? I went off to enjoy a life at court and left him, without a thought. While I cultivate a double chin at the king's expense, he's probably grown bowlegged from hunger, like Anani.*

Already close to drowning, Naheshi felt a new wave of deepest sorrow break over him. *Forgive me, forgive me.* Was Puzuzi glad when Naheshi's good luck had come apart, and he, Puzuzi, at least was free and a man?

And now Naheshi himself was trapped. He wanted to say to Urtenu that he had nothing to report because he'd been in bed for days, injured in a mugging in the Lower Town. He was more than willing to invoke whatever vices on his part might have taken him down to that unsavory quarter. What did people even do there? It might shame him, but he didn't care. No fictitious shame could compare to his real one.

Naheshi realized he was standing still and made himself open another chest, although his movements were dreamlike, his thoughts still floundering in the marsh of his dilemma.

If the attack had been orchestrated by the Old Dragon, then Urtenu would know exactly what the chamberlain had been doing down there, and Naheshi's lie would accuse him. If he did not report, then they might think he was really part of the plot himself, and considering what he now knew about the queen's plans, he supposed he was. *Would that she had never confided in me!* But he'd longed for her confidence. This awful burden was, ironically, the answer to his fondest prayer. The gods had a cruel sense of humor.

The next day, as Naheshi headed to work at daybreak, Agipsharri was waiting for him outside the queen's inner door. Naheshi met him with an icy glare that he hoped concealed the rush of blood from his face. The older eunuch was shrunken down, a little hunchbacked with age, making his arms and legs, inflated though they were, look even longer. With his wide, lipless mouth, he resembled a malevolent toad.

Naheshi made a point of looming over him. "You again?"

"*Karubu* face, my brother in genital deprivation." Agipsharri smirked.

"Don't be so crude, you disgusting thing. Let me pass."

"You survived this unfortunate run-in, Nahish-shulmanu. Can you be so sure that the next accident won't be fatal, eh?"

Naheshi's eyes grew wide in spite of himself. "The next...? What are you talking about?"

"Pretty face all black and blue, ears slit like a runaway's. How much silver did you lose?" Agipsharri's grin widened with malice.

"W-What business is it of yours?"

"It can be dangerous to follow the queen, *karubu* face. Such a nasty part of town, eh."

Naheshi's heart lurched. Did Agipsharri know about the queen and the conspiracy, then?

"'Take my purssse, but don't hurt me!'" Agipsharri mimicked Naheshi's hoarse, high-pitched voice and Assyrian accent. He pinched his nose and made a suggestive expression of olfactory disgust.

Naheshi froze. How often had he rehashed the whole scene over and over in his memory, hearing every word, feeling every blow, judging his spineless comportment, reordering events so that he came out a little more heroic? He had a distinct recollection of crying those very words, cowardly though they were, to his attackers. He'd certainly told no one such... unflattering details in his report of the incident. Had the footpads themselves laughed and joked about him to their superiors?

His voice dropped to a choked whisper. "How... how

N.L. HOLMES

did you know that? Did you have something to do with the attack?"

"You think I'm some despicable turd, but I'm much more important than that. Some people actually value my services, eh, Nahish-shulmanu. I am, in fact, party to quite a few important things. Let's just say that my information had something to do with it, eh. Important people base their actions on what I tell them."

Whose side is he on? Naheshi wondered feverishly. *Is he betraying me to the dowager queen, or do the conspirators want me dead?*

"So what is it you want me to do?" Naheshi kept his voice down, but it still wobbled. "You must want something, or you would have come out and said what you keep hinting at by now. Is it gold? And what do I get in return?"

"What do you get? You find out what I know about you and the queen, eh. And you get me not telling anyone else. And you get a chance to get out before it really gets dangerous."

"As if I'd believe you." Naheshi tried to laugh carelessly, but he trailed to a strangled halt.

"As if you have any choice."

Don't listen to him, Naheshi warned himself, starting to swallow with difficulty. *Remember what Anani said: nobody believes blackmailers anyway.*

But then he realized that Agipsharri and Anani might be working together to entrap him.

Oh, stupid one. You've all but admitted to the old rascal you have something to hide. What's the worst thing that could happen if he tells? They could find out that I know the queen is involved in a plot to overthrow the king, and that I, too, am involved and have said nothing. Torture. Evisceration. Impalement.

His bowels writhed at the thought of such pain. "How much do you want?"

Agipsharri bared his yellow teeth in a grin. "As much as you'll give me."

"What? How much do you think I have? My purse was just stolen, remember?"

The other eunuch emitted a wheezing laugh. "It's not your purse I'm demanding, *karubu* face. It's your body. Not forever. Just one night."

Naheshi recoiled as if a snake had just dropped down before him, his mouth twisted in horror. "Are you mad? Let me pass."

"You've heard the terms. A little roll in the hay, or I tell what I know to everyone but you."

Naheshi could not speak. He pushed past the older eunuch and burst into the queen's chamber, gasping like a man stricken. He slammed the door behind him and fell against it. Taddu was still in bed. She rolled over and eyed him groggily. The night maids grumbled from their pallets, rubbing their eyes.

"Naheshi? What is it? What time is it?"

"It's still early, my lady. Forgive me. I… I let the door slam by accident."

"For god's sake"—Taddu buried her face in her pillow—"you interrupted a beautiful dream…"

Naheshi dared not return to the anteroom lest Agipsharri still haunt it. He parted the curtains and let himself out onto the loggia overlooking the gardens. It was the magical hour of sunrise, a sweet summer morning. The outlines of trees were barely visible below in the shadow of the building, but the birds were singing ecstatically. Everything was faintly misty. A rosy luminosity filled the sky little by little, and color gradually seeped back into the world. A bit at a time, the palm fronds emerged green from the blue shadows in the depths of the courtyard, and the sun's gilding crept up the wall opposite.

But Naheshi experienced no pleasure in the mysteries of a summer dawn. He shook uncontrollably. Just when it seemed things couldn't get any worse, the ground under his feet had caved in yet again.

Was Agipsharri utterly mad? Could he think Naheshi had any feelings at all for him, after all the hostility the chamberlain had shown him? No, of course not. It had nothing to do with affection or even lust. The old toad simply wanted to dominate Naheshi. Agipsharri had him at his mercy and wanted to humiliate him. This was simply the worst thing he could think of to make Naheshi confess his powerlessness, the way captives were made to lick the dirt or kiss their conquerors' boots. Naheshi had no idea what was left of Agipsharri physically or what the vile toad envisioned doing to him, but the thought of bodily contact made him shudder. To expose his defenseless, naked body to that malicious old creature... it was all too reminiscent of other angry people who'd wanted to humiliate him.

Merciful gods, hasn't the world crushed me enough? Tears dribbled unwiped down his cheeks. *But do I dare refuse? What might Agipsharri do?* The old reprobate might report the queen to her mother-in-law. Anani could tell him about all Naheshi's conversations, and Agipsharri would make the connection between those hypothetical "friends" in need of advice and Naheshi's own real role in the conspiracy. They would throw him into prison. They would torture him.

He leaned on the balcony railing, and his shoulders shook with silent sobs. He couldn't, he couldn't. He didn't even take off all his clothes to shower. There was just so much reminding he could endure. If he didn't have to see himself, he could sometimes forget what had been done to him. But in front of Agipsharri? Never. He could not. What was the worst thing that could happen to him if the old dog shit reported him? Death? That was better. Let them display his body on the walls after his death, and he wouldn't care.

But the queen—what if he got her into trouble?

Naheshi wasn't sure how long he had hung there on the rail, wrapped in wordless misery, when Taddu's voice rose from within the room. "Naheshi? Are you still out there? Go get us some breakfast, will you? The girls are going off duty."

"Yes, my lady." He blew his nose between his fingers and wiped at his cheeks.

He dreaded opening the door to the antechamber, but in fact, it was empty.

Only later in the day did he see Agipsharri on duty. Naheshi made a point of sending him on errands as often as possible. He feared that his swollen red lids were a delectable victory for the slave, who eyed him with his usual insolence but said nothing.

Only at the end of the evening, as the day shift of servants departed and Naheshi himself prepared to leave, did Agipsharri address him, saying, "Think about it, eh."

CHAPTER 12

NAHESHI SAT BEFORE HIS DINNER, scarcely conscious of the savory smells that rose from the dishes. His face, he felt sure, was a mask of misery, but even with his hardest effort, he could not unknot his eyebrows.

Anani stood aside after serving his master and waited for him to start. After a long while, during which Naheshi continued to stare unseeing through the table, the slave asked cautiously, "Is master ill?"

"Never been sick a day in my life." Naheshi attempted to mount a smile, but it fell from his lips in shards. He was almost afraid of his servant, wondering what the man knew and what harm he wished his master—although Naheshi couldn't really believe that Anani was a spy.

"Master has... problems? Is everythin' good at work?"

"Master has problems; he certainly does." Naheshi hung his head, blinking back the tears. "I promise you, Anani, I'm not always like this. You've just caught me at a bad moment in my life. You must think I'm quite the weepy fellow. I apologize; it can't be pleasant to be around me..."

"Can I help, master?"

"I don't think so. But thank you. If I don't survive all this, know how grateful I am to you." And the sad thing was, he *was* grateful for the care, the apparent affection, and the little kindnesses. Even if it was all an act, he was grateful. But it wasn't an act, was it?

"Not survive? Ba'al's beard! Is things that bad, poor master?" Anani squatted at the chamberlain's side, scruffy face screwed up in a sympathy that could have been real or false—there was no way to tell.

"Quite possibly, quite possibly. Although death sounds like a better alternative to me at the moment, frankly."

"Perhaps a good dinner would make master feel better? I've noticed that helps..."

Naheshi buried his face in his hands. Did he dare say more? His heart was so full of confusion he felt he would burst if he could not confide in someone. Finally, his eyes scalded, the corners of his mouth weighted down with gloom, he looked up at his servant. "I have a friend who has a terrible decision to make, Anani. And he doesn't even know what the stakes are, which seems... cruel. I want to help him make the right choice, because on one hand, he'll be shamed and full of self-contempt. But on the other hand, someone who is precious to him may lose her—his—life."

Anani shook his head. "Great folks has a lotta sorrow in their lives, seems to me, master. Better to be a lowly slave and do what we're told, far as I can see."

But it's because I am a slave that all this becomes so complicated, Naheshi wanted to cry out. *Because one person tells me to do one thing, and another tells me to do something else, and I have to obey them both.*

"Remember I asked you a while back about a friend who was being blackmailed? This is the same person."

"Ah. Did he cave in, or did he stand up to the blackmailer, master?"

"Neither yet, but he's very close to caving in, because he's... so... afraid of what will happen if he doesn't."

"I can't tell him what to do, master, but it's a fac' that no matter what you give blackmailers, they always wants more. You gotta stop 'em col'."

"Cold? You mean kill them?"

"No, just tell 'em you're not playin' their game. Although killin' 'em sometimes sounds pretty good, too... but don't let anybody know I said that!" He grinned and winked.

Naheshi looked up at him with suddenly hopeful eyes. "If only this person *would* die. He's old. It could happen. But I don't think I could do it."

"This is gettin' serious, master. I'd do 'most anythin' for you, but I hope your... friend doesn't want nobody killed."

"No, no. I would never ask that, Anani. If I couldn't do it myself, I certainly wouldn't expect you to."

"Your nice dinner is gettin' col', master..."

"Yes, how thoughtless of me. It smells superb. You've really discovered a hidden talent for manipulating the kitchen staff. You seem to be able to get things done. You should have my job."

Anani grinned, ducking his head modestly, but his little black eyes sparkled with pleasure at the compliment. "Oh, no, master. I could never hobnob with royalty and all.

I don't have master's education and nice way of talkin' and all. Can I pour you some wine? Your fish won't be nice once the sauce gets col'."

Was his solicitude an act? Naheshi refused to believe it. He wasn't a good judge of character, perhaps, but if there was ever an honest man, it would seem to be Anani. Naheshi picked up a piece of succulent fish and popped it into his mouth, licking his fingers of the last delicious drops of sesame sauce. The knot in his stomach relaxed with a purr. For a few minutes, at least, his problems seemed far away.

The next day, Naheshi beckoned Agipsharri aside. As much as it revolted him, Naheshi drew close to the old eunuch so as to speak quietly, but he wouldn't look him in the eye. He already felt as if he were unraveling like a rag.

"A-Agipsharri."

"Yes, esteemed supervisor?" Agipsharri's mouth widened into a smug line.

Naheshi could scarcely breathe, the dread and loathing sat so heavily upon his chest. *But if I can save Taddu's honor by my own dishonor? Maybe Agipsharri really will keep his mouth shut if I give in to him. Or is it innocent of me to hope so?* He who had told himself so often that he would die for the queen—if he knew that this sacrifice might purchase her safety, he could not refuse to make it. He forced himself to say, "After the day shift this evening."

"Ah, a new day, a new chivalry, eh. In the storage room, then, next to the winter banquet hall."

"The storage room!" Naheshi bleated, horror-struck. "There may be people around downstairs."

"Not at that hour—fewer than in the staff quarters. Do you want your information or not, eh?"

Naheshi's voice fluttered in spite of himself. "All right. In the storage room, damn you." *Oh, please, gods, let me die before this comes to pass; let me not wake up after siesta. Or better still, take Agipsharri.*

He moved through the day in a fog of trepidation. The queen had to shout at him repeatedly for ignoring her orders. He simply had not heard her. *This is for you, my dearest lady,* he thought numbly. *This is for you. This is for you.*

※

Summer days usually lasted forever, but Shapshu flew through the sky this once. The evening Naheshi dreaded drew near. He watched the changing of the shifts, saw Agipsharri disappear with the other day servants, and ordered the queen's dinner. It wasn't too late to back out. He could run. He might run away, in fact; look at how completely Pilsiya had disappeared. He could run back to Amurru. But what would the Great Lady say if he abandoned her daughter? What would his conscience say?

With a thudding heart, he left the royal apartments and made his way to the stairs. Perhaps he could throw himself off and break his neck. But there was really no way to fall all the way to the bottom, and he would probably just fracture a leg. Naheshi wasn't sure he was brave enough to face slow death by black rot. He realized he didn't even know exactly which of several storage rooms he was seeking. Perhaps he could claim to have stood outside the wrong one and finally given up.

But no, there stood Agipsharri in the shadows with his yellow leer and slitted eyes, and in his hand was a broom. Naheshi's breath rasped loudly through his mouth; he was starting to swallow in choking gulps. He cast his eyes around, hoping no other servant was anywhere near. The vast banquet chamber was dark, empty, and echoing. He followed the older slave through an adjacent smaller hall with open columns at the far end. Agipsharri ushered him with exaggerated deference into the little storage room. It adjoined another, but the intervening door had been barred shut, the stacks of tables pushed to the walls. A single oil lamp with a double wick sat on top of the pile. Naheshi imagined himself pushing the old eunuch down, throttling him, running away—or pulling his penknife out and slitting his throat… but then he would not find out what Agipsharri knew. He would never have the nerve anyway. Perspiration ran down his temples.

"So tell me," he demanded in a cracking voice when the door had been shut and a chair pushed up under the latch.

"Tell you what?"

"What you know, damn it! Why do you think I'm here?"

"Certainly not out of any human feeling for a fellow unfortunate, eh?" Agipsharri snarled in a voice of such venomous bitterness that Naheshi's skin crawled. "Afterward. You pay me first. Take off your clothes."

Naheshi gritted his teeth, fixed his eyes on the ceiling, and began to untie the neck of his tunic with shaking hands. "Why are you doing this, Agipsharri?" To his shame, the tears trickled down his cheeks.

"Do you plan to keep talking the whole time, eh? Undress, I told you."

Naheshi stepped out of his breechclout but kept his tunic wadded up protectively in front of himself. His pretense of dignity had flown along with his clothing. He found himself huddled over like a girl trying to defend her breasts from view. He was covered in gooseflesh and shook convulsively, although it was not especially cold. He felt violated already, just by Agipsharri's eyes. He'd been judged and found flabby, weak, fat, thin, deformed, abhorrent, and utterly vulnerable.

"Get the shoes off, eh. I don't want you kicking me."

"Don't hurt me, Agipsharri, please," Naheshi whimpered. "I've never done anything to you."

But Agipsharri snarled. "Oh, haven't you? 'Dog turd'—I quote here. Haven't you, 'obscene toad'? Haven't you, 'lump of lard'? I seem to recall a slap in the face, you piece of self-pitying, hypocritical shit. I seem to recall more than one deliberate errand that was taxing for an old man just because you wanted to see me sweat, you vain, lying, self-absorbed, dewy-eyed piece of Assyrian shit. Everybody thinks you're so nicey-nice and never have a bad word for anyone, but I've heard a few for me. Saved them all for me, have you, you ass shit, eh? What are you concerned about, eh? Losing a little dignity? Dignity is not for the likes of us freaks. Throw the tunic over there, and get down on your pretty white hands and knees. I piss on your dignity."

Naheshi sank to his knees, weeping, more profoundly wounded by the truth of the accusations than the physical shame. The thought of fighting or escaping seemed as remote as the stars. He was broken. He realized that he deserved this. Agipsharri hefted his broom.

"I see they cut you clean. They must've wanted to make

themselves a woman. You'd be pissing yourself right now if I let you pull out the plug, right? Who are you to make fun of anybody, you freak? Let's see if we can't find a hole. Turn your fat butt this way, Assyrian. The invasion is about to begin."

Naheshi dropped to his hands, shuddering with fear and self-contempt.

"Now, say out loud, 'I respect you, Agipsharri.'"

Naheshi was sobbing too hard. The pain hit like a lightning bolt, and he jerked and screamed.

"Say it, Nahish-shulmanu. 'I respect you.'"

"I... I..." Tears were flooding down his cheeks, mucus running from his nose.

"Say it."

He screamed again, seared with the agony, and collapsed to his elbows.

"Say it! Say it!"

＊

It must have been midnight before Naheshi finally fled the scene of his shame, tunic awry and stained with blood, his shoes in his hand, lurching up the stairs like a drunk. He stopped and vomited repeatedly on the landing, as if to clear his body of any trace of Agipsharri. Someone else could worry about cleaning it up. Naheshi just wanted to get home and bar the door. He staggered past the queen's apartments and those of the other royal women. The guards watched him impassively. Let them laugh if they wanted to. No doubt, they thought he was returning from some escapade a little the worse for wear.

He hurt unspeakably. His body had not even healed

from its beating, and now this. Naheshi felt blood running down the back of his thigh. Pain and shame made him so nauseated and light-headed that he wasn't even sure he could make it back. But there was his familiar door. He rapped on it with his shoe, and Anani opened it immediately, looking first anxious, then horrified.

"Ba'al's beard, master! Not again!" The slave helped him over the threshold. Lamps were lit. The good man had not gone to bed. *How could I ever have suspected him?* The red walls glowed cozily; he should be safe here. "Sit down, my poor master. Oh, I was so worried about you."

Naheshi could not sit. He fell to his knees, hung there until he felt too weak to stay upright, and rolled onto his side on the floor. He longed for the purification of tears, but somehow, despite the dry sobs, he seemed to be drained of salt water. Anani pulled a blanket over him, tucked it in gently around his shoulders, and while he went to get a basin and towel, let him lie there, staring glassy-eyed at the wall, repeating in a broken voice, "Nothing. He knew nothing. All that for nothing. Gods have mercy on me, all for nothing."

"Does master want to tell me what happened to him?" Anani asked as he began to bathe Naheshi's face and push back the disheveled hair.

"I just fed myself to a jackal, that's what. I just told him 'Do whatever your vile old heart wants to me, but tell me what you have against *her*.' And he did everything he could think of, short of killing me... and then, and then... he admitted he knew nothing."

It occurred to him he had let slip his secret, but he did not care. He needed someone's pity. He refused to believe

Anani was deceiving him. He needed him. Now the tears came, and Naheshi wept with open mouth—*wah-wah*—like a child, burying his face in the blanket.

Anani stroked his hair, forgetting propriety in the ancient ritual of human comfort. "There's evil in this worl', for real, master. Sure, everybody suffers somethin' anyway, but sometimes people just sets out to make others suffer, and I call that evil."

Tell me why it is always against me, Naheshi begged the gods. *Why have I had so much more than my share? Do I draw it to me, the way tall trees attract lightning? Does my stupidity, my gullibility, make me a target? Or am I really cursed? Was it Kinnaru who cursed me, right from the first, as I feared? Has someone put a mark on me somehow? Cursed to make the wrong choices, cursed to be a failure...*

Even Agipsharri had been disappointed in him by the end of the night: "Do you believe everything anyone tells you, idiot foreigner? You don't deserve your position." And it was true.

Naheshi could not face returning to work the next day. He had Anani tell the queen that his master was suffering from a relapse of his injuries. Naheshi lay on his side on the pallet the good slave had prepared for him, rolling him over with gentle hands so he could repose in greater comfort than on the thinly carpeted floor. He just lay there, suffering dumbly, while Anani puttered around.

Naheshi knew objectively that Agipsharri's cruelty was more about his own bleak, frustrated, envious life than anything the chamberlain had done to him. No one would recognize that better than he, as bleak and frustrated as the best of them. But what sort of gormless idiot would walk right into such a manifest trap? His own bad conscience had set him up for the deception. Agipsharri had played it for all it was worth, admittedly, but Naheshi himself had put the weapon in his hand. The old bastard was right: he did not deserve his place of privilege. The queen should have a better protector than he.

But then, how had the awful toad known the details of the beating unless he really was somehow involved?

Naheshi moved painfully for the next few days but tried to dissemble it, not wanting anyone to remark on his mysterious relapse. Despite his need to rehash the details of his humiliation over and over in his mind—an impulse as imperative as the need to rub a sore muscle—he kept his attention fixed on the queen's every gesture, torn between his shame and a desire to serve his beloved mistress by even more attentive and loving service. He'd failed to get Agipsharri to reveal what he knew—if he knew anything— and neither was the old monster likely to hold his tongue. Naheshi refused to look Agipsharri in the eye. There was nothing there but the reflection of his own defenseless white body.

Eventually, he felt he had to take the risk and speak to Taddu. He had to warn her of her danger. He waited until the day servants had left.

"My lady, may I have your ear for just a moment?"

"Very well, but make it quick, Naheshi. What is it?" Taddu turned toward him and set down her tapestry shuttles impatiently.

"Agipsharri. I… I don't trust him."

The queen made a *psh* noise. "No one trusts Agipsharri, silly. He would sell his own mother."

"I mean, I think he is involved somehow in the plot, and I'm not sure his intentions are honorable."

Naheshi was starting to perspire and have trouble swallowing. "He seemed to know all about my beating, my lady. I think he had something to do with it, in fact. He made me a bargain that he would tell me what he knew, if... if..." He wrung his hands.

"Well? Out with it."

"If he could... have me." Naheshi hung his head, struggling for control. "But then he still wouldn't tell me." He stopped, choking on his tears for a moment, then bravely forged on. "I'm worried for you, my lady. What if he's spying for the dowager queen?"

"Agipsharri?" She gave a disparaging snort. "The Old Dragon hates eunuchs. If he has any loyalty, it's to the Old Cow. He probably wouldn't tell you anything because there was nothing he knew to tell. Honestly, Naheshi, you're so gullible. Did you really think he knew anything? He was just parading his importance. You know he hates you."

"He does." Naheshi remembered with a shudder the awful ordeal in the storage room, but he said—as if he could change the truth by refusing to acknowledge it—"I'm not even sure why."

"You're not?" She looked at him in astonishment. "I'm only twenty, and even I can figure that out. He sees himself in you, but you've been successful, and he hasn't. That, and you treat him like a worm."

It's true, thought Naheshi in misery. *I just can't help myself. Have I brought this whole thing upon myself and my dearest Taddu through my lack of self-control?* "My lady is right, as always. Just be careful, I beg you. He's full of malice, and he'll harm us both if he can."

She sighed and rolled her eyes.

CHAPTER 13

"NAHESHI," MURMURED THE QUEEN IN a half whisper as he collected her discarded clothing one evening, "I want you to stay after the maids have left. Tell the night shift I have no need of them, will you?" She continued to ply her tapestry shuttles, sitting propped up in bed, as she spoke. No one seeing her through the crack in the outer door would have observed that the two were conversing.

"Yes, my lady." His heart pounding, Naheshi bowed out the door and drew it shut behind him.

He tried to keep his mind on his duties for the rest of the evening, but more than once, he forgot what he was saying in midsentence and had to cover up his confusion. Agipsharri was grinning a more evil grin than usual. *Let the old turd think whatever he wants.* A magma of white-hot terror and anticipation simmered in Naheshi's gut. Something was going to happen. Taddu was going to get him involved in something. She was going to do something so imprudent that they would both end up with their heads on pikes over the gate, but he couldn't abandon her to face the danger alone. She needed him now more than ever. If he had to die, let his last memory be that divine vision of her dark hair falling down on the shoulders of the white linen nightgown as she bent over her tapestry work.

The Lady Shapshu was setting, leaving the room awash with the sun-warmed perfume of thyme and marjoram. The day maids left, and Agipsharri and the pages as well.

When the night maids knocked, Naheshi turned them away at the door with his suavest professional air. "Our lady has no need of you tonight, my beauties. I'll watch over her. Come back tomorrow evening."

They were only too happy to sleep in their own beds with no orders for midnight snacks to trouble them. They would ask no questions. Naheshi barred the outer door behind them. He noticed there was a guard on duty outside. That reassured him—the king's eyes were open.

The soles of his feet were prickling with anxiety as he knocked on the inner door and entered the queen's presence. She had gotten dressed again, still in the somber colors of mourning, and was wrapping herself in a dark, enveloping shawl.

"We'll give it some more time, Naheshi. Then you and I are going to make a little trip to Mahadu."

"The port, my lady!" He could not keep from gaping.

"Yes, the port. Don't worry; you won't have to walk. There will be a chariot ready for us outside the walls just after midnight."

"But the guards…?"

"They haven't been a problem yet, have they? I told you that important people were involved. They've taken care of everything. Just trust them, and make yourself useful."

A chariot galloping down the port road in the middle of the night, and no one will hear? No one will see? He forced a pallid smile and nodded, afraid to say anything. He didn't trust himself, let alone "them." Whatever his dear Taddu commanded. She cared about him and would surely do nothing that would endanger him. He needed to believe that. Even though he might be consumed by daft suspicions of everyone else, he had to trust her, the dear fixed point in his universe. She loved him, and that made all else possible. Abandon that sweet star of hope, and nothing else made any sense. If she could entrust her life to "them," then by the Gracious Gods, so could he.

His stomach growled. He wondered what Anani had laid hands on for supper that night. No one would eat it, it seemed.

⬥

There was a full moon. Naheshi reminded himself to trust, trust. *They have taken care of everything.* When it had begun to descend above the roof of the palace and across the garden, Taddu made a signal for Naheshi to extinguish the lamps and follow her. He stepped ahead of her to open the hall door and found, as he'd half expected, that the guard had disappeared. His heart sank. She tiptoed in front of him into the darkness and through the utter silence of the sleeping palace.

There was not a soul to be seen. The queen stopped at the foot of the stairs and lit a small lamp. The glow here was not too dangerous; the chances of meeting anyone in the public parts of the palace at that hour were slim. But instead of heading past the kitchens to the service gate, to

Naheshi's astonishment, she led him in the other direction, toward the ceremonial court and the royal tombs. Fear licked up his spine—midnight was the hour of the underworld and its denizens.

However, rather than entering the vaulted darkness that led down into the realm of the dynastic dead, Taddu passed into a small room and handed her lamp to Naheshi. Before them was a grated hatch in the floor. The queen stooped and pulled at the wooden grille, grunting and tugging, but she could scarcely budge it. Naheshi hurriedly set down the lamp and helped her lift it as best he could with his bandaged hand. They were soon panting and dirtied by the slimy wood. He dared not look her in the eye. This was wrong. Everything about it was wrong. The grate was the entrance to the sewer tunnel. Someone had pointed it out to him when he first arrived in Ugarit. The famous sewer took the storm water off the hill into the creeks that embraced the city—a network of clay pipes bigger around than a man's thigh to carry the water, while the tunnels served as mains. He knew that there was an entrance just north of the palace, too, in the royal plaza.

The queen had descended the steps and was moving ahead of him confidently, her little shoes clicking on the stone floor, and he hurried so as not to lose the light of her lamp. The damp stone was draped with unsavory-looking festoons of darkness—moss or cobwebs perhaps. Naheshi didn't know what they were, but they bore a terrible resemblance to clutching fingers and the wings of bats. The farther they proceeded, the more the bone-chilling dampness increased, until a trickle of water glittered blackly in the lamplight at their feet and splashed their hems as they walked. The tunnel exuded the smell of saltpeter and saturated stone, of effluents and stagnation. Naheshi had to bend to clear the ceiling—the thought of touching those hanging things filled him with horror—and soon he had to be careful not to slip as well.

What ungodly mission are we on, here in the underworld realm of Nergal?

No good could come of this. He should convince the queen to turn back. Yet she seemed to be confident and unafraid. Had she actually made this hellish expedition before?

Suddenly, something scurried, squeaking, almost underfoot. Naheshi and the queen simultaneously let out a squeal of fear, their voices echoing in the confined space like the gibbering cries of ghosts.

"A rat!" Taddu laughed nervously, her voice still high-pitched with fright. "It can't be much longer."

But in fact, the tunnel seemed to go on forever, getting slightly smaller as it proceeded. Naheshi's breath came raggedly. He felt the weight of the city above him, closing in, the darkness swallowing them up. What if the lamp went out? What if the tunnel became so small they had to crawl? A smear of white light ahead gave him a moment of hope. Stairs stretched up into the moonlight, crisscrossed by the shadow bars of a wooden grate.

"Not here," Taddu whispered, a finger across her lips. "This is the royal plaza. Be quiet; there are guards not far away."

They skirted the exit, and the tunnel made a turn, opening out a little so that he no longer had to walk crouched over. After what seemed an eternity, another grilled opening glared brightly straight ahead. Naheshi realized they were more or less under the Old Dragon's palace, where the sewer tunnel emptied into the ravine to the northwest of the city walls. He had never been so happy to see the welcoming glow of Yarikh's light in his life. By the time they reached the doorway, he was gasping for breath like a man saved from drowning.

Taddu extinguished her lamp and set it down. She waved her arm through the locked grille and called softly, "Abishu! Abishushu, my love!"

A figure stepped in front of the doorway, a silhouette of a man wrapped in a cloak. He reached through the grille and unlocked the gate, and Naheshi feared the screech and clatter of the mechanism would awaken the whole city. The grille swung open, and the queen threw herself into the man's arms.

"My lamb!" He kissed her, fierce with relief, and tucked the big key into his belt. "Come quickly. My horses are waiting below. Are you too tired to make the climb?"

Naheshi emerged from the dark tunnel in the queen's wake, and the man reflexively pulled Taddu behind him and clapped his hand to his sword hilt. "Who's there?"

"He's with us, my love," the queen reassured him. "That's my chamberlain."

The man stared for a moment. "Ah, your doe-eyed eunuch. But love, this is too dangerous. We can't involve anyone else without—"

"He's loyal, Abishu. He'll do whatever I tell him. And he already knows something anyway, remember. He can be useful."

Naheshi could not see the fellow's face, but he recognized

his voice as that of the man who had saved him from the footpads. He bowed humbly. "At your service, my lord."

The man called Abishu stood hesitating for a moment before he said grudgingly, "Come on, then." He took the queen's hand and helped her down the steep path that stretched obliquely across the slope of the ravine, from the tunnel exit to the road that ran along the west side of the city hill. Lord Yarikh, the moon, was setting, and his glow illumined the western wall so brightly that it cast shadows as sharp and black as obsidian. The sky was milky with his light, the very stars effaced. To the north, Naheshi saw the tenebrous line of the creek, dry at this season, where the drains of the city emptied. His relief at leaving behind that nightmarish underworld tunnel was so extreme that he almost forgot the peril in which he and the queen were still enmeshed, and he marveled at the transfigured beauty of the city, its walls and towers as white as chalk against the pearly darkness of the east. The pale flash of an owl in flight flickered soundlessly across the sky and disappeared into the woods, its shadow mounting the ravine and merging with the bird until the night swallowed them both.

He realized the others had pulled ahead of him while he gawped, and he stumbled after them in awkward haste across the loose scree of the trail. They would be clearly visible to anyone standing on the ramparts above, if he looked down close enough to the foot of the wall. Naheshi's heart began to pound again. His stomach was growling, he could scarcely set one foot before the other, and he needed to pee. He hoped his mistress was in better shape than he.

At last, they arrived at the road just below the guard post outside the Royal Gate, where two horses stood cropping weeds in the shadow of a little pine tree. Behind them, a light chariot was harnessed. This Abishu had to be someone important, then—a *maryannu*.

"You, my flower, sit next to me on the floor. Keep your head down so if anyone sees us, they'll think there's just one person." He helped the queen climb into the chariot box and added in a colder tone to Naheshi, "You, eunuch, fit yourself in somehow, and stay down, by the gods."

The man untied the animals and stepped up into the box next to Taddu, who was crouched low against its front wall, her skirts tucked around her ankles. Naheshi was preparing to climb up after her when a thin buzz sounded, like the passage of a wasp, followed by a *thunk*. The horses reared and whinnied. Naheshi fell backward to the ground, and the driver only managed to control the animals with difficulty.

The queen cried in shock, "An arrow!"

Naheshi stared up to see the quivering shaft of the missile projecting from the leather side of the chariot box. It had barely missed Taddu.

"We're betrayed! We need to get out of here!" Abishu whipped up his horses.

"Wait for me, my lord!" Naheshi called out, scrambling to his feet. But he would have been abandoned had a second arrow not buzzed and thunked against the yoke of one of the horses. The animal screamed wildly and reared up on its hind legs, causing the chariot to lurch and tilt, and while the man tried to calm the two panicked beasts, Naheshi threw himself into the chariot behind the queen, his feet braced against the opposite side, clinging for dear life to the struts. Abishu shook the reins furiously, and the horses broke into a gallop, clattering away in a thunder of hoofbeats and a jingling of harness. The horses' hooves and the cartwheels were muffled with leather, but they still rang as loud as an avalanche in the silence of the night. The chariot bounced and swayed with the desperation of their pace down the chalk-white road. It was all Naheshi could do to hang on. The vehicle was not designed to carry three. If they lost a wheel, they would all be dead.

"Did the soldiers see us?" gasped the queen.

"No, my love, it wasn't the soldiers. Those arrows came from the other side, from the trees on the opposite side of the ravine. If the archer had been as close as the wall, we would be dead."

"Who, then, Abishu?"

"I don't know, but let's not slow down to see if they'll come after us."

Her eyes glittering with excitement in the moonlight, Taddu shouted down at Naheshi over the clatter of the wheels, "Naheshi, is anyone coming behind us?"

"No, my lady," he assured her through his rattling teeth.

The port of Mahadu was less than a league away—barely an hour's journey, walking. At the crazy pace of their careening horses, they covered the distance in no time. Naheshi knew they were near the port by the effluvium of the dye works, a mingling of putrefied shellfish and the urine used as a mordant.

The horses slowed to a trot and then a walk, and Naheshi began to see houses behind him as they passed into the streets of the town. There was no wall; in case of attack, the inhabitants would seek protection in Ugarit itself. The night was black and silent, the moon nearly set.

He heard the horses blowing in exhaustion and the faint jingle of their harness, the muffled clop of their feet. The chariot stopped, and Naheshi uncurled his fingers from their frozen grip on the struts. His heart was pounding as if he had run the entire distance.

"We're here, my love. Get out, eunuch, and let your mistress down. Inside, quick."

Naheshi rolled out clumsily, feet first, and helped Taddu down. The driver rapped the hilt of his whip on a nail-studded door in the blank wall beside them, and it opened a crack.

"The lion will bring down the antelope," he whispered, and the door swung open in a wash of yellow lamplight.

They were bundled through the vestibule and a small court with a well. Abishu ordered a slave to bring in the chariot, and the servant ran to unbar the wicket gate. The man who had greeted them led them into a well-furnished small room that was crowded and pungent with the onion-like odor of perhaps ten or fifteen sweating men. They looked up then rose at the arrival of the newcomers, and one—a lean, wiry man of early middle age who had been sprawled on a chair by the door—stepped forward, his expression uncertain at first but then shifting into a smile. His beaky features were familiar. Could it be the king? But he was thinner, and his beard was dark. He had a look of watchful tension, like a dangerously uneasy carnivore.

"Ah, my sister-in-law," he said. "Welcome, Lady Taduhepa. May the gods bless your presence among us and make us successful."

Naheshi suddenly realized who this was: the king's elder brother, Heshmi-sharrumma. Abishu himself had to be the younger prince, Abdi-sharrumma. The two treacherous brothers who had tried and failed to overthrow the king five years earlier, just before the queen and Naheshi had come to Ugarit, were at it again, and Taddu and he were squarely involved. He felt faint and had to lean against the wall. *Treason, pure and simple.* His worst fears for the queen were realized.

"We were attacked, my brother, not far from the enceinte." The younger prince brandished one of the arrows, which he had plucked from the chariot box.

"The watchmen were supposed to ignore any movement out there," interrupted one of the men angrily.

"The attack didn't come from the wall. It came from the trees beyond the ravine to the northwest."

There was a rumble of alarm and speculation. Abdi-sharrumma addressed the gathering but was looking closely at his brother as he spoke. "Clearly, someone was aware of our plans, gentlemen. Someone knew we would emerge from the sewer tunnel and that the chariot would be tied up near the tree."

"Have we been betrayed?" a voice demanded uneasily.

"Some of us have."

"Who tipped them off, brother?" Heshmi-sharrumma met him with a level stare. "Not our dear sister, surely?"

"Most assuredly not!" Taddu said, her amber eyes glittering with outrage. "My life was in danger, too. This arrow barely missed my back."

"Who, then?" Abruptly, Prince Heshmi-sharrumma demanded in a harder voice, "Who is this?"

Naheshi looked up and realized they were speaking of him. His throat went dry.

"This is my chamberlain, Nahish-shulmanu. He's an Assyrian. You can imagine why he would wish to be part of us, my brother."

The elder prince eyed Naheshi's pallid face coolly. "Assyrian, is he? Ah, yes. Perhaps he can be useful to us. Have him listen to what our good allies say among themselves when they think we can't understand them."

"Brother," Abdi-sharrumma interrupted, "I have the feeling Lady Taduhepa may be hungry after her journey. Someone pass her some bread and wine, please." The slightly threatening tone in his voice gave way to good-humored charm. He guided the queen gently to a seat and settled her, gazing directly into her eyes with an intimate, white-toothed smile as if no one else were present in the room. He seated himself on a cushion at her feet.

Taddu did not seem to share Naheshi's exhaustion. Her eyes were fever bright with exhilaration, and she smiled coquettishly at her escort. *She's actually enjoying this,* Naheshi thought in amazement. *She's not afraid at all. She loves this danger. She devours excitement as a wolf devours flesh, and it makes her shine.* Someone thrust a piece of bread at him, and he stuffed it down gratefully. No one offered him a seat; he hoped his wobbling legs would keep him upright with the help of the wall.

"Permit me to introduce my advisors, sister." Heshmi-sharrumma gestured around him. "Some you no doubt already know, like the palace commandant, Kili'anu, here."

Naheshi recognized the man who had spoken about the watchmen. *So that's how the guards happened so conveniently to be absent when needed.*

"Lord Azzi-iltu, Lord Iwirikalli, Lord Tala'abi..." he

went on, each man nodding respectfully as his name was called.

The icy sweat began to trickle down Naheshi's scalp. *These are the cream of the* maryannuma*: officials, merchants. They may really succeed. They'll have me torn into pieces if they find out I'm spying for the regent.* He couldn't picture Agipsharri in such exalted company. Perhaps he was wrong about the old eunuch.

"Tonight, we have with us representatives of the king of Assyria, so you can see that our cause is fully supported. Let the Great King's viceroy try to come to the rescue; this time we'll be ready. Our own soldiers are poised to resist him, and the Assyrians will choose that moment to create a disturbance in the north that will force him to send his troops up there instead. For once, the fate of Ugarit will rest in the hands of us sons of Ugarit. Our days of slavery are almost over, gentlemen!" Heshmi-sharrumma bared his teeth in a predatory grin, and the men erupted into a rumble of enthusiasm. "My brother, please bring in the Assyrian ambassador."

Abdi-sharrumma obediently rose and exited.

"This is no low-level delegation, my friends," Heshmi-sharrumma assured them all. "He is Tukulti-ninurta's own princely cousin. We are supported in the highest places."

Abdi-sharrumma returned and ushered before him into the room three men, dressed after the fashion of Assyrians in short-sleeved tunics and fringed shawls, their long beards cropped square across the chest. The eldest—clearly the prince, based on the deference his fellows showed him—entered first and looked around the room with shrewd, appraising eyes. He was a squat old man, his shoulders still broad, his neckless head thrust forward like a vulture's. A sudden icy suspicion coursed up Naheshi's spine. He knew that face from somewhere.

"Gentlemen, Prince Shalim-ahum, ambassador of the King of Kings Tukulti-ninurta of Assyria."

It was all Naheshi could do not to slide down the wall with a whimper. Oh, cruel gods, ironic gods. He should have recognized that wide mouth, even though the thick lips were less thick. He should have known that predatory head, even though the hair was gray and sparse, the scalp spotted with age. Twenty-five years disappeared in an instant, and he was a cowering child, and Shalim-ahum was roaring, "He can't sing? What about my investment? I've been feeding this useless lump of meat for four years for nothing?"

It was his old master.

The blood drained from Naheshi's face. He shrank against the wall, willing himself to become invisible. His hands shook; he prayed his delicate stomach would not betray him. He could feel his bread boiling upward.

Heshmi-sharrumma introduced the conspirators, the Assyrian pinning each of them with a stare as if memorizing their faces. Naheshi knew how formidable the old diplomat's memory was. At last Shalim-ahum's gaze fell upon Naheshi, and the eunuch could see a slitting of the eyes as the old man shuffled through his mental archives.

Taddu spoke up brightly. "That's my chamberlain, Nahish-shulmanu, a countryman of yours."

Shalim-ahum's wide mouth pulled tighter in a wry smile of recognition. "Ah, yes," he said in thickly accented Ugaritic. Naheshi knew that sly, penetrating squint all too well. "Actually, Nahish-shulmanu and I share a long history, don't we?"

He sauntered over to his former slave and poked him in the belly, adding in Akkadian, "What are the chances, eh? You're looking well fed, Nahish-shulmanu; last time I saw you, you were skin and bones. I'm happy to see that the West has agreed with you." He turned back to the group. One of the men stood up and gave him his chair.

"Gentlemen, my lady queen," Shalim-ahum continued, "I believe your prince has informed you in general terms, but permit me to repeat more specifically what my master the King of Kings has in mind to do for you and what he expects in return."

Naheshi was in such turmoil that he heard nothing of the old man's speech. It was as if an abyss had opened at his feet—yet another—and he was sliding in. He felt he couldn't breathe. He wanted to run, but his legs would not have held him up. His mind was filled with the image of that face, contorted in rage... that wide, thick mouth with spittle flying... the little child cowering in fear. *I have disappointed master. It's all my fault.* He felt the tears scalding his eyelids; he wanted to curl up and die, melt away into oblivion. There was no enduring such self-contempt. He couldn't swallow.

Taddu shook his arm. "Naheshi, what's wrong with you? Are you awake? We have to go—come on."

He followed her like a half-wit, trying to work up enough saliva to warn her. "My lady, that man—"

"Later, later. We have to get back right now."

"Assyrian!"

Naheshi turned, cringing, expecting discovery.

Prince Heshmi-sharrumma stood at his elbow. "What did he say to you in Akkadian?"

"Remembering old times, my lord. He said I looked... pr-prosperous," Naheshi stammered, strangling on his spittle.

The prince nodded, but his eyes were narrowed.

Abdi-sharrumma shepherded them out into the dark street to his waiting chariot. The moon had set. The other men were dispersing in various directions through the night. Several of them agreed to pass along the wooded ravine bank to be sure no one was still lying in wait there. Naheshi and his companions climbed into their vehicle as before; they galloped with muffled hooves to the pine tree by the road as before. They picked their way—this time by the pale light of the star-glittering sky—across the ravine trail as before. Naheshi could have recounted none of his actions as they traveled. His thoughts were leagues—and years—away.

At the grate, Abdi-sharrumma embraced Taddu and urged her, "Hurry. Dawn is not far away. Be careful, my love." He got a spark going with a bow drill and handed her the lamp they had left, checking its oil. "Take no risks. Your life is more precious to me than anything."

"You, too, my dearest. Find out who ambushed us, and show him no pity!"

One last kiss, and he melted away into darkness. Naheshi heard the grate lock back into place. The queen led off through the dripping tunnel on quick little feet. He followed like a dumb animal, panting and shaking but this time not from fear of the underground hell. He carried his own hell with him.

The two passed the stairs that led up into the plaza, but no moonlight shone down. Turning, they followed the broader tunnel under the palace and eventually climbed the steps to the overhead grate, which Naheshi clumsily heaved open with his bruised shoulders. Side by side, the pair emerged into the little room by the royal tombs, and the queen extinguished her lamp. Through the utter blackness of the sleeping palace, they tiptoed. There was a light in the kitchen as they went up the staircase—the bakers were beginning their work—but no one acknowledged or stopped them until they passed through the unguarded door of the queen's apartments.

Naheshi pulled down the bar and leaned, trembling, against it. "My lady—"

"There! We're safe! Wasn't that thrilling, Naheshi?" She was dancing around on her toes in her excitement, hands clasped. "We're part of something really important, something that will change the course of the world! My baby will be the king, and I will be his regent with Abdi-sharrumma. And then, who knows? Heshmi might meet with an accident, and it will be Abishu and me—"

Naheshi blurted, "Please, my lady, that man—"

"What man?"

"Shalim-ahum. Don't trust him! He's... he's... a bad man." Naheshi's voice was tight and tremulous.

"What? The King of Kings's cousin?" The queen faced her chamberlain, hands on hips. Her excited expression chilled into severity. "See here, Naheshi, I think you're being a little judgmental of your betters, don't you? Who cares what kind of man he is? He represents the king of Assyria."

231

"Don't trust him, my lady. Oh, please. He was... he was my master. I know him. He... did awful things..." He could hear his voice shaking and rising in pitch. Taddu stared at him. "He... he raped me. I was just a little child. He was angry because... because... I couldn't... sing anymore. He'd bought me to make me a singer, and then somehow it didn't work..."

He knew he had told her that before. Naheshi couldn't think. He fell apart in sobs, sank to his knees, covered his face with his splinted fingers. "He was furious. He wanted to punish me, a little child. Don't trust him, don't trust him!"

The queen turned away with a swish of skirts and stalked to the window. There was no sound but his sobbing. He longed to feel her lift him up, to hear her say, "You poor thing, Naheshi. You've been through so much. I love you; you know that. Everything will be fine." He ached to feel her warm arms around him, comforting him, her soft breasts against his chest, her downy cheek against his brine-streaked face. He looked up at her pleadingly through his tears.

She stood for a moment with her back to him, then whirled and came to stand over him. But her eyes were not gentle. They glittered with outrage. "Naheshi, have you completely forgotten yourself? He is a prince, a prince, and you are a slave. Why shouldn't he use you if he wanted?" Her voice rose. "By all the gods, Naheshi, you were his slave, his property. He could do anything he wanted to you. Have you gone crazy? That doesn't make him a bad man."

She emitted a whoosh of frustration. "Naheshi, I hate to say this, but you are getting completely out of line lately. You seem to be somehow obsessed with the idea that everyone wants to ravish you. Believe me, you're not all that attractive to a normal person." Naheshi flinched as if he'd been struck, but she forged on, not appearing to notice. "Perhaps I've been too indulgent. Just remember you are a slave, a slave, Naheshi. Do I need to have you whipped to remind you of your place? Should I sell you? I'm fed up with it—spying, following me around, giving me orders. I am not *your* property. You are *my* property!"

She stood looming over him for a moment, her eyes blazing down. Naheshi gaped up at her, expressionless with shock. He felt his soul shriveling like a wick consumed by her flame.

"Get out," she said more calmly, "and come back when you're in control of yourself. Or else this is it. Do you understand? I'll get you a job in the chancery. But I won't have you telling me what to do."

He struggled to his feet, bowed deeply, fumbled open the bar, slipped into the corridor, and stood there for a moment, not even making the effort to wipe his nose. He heard footsteps coming; the day guard was taking up his post. Naheshi nodded to the soldier, walked stiffly down the corridor past the apartments of the king's women, to the staff area, to his own door. He unbarred it and entered with no attempt at being quiet. Anani popped up from his pallet on the floor.

"Who's there? Oh, master! Master! You're back! I was worried…"

Naheshi smiled mechanically but pushed past, snagged the chamber pot, and clumped up the stairs to the roof. Anani trailed after him.

"Does master need anything? Are you hungry?"

"No," Naheshi murmured. "I just want to be alone for a while. I need to think."

Anani backed down the stairs and left his master to his thoughts. Naheshi relieved his bladder, but the pressure was building unendurably in his mind. He sat down on the roof roller. The early-morning hour was cold, but so was his soul. The sky was lightening imperceptibly, the stars fading; he could see the silhouettes of trees and towers against the horizon, although there was still only the ghost of dawn. That would be coming from behind him, from the direction of Assyria.

Again and again, his memory replayed the image of Abdi-sharrumma and Taddu kissing—of the prince's broad hand against her back, the black hairs on his knuckles. Of course she loved him. He was a man. He was muscular and strong and built for... conjugation. He had a beard, he carried a sword, he was trim hipped and hard chested. That was the kind of person the queen loved. She would have loved the king, her husband, if he had loved her. But it was Abdi-sharrumma who loved her, and so she loved him.

Naheshi loved her, too, but he wasn't a man. He was *not* the kind of person the queen loved. The thing that had happened once with Naheshi meant nothing to her. She'd had a need, and he was the only object there to fulfill it for her. Naheshi meant no more to her than his chamber pot meant to him. He was her property, quite simply. He'd been serviceable, and it had meant nothing. He was a dog, a thing. The warm bath of happiness, the thought of being loved finally, of being freed from his failures, redeemed by her esteem—it had been an illusion all along. He knew nothing so beautiful was likely to happen to him; he was cursed of the gods. He'd offered himself to the most traumatic humiliation at the hands of Agipsharri for her sake, and he was just a thing to her.

Something in him had just died, he realized. The queen had daggered it to the heart. All his life, some abscess in his deepest core had been filled by the purulent mass of self-pity. It had weakened him, made him unable to make a decision, unable to trust himself. But that had drained out through the wound she'd just inflicted on him. And in its place was something equally painful but by whose cold light he could see a firm direction. A little fire, bitter cold but burning, had been ignited in him, like tiny flames licking invisibly in the grass before they caught and spread into a conflagration.

He'd thought he had been miserable before, but there was no misery like the crackling flame of rage. Naheshi did not picture himself as an angry person, had not permitted himself to be one. Bad people were angry. His father was angry. Shalim-ahum was angry. Agipsharri was angry. But there were moments—not a lot, but some—when wrath came over him, too, with its snarling face exposed, and he knew it for what it was. Instead of feeling sorry for himself, he found himself wanting to exact vengeance on those who had maligned him. And they were many.

He could usually wrestle down the worst of the anger by reminding himself that thousands of people were slaves; they had no rights, and so they could not be wronged. Thousands of little boys were castrated with or without their parents' collusion. Thousands of people lived in hostile territory, suspected and sneered at. Thousands of people were terrorized, ordered around, held in contempt—most people, in fact; the powerful were few. His anger was utterly futile, because he was completely helpless to change things. He would remind himself how fortunate he was in so many ways, how much worse things could be. He could be beaten by a cruel master, like Anani. He could be hungry and living on the street. He had a pliant nature; he was content to do what he was told without too much damage to his pride. Things were not so bad.

But then a kind of scalding misery would rise up inside him, half of himself screaming and gnashing its teeth like some barely leashed dragon, the other half weeping piteously, "Don't! Don't be like that!"

He didn't want to be angry, but he was. He was. And he had no intention of fighting it back anymore. Throbbing with envy, he thought of Ili-milku and the Lord Urtenu with their houses and their families, their ancestral tombs, their grandchildren. He thought of his Taddu, who might have had a kind word for him that night but did not. Instead, she'd kicked him down to his rightful place, trampled on his most intimate soul.

He thought of his mother weeping in the other room, wailing, "What have we done to him?" He thought of his father hissing, "Shut up, woman. This will solve our problem." The child's soul had shriveled with pain at the understanding that *he*, who only wanted to please, was their problem.

He thought of the Old Dragon eyeing him with bone-deep contempt, of Shalim-ahum roaring, "What do you mean, 'he can't sing'? What about my investment? You mean I've been feeding this useless piece of meat for four years for nothing?" He thought of Agipsharri and his hatred, his cruelty, and of all the snickering maids and sneering guards, mincing around behind his back, mocking him in falsetto. If he was ridiculous, who had made him ridiculous? He hadn't been born that way. He'd had some dignity once. And he felt as if he would simply incinerate with pain, as if he were an oil-soaked torch that would go up in a blaze that consumed everything around it.

But like all torchlit paths, his way forward had grown much clearer.

CHAPTER 14

A S SOON AS MORNING HAD decently risen, Naheshi made his way to the Old Dragon's residence, where Lord Urtenu would be ensconced. He'd had no breakfast, but he was so intent on his mission that he scarcely noticed.

The queen mother's secretary received him promptly. "Good morning, Nahish-shulmanu."

"My lord." Naheshi bowed, his hands clasped tensely.

"Have you anything to report this week? We notified the palace commandant about the guards going missing."

"They were missing again, my lord, but I can explain that easily now. Permit me to inform my lord that there is a palace coup afoot under the leadership of my lord the king's brothers, and my lady Queen Taduhepa and the commandant Kili'anu, among other notables, are involved."

Urtenu's caterpillar eyebrows rose in genuine surprise. "Well, well. You have had a busy few days, I see. Please, tell me what you know. We need names and exact dates."

✦

Around midmorning, Naheshi left Urtenu's office and made his way back to the queen's quarters. The maids told him she had taken the children down to the garden. He was relieved not to have to face her. He took advantage of her absence to arrange a thorough cleaning of the apartment. He'd never been so unsmiling and peremptory with the servants. There was much rolling of eyes behind his back. Naheshi saw it, but for once, he didn't care what they thought of him. He was not in a mood to tolerate laziness.

By midday, the place was spotless. The bedclothes, although unused the night before, had all been replaced, fresh flowers arranged. When the queen returned with Prince Utri-sharrumma and Princess Batashiya in tow, Naheshi bowed expressionlessly, took the order for lunch, and exited. He especially avoided catching the eyes of the royal children, who were fond of him. He could not let himself be distracted by a sweet smile or a little dimpled hand placed in his. The less he thought about the children, the better. No one had thought of him when he was a child.

⁂

Heshmi-sharrumma glared up at his henchman from dangerously narrowed eyes. "I warned you, Agipsharri. This was our last chance to deal with my brother before the king's return, and it failed. What have you to say for yourself?"

The old eunuch spread his hands in a gesture of sweet reason, although his small eyes evaded the prince's. "It was risky, my lord. The targets didn't appear until the moon had nearly set, and my archers tell me the shadows confused them."

Disgusted, Prince Heshmi-sharrumma snarled, "Damn it. What sort of people did you hire? I gave you plenty of silver. You should have gotten real professionals. I can't imagine that a former soldier or someone really skilled wouldn't have been able to adjust to a shadow, by the Lord Ba'al."

He surged up from his table with a bang of his palms on the surface and closed in on Agipsharri. He would not endure this foul-smelling piece of lard undermining all he had worked for so many years. "As a spy, you've had your value, but as an arranger of disappearances, you have not performed well. And now we've lost a critical amount of time. By your own admission, the king is returning and, with him, his loyal elite troops. You foul bastard. You may have cost us the revolution." Heshmi-sharrumma's jaw was so tense with barely controlled fury he could almost hear the grinding of his teeth.

The old eunuch's fat cheeks grew chalky, and his smile faltered. "I assure my lord, it can still be salvaged. Perhaps it's better after all to make use of my lord Abdi-sharrumma's charisma now and quietly remove him later, eh. I will—"

The prince, his mouth curled in a derisive smirk, cut Agipsharri off. "If you can't get rid of him now, when he's alone and exposed against a white hillside on a moonlit night, what's to make me think you can pick him off later, when he is more powerful and has the royal family of Amurru on his side? You botched this, eunuch. Don't expect a third chance. I know the only thing you are really concerned about in all this is to see the queen embarrassed. But if you work for me, you work toward *my* objectives. Is that clear?" He slapped the end of his belt rhythmically into the palm of one hand like an angry cat twitching its tail; the fatal pounce was imminent. He could see that his prey was afraid, and he savored it.

Agipsharri licked his lips. "Yes, my lord. Do permit me to remind my lord that I have saved his life by alerting him to his brother's treachery, I—"

"Our contract is terminated. Continue to keep your eyes open at the palace, but consider yourself relieved of this assassination." Heshmi-sharrumma drew closer to the eunuch, and although the prince was much the shorter of the two, he seemed to look down on the old wretch. He was the dominant animal here, no mistake. His voice grew slippery with sarcasm. "Oh, yes, and another thing: Kili'anu tells me someone reported the absence of the guards the other night. Don't suppose you'd happen to know who let slip that little detail, would you?"

"Absolutely not, my lord. It could have been anyone— the palace is full of officious servants looking to ingratiate themselves with the regent." But Agipsharri's little eyes dodged uneasily.

"Think about it, Agipsharri. The offenses are piling up. You're becoming less useful to us by the day." He raised his voice. "Tala'abi!"

The young nobleman appeared at the door. "Yes, my prince."

"See to it this fellow is shown out."

Tala'abi returned a moment later alone.

"How much of that did you hear?" said the prince.

"Enough, my lord. He was still prating about how much silver we owed him as I shoved him out the door.

Is he safe anymore, do you think? Or should we consider putting an end to him?"

"He should make a broader target than my brother." The prince's fists tightened. "Kill him."

※

"My lady does me too much honor." Agipsharri bowed obsequiously. He seemed to fill the dowager's office with his bulk. Even behind the buffer of her desk, she drew back a little, repulsed.

"You're right," she said, making minimal effort to control the expression of distaste that drew down the corners of her mouth. "So waste as little of my time as possible, eunuch. I wouldn't have received you had it not been for the recommendation of Lady Pizidku, who values your years of service. What do you want to tell me?"

The old eunuch smiled smugly. "There is a plot afoot, my lady, to overthrow my lord King Ammishtamru and ally the kingdom to Assyria."

"Yes. We are aware of that."

Agipsharri's smile faded, and his small eyes grew uneasy, shifting back and forth.

"It is led by my lady's two sons, Prince Heshmi-sharrumma and Prince Abdi-sharrumma."

"Yes, yes, that's old news." *Dear gods, he's only wasting my time.* "Have you nothing else to offer?"

Agipsharri looked up triumphantly. "Queen Taduhepa is involved. She is also adultering with Prince Abdi-sharrumma."

"Eunuch, your information is already well known.

You'll have to bring me something more surprising than that," said Ahat-milki.

The would-be informant pursed his lips, disappointed. "The queen's chamberlain is also involved."

At last, the old queen emitted her dry, barking laugh. "So we've heard. Nothing new there. I think you have no news at all worth paying for. The gods give you good day."

"My lady is amazingly well-informed," Agipsharri said unctuously. "Should you ever require any small tasks performed or a discreet ear among the conspirators, I assure you of my readiness to serve, eh."

"Fine. Good day." She observed with annoyance that the old eunuch had made no move toward the door. "Well, what? You didn't expect to be paid for this stale intelligence, did you? Go on. Out! Tatasshe, escort this fellow out, please."

What a malodorous, raddled old specimen. Have these people no self-respect?

But Agipsharri was not easy to eject. As he waddled after Tatasshe to the door, he turned a final time to the queen mother. "Perhaps my lady is unaware that the coup was delayed by a rift between the two princes. Prince Heshmi-sharrumma doesn't trust his brother and had actually contracted to have him killed, and vice versa. Fortunately, these plots within a plot were foiled. If I may say, it was I who was charged with assassinating the two princes… and I who managed to spare their lives, at risk to my own. Perhaps your sources neglected to tell you that, eh, my lady?"

Ahat-milki stiffened as if the temperature had suddenly dropped in the room. So her boys were tearing at one another. What could there possibly be that both of them wanted? She had a cynical presentiment that Taddu had something to do with the falling-out.

Perhaps this creature was telling the truth about his role in saving her sons' lives from one another; perhaps not. As a mother, she wanted to thank him. As the regent, she was indifferent to the life or death of the conspirators against the throne. Perhaps she should punish the fellow for failing to cut off the heads of rebellion when he had a chance.

"Old news," she growled as he was escorted through the door.

⚜

Ammishtamru would set foot in the palace within the hour. The king, on his way back from Hattusha, was making an effort to arrive before the fall rains began, according to his latest letter to his mother and regent. Just moments before, a courier had galloped up from Mahadu to say that the royal ship had cast anchor. It could not be soon enough for Ahat-milki. She was eager to turn the weight of the kingdom back over to her son. She'd kept him apprised in general of the rumblings of revolution—without naming names; he would be angry enough without picturing Heshmi-sharrumma at the head of a rebel army—but there were many details she needed to fill in for him. Her personal couriers and those of Lord Takhulinu were certainly secure, but it seemed clear that Ammi did not trust his own. His letters to her were terse, formulaic. He expected them to be read aloud to her, perhaps... as if she couldn't read. Men never seemed to understand women's capabilities, even when kings relied on their wives and mothers.

Yes, son, I can read.

Ahat-milki reread the next-to-last letter Ammi had sent her immediately after his audience with Tudhaliya:

"To the queen, my mother, say: message of the king, your son. I fall at my mother's feet. May all be well with my mother! May the gods guard you; may they keep you well. Here with me, everything is well. There with my mother, whatever is well, please send word of that back to me."

Yes, yes, all is well; everything to the ends of the earth is perfectly well. Someone needed to devise a seal that read "All is well" so that one could simply stamp one's letters.

She blew out a cynical "Tsh!"

So the Great King had not been furious that Ugarit was seeking to renege on its duty to provide soldiers, at least. No doubt the promise of gold was even more enticing than an army.

The letter continued: "They have promised a gift for the Great Queen out of our tribute. She accepted my greetings."

That was indeed important. The opinions of the Great Queen Mother Puduhepa were at least as weighty as those of her son, Tudhaliya. Ahat-milki dared to hope her own greetings and gifts to her counterpart in Hattusha had played some role in the success of the mission, in fact. How much more appropriate a word of salutation from the Great Queen's own granddaughter would have been. *But,* she thought bitterly, *that would have required some effort on Taddu's part. Mustn't expect miracles.*

When Ahat-milki read, "and the face of My Sun shone upon us," she snorted outright. She could see the cynical curl to Ammi's lip as he dictated that stock phrase. *My Sun, indeed.* Ammi might be politically indebted to the boy in Hattusha, but he was not half the fool his brothers seemed to think he was. The Great King held Ugarit by force and treaty, not because of some divine mandate. Every king in the world seemed to think he was the sun beside which all the other little lights paled. Egypt, Assyria, and even the powerless dregs of Mitanni had flaunted their winged sun disks. Come to think of it, there was one on the head of the royal bedstead here.

Her dry smile faded, and Ahat-milki tapped her fingers nervously on her desk. Within the hour, Ammi would be back. That meant many things, and one of those was that Heshmi had not managed to get his coup off the ground as quickly as he had hoped. And *that* meant that there was now personal danger to Ammishtamru; it would not be a bloodless uprising. Her sons would fight one another again for the throne.

She sighed deeply, wearily. *Athirat, mother of the gods, protect us all.*

The young queen had to go immediately; no question about that. Ammi would not be happy about it—or perhaps, underneath the indignation and humiliation, he would be. It was, at best, another time-consuming piece of business to attend to. The offense could be made public in discreet terms: her behavior had "sought to harm the king" or some such bland accusation. Ahat-milki had received Urtenu's latest report with a mixture of disgust and satisfaction. The young eunuch was working out well as a spy, she had to admit. She owed him a nice reward. It had not taken him long to discover that the queen was playing her royal husband false.

What a goose. Her niece was a hopeless goose. Ahat-milki gritted her teeth in annoyance. That marriage had been an enormous disappointment. It would be such a relief to have the young queen gone and Pizidku back on the throne where she belonged. They would write to Taddu's brother to take his sister back. Too bad dear old Benteshina was no longer alive. He'd understood the messy little exigencies of political marriage. One could not be sure of how a starry-eyed youngster like Shaushga-muwa might react, but Ahat-milki had already sent a letter in Ammi's name to Karkemish. If it persuaded the viceroy to support them, then Shaushga-muwa would have no choice but to cooperate. Vassalage could be a gift as well as a curse if you knew how to use it, and Ahat-milki did know.

She heard the distant clatter of chariots and horses in the street beyond the massive walls of the palace. There were trumpets and shouted orders, cheers of retainers and nobles. The royal party had arrived from Mahadu. If she'd been younger, the old queen would have gone out on the parapets of the wall to watch them come in. A royal procession entering the city was a thrilling sight, but at her age, it was too much trouble. And frankly, the prospect of fratricidal war among her boys had taken its toll on her spirit. Dread hung over her like a thunderhead. Ammi would come to her in good time.

Ba'al Haddu, protector of kings, just let him be watchful. Surely, Heshmi would not attempt anything with so many soldiers and officials about. But then, he had done it before.

Ahat-milki called her maids, who poured into the room like brightly feathered fowl shooed out of their birdhouse.

"Set up my chair here, girls," she ordered in her gravelly

voice. "And bring another, a finer one, for the king. And some chilled wine, the best we have."

They scattered to do her bidding, and she sank into her chair gratefully.

Her housekeeper entered with a deep bow. "My lady, our lord the king."

Ammishtamru son of Niqmepa, a deep-chested man in his midforties, strode into his mother's salon. It was hard to believe such a large, muscular personage had come from her own tiny, stick-thin body. She could hardly remember him as a child, unlike Abdi-sharrumma, who looked just the same as he had in childhood, his eyes bright with lies. Ammi had always had something middle-aged about him. He was steady, even stolid. He might sneer about his duties, but he fulfilled them. Despite Heshmi's talk of daring and imagination, of all her boys, Ammi was certainly the best suited to rule. The Great King had chosen wisely.

She smiled in delight at her middle son and stretched out her arms to him. "My son! The gods be praised, you have reached home safely."

"My mother!" he said, leaning down for an embrace. He stank of sweat and seawater—he'd been traveling for days. His reddish beard was full of dust from the road, and there were great dark ovals under the armpits of his short military tunic. He laughed. "Don't feel obliged to kiss me. I must be pretty foul."

"You're a welcome sight to these old eyes, my son. I have held my breath in fear until I saw you home safely. Things are, as you know, uneasy here."

He drew up his chair and helped himself to a cup of wine, rolling it around in his mouth and gulping down a copious draft with an "Aah!" of satisfaction. The king wiped his lips with the back of his hand and leaned back wearily. He stretched out his legs and crossed his booted ankles, reclining as best he could in the chair.

"So I understand. Tell me what's going on."

Ahat-milki considered her clasped hands while she composed her thoughts. She needed to make the story concise and compelling. She needed to arouse her son's outrage without making him feel humiliated.

"There are two issues, Ammi. One, as you know, is that there are rumbles of rebellion. It's not the first time." She raised her eyebrow significantly.

"You mean my godforsaken brother again?" the king exploded, starting to rise from his chair. He sank back, shaking his head bitterly. "Won't that son of a dog ever give up? I knew it was stupid to pardon his life before, but that's what the Great King wanted. The Hittites are so keen on looking merciful. I thought he was not supposed to leave Alashiya. Where is Pukanu in all this?"

"Who knows, my son? He is Heshmi's father-in-law, after all. I think he might be expected to side with him. If his daughter were on the throne, Alashiya would certainly occupy a privileged place in Ugarit's commerce. And how difficult is it to sail away from the island? Ships are coming and going all the time, and it's just off our coast. He's not under house arrest."

Ammi growled a reluctant agreement. "And I suppose Abishu is involved as well? Always big brother's loyal little shadow."

"That appears to be the case, but it's more complicated than that, my son," the queen replied carefully. "My sources tell me that they—the conspirators, I mean—had hoped to strike while you were gone, but apparently, things did not work out that way. I'll explain why in a moment. Now you must be especially on guard. They have eyes and ears in the palace itself and know all your movements."

"Whose eyes and ears?" the king demanded.

"I don't know for sure yet. But I do have some suspicions, and I'm following up on them. We, too, have our eyes and ears, you may be sure. Just be watchful. Heshmi is mad with ambition. He feels he has been wronged and will commit any folly to take back what he thinks should belong to him."

"Then let him complain to the Great King, not to me," said Ammishtamru. "Has he forgotten whose father set this all in motion?"

"I'm only too afraid he has not, my son. In fact, his plan is to break the treaty with the Great King. He thinks Hatti is poised to fall, and Ugarit will go down with her unless we act now to disengage from our vassalage."

"And turn to whom, by the beard of Ba'al? I don't suppose he's aware that Egypt is now Hatti's friend instead of a rival?"

She sighed grimly. "Rumor has it that he would turn to Assyria for protection."

"Assyria! That's rich. Does the imbecile not recall how Assyria protected the remains of Mitanni? By gobbling them up, that's how." The king's voice was thick with sarcasm. "Yes, I'm sure Assyria would love to protect us, right into the sea. She's been wanting access to the coast for a long, long time, and with us in her claws, there would be nothing to stop her."

"Well"—again Ahat-milki picked her words with

care—"perhaps the theory here is act before the inevitable happens and so be in a position to dictate more favorable terms for Ugarit."

"Ba'al's beard, you sound like a revolutionary yourself, Mother dear." Ammishtamru emitted his growly laugh, but it was not a wholly amused noise. "I have to disagree with you. Whatever our gripe with the Great King, he's still powerful, and he's still concerned for our welfare, believe me. Remember the last time your darling boys tried to assassinate their brother? It was the Great King's viceroy who came to my rescue, and the upshot is that I am in his debt. I can't throw that alliance in his face as if it meant nothing. Men have their honor—me included."

"Very well, my love. I am simply telling you what I've learned. I want to hear all about your visit with the Great King. But before you tell me, there is one more thing."

She fixed him gravely with her painted eyes until she was sure she had his attention. Then she said in a quiet voice, "Your queen, Lady Taduhepa."

"The Great Queen was a little surprised not to hear from her granddaughter, I think." Ammishtamru sipped his wine.

"No doubt, but the queen has been... busy, it seems. Ammi, there is evidence that she has been having an affair."

The king did not react with the skepticism that Ahatmilki had feared. Perhaps he was already more disenchanted with his Amurrite bride than she'd realized. He expelled a curse and slammed the arm of his chair with a furious palm. "That woman has been trouble from the moment she walked in the door. Do you have hard proof?"

"Reliable testimony, yes. She has been leaving the palace during the day and even in the middle of the night.

Her chamberlain has seen her. He followed her more than once."

"Who's her little friend? Some sailor from the port?" The king took a sip from his cup.

"It's your younger brother, my dear."

Ammi slung his cup to the table with such vehemence that it rolled to the floor with a clang, the last of the wine splashing out. His lips drew back in a string of oaths.

"Now, don't be profane," his mother cautioned. "You know how he is. It seems even Heshmi has turned against him and tried to have him removed. That's why the rebellion has been delayed."

The king snorted with grim laughter. "What a bunch of eggs you've hatched, Mother. Were we always like this?"

"I lay the blame on my niece," said Ahat-milki. "That girl has been a curse for our family since the moment she arrived. But we can't have her arrested on a slave's testimony; we need to catch her red-handed. In fact, I suggest that you act as if nothing is wrong when you're around her. We don't want to tip our hand, because we hope to intercept her tryst at some point soon, and that will give us the evidence we need. Then we'll send her back. She'll be disgraced, and her brother won't find it easy to marry her off again. Who would knowingly wed an adulteress?"

Ammishtamru looked uneasily at his mother. "I don't suppose there's any chance that the crown prince is... not..."

Ahat-milki smiled reassuringly. "I can't imagine that, Ammi. He looks so much like your father."

"Who is also Abishu's father, if we're not all deceived," grumbled the king. "Some comfort that is. And the other one, the little girl?"

"This all seems to be new, my dear. Abishu has been in Alashiya for the last five years. I wouldn't worry about the children." She patted her son's arm.

"I ask because I will not have that woman's bastard on the throne of Ugarit. If there's any doubt at all, the boy goes with his mother, and Ibi-ranu is back in line, understand? I don't care what the Great King wants. He has to see this for what it is." Ammishtamru's big hands clenched into fists that promised violence.

His mother said, "Of course, my dear. This is all terribly distressing, I know. I apologize for confronting you with such matters before you have so much as rested from your trip."

"No, no. I have to know what's going on. I assume she's part of the plot? She must know what Abishu is up to."

"One supposes so." Ahat-milki sighed. "I've taken the liberty of informing the viceroy about what we know so far. That way, he may feel out the Great King a bit before we confront him with a full-scale demand for a divorce."

"Clearly, the minute my back is turned, my whole family gets busy concocting treason—except you, Mother, of course. And Pizidku." The king's anger grew mellow at the name. A smile crinkled the edges of his eyes. "I appreciate her more every day. I should never have agreed to set her aside." Ammishtamru bent over to pick up his cup and set it on the tabletop. He leaned back in his chair with a gusty sigh. "Well, we'll deal with all this later, and I'll catch up with correspondence. First let me tell you about what happened in Hattusha. I was lucky to find the Great King in his capital. He's doing some sort of religious walkabout all over the kingdom."

CHAPTER 15

THE RETURN OF THE KING both complicated Naheshi's duties and made it possible for him to keep his distance from Taddu. It coincided with the harvest festivals of late summer, and the queen's presence was required at numerous ceremonial events. The king also summoned her to his bedchamber for the first time in a good many months, which should have made her triumphantly happy but in fact aroused considerable resentment in the first royal wife. She returned to her apartments angry to tears, grumbling to Naheshi about Ammishtamru's brutality and how glad she'd be to see the last of him. It was plain that every night spent with her husband meant one more night away from his brother. Taddu was not a patient woman, and when she was provoked with the king, the servants knew to lie low. That served Naheshi's inclinations perfectly well.

The next time the queen told her chamberlain to send away the night maids, she fixed him with a long, penetrating look. But he simply bowed without a word and went to carry out her will. He spoke to her as little as possible, keeping his face a smooth mask of professional complaisance. The queen might wonder what was going on behind that expressionless veneer, but she did not seem displeased by the new Naheshi. He'd become more than ever the ideal servant, the good dog. She was no doubt glad his overwrought tears and pleadings had ended.

After dark, they made their way into the city once more—thank the gods, not that hellish tunnel again—Abdi-sharrumma in the lead, down through the tatty neighborhoods just inside the South Gate. Naheshi's skin crawled at the memory of his first adventure there, and he stayed close to the queen and her sword-bearing lover. As they turned into the little alley where they'd first disappeared some weeks earlier, a wicket gate opened for them, and they passed inside a courtyard where a number of wagons stood, their traces empty. A servant led them through a door into the house, and they found themselves in the presence of many of the conspirators from the port. As the men looked up from conversation, the flickering lamps reduced their eye sockets to lightless holes, turning them momentarily into a confederacy of death's-heads.

"Abdi-sharrumma," said the prince's brother. "My lady. Our token Assyrian. Be welcome."

Someone handed Taddu and Abdi-sharrumma a cup of wine. They settled themselves on stools and drew into the circle of conversation. Naheshi stood attentively at their backs, and this time, he was indeed attentive, his ears fully cocked. They spoke of their glorious plans for Ugarit's future, of the better world that Heshmi-sharrumma's reign would bring under the kindly aegis of Assyria. Naheshi found himself thinking that these people, for all their learning and blue blood, were more innocent than he if they really believed Assyria would leave them free once it had secured their obedience. His countrymen were predators—no one knew it better than he, the prey they had savaged and vomited out.

"We missed our opportunity to strike before Ammi's return," Heshmi-sharrumma was saying. "Things simply weren't in place soon enough. But that won't stop us now. We have Shalim-ahum's word that the King of Kings will distract Tudhaliya and his viceroy before New Year's Day. Tukulti-ninurta plans to invade the area around Nihriya. It will take the Hittites a while to get up there, and no doubt, they'll dicker first—they've been trying to talk him into a peace treaty for months, and he's pretended to go along with it. But Tudhaliya won't take chances. He'll call in his vassals, and Ini-tesshub will be there with troops from Mukesh and Shiyannu as well as Karkemish. He'll be the first to go, in fact. And that will leave the West undefended. It's then we move, gentlemen."

The prince's dark, intense face brightened. "With the help of the commandant here, we will have at least half of our own army to count on. Some of the officers won't join us, so we need to be prepared to take them out expeditiously. The New Year's festival makes the perfect moment. They won't expect us to dare repeat the same ploy." He grinned. "Any questions?"

There were a few. Naheshi registered them with his sharpened ears. So the coup would again fall on New Year's Day, when the whole court would be gathered in the plaza around the royal chapel. If the guards were complicit, it would be easy enough to surround the king, who would be presiding as high priest. This time, the viceroy would not gallop to the rescue. The slaughter would be complete. Heshmi-sharrumma would reascend the throne after the Days of Deconsecration, in the place of his brother—Athtar the vassal to the divine Great King Ba'al... in Asshur, not in Hattusha.

"And Prince Utri-sharrumma will succeed you, my brother? Is that not the plan?" Taddu said, her little-girl voice cutting through the baritone rumble of men.

Heshmi-sharrumma turned his black gaze upon her. "Yes, my dear sister." His lips spread in a brittle smile. "That's the plan we've discussed."

Naheshi neither liked nor trusted this man's smile. *May the gods give King Ammishtamru the strength to unmask him.*

The commandant spoke up. "We need to set up the movement of our forces down to the last detail. Everyone has to know exactly what his assignment will be. We must know the signs and countersigns."

"Yes," said someone else. "Let's meet one more time."

Heshmi-sharrumma nodded. "The night after the full-moon festival, then? In this same house. *The lion smells prey.*"

The others assented, and the meeting broke up. Abdi-sharrumma hustled the queen into the courtyard, Naheshi at their heels.

"It's really going to happen, isn't it, Abishushu?" breathed Taddu.

"Yes, my flower. And then our new life together begins. I count the hours." He kissed her hands as if he wanted to eat them. Naheshi, with ice in his heart, observed the man's handsome profile and white teeth.

They made their way by torchlight up to the service gate of the palace, where Abdi-sharrumma bade the queen an enflamed goodbye, and Naheshi held the gate open for her to pass inside to safety. She released him at her door, and he bowed profoundly before returning to his own apartment.

The next morning, he met Lord Urtenu.

Morning was still young when Naheshi left the queen mother's dwelling and directed his steps across the royal plaza, heading for the main entrance of the palace compound. A group of foreign diplomats had gathered outside the broad porch with its cherubim columns. Their chariots were turning around with a clatter of hoofs and the protesting whinnies of horses, and wagons of gifts were being unloaded. The king was holding an audience that morning. Naheshi had no desire to call attention to his early jaunt, so instead of entering by the ceremonial porch, he passed through the gate that connected the palace to the city fortifications. Footsteps echoing, he continued down the west side of the massive palace wall toward the Rampart Street entrance.

To his amazement and horror, he saw Agipsharri's turnip-like form approaching from the other direction, his skirts swaying with the rhythm of his hurried steps. The old eunuch had not yet spotted Naheshi, but there was no place for the latter to hide. The two would surely collide at the entrance in the narrow street, that canyon between the walls. Naheshi stopped, his heart sticking in his throat, and he considered taking openly to his heels. But then

Agipsharri looked up and saw him. The old eunuch's face split in a malevolent leer. Naheshi froze, his saliva gagging him.

"Well, if Nahish-shulmanu it isssn't!" the queen's slave said, gloating. "So eager for more that we're following me around, is that it, *karubu* face, eh?"

"N-No—" Naheshi began to stammer, robbed of any disdainful witticisms by sheer consternation, when... he glimpsed something plummet from the sky.

A heavy crash resounded at his feet. Agipsharri flew up into the air and slammed backward to the street with a ground-shaking thud and a yelp of horror.

Naheshi jumped away, raising his arm against the cutting projectiles that peppered him, and stared around in terror, cowering against the fortification wall. A large amphora of grain—a hip-high vessel with clay walls as thick as the joint of a man's finger—had exploded on the cobbles not a cubit away from him, spraying razor-edged potsherds and kernels of wheat across the width of the road. It had clearly struck Agipsharri in its fall, although not fatally. The eunuch was screeching in pain and shock, clutching his shoulder. Like Naheshi, he was bleeding from the jar fragments that had flown out everywhere. Naheshi stared at him wide-eyed, wringing his hands, not knowing what to do. Then he cut his eyes upward, goggling at the upstairs windows of the palace, whence the jar had almost certainly come.

"Help me, you misbegotten dog turd!" cried Agipsharri.

Naheshi, his mind in turmoil, drew near as gingerly as if a snake lay writhing on the ground. *Should I help the vile creature or flee and leave him to the mercies of his attackers, whoever they might be?* The thought of touching Agipsharri again was so repugnant as to turn Naheshi's stomach inside out, but the old eunuch *was* the queen's property. And if he refused to help, would Agipsharri not report him?

Naheshi, weak-kneed and splattered with blood, gaped first at the other eunuch then at the windows. His heart was drumming. *Agipsharri will report me...*

"Help me up, damn you, you Assyrian dog!"

If people hear him calling me an Assyrian, some mob is likely to come and beat me up, thought Naheshi, the perspiration beginning to bead his face.

After what seemed like an interminable moment of indecision, he leaned over and, swallowing his revulsion, tried to pull Agipsharri up by the other armpit.

He panted. *Gods, he must outweigh me by three times. I'm going to hurt my back.*

His fingers sank deep into the other's fat arm, but he could not budge Agipsharri. The old eunuch screamed in pain, cursing Naheshi plentifully.

"Help! Help!" Naheshi yelled in his hoarse, ineffectual voice. The guards on the wall had already noticed the ruckus, and a soldier came running from the gatehouse, a spear in his hand. Yet another approached from the side entrance to the palace.

"Here, what's going on?" one of them demanded.

"Murder! They tried to murder me!" Agipsharri cried shrilly, floundering belly-up on the packed earth of the street like an overturned tortoise.

"Who, old fellow? There's no one else around. This boy?" One of the soldiers indicated Naheshi with a thumb, but apparently, the improbable image of the timid young eunuch, with his spindly limbs, heaving the enormous grain jar spoke for itself. The man answered his own question with a dubious shake of the head.

"It fell from above, sir," explained Naheshi, trying to control his chattering teeth. "It could have killed us both."

"Who would want to kill you two? Some jealous husband?" the other soldier asked, grinning.

"Perhaps it was an accident," Naheshi murmured, looking up at the window. But the rooms above him were part of the chancery, and grain jars were not to be found in the king's chancery by accident. Had it been dropped from the roof, then? In any case, someone had purposely heaved it out with intent to kill one or both of them. Were the conspirators aware that he was reporting to Urtenu?

"Well, don't just leave me lying here in the street in pain, damn it," snapped Agipsharri.

The soldiers eyed his bulk and hailed one of their fellows from the wall, and the three of them began to lever the old eunuch to his feet. Naheshi managed to retreat into the doorway before anyone could ask him any questions.

Ten days had passed. The fall equinox was upon them, and the autumn storms had come in early, to Naheshi's distress. Roiling black clouds galloped in from the sea like a chariot division, the riders of the Lord Haddu, bringing with them rain and thunder, their banners unfurled across the western sky, snagging inland on the mountain peaks, leaving Mount Sapunu wreathed in indigo darkness. Naheshi kept the torches lit all day throughout the queen's apartment. Evenings came early.

Lord Yarikh chose to remain invisible behind the screens of cloud and took no part in his festival of the new moon that month. But the rain held off long enough for the king to offer sacrifices, and the participants—including Naheshi and his staff—were able to withdraw into the ritual banquet hall adjacent to the chapel for the final prayers.

In another week, Ammishtamru would preside over the New Year's celebration, and if the conspirators had their way, that would be his last living act.

Naheshi expected some intervention on the part of Lord Urtenu at any moment. Time was running out, and the chamberlain's nerves were stretched as taut as the strings of a harp.

The following night, the queen instructed Naheshi to send away her night servants and remain in the apartment. He wondered what Anani made of these evenings when his master did not return. Naheshi thought ruefully of the dinners left uneaten during the last few months. Perhaps he should have warned his slave ahead of time, but he hadn't wanted to call attention to the absences. *Let Anani think whatever he likes.* Perhaps he was telling his masters, whoever they were, about every nocturnal jaunt. Or more likely, he was perfectly innocent, the poor fellow, and Naheshi had simply overestimated his own importance. More and more, Naheshi was sure the latter case was true.

That near disaster in the Rampart Street still haunted him. His mind ran over and over the list of possible perpetrators. Was it the queen mother, out to silence him now that he had served his purpose? Or was it the conspirators themselves? Perhaps Prince Abdi-sharrumma wanted to rid his lover of her watchdog.

Without a moon visible, Naheshi had no clear way to gauge its setting. He rigged a water clock for the queen and turned it again and again until it seemed the proper time should have elapsed. This struck him as dangerously imprecise for the most important meeting of the conspiracy, but apart from a quiet fluttering in his belly, Naheshi felt only moderately frightened. He'd turned responsibility over to Urtenu and the king and could permit himself to be swept along with whatever happened. Indeed, Naheshi felt within him a curious vacuum of emotion, like that strange feeling before a storm when the wind seemed to have sucked itself up into a silence devoid of all movement. His feelings toward the queen were no longer actively angry— he found he could not maintain the painful fire of rage for very long; it was too exhausting—but like a dog with its teeth in its prey, he would not relent in his campaign of vengeance. Every time he saw her with the prince, her lover, it reminded him of what he had suffered, and that was enough to keep him on course. For the moment, he simply awaited what the gods would send.

When the clock had flowed empty for the sixth time, he and the queen slipped quietly into the corridor, unwatched by any guard. They passed silently down the stairs, around the courtyard in the darkness of the loggias, and out the service gate in the now-familiar trajectory. The dripping of water from the rainspouts drummed a loud tattoo that helped mask their steps.

There was Abdi-sharrumma, torch in hand, enveloped in a cloak drawn over his head like a hood. He embraced the queen, drawing her into the darkness of his capuche, and kissed her passionately on the mouth—their desire,

Naheshi noticed with dull hostility, whetted by the danger of the moment. Down the rain-slippery streets they moved, the two with the torch ahead, Naheshi following as closely as he could, although he mistrusted his balance on the muddy slope. The brand created a globe of misty light in the moisture-saturated air, silhouetting the queen and her lover. Dampness had penetrated Naheshi's woolen cloak, and he was starting to shake. As he eased his way down the slick, stepped street, the others drew ahead. They passed into the warren of dark alleys. Rank smells brought to life by the water assailed his nose, and he buried it in his cloak, trying not to gag. His shoes splashed in unsavory puddles.

A jagged spear of lightning flared overhead. Naheshi jumped, the fine hairs standing up on his arms. In a heartbeat, the Storm God's chariot rolled thundering down the narrow space between peeling walls. Naheshi's pulse was pounding. Ahead, he saw the door open.

"The lion smells prey," murmured the prince, and Abdi-sharrumma and the queen slipped inside. Naheshi scurried to catch up and was ushered into the lamplight at their heels.

Heshmi-sharrumma had risen to greet the latest arrivals, when a hollow crash that shook the house resounded. Naheshi's first thought was that the storm had broken. The others stared around, hands on sword hilts. And then came a second crash, immense, and the sound of splintering wood followed by shouting and the clash of metal.

The king's men had arrived.

Shouts of confusion and fear rose from the conspirators as they jerked their weapons, hissing, from their scabbards. The men scrambled in all directions, colliding with one another, knocking the smaller of them down. A table crashed to the floor. Several plotters attempted to gain the stairs, hoping to escape across the roof, but soldiers poured down the staircase in a clatter of boots and a clash of shields. In through the door of the room came more armed guards. The courtyard outside was flaring with torches, revealing the street gate in ruins on the ground, ripped from its hinges. Terrified horses plunged in their traces, eyes rolling, hooves flailing. Bronze flashed and screamed as it slid off bronze. The conspirators had nothing to lose—if they were captured, their lives would be horribly forfeit—and they fought like wild animals. Naheshi saw Abdi-sharrumma pull the queen away from the melee and try to draw her back toward the interior, but although Naheshi cried out, he could not reach her through the welter of shields and swinging arms. The two disappeared into the darkness.

Not a cubit in front of his eyes, someone severed a head from its body. It toppled to the flagstones of the court, a great, pulsing fountain of bright blood spraying all over Naheshi's face and cloak. A soldier drew back his hand with reddened blade to swing again, but Naheshi felt his bile rising and doubled over, heaving, which undoubtedly saved his life.

He pulled as far back against the wall as he could, appalled by the carnage, frightened in earnest for himself and for the queen. *Where is she? Has she escaped? Does she lie dead somewhere?* He saw Heshmi-sharrumma at the door, his teeth bared, slashing desperately at the shielded soldiers who confronted him, and then the prince went down into a pile of the dead and wounded. Naheshi crawled over the bodies into the space below the staircase and huddled there.

The conspirators were few, the king's men many. The battle was over in minutes, although they were the longest minutes of Naheshi's life. After the clang of bronze and the cries of the wounded, the silence was as thick as the darkness, broken only by panting and the groans of survivors.

Then the soldiers began to collect the dropped weapons and haul out the dead. Someone grabbed Naheshi by the arm, dragged him to his feet, and pushed him roughly toward the door. As he stumbled out in the man's grip, he heard a furious female shriek, and turning, he saw the queen carried down the stairs under another soldier's arm. She was reviling him and pounding at his chest with her fists. Naheshi's heart sank for her—her dress falling up around her knees, her hair disheveled and unveiled in front of all those men. She saw him and screamed for his help, but he was held fast and could only look on with pity.

Outside, soldiers filled the narrow street. The rain had not yet fallen, but the atmosphere was heavy with its threat. Every so often, a flash of distant lightning pulsed silently across the darkness. By the light of the torches, Naheshi could see that chariots blocked the entrance to the alley.

In one of them stood the king, helmeted and cuirassed, a battle-ax in hand.

"My brothers?" he demanded of the officer who was supervising the removal of bodies.

"Prince Heshmi-sharrumma is here, dead, my lord. No sign of Prince Abdi-sharrumma."

"Here is the queen, my lord," called the man who had brought her down the stairs. He held her, arms tied behind her at the elbows, but she was shrieking and trying to kick him.

"Let me go, you cur!"

The king stared at his wife for several moments then shook his head in disgust. "Tie her feet and gag her," he snapped. "Put the wounded and the dead in separate wagons. I'll take the prince's body."

"The prince?" Taddu cried in horror. "Say he's not dead! No! Nooo! Abishu, my love!"

Ammishtamru growled, "Gag her, I said."

Her screams grew muffled as they tied the rolled-up cloth around her mouth. *She is like a fox in a trap,* Naheshi thought, *writhing and furious and incoherent.* He himself felt emptied of life and feeling, as if he'd heaved up his heart along with the contents of his stomach. He wished he'd never seen what he had seen that night, the least horrific of which was the drying blood all over him. The soldiers must have thought it was his own, because he was pushed into a wagon with several men in various stages of disembowelment and severance of limb. He had the sense that they were all just beasts, penned up for the hunt and slaughtered like lions in a hunting park... and it was he whose testimony had baited the trap.

What have I done?

It was daylight by the time they regained the palace, heavy and dark still with the threatened rain. The queen was put under house arrest in her own apartment. Her maids were permitted to attend her, but there were guards under the loggia in the garden below and outside the inner entrance.

The day shift had just taken up duty as the grim procession entered the royal apartments, flinging the heavy doors unceremoniously back against the wall. The girls, huddled together, met their mistress with round, fearful eyes, staring back and forth at one another, at her shackles, and at the soldiers who hustled her into the room and unbound her. The maids' terrified glances sought Naheshi for an explanation, but he avoided their eyes. After the departure of the guards, the room was strangely hushed. No one had the heart to talk; no one dared to ask questions. Naheshi sent the maids to draw the royal bath, and they did it without the normal chatter and laughter. The queen demanded fresh clothing, and the girls hastened silently to obey.

After her first hysterical resistance, Taddu had regained some dignity and was now acting as if she had been wronged. She sat straight and queenly under the ministrations of Ishtar-ummiya who, big-eyed with fearful curiosity, combed and rebraided the royal hair. Doubtless, the handmaids were all dying to know what had happened. They would find out soon enough; their lives would change, too.

Naheshi had managed to convince the soldiers he was not among the injured, and they had turned him back over to his mistress. He was afraid to leave, lest she realize that he was not as much of a prisoner as she and so work out that he was the source of their downfall, but she ordered, "Naheshi, change your clothes. You're disgusting to be around. They'll find out they can't treat me like this. My brother will start a war if he hears about this outrage."

He bowed out in great relief and tottered, dog-tired, to his apartment. Anani opened the door anxiously and almost fell down with shock when his master walked in, covered in blood and vomit.

"Master! Oh no! What've they done to you this time? Oh, come in; let me help you. Are you badly hurt?"

"I'm not hurt at all." Naheshi's voice was as flat as that of ghost.

He peeled off his filthy cloak and shawl and handed them to the slave. He sank, suddenly weak-kneed, into his chair and dropped his face into his hands. *What have I done?* he asked himself hollowly. *Is this what I wanted to happen?*

"Lemme get somethin' for poor master to eat. Lemme give you a bath."

Naheshi didn't have the energy to answer. He just hung there, braced by his elbows on his knees, tasting the bitter dregs of his bile in his mouth, the bitter dregs of his honor. He saw in his mind's eye the man's head falling sideways to the ground and that ghastly red fountain springing up.

Is this a victory? Has the kingdom been saved? But my Taddu, humiliated and dishonored… was this what I wanted? Am I supposed to feel satisfied? People are dead, fathers of families; children are orphans because of me.

He let Anani pull off his tunic, wrap a towel around his hips, and lead him into the room with the drain in the floor. He stood like a dumb sheep, not even bothering to suck in his stomach, while the little man climbed a stool and showered hot water over him from a pierced jug. Naheshi sank down on the stool while his slave pulled a clean tunic on over his head, combed and arranged his wet curls, tied his belt back on, and tugged on his shoes.

"There, master looks nice and neat again. Lemme run down to the kitchen and see what they have—"

"D-Don't go, Anani. Just a cup of wine. I just want to clear my mouth."

"Master..." Anani began timidly. "I know it's not my place to ask, but... what happened to you?"

"I think I lost my soul, Anani."

The slave looked at him, fuzzy brows furrowed with incomprehension, but was too discreet to ask more. Naheshi ached to tell him everything, to hear him say, "Anyone would have done the same!" But the habit of silence was too strong. And Anani might be trying to entrap him... no, that idea took too much effort to believe, Naheshi found. Suspicion was like anger: a state of mind that demanded more tenacity to sustain than he had in him. It couldn't possibly matter anymore. The worst had happened.

"Listen, Anani, I may have to leave. I may have to go back to Amurru with the queen. I don't know if I'll be able to bring you with me. If that happens, go to Ili-milku. He'll employ you. Do you hear me?"

Anani's face crumpled like a leaf in the fire. "Yes, master."

"Anani?"

"Yes, master?"

"Forgive me."

"What for, master?"

For not trusting you. I didn't know an honorable man when I met one. He said nothing but tried to smile, a smile that trembled and collapsed, dragging the corners of his mouth down with it.

CHAPTER 16

THREE DAYS LATER, AROUND MIDDAY, the king's soldiers came for the queen. It was still gray outside, so Naheshi could not be sure of the hour, but his stomach told him lunchtime was nigh. Two of them led her, each taking an elbow, ready to truss her up if she fought, but her comportment was every bit that of a queen—head high, shoulders straight, no shame or fear. Her face was pale but composed and even disdainful. Naheshi knew that, like him, she hadn't slept all night.

He was watching her go, his mind an incoherent and conflicted jumble of pity and relief, when the other two guards laid hands on him as well. "You, too, eunuch."

They drew Naheshi out into the hall, and suddenly his throat constricted. *Is this normal?* The king did know he was on their side, did he not?

The block of soldiers marched the two of them down the corridor to the stairs that served as the king's private entrance to his throne room. That way, they would encounter no one en route. They entered the room at the left of the dais where King Ammishtamru sat on his inlaid ivory throne. Before them stood some twenty men, the merchant lords of Ugarit who made up its council. Several Hittites also stood among the group, recognizable by their shaven faces and long hair. There were soldiers at every entrance, bronze weapons glittering. The queen mother sat beside her son at the king's right hand, a tiny figure, her back straight but her face sagging and somber. Prince Ibi-ranu, the king's eldest son, not much older than Taddu, stood at the other side of the throne, his young face equally grim. He was tall and had fairish hair like his mother.

Naheshi's stomach was knotted with anxiety. What troubled him most of all was the presence of Prince Utri-sharrumma and his sister in the arms of their nurses. *They should not have to witness their mother's shame like this.*

Naheshi was led to the nurses' side, and the queen was made to stand alone at the foot of her husband's throne. Little Utri-sharrumma stretched out a dimpled hand to Naheshi, but the chamberlain cut his gaze away, not daring to look at the child. Naheshi had eyes only for his mistress. He, who knew her so well, could see fear in her movements, but she held herself erect and dignified.

Taddu curtsied deeply and with considerable consciousness of her beauty. Her face turned up to the king with a smile. "My husband has summoned me?"

Ammishtamru eyed her with contempt. He spoke through his clenched teeth in an undertone that was meant only for her ears, and yet Naheshi and no doubt everyone else could hear. "Yes, you whore, and this is one command you do well to heed. Do you deny that you have been having an affair with my brother while I've been gone? Feel free to deny it, and so add perjury to your other crimes."

"My lord, I answer proudly that I have sought the good of the kingdom. I—"

"Since when is the good of the kingdom served by the spectacle of a queen who is unfaithful to her husband, 'my flower'?" The king pronounced the word in sarcastic imitation of a lover's whispered endearments. Taddu blanched, touched momentarily by shame, and Naheshi's guilt blossomed like red-hot coals upon his cheeks. "Eyewitnesses have seen you together, meeting in the Lower Town, at Mahadu, at the entrance to the sewer tunnel, even at the very gate of the palace. By night and by broad daylight. A fine display for my subjects, eh, you trollop?" the king growled.

The assembled courtiers looked down discreetly at their shoes. Naheshi felt as if his face were on fire. *She'll know it was I who betrayed her. She'll know.*

"If it were just me, I'd take off your pretty, empty little head, as is the right of any husband whose woman has dishonored him. You can't be ignorant of how tenuous my grasp on the throne is, with a never-ending tide of brotherly revolutions breaking against us, and looking unable to control my own household is not exactly to the advantage of a ruler. Is it coincidence that you were taken at a meeting of conspirators?" He snorted skeptically, as if not at all inclined to accept this as coincidence.

"But fortunately for you, since our marriage was contracted under the auspices of the Great King, he has the final say on what to do about this little breach of obligation on your part, my wife, and we all know how fond of clemency the Great King is. Believe me, I would have brought this all to a conclusion before now if we had not been waiting for word from Hattusha."

The king gestured to his guards to pull the queen back, but she shook off their hands and stepped to the center of the hall without aid. Her face was pale but controlled.

Ammishtamru's voice—as gruff as a bear pelt, as rough as the bark of an immutable oak—rose to draw in the court. "My Lord Ini-tesshub, would you be so kind as to read our suzerain's letter to this woman?"

One of the Hittites stepped forward. He was a tall, thin-cheeked man with hooded eyes and long gray hair, whom Naheshi had seen from a distance at festivals. His clean-shaven face was mournful. "My son, I thank you on behalf of the Great King. I have presented your case to him, and the judgment is as follows." Ini-tesshub held up a tablet and read out in his orotund baritone, "In the presence of My Sun Tudhaliya, Great King, King of Hatti:

"Ammishtamru king of Ugarit took as his wife the daughter of Benteshina king of Amurru. With respect to Ammishtamru, she has sought, despite all, to do him harm." He paused for effect. "Therefore, Ammishtamru has repudiated the daughter of Benteshina for all time."

There was a gasp from the servants but not from the councilors—they looked grimly unsurprised. Taddu seemed to reel a bit but held her head high. Naheshi felt profoundly queasy. Things, including his own judgment of the situation, had gotten out of his control. The king had thought his love was returned, but it had been cast back in his teeth—that was where Naheshi's sympathies should have lain. And yet he felt nothing for the king, and his pity flew out and enveloped the little queen like a swarm of bees circling their hive, the dear home of their heart. Her crime was that she had loved the wrong person—how well Naheshi knew what that was like. But perhaps her real crime was to have *trusted* the wrong person—*him*. She'd been betrayed. He had betrayed her. And the repercussions of that betrayal were taking on a horrid, hard-edged reality.

Ini-tesshub continued to read: "Whatever possessions the daughter of Benteshina has brought with her she shall take away with her. She shall leave the household of Ammishtamru.

"Utri-sharrumma, the crown prince of Ugarit, shall have a choice. If he says 'I want to go with my mother,' he shall leave behind his possessions and depart, and Ammishtamru will install another of his sons in the office of crown prince in the land of Ugarit. When Ammishtamru joins his ancestors, if Utri-sharrumma takes the throne and attempts to return his mother to the office of queen in Ugarit, the Great King shall depose him and place another of Ammishtamru's sons on the throne."

The queen mother rose from her throne, stepped forward, and called out to the young prince, "Utri-sharrumma, my dear, come to Grandma."

Released by his nurse, Utri-sharrumma toddled forward, looking uneasily back at his mother. Ahat-milki captured his little hand and patted it. "Now, my dear, Mama and Papa are separating. Who do you want to go with?"

"Go with Papa!" Taddu cried urgently, shooing him with her hands.

Utri-sharrumma looked confused and ready to cry.

"Go on, sweets. Go with Papa so you can be king! Go with Papa!"

But the little prince had no idea why his mother did not seem to want him, and he began to whimper.

Her voice grew shriller and more desperate, but the elevated tone served only to frighten him the more. "Go to Papa, Utrishu. Papa! No, don't come to me; you'll lose everything! Go, go to Papa!"

"Papa?" He stood rocking back and forth, looking uncertainly up at his father, who was seated grim-faced on his throne.

"Go to Mama, then," urged Ahat-milki softly, and the little boy, released, rushed to his mother and buried his face in her skirts.

"So be it," declared the viceroy. "Let every man here and all the gods of Hatti and Ugarit bear witness. The crown prince has chosen to go with his mother into exile. Let another be chosen from the king's sons."

"You tricked him!" the queen shrieked at her mother-in-law, her eyes starting from her face like a madwoman's. "It's not fair to make him choose. He's only a little boy! It was a trick to rob him of his birthright! You evil old witch!"

She made as if to fly at the queen mother, but the guards held her back. She struggled, howling with fury, and the little prince, still hugging her legs, howled, too. Batashiya, his three-year-old sister, joined in from her nurse's arms. Meanwhile, Ammishtamru had risen from his throne, his face crimson with anger. Ibi-ranu stood at his side, looking grim.

"Shut your mouth, woman!" roared the king. "Are you the only one permitted to trick people? Is that it? While the queen mother has been serving the kingdom with all her heart and breath, you've been plotting, making sheep's eyes at lovers, and taking part in a conspiracy against your king and husband. Go back to Amurru, and may we never look at your face again. Guards, take her away. The little girl stays here; she may be useful."

Over the protesting screams of the queen, the throne room erupted into a roar—cries of shock and distress, rumbles of righteous indignation, and the shrill tears of the nurses.

Ahat-milki's gravelly voice made itself heard above the chaos. "One more thing, gentlemen. The king has bestowed many gifts upon Taduhepa while she has been here: orchards and horses and slaves and jewelry. All that should stay here as well. She must not be rewarded for her evildoing by being permitted to keep so much as a shawl."

The viceroy nodded, raising his hand, and the babble subsided. "If that is the wish of my son the king, we can draw up an arrangement to that effect right now." He motioned to his secretary, who stepped to his side, tablet and stylus in hand, and the viceroy added in an undertone, "Make a note that the young princess remains with her father."

"You bitch!" shrilled the queen, clutching her son. "You're taking my baby from me, and now you're going to strip me even of my clothes? Do you hate me so much you want to see me go home in rags?"

But Ahat-milki had won, and she saw no point in engaging with the vanquished. She ordered levelly, "Let her chamberlain gather her possessions and take them with her."

Naheshi bowed and stayed down while the queen was dragged past him, screaming imprecations. He wished at all costs to avoid her eyes.

If anyone had asked Ahat-milki whether she'd really won, she might have had a hard time answering. The very ill she'd tried so hard to avoid had taken place despite her best efforts. Her eldest son was dead, cut down in an attempt to usurp his brother's kingdom. Her curse had come home. She sat on her ivory throne for a long while after the others had left, upright and dry-eyed. It was no comfort to her that she'd been right about Taddu's complicity. *The fool.*

Nothing but tragedy had come of all this. Her firstborn was dead, the child of her tenderest years, the fruit of her and Niqmepa's first love. But Heshmi had let hatred and anger undermine his intelligence, something a ruler could never afford to do, no matter how bitter or humiliated he felt. The kingdom's welfare had to come first. Her Heshmi-sharrumma had paid for it with his life.

Ahat-milki closed her eyes for a moment to gather strength, but the memories assailed her. Heshmi had always been too intense. She could remember him sobbing with fury as a thwarted child, unappeasable. He could never bend and so was doomed to break. She must have failed him somehow. Had she not shown him enough love?

She felt the fist of Tsaduk, god of justice, squeezing tighter and tighter around her. The fate she had dreaded was coming to pass: to see her children all die before her. Like any mother, she wanted to throw herself on his body and wail, to tear her hair and cover her face with dust, but that was denied her. Heshmi had died in treason. There would be no funeral; there would be no mourning clothes.

His body—the flesh of her flesh—would be thrown to the dogs somewhere.

Would Pukanu of Alashiya, his father-in-law, make any trouble? Not if he didn't want to reveal any implication on his part. The Assyrians would pretend to know nothing about it, although the eunuch had been very clear about their participation at the highest level. Takhulinu had already sent a message to the Great King, warning him of the diversion in the north in a week's time, but what could he do? A challenge was a challenge. Tudhaliya would have to call them out. In fact, before that message could possibly have reached Hattusha, the Great King had written to Ammi, ordering him to provide troops instead of money, despite their exemption.

Too bad. They could certainly spare no troops at the moment, because Abdi-sharrumma had escaped. As a statesman, Ahat-milki knew she should be chagrined, but as a mother, relief had flooded through her when she heard that neither his body nor his living person had been found. The scapegrace had made it out alive. He might or might not plan to continue the revolt. That depended on which of the men had not been captured or killed the other night. She wondered if he had the ambition without his brother. He was motivated not by power but, rather, by attracting people's affection. He'd managed to charm the little queen right out of her marriage bed and into his own. Perhaps that had been his way of flaunting himself to his older brother. Ammi had never hated him before, even after the first rebellion—Abishu seemed too ineffectual to fear—but now her middle son loathed him. If the prince ever showed his nose in Ugarit again, he would die a horrible death.

Somehow, the adultery had struck Ammi more forcefully than the treason.

Men.

She sighed, a deeply weary sigh. She had lived too long. There was only so much capacity for sacrifice in the human soul, and her store was running out. The queen mother was tired, tired, tired.

※

But her work was not finished. The former queen's ship had sailed at first light, and only hours later, Ahat-milki was in the king's apartment with her son, his once-again queen, and their eldest son, Ibi-ranu. They were all snappish and glassy-eyed with sleeplessness. The coup had been deflected, but no one knew what would happen next. Influential people had been involved, and some of them had survived. Their families would make every effort to buy them clemency, and the council would henceforth be filled with marginally loyal men who wanted to break their treaty with Hatti. And then there was the unknown quantity of Abdi-sharrumma. Ruling had suddenly become much more difficult, the king's task a walk along a knife's blade.

Ammi had already taken more than one drink since daybreak, his mother noted with disgust. He was usually fairly temperate. This business had apparently troubled him more than he wanted to admit.

"Well, she's gone," the king announced, his arm around Pizidku, "and good riddance, although I would rather have had her head. I don't give a rat's ass for what the Great King says. It's important that Ibi-ranu be back in line for the throne. He's been trained to the job, and he's old enough to take over if anything should happen to me. Uncle Benteshina's dead, so this won't break his heart too badly."

"What do we do now, my father?" Ibi-ranu asked him.

Ammishtamru lifted his cup. "We drink to the disappearance of Taduhepa, the treacherous harlot." He drained his wine with a smack of the lips. "And anyway, she had skinny legs."

Ibi-ranu snickered, but the queen mother snapped, "Don't be so coarse, for god's sake, Ammi. This divorce could touch off an international incident. We don't know how her brother Shaushga-muwa will react."

"Everyone's tense," Pizidku interjected mildly. "Nothing we say this morning should be taken seriously."

"If he values his skin, he'd better toe the line," said the king with an evil grin. "Our esteemed viceroy Ini-tesshub will be right there, blowing Hittite breath down his neck."

Ahat-milki pursed her lips disapprovingly. "Well, he may not. He may take off for Nihriya, if the eunuch's report about Assyrian provocation was accurate. It's nearly New Year's."

"Frankly, I think Shaushga-muwa'll realize his sister got off lightly. Ba'al's beard, Mother; she was not only caught in adultery, but also involved in a plot to overthrow the crown. She should have been beheaded on the spot. I've been brooding over this mess for three days—"

"He has," confirmed Pizidku. "Positively seething."

"And this whole idea of a peaceful divorce is sounding more and more unjust. You divorce a woman because she can't have children, not because she cuckolds you with your brother and plots to kill you. The more I think about it, the more I feel I've been cheated."

"Of what? Your revenge? And she wasn't really *caught* in adultery. Just because she was in the room with Abishu doesn't mean they were lovers."

Don't be such an asinine male, the dowager thought. *This solution was cheap and painless. Just accept it. If the Great King does one thing well, it's clemency.*

"Cheated of my *justice!*" roared the king, red-faced. "You weren't there, Mother dear, and I was. I heard her crying out, 'Abishushu, my love.' Trust me, I don't have to see them in bed together to know that they were more than fellow conspirators. The least little day laborer in the kingdom has the right to vindicate his honor if his wife betrays him. Doesn't the king deserve the same?"

The king pounded the arm of his chair for emphasis and leaned forward over the table. "As Shapshu is my witness, justice has not been done! She'll live a life of ease in her brother's court until Gasshulawiya marries her off to the next poor ignoramus. The more I think about it, the madder it makes me." Ammishtamru filled his goblet from the ewer on the table and gulped down a draft with the ferocity he might have liked to apply to slicing off Taddu's head.

"And frankly," he added, wiping his mustache with the back of his hand, "I'm a little tired of the Great King telling me how to live my private life. This divorce was his idea. He doesn't want to alienate Amurru any worse than he has to. I understand that. But mark my words: every great family in Ugarit who might have taken part in this conspiracy but held back for fear of the consequences will be thinking, 'Look how easy it is to get away with something. Ammishtamru is afraid to assert the full force of the law.' I'm going to come out of this looking like a damned goat." He set down the cup fiercely and crossed his arms. "Don't protect her just because she's Benteshina's daughter. He spoiled her rotten."

Ahat-milki felt her own patience snap. "Is that meant to be joke, Ammi? I never liked her, and I think that was quite obvious to everybody, except you, apparently."

"You're missing my point—"

"No, I think I understand your point quite well, son. You want to execute Taddu because she humiliated you. But think about how Amurru will react. Things are going to be tense enough with a divorce. We don't need a war any more than the Great King does."

"Please, everyone"—Pizidku held out her hands in a gesture of peacemaking—"let's stand by one another instead of saying things we'll regret."

"I want her extradited," Ammishtamru insisted.

"But is it worth risking a war for, my son? Can you not be satisfied? Haven't there been enough deaths?"

"That's it, isn't it?" The king stood abruptly and stalked over to his mother, standing above her, his face inflamed. She could smell the wine on his breath. "It's because now that your precious Heshmi-sharrumma is dead, you've lost your stomach for a fight. You're hoping that Abishu will get away safely."

Ahat-milki snorted. "What does that have to do with a war with Amurru? You're drunk, Ammi. I have nothing more to say to you. I just hope you'll give yourself time to sober up before you take steps you'll regret." She clamped her lips to bite back all the other words she wanted to cast at her son.

Ibi-ranu spoke up. "Don't talk to my father like that, Grandma."

His mother looked around at him, shocked, and tried to say something, but the old queen interrupted, her voice grave. "You'd better hope that *someone* talks truth and good sense to your king, boy. And you'd better hope there's someone there to do the same for you when you're on the throne, because I won't be around forever. Kings are anointed by the gods, but until they die, they're just men, and they can make mistakes. That's why they have advisers; that's why there's a council."

The crown prince subsided, chastened, but his father slammed his fist down on the table.

"Merely anointed though I am, here's what I want to see happen: Ini-tesshub gives us the clearance to extradite her, and we bring her home and take off her pretty but disloyal little head. The message to all conspirators is clear: you'd better watch your step, or you're next, because nobody is sacred. Shapshu sees all." Ammishtamru threw himself back into his chair.

There was a moment of silence as the family digested this scenario. Pizidku hung her head, her eyes fixed on her hands, which were twisted together in her lap. Ahat-milki, despite her anger, had to admit that her son's plan was useful. There were those soon-to-be-pardoned conspirators to think about. The *maryannuma* were too powerful to alienate with a direct attack, but it certainly couldn't hurt to keep them in line with a salutary example of strength. Unlike a man, she could back off from her position if the good of the kingdom required it.

She could feel Ibi-ranu's eyes on her.

"Well," she began, "I can see the value of that if the viceroy will agree. But will he? How will Shaushga-muwa react? What if he refuses? What if her brother lets Taddu 'escape'? It might occur to him that that would be a good way to save her without looking disobedient. We just don't know him very well. He's so new on the throne.

"What do *you* think, my dear?" she urged Pizidku. *The woman is quite sensible, really. It will be interesting to see which will win—her natural kindness or her political good sense. She'll be the regent before too many years. It's prudent to sound her out.*

The king's wife spoke thoughtfully, her gentle face grave. "What my mother says is true. The young king is an unknown quantity. But we know well how his mother, the Great Lady, would react. She would do the honorable thing as a vassal. She would obey her brother's viceroy, no matter how much it broke her heart."

"Well said, my dear." Ahat-milki smiled. The king sank back into his chair next to Pizidku and stroked her neck proudly.

"But, Mother, do we know if the young king will listen to the Great Lady?" interjected Ibi-ranu.

Aha. Do we know if Ibi-ranu will listen to his *mother when he is king?* The dear youth looked so earnest, with his little beard. Ammi had been wise to bring him into such discussions and let him learn of the complexities that surrounded every situation.

"What if he does as Grandma suggests and tries to sneak her out then claims she escaped? Then Papa looks foolish, and that's dangerous, as he said the other morning."

"What if we send a message to Taddu," the dowager

mused, "pretending to be her lover, and say, 'Come back without fear; I'm going to save you at the last minute'? She won't be tempted to flee."

The king looked at his mother with renewed respect and raised his cup to her. "You're quite the old plotter, aren't you, Mother mine? Would she believe it, do you think?"

"People believe what they want to." Ahat-milki shrugged. "I think I could imitate your little brother's style sufficiently well. Now, the handwriting... that won't be so easy. I may have a letter of his somewhere. It will have to be slipped into the palace by some means. Shaushga-muwa would never let her receive a letter like this if he knew about it. Have we any spies in Amurru? We need to put it where only she will be able to read it."

Ammi's face grew momentarily dark. No doubt, he was picturing Taddu swooning over his brother's false letter, clutched to her heart. "I think we can find somebody to slip into Shaushga-muwa's palace with a letter easily enough," he said, looking up. "Let's talk to Ini-tesshub before he leaves. This all falls apart if he is unwilling to support us."

"Let me speak with Ini-tesshub, then, son. We are old collaborators. Call Takhulinu—and Urtenu as well; he's been in charge of gathering intelligence on all of this. We'll need to present at least the basic change of plan to the council, and we'd better do it before the ex-conspirators are back in their seats. Did Takhulinu have any family in on the plot?"

The king shook his head.

"No? Then maybe he can talk it up to the council before we meet."

Ibi-ranu jumped up and went to the door. Ahat-milki

could hear him ordering the soldier on duty to fetch the Lords Takhulinu and Urtenu.

"Is that all, my son?" she asked in a tone that implied that it was. "I have a letter to write."

"Wait, Mother. I think there's another letter we need to manufacture, one that will finally put an end to all this business."

Ahat-milki froze, fearing that he was going to voice the same idea that had passed through her own mind. In her weakness, she had rejected it. Perhaps it was the gods' will after all.

"What if we send the same sort of faked message to Abishu in my esteemed wife's name? We could beg him to come and rescue her at such and such a time and place—"

"That would draw my uncle out," agreed Ibi-ranu enthusiastically.

"But instead of Taddu, he would find a detachment of soldiers waiting for him. What do you think?"

I think I would rather lie in my tomb than betray my baby boy to his death, the queen thought in anguish. But this was what it meant to be given to the kingdom. The security of the throne came before everything else. Everything. The curse she'd been made to lay on her sons was inexorably at work.

She schooled her face to blankness and said with only the slightest tremor, "Very well. It's worth a try."

Ibi-ranu's eager grin suddenly faded, and he said uncertainly, "But we don't know where he is, do we, to send the message to him?"

A disappointed silence sat upon them.

"Mother dear," said the king at last, turning to Ahat-milki. "Any chance that your network of eyes and ears can winkle him out?"

"I... I may be able to take care of that." *Gods help me, what have I offered?*

"Well, then, Mother, I leave the two letters to you."

She rose and bowed, unable to speak and, turning with a flurry of skirts, departed before she lost her composure utterly.

CHAPTER 17

T HAT EVENING, THE DOWAGER QUEEN called discreetly to her palace the person most likely to be able to find Abdi-sharrumma. She had invited young Ibi-ranu to be present as well. This was the dirty reality of royal rule that he needed to know about. Ammishtamru had agreed, and the youth sat at her side, outwardly contained, as always. This air of serenity was his heritage from his mother, along with his light-brown hair. Only his fingertips, twitching back and forth upon his thigh, betrayed his tension.

"Grandmother, I want to apologize about this morning," he said, his eyes lowered in shame. "You were absolutely right about a king needing to be able to hear the truth from his advisors."

"Yes, my dear. Nobody gets everything right all the time. Not even me."

She smiled thinly up at him, but there wasn't much mirth in her eyes. These days were hard, very hard. She felt as if she were nearing the limits of her strength. Perhaps that was one reason she needed a strong, young grandson at her side when she did what she had to do.

"I want to admit something to you, Grandma. I... I, too, feel we should leave our Hittite vassalage and go over to Assyria."

She shot him a shrewd sidelong glance. He kept his eyes on his lap.

"Your father will never agree," she replied flatly.

"I realize that, and I understand why. Is it disloyal, do you think, to disagree with him on something so crucial to our foreign policy? I know I'm young and don't know everything, but it just seems obvious."

"My dear boy, the time will eventually come when it is you on the throne of Ugarit, and then you must do what *you* think is best, not what your father might have done. Listen to your mother and your advisers, but you will need to make your own decisions. You don't have to be ashamed of holding opinions of your own." She laid her hand affectionately upon his forearm. "Your father is very proud of you. We all are."

The young man smiled gratefully down at her, but she gripped his arm harder and fixed him with her serious painted eyes. "I just pray the gods that you and your brother Niqmaddu will be true friends, Ibi-ranu. Be loyal to one another. Remember the horrors my sons have let loose on one another, and swear that won't happen again, for the love of your people."

"Yes, Grandma. I swear by all the gods."

There was a long silence. Ahat-milki finally demanded softly in her deep, throaty voice, "Ibi-ranu, my son, what would you have done if... all this had not happened? What if Utri-sharrumma had come to the throne? You're nearly twenty years older than he. What would you have done if he'd become king, and you were left standing off to the side?"

Another silence. The boy bit his lip and studied the floor in front of him, as if he were struggling between answering in a way that would please his grandmother and saying what he really thought.

"I... I think I would have fought him for it, Grandma. It would have been so manifestly unfair."

"Then learn from that, my son. Try always to do what's honorable and fair, because nothing drives people to desperate acts faster than unfairness. But realize that not even the gods can succeed all the time." The weight of her own deceits lay upon her, crushing her.

Ahat-milki's housekeeper announced the arrival of her visitor.

He waddled into her presence with an inscrutable smirk and bowed low. She controlled her disgust with difficulty.

"My lady has summoned me?"

"Where is the prince, Agipsharri?"

"Which, my lady? Prince Utri-sharrumma? No doubt he is on his way back to Amurru with his mother, eh." The old eunuch's smile widened into a lipless line that seemed to split his fat face in two.

"No," said the queen dryly. "The king's brother. The man you so gallantly declined to assassinate time and again. I assume a person of your indispensability would know where he has gone to ground."

"It's possible that I might be able to locate people who might know people who know, my lady, and for a very reasonable sum, I can probably arrange to have him found." Agipsharri smirked, his hands joined over his belly.

Suddenly, Ahat-milki had had enough of this obscene creature and his perpetual haggling. She snapped, "Let me remind you, slave, that as a party to this conspiracy, you are guilty of treason. I would think you might be satisfied with the reward of having your complicity overlooked in exchange for serving as our agent. Try to control your greed, will you?" Aware of her grandson's eyes upon her, she fought down her anger and added in a carnivorous purr, "Or do you prefer that the king's soldiers torture out of you the information you seem so reluctant to give up?"

The old eunuch spread his hands deprecatingly. "My lady can have me tortured if she likes, but I can only give her the next step in the chain of contacts, eh. I myself don't know the prince's whereabouts, remember. By the time the king's men have found and tortured everyone in the chain, the prince will be long gone."

So he had her. She needed his knowledge. The queen mother said levelly, as if threats had not been exchanged, "I have a written message for him. I want it delivered as soon as possible. You will be rewarded when the message is successfully transmitted."

"But my dear lady, in order to locate him and have the letter carried and delivered into his hand, I will have to hire several professionals, eh. I certainly can't do it myself, as old and slow as I am. And so it may be necessary to be paid a little something up front, since I have no personal funds—as glad as I would be to expend them in the interests of the kingdom."

A pox on you, you greedy capon, she thought furiously,

but the fifty-years-long habit of diplomacy kept her outer expression bland.

"Very well." Ahat-milki withdrew from a coffer on her writing table a small leather bag, clinking with silver. "Take this for now. It should be sufficient. You'll be paid more when the mission is carried out."

"I promise, my lady, that Prince Abdi-sharrumma will have the letter by tomorrow."

The queen mother flinched. He had spoken Abishu's name. The reality of what she was doing could no longer be evaded—she was betraying her son to his death.

"Here is the letter." She passed it to him with her fingertips, loath to touch his long, puffy hand with its bitten nails. She knew the contents by heart: *My love, don't let them take me back to Ugarit. When the ship is unloaded at Maradu, the guard will be at its smallest. Strike then, and you can save me. Your dove who loves you.* "Be sure that he reads it, eunuch. Let nothing come between you and the delivery of this letter. And bring me back his reply."

Agipsharri inclined, pressing the clay envelope to his breast. "I live to serve, my lady."

He bowed his way from the room, and Ahat-milki was left staring at the door, her face expressionless but her heart in tatters.

CHAPTER 18

T HUS IT WAS THAT FIVE years after he had left, Naheshi arrived back in Amurru, the place that, as much as any other, he considered home. It was a small country, its capital a small city, the king's house a small palace after the splendor of Ugarit. The southern coastal plain lay under a pall of drizzle, and the rain-streaked walls of the little citadel were dismal. The new king and his mother received the young queen as soon as she'd disembarked from her ship and made her way under guard to the royal residence, where Naheshi prepared her old apartments for occupation. He had just set out flowers and fluffed the pillows when approaching footsteps made him look up. Taddu, with her brother Shaushga-muwa and the Great Lady, had entered the room. Naheshi bowed and stepped respectfully against the wall.

"Here are your rooms back, sister," said the young king. His face was haggard. No matter how much he might rejoice to see his sister again, the present circumstances were humiliating, perhaps even dangerous. Naheshi recalled that

Shaushga-muwa had barely even sprouted his first beard the last time he'd seen him.

The Great Lady squeezed her daughter's hands, her face sorrowful. "Please try to comport yourself with dignity, my dear. Don't feel like your life is over. You're young and still able to bear children. Perhaps it will be possible to marry you to someone else. In the meantime, Utrishu will be in your old nursery."

The king turned and left with no more than a melancholy glance at his sister. The queen mother embraced her tearful daughter and headed to the door, but then she saw Naheshi. Her troubled eyes lit up, and she beckoned him outside into the corridor. She was no great beauty, with her equine face and mousy graying hair, but goodness and intelligence radiated from her countenance. Naheshi longed to fall at her feet and cling to her knees.

"Nahish-shulmanu, my dear old secretary. I never expected to see you again under such sad circumstances."

"No one is sadder about this than I, my lady."

"It gives me a certain contentment at least to think that you were with Taddu through all this. I know how kindly and supportive you are. You've always loved her." She touched his arm gratefully then noticed his bandaged fingers. "What happened?" She looked up at him, and her gaze fell upon the crusty slits in his earlobes. Her eyes widened. "And your ears? My poor boy! Whatever can have happened?"

"A mishap, my lady. Thank you for asking."

Her regard lingered in concern upon his face, but he kept his expression bland. At last, she moved past the pleasantries. "Tell me, Nahish-shulmanu"—her voice dropped—"are the charges against my daughter true? Surely, they are exaggerated a little?"

"My lady, I am grieved to tell you they're true. But who knows what was in her heart? My lady the queen is high-spirited. I think the discipline of her routine was hard on her. I feel sure she meant no harm."

To his surprise, Naheshi found that he believed what he was saying. He wanted there to be some innocuous explanation: she hadn't understood—they had tricked her, perhaps, or promised her things. He wanted her to be innocent. Indeed, he wanted badly to be innocent again himself.

The Great Lady squeezed his arm, her smile tender. "You've never been able to think ill of anyone, have you? I very much fear that Taddu is a headstrong girl who can't bear to be idle. She was always up to something as a child... well, you remember how she was. No amount of reminding her of her duty could convince her. And I'm afraid that her father, may he rejoice among the Rapi'uma, encouraged her in that. She was not well prepared for being an adult and a queen, alas, and I bear part of the responsibility. I do hope this disgrace won't cast her down too badly. She's not used to being thwarted."

"No, my lady."

"Stay by her. Perhaps she'll feel she can confide in you. She seems little inclined to take me into her confidence. Maybe that will change. I hope so." She gazed sorrowfully into space and sighed. "So very foolish. What a waste. And I feel bad for Shaushga-muwa, too. He has recently been betrothed to one of my younger half sisters. This divorce has cast a pall of gloom over what should be a happy time. We had just started to come out of mourning."

She turned back to Naheshi, her gaze moving up and down to take him in. "You seem subdued, Nahish-shulmanu. Are you well? This has been hard on you, too, hasn't it? You were always sensitive. But loyal, my dear boy, and how rare that is. You know, I remember very well when that diplomat from the Assyrian court gave you to me. He pointed out that *shulmanu* was the name of a god, of course, but that it also could mean 'gifts of well-wishing.' I thought that was so sweet. That's the way I have always thought of you—as a gift to my family. Well, welcome home." She reached up and patted his cheek.

He wanted to cling to her hand and beg her absolution, but he just smiled wanly as she continued.

"I know you will try to help Taddu recover her good cheer. Hopefully, we can find her another royal husband. She's still young. And indeed, so are you. How old *are* you now, Nahish-shulmanu?"

"Thirty-eight, my lady."

"I can hardly believe it! You haven't changed at all since you first arrived twenty years ago. I wish I could say the same for myself."

Naheshi appreciated the discretion of his former mistress. He'd changed by several times his earlier body weight, in fact. He had to admit, however, that his former mistress did look older even since he'd last seen her, five years before. Her long Hittite face was worn and colorless. But then, a lot had happened in the last few months. Her husband's sickness and death and her daughter's ignominious divorce must have aged the whole family.

The Great Lady wasn't really much older than Naheshi, as incredible as that seemed to him. He thought of her as a kind of mother. How he wished that he could crawl into her lap right then and feel her arms around him, making everything right.

"My lady is always perfect in beauty to my eyes."

She laughed wearily. "We need more like you, my dear boy. I leave my daughter in your hands." The queen gathered her skirts and turned away.

Naheshi watched her go with a sense of his world falling apart. *If you only knew what grief I have brought upon you and your house, my dearest lady. You who were so kind to me. I am a poisoned gift. Oh, what have I done?*

He had sought to please the king. Wasn't that what his pangs of confused conscience had been about? Had he not tried to carry out his primary loyalty, which was to the king? Perhaps Ammishtamru was satisfied… if he'd really wanted to know his wife was betraying him. But also, Naheshi had thought to visit—*say it*—revenge on Taddu for her cruelty. In fact, he had to admit he'd tried to make Taddu pay for all the humiliations he had ever suffered. But was this grief and shame what he wanted? Little Utri-sharrumma had been deprived of the throne. How his heart ached for this child, whose life was forever changed because of a choice he was too young to understand. Princess Batashiya had been torn from her mother, and the Great Lady and her son had been plunged into dishonor and sorrow. Ugarit and Amurru were perhaps on the brink of war and the Great King's alliance against the Assyrians' way to the sea jeopardized. Naheshi cared little enough about politics, but any policy that slapped his countrymen in their faces seemed attractive, and he might have destabilized it.

He gnawed his lip in misery. So much for his dreams of being valuable. He had dragged many lives down to ruin. He was an idiot, playing not only at being chamberlain but at being a human.

※

With the eagerness of a child begging to hear a favorite story, Taddu demanded, "Tell me again, Naheshi. Did Abishushu get away?"

"As far as I know, my lady." Naheshi felt weary and incapable of sentiment. He painted a dull smile on his face.

"You never saw his body, did you?" Anxiety wrinkled the queen's brows adorably.

"No, my lady."

Naheshi had hoped to see the mangled corpse and add his own little desecration to it, but in all the carnage, that had not come to pass. How often had he replayed in his mind's eye the prince's white grin and bright eyes as he leaned over to kiss Taddu, and her hungry, gaping lips locking onto his? How often had he envisioned other parts of them locking together in the sacred action of which his own brief moment of ecstasy had only been a cruel parody? That was the tinder that had finally ignited him, illumining the path of duty. But the fire had burned itself out thoroughly, and he felt cold and directionless once more.

"If he got away, then all is not lost. They'll remount the rebellion, and he'll come to get me!"

"Yes, my lady."

"Who do you think betrayed us, Naheshi?"

Naheshi felt his blood run icy.

"I'll bet it was that monstrous old Agipsharri. He's hated me since the beginning. He was nothing but a spy for Pizidku all along, the hateful old bucket of lard." Animosity glittered in her stare.

Naheshi swallowed with difficulty. "No doubt, my lady."

"You're certainly very pale and hangdog these days, Naheshi. My mother is counting on you to brace me up, and look at you. Are you sick?"

"No, my lady." He forced a smile. "I... I just feel sorry to see you shamed like this."

"Who's shamed?" she demanded, her eyes blazing with indignation. "Shame on those who betrayed us! Shame on those who slaughtered those patriotic nobles! Shame on those who are so insecure in their own manhood that they can't but suspect their wives in the presence of a younger man!"

But were you not guilty? he thought wryly. *Was it all the king's suspicion?* Aloud, he simply said, "My lady is right, as always."

Yet at other times, Taddu was as desolate as Naheshi, sitting sunk in gloom by the window she'd looked out as a girl, her tapestry shuttles idle in her lap. He brought her flowers; he directed the maids in songs and games for the queen's amusement; he found her a caged songbird. He sat at her side on the floor while she stared and sighed and stared again as if she expected Abdi-sharrumma to come riding up to her window. Naheshi forced himself to smile when he felt that his mouth wanted to make one of those inverted sickles that the moon made when rain was coming.

The Great Lady came from time to time to sit with her daughter and try to discuss a possible future for her, but Taddu was little inclined to talk matrimony with the petty kings of neighboring kingdoms. "I've told you, Mama. I will not remarry unless Abdi-sharrumma comes back."

"My sweet, you can't be so intransigent," said her mother with the weary air of one who had said the same thing over and over. "You're damaged goods in the eyes of men. If we can arrange a marriage at all, it will be with someone who feels so honored to ally with Amurru and Hatti that they won't ask too many questions. You must realize this prince is outlawed. If his brother ever catches him, he will put him to death. There can be no future with him. Surely, you see that."

Taddu bridled, chin lifted in defiance. "My father's ancestors were outlaws, too, but they were smart and strong enough that the great powers had to recognize them as real kings. The other kings will see that Abdi-sharrumma should be on the throne somewhere. Let your brother make him ruler of someplace in the interior. I don't even care where, as long as I'm at his side."

Gasshulawiya shook her head, her eyes dark with sorrow. "Times have changed, my daughter. Your father's ancestors could play Hatti and Mizri off against one another, but today, those kingdoms are at peace. And even then, they could only weld a band of brigands into a kingdom through the legitimation given them by a great kingdom, remember. A small nation like Amurru must have a protector, and for that protection, it must pay in obedience. Tudhaliya was as much dishonored by your adultery as Ammishtamru was. He was the one who arranged your marriage, to cement the friendship between our kingdoms. He's not a vengeful man, but I don't think he'll be very indulgent toward you and your wayward prince."

"Well, he betrothed me to the wrong brother." Taddu was adamant. "Ammi was the dullest old stone I've ever met. It made me feel a hundred years old just to be around him. He's old enough to be my father."

Her mother exchanged exasperated glances with Naheshi then turned patiently to her daughter. "My dearest, princesses don't always have the luxury of marrying handsome young stallions. Our duty is to make alliances between countries, and in doing that duty, we also find our fulfillment as women. Your father was considerably older than I was, yet we discovered happiness together. Ammishtamru is a decent man and a powerful king; his country is rich and important. And he's rather nice-looking and not even especially old."

"Then why don't *you* marry him?" her daughter said.

The Great Lady stood up with a sigh. Her voice was calm, as always, but a muscle ticked in her cheek. "If you won't listen to reason, Taddu, my dear, you have a very lonely life ahead of you. Your brother and I are doing our best to help you regain your status, but you refuse to cooperate. You're pinning your hopes on dreams, my daughter." She swept to the door. "Nahish-shulmanu, can you accompany me for a moment?"

Naheshi got awkwardly to his feet from his place on the floor and followed the queen mother out into the hall.

"Can you please try to talk to her?" she whispered,

gripping his arm. "You see how much impact anything I say has. Maybe she will listen to you."

"I doubt it, my lady. She very emphatically doesn't want *me* to tell her what to do."

The Great Lady looked at him hard then said in a gentle voice, "Are you sure you're all right, dear boy? You look very pale."

"As healthy as a horse, my lady." He forced a smile.

"Talk to her." There was pleading in her eyes, Great King's sister though she was.

"I will, my lady."

She returned his smile and moved away.

When Naheshi turned back, Taddu was standing in the door, her fist on her hip. "Well, what did she want, Naheshi? Did she tell you to spy on me?"

Naheshi froze; his heart seemed to stop. "Why would you ask that, my lady?"

"She probably told you to talk me into marrying some grim old vassal of her brother, didn't she? She knows I don't listen to her. I never have. My father knew how to get me to do things. He respected me." She fell silent. Then in a fainter voice, she murmured, "Nothing is the same around here now. It doesn't even feel like home anymore."

"We all miss your royal father, my lady." *Don't ask if I have ever lost anyone,* Naheshi thought, remembering the sublime folly to which his commiseration had led him once before.

A loud knock at the door preempted the queen's next words. The panel slammed open, and the young king strode in, jaw set and eyes fixed. His mother hurried inside after him and closed the door behind her, leaning against it. The Great Lady's face was blanched and twisted.

The young queen started. "My brother! You frightened me. What brings you here in such a whirlwind? Mother, is something wrong? Why are you back so quickly?"

Shaushga-muwa seemed to advance on his sister but stalked past her and announced to the air, his voice shaking, "I just this moment received an ambassador from Ugarit. Your husband has decided he wants you extradited. I told him no. So he is sending ships and soldiers." He turned and stared, wild-eyed, at Taddu. "He is, in short, invading my kingdom."

"Invading?" Taddu's eyes grew round. She clutched at the king's arm. "But you won't let him have me, will you? This is outrageous! I don't want to go back."

"I'll fight for you, Taddu, but I really don't think we can win against Ugarit. You've brought a war down upon us, sister." He shook her hand off. "Instead of a marriage, my first royal act is going to be a damned war, which we'll probably lose."

"But you can't send me back, Shushi. What will he do to me?" Taddu's voice rose in desperation. "Ammi can have a dreadful temper. You should have seen him when he sent me away. He called me terrible, humiliating names. He was yelling so loudly it nearly blew back my hair, and he frightened little Utrishu. They were all in league against me to take Utrishushu's throne from him. You—"

"He's talking about 'fitting punishment,' sister." Shaushga-muwa exchanged afflicted glances with his mother. "I don't know precisely what he has in mind, but I can certainly guess. I have to say, I was surprised he settled for a divorce and exile if he believed the charges against you. You… you have to know what the punishment for treason and adultery is. I've told you, my sister, I will do what I can to prevent this extradition. I may have to appeal to the viceroy. I know the Great King doesn't want his vassals at war with one another. But the simple fact is, Ammishtamru is stronger than I am—more ships, more men, more gold. If it comes to a fight, don't expect miracles, Taddu."

"My daughter, you've put us in a terrible position." The Great Lady stepped forward and addressed her youngest child, her long face somber. She took the girl's hands in hers. "Amurrite lives will be lost. There will be reparations to pay, the city or the fleet may be damaged… and we will still have to give you up."

Taddu's voice was shrill. "A pox on Ammi! Isn't it enough to ruin my life? Why must he be so vengeful? He seemed eager enough to be rid of me then. He said he never wanted to set eyes on me again, and now he's changed his mind. Well, I never want to see him again, either. It had to be the Old Dragon that has put him up to this."

The Great Lady cast an interrogatory glance at Naheshi, who whispered, "The queen mother."

"My dear, I fear you can't in all honesty blame Ammishtamru or his mother for this debacle. He's well within his rights. Oh, Taddu, my sweet, why? Why did you do this? It was so foolish. So much harm will come of it all." Gasshulawiya buried her face in her hands, and Naheshi felt his heart crack and shatter like a glass vase, the sharp pieces imbedding themselves in his chest.

The king said, "He wants us to put you under

house arrest someplace away from the palace until the extradition—"

"What? So I can't even see my own family? How utterly cruel!"

"He feels it's not sufficiently punitive to house you under the roof of your kin," Shaushga-muwa explained with a huff of fury. He began to pace back and forth, filling the small room with the musk of his frustration. "How I wish I could teach this arrogant dog shit not to meddle in the affairs of my kingdom and my family! But alas, I'm very much afraid that we're in no position to do that." The king stopped pacing and turned to stare his sister in the eye, his dark-browed gaze ravaged but determined. "At least I will fight like a man to defend you, sister. We'll go down trying to save you. I only wish I honestly believed that you were worth it."

"Shushi!" Taddu cried. "What an awful thing to say!"

Her mother took her in her arms, crushing her to her breast, her stricken face upon her daughter's head. "He doesn't mean it that way. But oh, my darling, do you understand even yet what a terrible thing you have brought upon us? A war, Taddu, a war. Was your love affair worth such a price? And if we lose—"

"And barring a miracle" interjected Shaushga-muwa bitterly, "we *will* lose."

"What will become of you, my dearest?"

At last, the little queen had no answer. She clung to her mother with big, frightened eyes. Naheshi, looking on, felt as if every bit of himself were in danger of shattering like his heart, tinkling to the floor, blowing away like sand in the wind, and simply ceasing to be. He had brought this on those he loved, including his dear Great Lady, who had been so kind—a real mother—to him. Now she was broken with grief and shame. He was a poisoned gift indeed.

※

The city was preparing for war: the chain was up across the mouth of the long, pronged harbor, and inhabitants of the Lower City had crowded themselves within the citadel, bringing as much food as they could carry. Watchmen patrolled the palace walls day and night, their eyes keen for a fire signal from up the coast that would announce the approach of a hostile fleet from Ugarit.

Naheshi stared out into the gray garden, which was dissolved into a dreamlike landscape by the fine drizzle that hung in the air, its paths and beds no more substantial than the gray sky. Again, he felt as if the world had drawn away from him like the retreating tide, leaving him completely alone to float in a colorless mist of half truth, half goodness, half reality. Nothing made sense anymore. The city was going to war, a war he had caused. Yet there went a gardener, ambling across the courtyard, poking about with his spade, doing his concrete, everyday task. It seemed hard to reconcile. How could things go on as usual for anyone when they might all be dead in days? *Odd, that gardener.*

Queen Taduhepa was subdued at first, but before long, she began to look upon the idea of girding for war as exciting, and her spirits rose.

"I think Shushi is too pessimistic, Naheshi," she said, pacing the room. "Look at this town. It's set high on its mound, the walls are as thick as anything, and there are all these people inside, ready to fight. I bet we can hold off Ammi's stupid army easily. He isn't taking into account what fighters we are. My father used to tell me about his great-grandfather Aziru and *his* father Abdi-ashirta. They were mighty brigands in the wilderness, and no one could catch them. They would raid cities and run away, laughing at the great kings, even Mizri. No one could ever pin them down. Kings would send out armies to put an end to them, but the Amurrites would manage to rout the armies entirely."

She faced Naheshi, her eyes glowing. "My father himself stood up to the Great King when he was young. They took him off to Hattusha, and he only left after he had made his point. We're not so easy to defeat. If some soldier tried to lay a hand on me, I'd fight, and you would, too, wouldn't you, Naheshi?"

Most people interpreted her father's sojourn in Hattusha as an arrest for disloyalty. He had been freed after fourteen years—only when he swore he would be a good vassal.

"Yes, my lady."

"You could slap them like you did Agipsharri that time!" She laughed. "But no, look how you fought to save my seals. You see? You're something of a warrior, too. Everybody knows what warriors the Assyrians are."

"Yes, my lady."

"Try not to look so gloomy, Naheshi. We need to keep up our spirits here." She turned to the window. Outside, against the flat gray sky, two seabirds were wheeling. Suddenly she glanced down at the floor and stooped to pick something up. "What's this?" Taddu turned and held out a small clay envelope.

He stared at it, slack-jawed. A letter? Where had that

come from? He would have sworn it was not there in the morning, when he had laid out the queen's clothing for the day. "I... I have no idea, my lady. Could your lady mother have dropped it when she was here last?"

"We would have heard it if it had fallen on the floor. Someone must have slipped it through the window somehow." She looked up at Naheshi, eyes aglow like bright gems of amber. "Oh, Naheshi! Do you suppose...?"

He did not know what to suppose. *Does she think Abishu sneaked into a hostile city and palace to deliver a billet-doux?* He babbled a little, trying to think of something to say. The queen demanded his penknife and cracked open the clay cover. He watched her eyes devour the characters, her lips moving silently. Then she beamed up at him, and it was as if Shapshu's shining rays had melted back the clouds. The little room was gilded with her joy.

"It *is* him, Naheshi! He's alive! Oh, blessed gods! He's going to save me! I knew it."

Naheshi repressed a rancid pang of jealousy, stunned that the prince had managed such a trick. Someone in the palace had to be in his pay. Suddenly, the image of the mysterious gardener came to mind. Who planted things in the rain? There was something odd about that; Naheshi had felt it immediately. Perhaps Abdi-sharrumma had hired the man to deliver the letter. It was almost unbelievable, such an infiltration, but perhaps every prince had his network of spies. Naheshi, if anyone, would understand that.

He managed to shape his lips into a smile. "What wonderful news, my lady."

"Read it aloud to me, Naheshi. It hardly seems real

until I've heard it aloud." The queen thrust the tablet at him. She hugged herself blissfully while he read:

"My beloved, I am well. Do not fear to return to the city. There will be a rescue en route at the port. All will be well. Trust me, the one who loves you."

Naheshi stared unseeingly at the tablet, struggling with the bitterness that welled up inside him. His heart was so full of bile he could have wrung it out into a bucket. There was silence in the room.

Then the queen said pensively, "Naheshi, could you take a message back to Ugarit for me?"

"I... I... isn't the port blockaded, my lady?"

She turned to face him, her eyes bright. "Go by land. They can't have put up a fence around the whole country."

"By land?" He stared at her in disbelief. "Ride a horse? I don't know how." The idea of him clinging to the back of a galloping horse was so ludicrous that he wondered if she were making fun of him.

"Then take a ship." She shrugged. "Shushi will let you through if I tell him to. It's a diplomatic mission."

"Where does my lady want me to go in Ugarit?"

"Well, I don't actually know. Where do you think Abishu would be?"

"I have no idea, my lady. Isn't this extremely dangerous? What if someone follows me? Everyone at the palace there knows I belong to you..." He prayed that she would not send him back on a ship.

"But you won't go to the palace, Naheshi. You'll find one of the conspirators and ask him discreetly where Abishu is." The young queen was twinkling with excitement, her cheeks flushed.

"What will your mother and your royal brother say? Won't they wonder—"

She cut him off, her voice rising, her eyes flashing with quick anger. "Enough objections, Naheshi. Haven't we discussed this sort of thing? You are my slave. Do what I tell you." The queen smiled suddenly, dangerously beguiling, and laid her hand on his arm. "You're smart. Think of how to get it done. Just go do it, by the Gracious Gods."

CHAPTER 19

S HAUSHGA-MUWA HAD DECIDED, AT HIS mother's urging, to send an ambassador to Ugarit to attempt one last peaceful settlement before the two countries went to war. He was counting heavily on the Great King's support, which the viceroy had almost promised him he would receive. It was unimaginable that Tudhaliya would permit a war between two of his vassals when he was on the brink of open hostilities with Assyria.

In order to justify his participation in the mission, Naheshi had crafted a message to King Ammishtamru that might sound plausible in the mouth of the latter's former wife. It was a delicate job, to show her pleading for mercy without outright confessing the crimes of which she was accused. There could be no confession, because that would harden the king in his demand for her head, whereas Shaushga-muwa was going to argue for the original sentence of divorce and exile.

Of course, Naheshi's real message was not on that tablet, nor was it addressed to the king.

"Don't make me sound so abject," Taddu complained

after he'd read the contents to her. "It sounds like I'm in the wrong. What's this about—'I realize my youth and inexperience have led me into imprudent acts'? I would never say that."

"My queen, the Great Lady and your brother the king will certainly read this over before I deliver it. It has to sound convincingly repentant, or my lady's former husband will not receive it."

"Well, do whatever you think will work. It's all a lie anyway. You're good at this sort of thing."

Ah, yes, Naheshi thought grimly. *I* am *good at lying.* Lying had become a veritable second nature to him lately. There he was, deceiving his beloved Great Lady in order to serve the mistress he had betrayed. His loyalties were hopelessly confused again. If he was still in the service of the queen mother of Ugarit, he shouldn't be arranging a tryst with the rebel prince. It was all too much. He wanted someone else to make decisions for him and take away this awful burden of confusion.

He wondered where Anani was and if he had, in fact, made it to Ili-milku's household. He found himself mightily reluctant to believe the slave had been spying on him, but that was because he wanted to think his servant loved him. He wanted to think *someone* loved him—undeserving though he was—even an illiterate little slave. He'd wanted to believe his Taddu had loved him, but it turned out to be an illusion. That was where everything had gone wrong. And yet he hadn't learned his lesson at all. He wanted the Great Lady to love him, but he wanted Taddu to think well of him too. He wanted Ammishtamru and the queen mother to believe he was a valuable servant, yet he couldn't make up his mind to earn that admiration at the price of Taddu's contempt. He just wanted someone to love him, without his having to make so many decisions. It was almost a physical need, like hunger.

He looked down at his mistress, trying to clear the anxiety from his brows, but his face felt permanently crumpled. Perhaps this was how the wrinkled countenances of the old began— here a worry, there a sorrow, until life had written the history of their failures upon their aged cheeks.

"Do I have my lady's permission to submit the letter, then?"

"Do it, Naheshi," she said. "Just get to Ugarit and find Abishu for me, whatever lies you have to tell my husband."

The next morning, Naheshi was among the people gathered at the quay to embark on the king's ship, which lay rocking at anchor, its royal pennants drooping in the fine rain that dampened and chilled everything. The drizzle showed no sign of holding off for a diplomatic mission between Amurru and Ugarit.

Naheshi, wrapped in his cloak in an unsuccessful attempt to stay dry, had scurried down to the harbor just in time to see his fellows moving up the slippery gangplank. Taddu had engaged him until the final minute with the details of her message, and as a result, he'd been the last one of the group to show up. The chariot horses had already been picketed on the deck by strong ropes held in four directions, and the rowers were all in place at their oars, ready to maneuver the ship out of the harbor.

To his horror, Naheshi found that the ambassador of King Shaushga-muwa was a certain Lord Bayaya, whom the chamberlain remembered only too well from his days as a scribe. The man had never taken him seriously as a professional, always seeing in him a pretty-boy eunuch who was decorative at best. And then Naheshi had made the mistake of correcting the man's Akkadian. Bayaya had made it abundantly clear from then on that he thought Naheshi was a dog turd—an opinion he had not changed.

The diplomat wasted no time before jerking Naheshi aside and telling him bluntly, down the length of his aristocratic nose, "Look you, Nahish-shulmanu, this is a serious life-or-death mission. If you can't be on time, I'm not going to bother with you. Do you hear? We don't need your separate message to the king. What really matters is that the viceroy supports us. So get it through your head: either you're on time from now on, or I leave you. Is that clear?"

"Yes, my lord," Naheshi murmured contritely. *It wasn't my fault* were words a slave might never utter. And it *was* his fault, all of it: the war, the 'fitting punishment'—he knew what that meant even if the young queen didn't—and the broken hearts. They were all his fault.

He followed Bayaya up the gangplank, and the sailors began to haul up the stone anchors. At the mouth of the basin, the chain was lifted, and the rowers pulled in their oars. The square linen sail dropped jerkily on its brails, filling with wind, and the little ship set out upon the great black sea to try to stop a war.

⁂

It was evening and already dark when the vessel arrived at Mahadu harbor. There was a tense moment while Bayaya dickered with Ammishtamru's soldiers; the ship was, after all, flying enemy colors. The viceroy's safe-conduct seemed to sway them, and the small party of Amurrites disembarked in a driving rain. Naheshi reeled immediately to the edge of the quay and began to spew the remains of his breakfast into the harbor.

When the chariot was reassembled and the sore-tried horses hitched up to it, Lord Bayaya called out impatiently to Naheshi, "You, eunuch. Get in the chariot now if you want a ride to the palace. I told you, I'm not waiting for you. The guards say we have to be out of here tonight."

"Yes, my lord. I... I'll be with you in a—" Naheshi lunged for the water, retching.

Bayaya rolled his eyes and thrust out an impatient hand. "Give me that letter, Nahish-shulmanu. I knew we shouldn't have brought you, you buffoon. As if you could go into the king's presence looking like that."

"But, my lord—"

"Give me the letter." Bayaya waggled his fingers impatiently. "I can present it to Ammishtamru as well as you can. Hurry up. They said they'd imprison us if we weren't out of here promptly."

Naheshi heaved again, and before he could wipe his mouth and stand up to dig the letter out of his pouch, the ambassador had motioned his servant over to snatch it away, toppling the eunuch to the wet pavement. Naheshi felt a moment's panic, hoping the fellow would not pull out the wrong letter.

"I've warned you, Nahish-shulmanu. I don't know how

long we'll be, so just stay with the ship if you want a ride back. Otherwise, you're on your own. Do you hear me?"

Naheshi climbed unsteadily to his feet as the chariot clattered off into the rainy darkness, accompanied by Ammishtamru's soldiers. He almost envied the relish with which Bayaya inflicted humiliation upon his enemy. If only Naheshi's own vengeance might have brought him a little more satisfaction. But nothing was that straightforward in his life; his heart was in too many places at once. He cast a worried look in his pouch to be sure the prince's letter was still there and exhaled in relief as his fingers encountered the clay envelope.

Naheshi wasn't even clear in his own mind where he ought to go. Whom exactly did he plan to see? Should he try to catch up to Bayaya and insist on presenting the queen's letter? He wondered if he should make a real effort to contact the prince, but what purpose could that possibly serve? It might get him in trouble, and who would know where the rebel was, anyway?

He just wanted to lie down and get warm. The terrible lethargy that had possessed him since they arrived in Amurru still had him in its grip. *What do I do now?*

The quayside was nearly empty except for the crew on board the ship, who were securing it and lighting lanterns. Two soldiers huddled on the breakwater, standing guard. The Amurrites were really being treated like enemies, Naheshi realized. The soldiers watched him with narrowed eyes as he stumbled off into the town on foot.

A few minutes later, he was trudging in the darkness up the steep, mud-slippery road to the city, with the rain sheeting down on him, penetrating his boiled-wool cloak.

He wondered if the tablet with the queen's letter to her lover would even survive, tucked inside a leather pouch though it was. It seemed to take forever to traverse one league, and then, of course, he found the Royal Gate closed for the night.

The soldiers at the guard post stopped him well outside the entrance. "Whoa there, fellow." Two of them crossed their spears before him. "City's sealed for the night. Better come back in the morning."

Naheshi cast them a piteous look. "But I've just arrived from Amurru with a message for... for the queen mother," he improvised. *Where did that come from? What have I just committed myself to?* But then, had his lady not told him, "Do whatever works"? It was all a lie anyway. He could still see Taddu's transfigured face drinking in Prince Abdi-sharrumma's letter, and he hardened his heart. "It has to do with the former queen. Surely she wants to hear it. I... I... where else can I go?"

"Hey, don't I know you, eunuch?" demanded one of the soldiers, peering up at his face. "You're one of the ones that amphora dropped on!" He turned to his comrades. "Remember? I told you about that. It was the funniest thing I ever saw." They all laughed uproariously, recounting the image of the floundering old Agipsharri and his timid companion crying for help in a piping treble.

Naheshi felt more weary than humiliated. *Can't you even see me here, freezing in front of you?*

But at last the soldier turned back to him.

"I know you're with the palace staff. We'll let you in, but I can't be sure the queen mother will see you this late."

"The Lord Urtenu, perhaps?"

The soldier shrugged. "I don't know. Probably they're all at dinner by now. You can try."

The men opened the massive gates one after another, and Naheshi scuttled through. Then he stood alone in the dark royal plaza, the rain falling more softly than before and the only sound the gurgling of the drains. He saw torches blazing cozily under the porch where the cherubim columns stood, and soldiers on guard, but the old queen would not be in the royal palace at this hour. How tempting the dry porch appeared, nonetheless. He slogged through ankle-deep water across the plaza and approached the gate that separated the royal precinct from the city at large. He hailed the soldiers, and they went through the ritual of identification. The young queen's seals at his belt no longer had any cachet, but one of the guards said he would accompany Naheshi to the dowager's door.

His nausea had worn off, and Naheshi was hungry and shaking with emptiness—emptiness of soul as well as body. He had let the soldiers decide where he was going to take his message. "I'm going to the queen" had seemed more likely to get him through the gates than "I've got a message for the outlawed prince." And in all frankness, he'd feared to face Bayaya if he showed up, late again, in the royal audience hall. He was scarcely a decision-making human anymore—just a dumb animal reacting to things around him. He felt reluctant to acknowledge the flare of bitterness, like a bite of wormwood, that accompanied his memory of Taddu and the letter, her beaming face, the heroic promises of the prince. *There is no malice here, surely, oh surely. I'm just weak, not bad.* But the icy flame in his breast as he remembered made him wonder.

The old queen's housekeeper opened and, seeing the soldier escorting him, let Naheshi in. He had to clear his throat several times—he'd become so hoarse. "News of the former queen," he croaked. "I've just arrived from Amurru."

"One moment, then. I'll have someone bring you a towel, so you don't get water all over my lady's floor."

Naheshi felt so drained he had to sit on the floor of the vestibule while she was gone. *What have I done? What have I done? Why betray Taddu again? The storm has already broken over her head. I just took the easiest course to get into the city because I was tired and cold... and because I want someone to say, 'Well done.' Coward.*

And she loves him...

A moment later, the housekeeper returned, a bundle of towels in her arms. "Our lady will see you, but dry yourself off first."

He hauled himself laboriously to his feet and stripped off the dripping outer layer of his garments. Even his shawl and tunic were soaked, but he would have to endure that. He barely had the energy to towel off his curls so that they did not dribble in his face. The housekeeper pursed her lips disapprovingly but led him up the stairs.

The dowager queen was sitting in her salon with several lamps lit, but the room was still mostly in darkness. Her somber clothing almost disappeared into the shadows, leaving only the ghastly apparition of her gaunt old face, harshly lit by the flickering light.

"Well?" she said brusquely in her deep voice.

"My lady, I... I just arrived by ship from Amurru, carrying a message from Lady Taduhepa for ... your son, Lord Abdi-sharrumma. I didn't know if Lord Urtenu was still on duty or not, and I... they were going to turn me back at the gates, so I... took the liberty of saying I was bringing news to you." He was panting, exhausted, his stomach cramping with hunger.

"And are you, eunuch?" she demanded dryly.

He fumbled the leather pouch from its strap and drew out the tablet. *Intact, gods be praised.* He offered it to her, lowering himself to his knee and averting his eyes. She took it from his hands and cracked open the clay envelope with a long gold knife that lay on her table then shook out the tablet. Her eyes traversed the script, her lips moving silently.

"Very well, eunuch—I forget your name. Something Assyrian, was it not? How would you like to take a replacement message to my son after all?"

He wanted to cry out in protest, "Now?" but instead, he responded meekly, "I am at my lady's service."

"I have someone who can find him. I'll put you in contact with him. Actually, you must know him; he's one of your kind and formerly of Taduhepa's household—a certain Agipsharri."

Dear gods—Agipsharri, of all people? Fear shivered like an icicle up Naheshi's back, but he managed to control his face.

"You can write out what I tell you. Deliver it this evening. Deliver it yourself. That will make it all the more convincing. I think we need to move directly on this. Are you prepared to take dictation?"

His mouth was saying, "Yes, my lady," and his hands were opening the wooden leaves of his wax tablet and drawing out a stylus, but his mind was babbling noises of horror. Of all the dreadful unlikelihoods: Agipsharri. He felt he didn't have the strength to confront the old reprobate that night. He was so tired, so hungry, so vulnerable. *What if Agipsharri should try to—*

"Eunuch? Are you listening? Keep the greeting as 'My love, I pray that you are well.'" The dowager mused aloud, staring without focus for a moment as she consulted her memory, "She doesn't know what his last letter actually said, but we have to seem to respond to it. So add—let's see—'I am indeed in good health.' Then… 'We will land in Mahadu five nights after the festival of the New Year. Don't forget: that will be an unguarded moment. I await your intervention at the docks. We should arrive around sundown.' What else? How to be sure the would-be rescuers don't really encounter the princess? 'Come by way of the Mukesh road. I… I long to see you again. Signed, your dove who loves you.'"

This will not cause any further harm for Taddu. It will only bring down the prince. They have already decided she is guilty, that she will receive a 'fitting punishment,' and we know what that means. This will not make things any worse. It can't be any worse for her. But it will bring down Abdi-sharrumma. Naheshi saw the prince's white grin, his possessive arm around the queen's shoulders, and he wanted to gloat. But he lacked Bayaya's talent for enjoying revenge. Instead, he felt an uneasy creeping of his scalp. He tried to call to mind something that could become worse as a result of his action, but he was too tired to think straight. What he needed to come up with was a real plan to help her escape.

Naheshi looked up, waiting for the next line, but the

queen said, "There. Now, give me your tablet, and I will write a safe-conduct to the palace for you. You can make a good copy at the chancery. If she has ever corresponded with her lover before, try to imitate her handwriting."

"I write her letters anyway, my lady."

"Perfect." The queen mother pressed the letters into the wax then drew her seal from its little case on her desk and rolled it across the bottom.

"Go on. Do this right away. You know better than I where this Agipsharri lives, no doubt."

Ahat-milki rose and left before Naheshi, who was moving like a sleepwalker, could even make his bow.

The dowager queen had immediately sent a message to her son that she was on her way to the palace, and now she stood before him and Pizidku as they dined in the royal apartment. "Forgive me for appearing at this hour, my son, but I think you will agree that it's an important turn of affairs I report."

"Think nothing of it, Mother. I trust your judgment. Care to join us for a bite to eat?"

Ahat-milki waved a hand to decline, but she took a seat across from Ammishtamru at the table where he reclined and Pizidku sat. The latter passed her goblet of wine to her mother-in-law with a welcoming smile. The old queen squeezed Pizidku's hand and took a sip. Musicians were playing softly in the corner.

"You may have the excuse you need now to extradite and put to death your former wife," she said.

"The gods are good!" The king chortled. "What's

happened? As things stand at present, I fear this threat to attack the Amurrites if they don't send Taddu back is going to escape from our control. There's an ambassador from Amurru in the palace as we speak. We just palavered, and I don't much like the way things look. Shaushga-muwa is standing his ground, and the viceroy is extremely unwilling to play our game. He keeps talking about going to Tudhaliya in person to stop us. Apparently, this is the very last thing Our Lord and Sun wants: for his vassals to go to war while Assyria is growling at him in the east."

"Yes, well, I daresay this may convince Ini-tesshub that she is incorrigible. She is continuing to plot against you even from exile."

The king threw back his head and laughed. "Excellent! What's come up?"

"Her eunuch brought me a message directly from her in Amurru, which was destined for your brother. She pledged her love, told him Shaushga-muwa would defeat your forces, and swore she would rejoin him to continue the fight. Of course, she thinks he is planning to intercept her en route here." Ahat-milki laid the tablet on the table.

"Can you believe it? It's just what we hoped for!" The king planted a celebratory kiss on the cheek of Pizidku, who looked away, her brows creased.

The queen mother set her face, at the price of great effort, and continued, "I took the liberty of replacing the message with another. He will think Taddu has begged him to rescue her as the ship docks at the harbor. That's what we put in our letter to her as well. I... I told him to come in by the Mukesh road. That assures that he won't run into the real Taddu—if in fact we can get her back, which is far from certain but getting more likely at this point—and it also gives us several excellent spots for an ambush. I dare to think that the presence of her chamberlain in person will lay to rest any suspicions he… your brother might have."

She'd done it. She had laid a trap that would lure her son to his death. Her life was nearly over. There could be no pain that compared to this.

"Ha ha! You are worthy of an epic, Mother! Listen closely, my dear"—the king beamed at his wife—"and learn at the knee of a master." His hilarity faded as he saw her face. "What, my treasure? You don't look very happy."

Lady Pizidku turned a sorrowful smile upon Ammishtamru and laid a hand on his arm. "It gives me no satisfaction to see the daughter of a king humiliated like this, my husband. Forgive me; I know it's a victory for justice."

"It's her own damned actions that are bringing humiliation down on her, not anything we're doing," grumbled the king.

"You're right, of course. And I suppose I would do the same were I in my mother's place."

"You would," agreed Ahat-milki, grim lipped. "You would derive no pleasure from any of it, believe me, but you would still do it."

Ammishtamru poured himself a measure of wine. "To hear you ladies talk, ruling a kingdom is the worst burden in the world. Should we envy your eunuch slave, then? Not me. I have to say I rather enjoy all this." He winked at his wife and popped a bit of meat into his mouth.

Pizidku said gently, "My husband, your mother has just

seen one of her children slain and is anticipating the death of the second one. This isn't pleasurable."

The king snorted. "My dear brothers are reaping what they have sown, my lamb. Kill or be killed."

"Enough of this theological discussion, Ammi." Ahat-milki stopped him with rather more bitterness than she'd intended to show. *The lout.* He had no idea what this was costing her. Pizidku gazed at her with compassionate, bovine eyes but said nothing. "We have the proof of Taddu's misdeeds in hand. I say we petition the Great King directly for her extradition. Let Ini-tesshub dawdle all he likes, trying to avoid a judgment; if his suzerain speaks, he will have no more choice than Shaushga-muwa. Put it squarely to the Great King that she's still plotting against you, and show him the proof. Then we can drop this posturing about a war. It makes me uneasy."

"Yes," the king said with a satisfied grin, "and I'd like to see Tudhaliya say no, since he has been begging us to send him troops despite our exemption. At last we have some leverage. Fine, Mother; I'll get Takhulinu on it this very night."

CHAPTER 20

NAHESHI RETIRED FROM THE DARK house and crossed the plaza again, relieved that the rain had stopped. He'd left his cloak in the queen's vestibule. His feet, in their sodden leather shoes, were like uncontrollably clumsy blocks of ice. At the cherubim porch, he showed his safe-conduct to the guards, who let him enter, and he squished through the unlit ceremonial rooms to the servants' stairs and up to the second floor, his chest heaving. So much for all those years of breath-control exercises.

No one was in the chancery. He could write out the queen's false letter without anyone asking questions. Naheshi lit a lamp from one of the torches in the hall and dropped to a stool at the secretaries' table, water pooling at his feet. But there were no damp tablets or bucket of wet clay. Just his luck; everything had been emptied out for the day. Only a few discarded half-dry blanks lay on the table, overlooked. Squeezing water out of the hem of his tunic, he managed to dampen a drying tablet well enough to poke letters into it and shoved it with shaking hands into his leather pouch. He hoped the prince wouldn't wonder about the quality of the writing.

Naheshi took the lamp with him when he left—what was a little theft compared to the black stains on his conscience?—and stumbled down the corridor to the servants' quarters. There were the queen's old rooms, those of the Lady Pizidku and the concubines, and his own little nest among the high-ranking servants' apartments. Then he passed the labyrinth of small cubicles and dormitories for the lower slaves. He realized he didn't know exactly where Agipsharri lived, but he could recall a few clues the old eunuch had dropped over the years. He knocked on a door that had to be the right one. The panel swung open, letting out a strong odor of urine and cooked food. Despite his revulsion, Naheshi's mouth began to water uncontrollably.

"Who's there?" Agipsharri stared at Naheshi with his little eyes wide, for once deprived of speech, then his sly grin split open. "My, my. Look who's back, eh."

"Just don't say anything more, Agipsharri. Please let me in. If I don't sit down, I'll fall on the floor." Naheshi felt tears starting to well under his eyelids, but he didn't care. Agipsharri stepped back from the door, and Naheshi sidled past, their bellies brushing in the narrow space. The chamberlain sank to a cushion, huddled and shivering, the tears running down his cheeks.

"And I owe the honor of this visit to…?"

"A truce, I beg you, Agipsharri. I am here on the queen mother's business. But please let me have something to eat. I'm so tired. Dear gods, I'm so tired…" He dropped his head into unsteady hands.

Agipsharri called out to his slave, who was ladling

something stew-like and savory smelling from a round ceramic pot in the far corner of the room. *Slave?* wondered a remote part of Naheshi's mind. *How does he afford a slave?*

"Serve up a second bowl for my friend here, eh." Agipsharri leveled his narrow, malevolent gaze at Naheshi. "You *are* my friend, aren't you, Nahish-shulmanu?"

"Yes, I'm your friend, Agipsharri." Naheshi forced himself to say the words the other had demanded that night in the storage room: "I... I respect you. Just let me have something to eat, I beg."

"See? That gets easier with practice. And now that you are no longer my supervisor, what's to prevent us from being friends, eh, Nahish-shulmanu? Bring him a blanket as well, Arsuwanu."

Agipsharri lowered his spreading bulk to a stool, still fixing Naheshi with his small eyes.

"A little less high-and-mighty all of a sudden, I see. Not too proud to beg. No insults for your old colleague?"

Naheshi hung his head and bit his lip, not trusting himself to speak. His heart was pounding like a cornered animal's.

"Well, then. Maybe a little rough treatment is good for you, eh."

Naheshi's head snapped up in a reflex of terror, but the other eunuch was chuckling, his belly wobbling, and made no move toward him. *If he tries anything, I'm too tired to run.*

The slave placed the small table full of food in front of the two eunuchs and handed the guest his heaped plate. Naheshi practically fell into it face-first, shaking so hard he could hardly hold the dish. Agipsharri still eyed him, his expression neither hostile nor friendly but evaluating. The slave returned with a blanket, which the old eunuch draped over Naheshi's shoulders while the latter shoveled food into his mouth with a trembling hand, mopping up the last drops with a piece of bread.

Agipsharri waited till Naheshi leaned back against the wall, still exhausted but sated, then said again, "So?"

"Thank… thank you, Agipsharri." Naheshi breathed with difficulty. "I come to you seeking a favor. I need to find Prince Abdi-sharrumma. I have a message for him from the dowager queen, and I have to deliver it immediately."

"Ah, the artistically crafted correspondence continues, I see. Although I must say, you don't look to be in very good shape for a jaunt through the city tonight, Nahish-shulmanu."

"I have no choice. I'm a slave." A rueful laugh escaped Naheshi's lips.

"Aren't we all; aren't we all? And why do you think *I* know where the prince is, eh?"

"The queen mother told me so. I know, I know," the chamberlain added hastily, hoping he wouldn't arouse Agipsharri's anger again, "you weren't lying when you said you were important. I respect you, Agipsharri, I—"

"Yes, yes." Agipsharri's thin grin showed he was not so displeased to hear Naheshi grovel. "You know, Nahish-shulmanu, I was the one who started off this series of false letters to the prince. I was the one who delivered his reply… to the dowager. So the work of saving the kingdom goes on, with the help of its unlikely little heroes, eh? Arsuwanu!" he called to the slave. "Go get you-know-who. And hurry."

The slave bowed and scurried out without a word.

Naheshi wondered if the man were mute. Agipsharri sat enthroned toad-like on his seat, still considering the spectacle before him. Naheshi seemed to himself a little less insubstantial with something in his stomach, but he was still utterly exhausted and only gradually beginning to stop shaking from the cold of his wet clothes. He felt like a small, helpless creature transfixed by the stare of a serpent. And yet Agipsharri's gaze was not wholly inimical. Naheshi drew the blanket closer around his shivering shoulders and wiped his tears and the meat sauce from his face with the back of his hand. He had no dignity left. He remembered Agipsharri saying that the likes of them had no dignity anyway. Naheshi did not even care that he appeared pitiable in the presence of his enemy.

"So," said the old eunuch for the third time. "I will help you, Nahish-shulmanu, just to show you that the household of Lady Pizidku is magnanimous in victory, eh. And... because you showed yourself willing to help me."

They sat silently eyeing one another for a moment. *When have I ever helped him?* wondered Naheshi. But then he recalled his half-hearted efforts to pick the old eunuch up out of the street when he'd been hit by the falling amphora.

"You know, I actually considered revealing your— shall we say—*perfidy* to the rebel princes at one point. We educated folks do like those big words, don't we?" continued Agipsharri, his lipless mouth stretched to the side in an expression somewhere between bitterness and amusement. "But then... then said princes had perhaps just tried to murder me, and I had to ask myself whether it was appropriate, whether you were deserving of that kind of revenge after all. A helping hand to a brother in need...

331

maybe that was worth something. Maybe that meant something, eh."

Can one little moment like that change a person's whole attitude toward someone, then? Naheshi marveled. He remembered, his face burning even after all these weeks, that night when Taddu had turned on him in anger—and he knew that it could, for good or ill. That very moment had started him down the steep path upon which he still slipped and slid. Agipsharri was no more a free man than Naheshi was. Agipsharri, too, was desperate for whatever little scraps of his superiors' esteem fell his way. And Naheshi had refused to show him any respect at all. The horrible episode in the storage room had made it clear how central that was to their curdled relationship.

Why was I so hateful? he asked himself in misery. *I thought he hated me, but which came first? I was afraid of him. He was old and ugly and... and a eunuch. And everyone knows that eunuchs are awful, spiteful, gossipy, corrupt.*

Naheshi felt his hatred begin to liquefy into pity, which was also self-pity. It dribbled downward through his chest, where his heart huddled like a frightened rabbit, and over his bowels, and down to that empty terrain that should have established him as a man but didn't, and seemed to dissolve his too-ample flesh from the inside like salt on a snail.

What have I done to him? What have I done to me?

He pressed his lips together to keep them from wobbling. At last, when the quiet became too painful to bear, he spoke in a shaky voice. "There's going to be a war, isn't there?"

Agipsharri shrugged. There was another silence broken only by his wheezing breath.

"Who do you really work for, Agipsharri?" Naheshi said.

"For now? The queen mother, the king, the forces of good… because they appear to be winning at the moment. I am what is commonly called a spy, eh."

"Me, too." Naheshi coughed out a humorless little laugh, closing his eyes at the absurdity of it. He was a bungler, a botcher, a ruiner of lives, a liar, a causer of wars. "But you figured that out, didn't you? Was it really you, or was it me they were after when they pushed that big amphora over the edge of the roof?"

"Ah, that! One of life's great mysteries, eh? We're both spies, after all, and no one loves a spy." Agipsharri grinned. "Brother spies."

"Yes, b-brothers." Naheshi had to admit it. They were part of the brotherhood of earth's most contemptible beings, and he did not mean spies. But he forced himself to ask, "Why do *you* do it—spy, I mean?"

"For gold, Nahish-shulmanu, as crass as it may sound to an idealistic young fellow like you. Some of us are not so well recompensed for our household services as others. But then, we're not a multilingual scribe. Yet we like our little comforts just as well as the better educated, eh. Besides"—his voice hardened—"what finer way to pay back the disappointments the powers on high have inflicted than by taking as much of their gold as one can, eh? And you?"

"I… I don't know why. Not gold. For love, I think. For hatred. B-Because I feel sorry for myself." Naheshi's mouth writhed with the effort to hold back his tears.

Agipsharri twisted his lips in a cynical smile. "Ah, but those are the reasons eunuchs and slaves do everything, eh, even eating and breathing. That's no reason at all. You have no noble political motives?"

Naheshi shook his head.

"Love or hatred, then. You love the Amurrite, don't you?"

"I used to, but she was cruel. So I hated her instead. Or rather I used to. Now, I… I just feel sorry for myself again. There was a moment when I didn't, but it was even worse. I did terrible things, thinking I was being good, Agipsharri, pretending I was being a good servant." Naheshi's voice broke and slid up so that he sounded like a small child.

The old eunuch laid a fat hand on Naheshi's shoulder. It rested there heavily for a moment, then the fingers slid inward in a caress. Naheshi froze, fearing the worst, but when Agipsharri spoke, it was with an unaccustomed softness. "I might have loved you, Nahish-shulmanu, but you were cruel. So I hated you instead."

Naheshi was absorbing those words numbly when the slave Arsuwanu tapped on the door and thrust his head inside. "Master, he's out here."

"Send him in." Agipsharri's hand slid from Naheshi's shoulder as a lean, ragged fellow wrapped in a dark cloak edged warily into the room.

"What's afoot, master?" the man demanded.

"Matan, take this fellow to the Visitor." Agipsharri fingered a piece or two of silver from his purse and dropped it into the man's outstretched palm.

"You got it, master. Come on, boy." He slid out the

door, and Naheshi struggled to his feet and stumbled after him.

At the threshold, Naheshi turned back to Agipsharri. "Thank you."

"Come back tonight if you need a place to stay, eh."

"Thank you. Th-Thank you." In his mind's eye, he saw the old eunuch lying helpless in the street, in pain. *Helpless and in pain, like all of us.* "I... I hope your shoulder is better, Agipsharri." He turned quickly away, afraid to look at the other, and slipped out into the corridor after his guide.

The man called Matan led Naheshi briskly to the service entrance of the palace, where he showed a safe-conduct to the guards, and the two struck out down the streets of the citadel toward the lower city. It was still drizzling, and the autumn night was cold. They had not so much as the light of a lamp to guide them. Naheshi found himself without a cloak yet again, and his clothes were soaked and bone chilling. He smelled like a wet dog.

He followed the quick steps of Matan as best he could, but they didn't go into the sleazy neighborhoods in the Lower City that Naheshi remembered from his previous visits. Instead, they moved across the hilltop into the temple district, where huge aristocratic mansions rubbed shoulders with more modest but still-respectable merchant dwellings. They stopped in front of the bronze-studded door of a palatial house.

Some maryannu *lives here.*

"There y'are." Matan made as if to fade away.

"Wait," Naheshi called out in an uneasy voice. "Are they going to skewer me if I just knock on the door? Is there some countersign?"

Matan shrugged and disappeared into the darkness. Naheshi turned to the door and, with clenching stomach, knocked. His fist made no sound, and he was afraid of hurting his knuckles, so he took out his wooden tablet and clicked on the panel with its corner.

Long ages seemed to pass. He felt himself growing faint. Things were beginning to sparkle in front of his eyes, and he put a hand against the wall to steady himself. A servant finally appeared, eyed Naheshi haughtily, and demanded, "What can I do for you?"

The question caught Naheshi off guard. Could he just ask to see Prince Abdi-sharrumma? Not likely, if the man was outlawed. He remembered how Agipsharri had referred to him. "I come from Amurru. I have a message for... the Visitor."

"One minute." The door closed in his face.

A moment later, the leaf opened a crack. Within, he could see one of the men from the conspirators' meetings. The man seemed to recognize him as well, and he opened the door a bit more. Thank the gods he was unaware of who had betrayed them.

"A message from Amurru," croaked Naheshi, his voice a hoarse shell. The man threw back the door panel fully, and before Naheshi could even step inside the vestibule, Abdi-sharrumma himself peered around the interior door.

"Who's there?" His eyes lit up at the sight of Naheshi. "By the gods! It's you! Is Taddu well, boy? Are our plans still on? Does she know when she's arriving?"

"My lord." Naheshi struggled to detach his pouch from its strap. "A letter for you."

The prince snatched the pouch and dug it open. He

tore out the letter and held it sideways to make out the scratching on its half-dry surface.

"Ha ha! Shaushga be praised! She's worth all my brother's armies put together! What a woman! Your mistress is a pearl, you know that, Assyrian?"

"Yes, my lord."

"Can you take a return message?"

"It might be risky, my lord. I'm not sure how I'll get back; I came with King Shaushga-muwa's diplomatic ship, but I don't know when it's leaving. I can take a verbal message, however."

"Kiss her for me!"

"Uh... perhaps I'd better not, my lord."

"Oh, that's right. 'We have standards of propriety at this court,' or whatever you said. You didn't know that was me showing her the jewels, did you? The diplomats, the relatives of Pukanu? Heshmi really is—was—his son-in-law."

Naheshi had not, in fact, known that the diplomats were the princes, but he realized in retrospect how very clear it was. So many things were clearer in retrospect.

"As you see, my lodgings here are not so bad. This is Lord Iwirikalli's house. He's being held at the moment, but his family isn't about to let him be executed. They'll pay Ammi to free him—everybody knows gold is my brother's little weakness—so nothing here is attainted or under watch. I'm hiding in plain sight among Wiri's servants. When he gets out, we'll be back in business, and my sweet flower will be at my side."

"Yes, my lord. Is that your message, my lord?"

"Yes, why not? That will relieve her mind. Well, my

fine, loyal fellow, go with the gods. Give my dearest lady comfort, and tell her I love her and I'll be there by the Mukesh road at the appointed time. She need fear nothing."

Naheshi was let out into the night. He debated returning to the dockside to see if Bayaya's ship had left for Amurru, but he didn't have the strength. Instead, he asked the guard at the palace if he knew whether the Amurrite delegation had weighed anchor. To his relief, the interview with the king had gone on so long that the embassy had been invited, at the urging of the viceroy, to stay overnight and depart at first light. He squished his way wearily up the back stairs in the familiar trajectory toward the staff quarters. But he wasn't heading to his own apartment.

How strangely and suddenly things had changed between him and Agipsharri, he thought, still a little dazed. After all that had happened, Naheshi felt he could understand the old eunuch's desire for vengeance all too well. Had he not dreamed of similarly extravagant revenges? Some, alas, had made it out of the realm of dreams. And perhaps that was the most pitiable thing about them both. His own experience, at least, had been that he himself had suffered more than anyone from his efforts at requital. Was Agipsharri, too, tortured by his anger? As Naheshi turned the corner into the lower staff residences, Agipsharri's mysterious words came back to him: *I might have loved you.* Naheshi wanted to weep for all that he had denied himself through his stupidity and fear.

"Well, well. We did come back after all, eh," said Agipsharri.

"Come in and dry off. I had Arsuwanu make you up a pallet, just in case."

Naheshi staggered into the room, water puddling around him. The silent slave stepped forward to relieve the newcomer of his shawl. There was a brazier lit in the middle of the room, and it was enticingly cozy. Someone seemed to have emptied the chamber pot—Naheshi was aware of an improvement in the atmosphere.

"Thank you, Agipsharri." Naheshi ached to say something warmer that would tell his host that he was grateful not just for shelter but for showing Naheshi himself. But part of him was still afraid.

Agipsharri approached him with a tunic of vast proportions, its seams enriched with colored bands of embroidery.

"This won't fit you, but at least it's dry to sleep in. Yours will dry overnight if it's spread out, eh."

Naheshi felt his throat constrict, remembering the last time he had undressed in front of Agipsharri. He backed away in spite of himself, threw the tunic over his head and pulled off his own wet clothes underneath, watching Agipsharri through the neck hole for any move that might be a threat. The texture of the wool was astonishingly soft; this garment had cost a lot. He could only imagine where Agipsharri had gotten the gold to buy such a piece of stuff. It was heavenly. He nuzzled it, distracted from his wariness, and sniffed the clean smell. His head emerged from the neck hole, but the rest enveloped him like a blanket, the decorated shoulder seams halfway down his arms. It was as big as a tent.

Suddenly, he snorted with laughter, and once it had started, he couldn't hold it back.

"I'm living like my ancestors—in a tent!" He giggled helplessly. "That's what we say back home: our ancestors lived in tents." He was close to sobs, his shoulders shaking with giddy hilarity. By the gods, he was tired. He tried to sit on the floor but fell backwards, entrapping himself. The harder he tried to sit up, the harder he laughed: a racking, painful, silent paroxysm that had very little to do with humor.

Agipsharri watched, his lips in a thin smile, and finally held out a cup of wine to his guest. "I don't know if you need this or not, eh. You already seem to be drunk."

Naheshi managed to control himself at last and gratefully sipped the wine, which was heated, while his stomach muscles relaxed. He felt himself going limp all over. "I'm sorry, I'm sorry, Agipsharri. In fact, this is a wonderful tunic. Thank you again."

"Think nothing of it. It was well worth it for the spectacle. Glad to see we have a sense of humor under everything, Nahish-shulmanu; we've always seemed to take ourself rather seriously. Perhaps I've yet to meet the real you, eh."

"I'm not sure you'd like the real me, Agipsharri," Naheshi said, his words slurring a little in spite of the care he took to enunciate them. "I don't think the real me is a very nice person. He's done some awful things, and they just seem to get worse and worse."

"Perhaps it's the false you that has done awful things, and the real you is innocent, eh."

"I'm afraid the real me *is* false…"

"My, we're wading into deep waters here. Perhaps I need some wine, too." Agipsharri poured himself a cup and set the ewer down on the floor with a grunt.

There was an extended silence. Naheshi longed to unburden himself but scarcely dared. At last, under the impulsion of the wine, he murmured, "Why is my life such a disaster, Agipsharri? What's the matter with me?"

"The matter with you, Nahish-shulmanu, is that you have 'abuse me' written all over your face. It's such delicious pleasure to be unkind to you and watch you crumple that even the gods have taken it up, eh."

"Is that what's wrong?" Naheshi looked up at him earnestly, his thoughts unfocused. The chamberlain's mind seemed to be wandering, and it was harder and harder to get his words out. His body felt boneless.

"Yes, indeed," agreed Agipsharri, sipping from his cup. "What earthworm taught you how to be a human being, eh?"

"My mother." Naheshi saw her meekly absorbing the perpetual criticisms of his father. *Good people don't get angry. Don't antagonize him, my dear; he has a hard life. He's right, you know; it's my fault. He's right; we really couldn't afford another child. Still, we love you anyway.*

But she was poor, powerless; that was how powerless people *had* to be. Tears began to trickle out from under his lids. He was cursed.

"Not again. I thought we had a truce, Nahish-shulmanu. What you're wielding now is a weapon."

Naheshi hid his face in his hands. "Oh, Agipsharri. I can't live with myself. I've done such awful things. All this is my fault."

"Ah? Then since you're so powerful, while you're at it, you might do something about this weather, too, eh."

Naheshi goggled at him uncomprehendingly, his head growing thicker and thicker.

The old eunuch snorted. "Why don't you go to sleep. I don't know when you have to leave in the morning, but I have duties to attend to for Lady Pizidku."

"Thank you for everything, Agipsharri. I really mean it." Naheshi made a little gesture as if to touch the other's arm but drew back, afraid to be met by some sarcasm.

"Yes, yes. Good night." Agipsharri blew out the lamp and settled his enormous body laboriously upon his pallet on the other side of the brazier, wheezing and grunting.

Arsuwanu the slave seemed to be nowhere around, and indeed, Naheshi had no idea where he might have fit. As tired as he was, he lay staring into the pulsing coals. Their rhythm almost began to form a melody, and without realizing that he had uttered an actual sound, Naheshi found himself humming a sad song from his childhood.

"Shut up, Nahish-shulmanu."

"Sorry, sorry. For someone so big, I don't hold my drink very well."

"No, you're rather like a child, aren't you? Nighty night, little Nahish-shulmanu."

A minute later, Naheshi said, "Did you know I used to sing? I had a beautiful voice."

"No, never would have known."

"I was supposed to become a singer for the King of Kings, but I lost my voice."

"Sad story. Good night, Nahish-shulmanu."

Silence fell, disturbed only by an occasional crackle of the invisible flames among the embers.

"Where are you from, Agipsharri?" Naheshi felt he needed to know something about Agipsharri. He had a past; he'd been a little boy once. Perhaps people had done terrible things to him, too.

"Good night, Nahish-shulmanu."

"No, really." Naheshi could hear how childlike his voice sounded, but he was too befuddled to care.

"Born right here in the palace."

"Were your parents...?"

"Eunuchs, too? No, Nahish-shulmanu." Agipsharri gave a puff of amusement or disgust. "My mother was a slave. She used to tell me King Niqmaddu was my father. So maybe I'm a prince, eh. Maybe I'm the king's uncle. Who can disprove it?"

Naheshi, whose thoughts were already sinking into confusion, didn't know whether his host was serious or joking or even lying, but the very possibility shocked him profoundly. Such things did happen between kings and slave girls. It seemed to make life's cruelty—his own cruelty—to Agipsharri all the more appalling.

He started to say something, but Agipsharri cut him off. "Enough, Nahish-shulmanu. Listen, I'm doing you a favor, but don't press your luck, eh. I need to get up early. Good night."

Naheshi snuggled into the enormous tunic and lay there until he heard Agipsharri begin to snore. After a moment, he reached across the space between their pallets and found the older eunuch's hand. He fell asleep with it pressed against his cheek.

CHAPTER 21

NAHESHI HOPED NEVER TO SEE the sea again. He and the blue-bearded Lord Yammu did not get on well. Perhaps none of the gods liked him. That was something he could understand; he was a despicable person. Taddu, on the other hand, welcomed him back with great eagerness, ignoring his green face and tottering gait.

"Naheshi, what news? Did you find him?" she whispered excitedly, taking him aside.

"Yes, my lady. He said to tell you he was well and safe. He is concealed at the house of one of the noble conspirators, who is not being watched." There was more to the message, but it was in response to the Old Dragon's concocted letter, so he had to be careful about what else he said. "The rescue plans are still in force. He added that he loves you and that I should kiss you for him."

She laughed in delight as if that were the most amusing idea in the world.

But you did kiss me once, he thought, *even without Lord Abdi-sharrumma's shadow over me.*

"Ah, Naheshi, how wonderful it is to be loved! Thank the gods he is safe. Tell me, did he look well?"

"Yes, my lady."

Taddu closed her eyes ecstatically, no doubt picturing the handsome, eager face of her prince. After a moment, she added as if in afterthought, "How did you finally get back?"

"In your brother's diplomatic ship, just as I went, my lady."

The autumn equinox, New Year's Day, came and went. Amurru made the customary sacrifices, but there was no joyful celebration in a city uneasily awaiting attack.

Gods defend us from another year like the last one, Naheshi thought miserably.

Taddu was full of a brittle good humor, sparkling with nervous energy. Her mother eyed her strangely, as if she could not comprehend such jollity in the face of humiliation and impending war. Naheshi knew very well what hope illumined Taddu's days. If only he could have shared it.

Although Shaushga-muwa refused to send his sister off to house arrest in some lonely backwater, he did, for propriety's sake, discharge her maids. Naheshi made his best effort to straighten her room and keep her clothes in order. He slept—badly—in the antechamber. Every afternoon, the Great Lady brought her grandson to see his mother, which lent a comforting warmth to the chilly little apartment. Prince Utri-sharrumma kept Naheshi busy telling stories and made him pull him up and down in his toy chariot. It was a welcome distraction from the chamberlain's gloomy thoughts.

One morning, not long after the first day of the year, he was looking out the window at the harbor when he saw sailors taking down the chain across the entrance.

"My lady, look. A ship is entering the harbor. And there are two more with it."

"Oh?" Taddu came over and leaned against him for balance while she stood on her toes to see. He tingled at her touch but kept his face impassive. "More diplomatic ships, do you think?" she asked. "Have they called off the war?" She threw Naheshi a triumphant grin. "Shushi held out against them, and look: Ugarit caved in. It was all for show, I bet. Ammi hates to lose face; he had to go through these motions."

May it be so, Naheshi thought with little hope.

They found out quickly enough why the ships had come. Not much time elapsed before there was a knock at the door. Naheshi opened it to find a red-faced page panting there. He'd clearly run to the apartment.

"The king requires his sister's presence urgently in the throne room, sir. He said not a minute's delay if she knows what's good for her."

Alarmed, Naheshi turned back to the queen. She'd heard the boy's words, and her cheeks drained of color. "Come with me, Naheshi. Don't leave me by myself. Something's going on. Oh, gods in heaven, have they caught Abishu?"

Naheshi turned back to the messenger. "The lady is on her way. I will see to her prompt arrival."

The page ran off like a hunted deer.

"Let me just get on something nicer..." the queen murmured, staring about.

"No, no, my lady. Go as you are right now, I beg you. This seems serious."

He herded her out the door, careful not to touch her. She half ran ahead of him, her neat steps clicking on the floor. She had on those embroidered red shoes that he loved. She looked so small and fragile, with her cylindrical cap and her long braids hanging below the end of her veil like a little girl's, that he felt his heart crumble. Had he been wrong to show her letter to the queen mother? He couldn't bear the thought that some terrible consequence of his own actions might harm her. All he'd meant to do was help to trap the prince.

He almost had a stitch in his side by the time they reached the throne room. It was by no means as grand or beautiful as the one at Ugarit, but it was impressive enough, with clerestory windows and a broad dais at one end. The king was sitting hunched in his throne, his hands on its arms. He was small and slight like his father and, at twenty-two, looked terribly young. His mother sat beside him, her hand hiding her mouth. Ini-tesshub and his Hittites stood before the king. Taddu stopped dead when she saw the viceroy. This could mean nothing good. Naheshi started to bow back out of the room, but the Great Lady gestured to him to stay. Her face was stricken.

Taddu looked from one to another with the wild fear of a fox at bay. "What's this about, Mama? Why is the viceroy here?"

Shaushga-muwa was the one to speak, his voice

unsteady. "As you know, your former husband has changed his mind, sister. He wants you back."

"I thought you were going to fight for me, Shushi. I don't want to go back to him. I—"

"Not to be his wife, my sister." Shaushga-muwa's voice broke. "He wants... he wants to put you to death. Haven't you understood that yet? What did you think this 'fitting punishment' we all kept talking about meant? And now we *have* to send you back, like it or not."

"What?" Taddu looked back and forth wildly from her brother to her mother. "What are you saying, Shushi? Mama—?"

Ini-tesshub interrupted in his mournful baritone. "King Ammishtamru son of Niqmepa went over my head, my daughter. He went directly to the Great King himself. The Great King has accepted his petition to put his former wife to death for her crimes. He has charged me to convey you back to Ugarit. I have here the order to my son, King Shaushga-muwa son of Benteshina, cautioning him not to try to stop the men or ships that have come for this purpose."

There was a long beat during which Naheshi watched in Taddu's face the dawning realization that it would be the viceroy of the Great King who took her back to Ugarit to her death. Her lover's small band stood no chance against Ini-tesshub's heavily armed troops. Who would ever shelter a man who had raised his hand against the Great King?

Her expression shifted from apprehension to horror. "Oh, all you gods, help me! No! No! Mama!" Taddu threw herself into her mother's arms, wailing. "No! Don't let them kill me! Shushi! Don't let them! Fight for me like you said you would!"

The king put his face in his hands, his shoulders slumping. The Great Lady rocked her daughter back and forth. Over the girl's veiled head, her cheeks were streaming with tears.

Shaushga-muwa, his face stretched into a mask of grief, murmured into his lap, "Sister, we can do nothing. It's your husband's right to punish you how he sees fit. He has the Great King's approval—that changes everything." He looked up at her, bitter in his helplessness. "That changes everything, don't you see? What can I do now?"

He dragged his eyes away. "Take her, Ini-tesshub, and tell my uncle that I am his loyal vassal. Take her, kill her, and throw her into the sea—there is nothing I can do about it." His voice shredded, and he struggled to regain control of himself. "Tell him... tell him I look forward to being his brother-in-law if he's still pleased to grant me the hand of his sister."

Taddu shrieked, "You coward! You're a coward! Our father would never have done this! You're all cowards! You're selling out your own sister to curry favor with Tudhaliya! Won't anyone stand up to that man?"

Gasshulawiya tried to shush her, but Taddu was sobbing and pounding on the arm of her mother's chair.

"My cousin, is there nothing we can do to soften this sentence?" The Great Lady addressed the viceroy in quiet desperation.

But he shook his head. "Not unless Ammishtamru relents. He is within his rights to punish an adulterous wife by death. And the Great King is currently in considerable need of Ugaritic troops; he's perhaps more than usually receptive to a petition from the king."

"But why did Ammishtamru change his mind?"

"You'll have to ask him, my cousin."

"The Old Dragon probably put him up to it," raged Taddu between clenched teeth. "She's had it in for me since the day I married her son. I hate her; I hate her! May she rot in the jaws of the underworld!"

"Quiet, my dearest. The gods might hear your curse and turn it upon you," murmured her mother, her eyes uneasy, and she spat over her own shoulder.

"So what happens now?" Shaushga-muwa asked bleakly.

Ini-tesshub responded, "The crew needs to reprovision the ship before we set off again, as I understand it. Let the young queen take with her enough clothes for a few days."

The Great Lady flinched as if an arrow had shot her through the heart.

"And we will embark two mornings hence at first light. I suggest a guard watch her tonight if you think she is likely to attempt an escape. I can provide soldiers if—"

"I have soldiers," said the king.

"Very well, my son." The viceroy pretended not to hear the fury quivering in Shaushga-muwa's voice. After a pause, he added gravely, "My condolences to the family. None of us, including the Great King, takes any pleasure in this business; believe me. It's a serious complication for his foreign policy. But he will applaud your selflessness. A war between vassals would be a very bad thing at the moment." He looked almost embarrassed. "I... have been authorized by King Ammishtamru to offer you a handsome recompense for the life of your sister: a sum of fourteen thousand gold shekels. But he will go no higher. No doubt the treasury—"

"Damn the treasury!" cried Shaushga-muwa. "Does that dog shit think he can buy my sister's life? That I would haggle for it? I give her up because I should, because I must."

The viceroy and his men took their leave of the king and queen mother. Taddu continued to wail in her mother's arms. Shaushga-muwa stared blankly in front of him, then he suddenly strode out of the room so fast he overturned his footstool, his mouth a thin, trembling line of rage.

No one remembered Naheshi in the other doorway. His legs had become so unsteady that he sank down on the floor, his hands over his eyes, his face against his knees.

Oh gods, oh gods, he thought hopelessly. *We are all slaves. We are all castrated.*

CHAPTER 22

"WELL, THEY'LL SEE I'M NOT going back
like a lamb to the slaughter. They're all
crazy if they think I will," the young
queen stormed as she paced back and forth in her room.
After the shock of finding herself under sentence of death,
she'd reorganized her hopes around the promised last-
minute rescue. "If only my father were here! He'd gallop
up in his chariot and take me away from this awful place.
We'd go where the damned Great King couldn't touch us.
We'd go to Assyria! Oh, Naheshi! When Abishu carries me
off, that's where we'll go. I do hope everything comes off
well. It's so hard not knowing when he will actually step
in. There's such danger for him. Could you get us back to
Assyria, do you think? Shalim-ahum would take us in."

*How can she even think of fleeing to that monster's
protection?* Naheshi asked himself with a stab of pain. She
had no care at all for what he'd suffered under the diplomat's
roof. She really didn't love him. He was just her dog, whose
loyalty was taken for granted. Once, that realization had
made him hate her, but he couldn't hate her any longer—

not when he saw her in her little red shoes. Not when she touched him with the unthinking innocence of a child.

Naheshi felt paralyzed. He could neither speak nor even move without an enormous effort. Guilt enveloped him like a great blanket of wool, clogging his nose and his throat and weighing down his hands. Poor Taddu was asking him to help her escape, little dreaming that it was he who had brought this ghastly fate upon her. *No, no. This wasn't what I wanted at all. I need to find a real way to get her to safety.*

To go crawling back to Shalim-ahum and beg for help, though? Naheshi wasn't sure he could do it. He would probably just collapse and die of shame right on his old master's doorstep. But then, he would have said the same about Agipsharri only a few days earlier, and after all, it hadn't been so awful. Naheshi had completely changed his mind about the old eunuch, in fact. *I'm like a cheap penknife that doesn't hold an edge; I can't even hate people consistently.* Would he be able to humble himself to Shalim-ahum to save Taddu's life? He'd already sacrificed all his little dignity on her altar. But he remembered that there would probably be no real rescue, unless Abdi-sharrumma were extraordinarily lucky.

No, he needed to come up with a plan himself. But he couldn't think; he couldn't make his mind work.

The kindly, maternal image of the Great Lady came into his head. "Should we perhaps tell your mother about the prince's rescue plan so she can stop worrying herself sick?" he suggested. That would at least buy a few days' peace of mind for Gasshulawiya.

Taddu bit her lip pensively. "What do you think,

Naheshi? It seems to me that the fewer people who know about this, the better."

"But it would relieve her mind to—"

"No, don't tell her. I forbid you. Let her be surprised like everyone else."

How like me to want to make someone feel better with a lie, only to have the terrible truth fall on them at the end. His impulse to lie was cowardly, but he could hardly bear to see his Great Lady in such pain. He felt that if he could just leave the truth unsaid long enough, someone might come along and change things. Maybe there really would be a rescue. He could almost make himself believe it. Yes, it could happen.

"One more thing, my lady. It's none of my business, but… if the Lord Abdi-sharrumma carries you away en route… what happens to your son?"

Taddu froze for a moment then laughed brightly. "He'll be safe here with my brother. Mama will see to it nothing happens to him. I'll get him back somehow, and little Utrishu will become crown prince of wherever we find ourselves."

No, he won't, thought Naheshi with a leaden heart. *Abdi-sharrumma will make sure that his own flesh and blood gets any throne he leaves. Utrishu will be the dangerous elder half brother pushed out of the line of succession until someone gets the idea to kill him. More blood on my hands.* But then there would be no children of Abdi-sharrumma and Taddu, would there? Any children the prince did have were somewhere in Alashiya with his wife, no doubt. A man his age was almost certainly married.

The last day of their stay in Amurru dragged on endlessly.

Although Taddu had only the few garments Ahat-milki had permitted her to take away with her, Naheshi saw to it that they were packed up tightly in a waterproof roll of thin leather. He'd left almost all his own things behind in his apartment. *Has someone else had taken it over by now? Who has my laboriously copied music texts?* He wondered wistfully if Anani had gone off to Ili-milku's house or if he might still be around. What a sweet relief it would be to leave himself in his slave's capable hands again. He didn't feel very well. Far too late, it occurred to him that he should have freed the man.

On the morning of their departure, the young king and the queen mother came to the apartment to say farewell in private. The dock at the harbor would be all about official public façades, but here, with no one to observe them, they fell on Taddu's neck and wept.

Shaushga-muwa sobbed, "I can't do anything to stop it. I can't do anything, little sister. I can't go against the Great King now that he has taken sides. Forgive me."

The Great Lady tried to be strong for her daughter's sake, holding back her tears, but she clasped the younger woman to her bosom and held her there as if Motu himself should not tear her loose. When she drew back, her face had aged ten years. "Meet death like a queen and like a daughter of Amurru, my child. Utrishushu will be safe with us. We'll tell him that you loved him."

"Yes, Mama," Taddu replied dutifully. She managed to look serious, if rather less distraught than someone facing execution might be expected to. The soldiers—her brother's guards—arrived, and they marched the two off to the gate of the palace.

"Stay with her, Naheshi," called the queen. "Don't let her die alone."

He longed to reassure her that all would be well, but his mistress had forbidden that, and he knew what was coming anyway. All would *not* be well. Not ever again.

At the harbor, the autumn wind was blowing unseasonably frigid and damp, now and again gusting sheets of rain. The sun had not even risen. The cold blew up under Naheshi's tunic, despite the shawl he'd wrapped around his hips and over his shoulders and the heavy cloak over that. His thin, bare ankles were freezing. It was almost as late in the year as a ship would dare to sail, with the storms already lashing the coast. *What if we are shipwrecked? Such perfect irony. Dead before we ever reach the rendezvous that is to save us from death but which isn't really going to happen.*

To see the ship off, the king and his mother stood blank-faced on the quay, as if they were part of its stone, only their skirts whipping in the wind. *What a hard lesson for young Shaushga-muwa,* Naheshi thought, swallowing with difficulty. *I watched this boy grow up alongside Taddu. Welcome to the life of a vassal, my prince.*

Taddu waved back, forcing herself to look serious, but as soon as the ship leaned out through the mouth of the harbor, she began to grin and dance around. The viceroy was in his cabin, and if the soldiers or sailors noticed anything strange about her, they said nothing. Everyone's eyes, in fact, remained discreetly averted from the condemned and her servant.

The west wind hit the ship broadside as it turned north, filling the sail with an explosive crack, and the vessel started to roll on the dark waves. Naheshi fell on the slick deck and, before he could even get to his feet, was throwing up his breakfast and then dry heaving until his sides ached. The queen retreated to the little shelter that had been erected to give her some privacy as the lone woman on board. Eventually, Naheshi, emptied out and longing to lie down, crawled in after her. He was wet and shivering.

"Ah, you found me," she said. "Oh, Naheshi, I can't wait; I can't wait! But I'm afraid it will be quite dark by the time we reach Maradu. I heard someone say the trip northward takes a whole day even without a headwind. What if the boat has to put in somewhere in another port to wait for better weather and we miss each other?" She seemed to notice his green face for the first time then eyed him up and down. "Gods, look at you. Every time I see you, you're covered in vomit. Go outside, will you? You smell."

He struggled to throw off his befouled shawl and kicked it out from under the tent cloth then collapsed on his back, repressing a moan.

The queen shrugged. "You're such a landlubber. I guess the sea is in my blood."

Mercifully, the rain stopped by midafternoon, and the storm wind slackened a little. The sailors were able to let out more sail, and the ship made better time. The weak rays of Shapshu even shone briefly through the flying clouds. One of the viceroy's soldiers brought them bread and cheese for a late lunch, but Naheshi couldn't look at it. He was almost grateful to be so nauseated. It kept him from having to think about the leagues of black water swarming with monsters beneath the little wooden cockleshell that held them.

The sun had set by the time the captain turned the ship into the mouth of Maradu harbor, guided only by the fitfully visible stars and the lights of the city on its nearby hill.

Here we go. Naheshi's whole body ached from his fall on the deck and from the cold. *Here we go. "One Who Loves Her" should be around here somewhere, waiting to make his daring rescue. I wonder if he plans to take me along. Perhaps the queen will say, "You must take him, too, my love, or I won't go! I can't even remember when dear Naheshi hasn't been part of my life!" Or perhaps she will just run into the prince's arms and forget all about me. And maybe that would be better.* But no doubt the king's troops had already caught the man, and none of that would happen.

Yet if it did by some miracle? The gods alone knew where the renegade prince and his lover would be able to go and who would risk taking them in—maybe the king of Alashiya. Which meant another sea voyage, Yammu help them. Naheshi longed for nothing grander than a comfortable little job as a scribe at the palace, his cozy apartment, the friendship of Ili-milku, and Anani setting out his dinner and offering him homespun wisdom.

The viceroy and his soldiers gathered on the deck as the sailors heaved the big stone anchors into the water, one after another, and made the ship fast. There were men on the quay with torches, but nothing could be seen of their faces, and everyone was dressed in heavy, dark cloaks. Taddu craned her neck, trying to glimpse the face of her prince. The gangplank was run out, and Ini-tesshub took the queen's hand and helped her to shore. Naheshi stumbled along as best he could, still wobbly on his feet, carrying her parcels. The men with torches turned out to be soldiers and servants of Ammishtamru. They surrounded the party, speaking to the viceroy, and all together they moved up the quay to where horses could be heard, stamping and blowing and jangling their harnesses.

Taddu still scanned the crowd for any sign of her rescuers, but her face was taking on a pinched and anxious look. "You're taller, Naheshi. Try to see if they're around," she whispered.

There were people all over the docks, to be sure, but they seemed to be sailors or longshoremen. A few ships had lanterns lit on board—probably they were guarded—but for the most part, it was extraordinarily dark at the water's edge. Farther away, the rain-slick streets of the port town were still full of people coming and going, far busier than the city itself at that hour. At the palace, everyone was probably sitting down to dinner, the day's work ended. Suddenly, Naheshi's stomach remembered that it had been deprived of two meals that day.

"I don't know, my lady. Everyone looks the same in the dark." *There will be no rescue,* he wanted to tell her. But it seemed cruel to dispossess her of hope.

The guards hustled them along to the waiting chariots. One of the soldiers made a step of his hands for Taddu to mount behind the driver, and Naheshi climbed in as best he could and sat at the back, braced against the struts, his filthy shawl trailing. It was an uphill drive to the city. He could imagine himself rolling out and being left behind on the road.

Naheshi could see Taddu's growing anxiety even by the tension in her back. The queen had to be asking herself where the rescuers were. The chariots rattled into movement with a whistle and a crack of whips. The horses clopped and blew. The viceroy's vehicle led the way through the narrow streets, surrounded by soldiers on foot, their spears glittering in the light of the torches they carried. The oily flames guttered in the rain, making macabre shadows dance across the walls.

Where was it that the conspirators had met around here, weeks before? Perhaps they would come pouring out of the door any minute and overwhelm the guards. Naheshi wanted to think that the prince had somehow detected the presence of a trap and changed his plans; perhaps there really would be a rescue.

But they clattered up the road to the capital without incident. They passed the guard post outside the Royal Gate, and no one was there but soldiers of the king. They turned sharply right into the massive royal gateway and shouted signs and countersigns. The four great sets of doors were thrown open one by one then slammed and barred behind Naheshi, Taddu, and the guards as they passed under the tower that guarded the western entrance to the city. At each echoing clang of hardware, the chances of a rescue fell away. Finally, they clopped across the plaza and drew to a halt.

Naheshi rolled out of the chariot box and helped his mistress down. Even in the dark, he could see the growing panic on her face. Soldiers hustled them into the palace, and the last hope died.

It occurred to him—only now—that it had been within his power to alert Abdi-sharrumma to the ambush. He could have changed Taddu's fate even after he'd seen the queen mother. But he had been too cowardly, too slow thinking, and too bent on taking revenge on the prince. He'd wanted to dream up a rescue himself, to be his mistress's hero… but instead, he was her executioner. The realization of this added guilt hung like a stone anchor around his neck, crushing his heart, bowing his meager shoulders.

The main entrance to the palace was magnificent, even in torchlight. The two columns that marked the porch rose up from their carved stone *karubuma*, those sphinxlike royal man-beasts with their smooth, sexless faces. Not the king but Takhulinu met them in the columned porch, his thickset shadow wavering in the light of the flames.

He bowed respectfully to the woman who had been his queen, but his words were firm.

"My lady will be spared sequestration in the guard house overnight. An empty apartment has been set aside in the residential section of the palace." He eyed Naheshi hovering in Taddu's wake. "Who are you, eunuch?"

"I am my lady's chamberlain."

"Very well. You may remain with her if she desires. Food will be brought to you tonight. In the morning… the king's justice will be done. May the Lord Motu receive you gently, my lady." He bowed slightly and faded back into the darkness.

The guards escorted Taddu through the throne room and up the king's private stairs, Naheshi trailing along. The queen had not been bound in any way, but the four stalwart soldiers blocked her in—she could hardly have made a dash for it. In fact, she was subdued and stunned. She hadn't reacted to Takhulinu's words at all, and Naheshi wondered if she'd even heard. Her eyes kept cutting around as if she were still watching for her rescuer. Pity wrung Naheshi's heart. No doubt, she was wondering if Abdi-sharrumma had been prevented from enacting his plan or had been caught… or had simply run away. She would never have guessed that the whole thing had been a cruel trick.

In a few hours, any such speculations would be supremely unimportant, and she would be dead.

The clatter of soldierly footsteps echoed down the empty corridor. The chancery was vacant at that time of night. They passed the queen's apartments, which had once been Taddu's and now, no doubt, were occupied by Lady Pizidku. No light shone under the door. They passed the rooms of the other royal women. They entered the staff quarters, and Naheshi saw with a hollow smile that, by some superb divine irony, his own apartment was to be their prison.

One of the guards unbarred the door. The few pieces of furniture remaining had all been stacked against the wall. The window to the balcony was nailed shut, and Naheshi assumed the door to the roof had been as well. His personal belongings were gone, including his beloved tablets. The little salon looked cold and grim by torchlight, somehow more forlorn than a stone cell in the guardhouse.

"We'll bring you food. There are some blankets in the other room if you want to sleep," said the guard.

And the soldiers withdrew, taking their torches and the only light with them. The door thudded shut. Naheshi heard an exterior bolt being shot—that was new—and the queen and he were alone in the darkness.

The moment of dreadful silence was broken at last by a smothered sob.

"My lady," cried Naheshi, tears stinging his eyelids. "Where are you? Here is my hand." He groped around like a blind man, and the queen caught his good hand in a trembling grip.

"Oh, Naheshi, it's really going to happen. I'm going to die!" Taddu's voice quivered. She felt her way up his arm and clung to him.

He could feel silent sobs racking her little body, and his own tears began to flow. "Be brave, my sweet lady. Face it like the queen you are."

"Where is Abishu, Naheshi? Why didn't he come?" Her voice rose in a frightened wail, the uncomprehending cry of an abandoned child.

He eased her to the floor and sat awkwardly beside her without withdrawing his hand. "There could be many reasons, my lady. It's the will of the gods."

How empty those words sounded—yet it was true that the gods ruled everything. Did the stupid choices of human beings count for nothing, then? Would all this still be happening if he had not betrayed her? Did that relieve him of his guilt? As much as he would have liked to believe it, the icy lump in his heart warned him that his culpability was real. He felt it was his own death that was coming with the dawn. Such shame was unsurvivable.

Taddu sniffed. "Did they catch him, do you think? I can't bear the thought of them torturing him. Ammi will do awful things to him. I've never seen him so mad."

"I... I don't know, my lady."

"Maybe Abishu escaped and will come back for me. Yes! I'll bet that's what happened." Her voice grew bright with hope.

Naheshi hated the ice crystals forming in his heart. How had he never known he was such a dreadful, jealous person? Defective to the last. But he forced himself to sound happy. He *was* happy; his beloved Taddu was clinging to his arm. He could feel the warmth of her hip against his own and her face against his shoulder. He could hear her snuffling up the tears as she grew more hopeful. He wanted to melt in that primal happiness her touch had ignited in him before, but his guilt lay between them like a block of ice. The awareness of his iniquity was a physical pain in his chest that made swallowing hard.

"No doubt, my lady."

"Perhaps he'll come at the very last moment and snatch me right out from under Ammi's nose. Wouldn't that be exciting? Won't the Old Dragon be shocked?" Taddu's voice sparkled with brittle hope.

Naheshi supposed such a rescue was possible, but he didn't have much expectation of it. He could imagine it, though. They would certainly leave him behind; Prince Abdi-sharrumma had only just tolerated his presence all along. The silence stretched out while each of them envisioned the unfolding of the future.

At last, the queen murmured, "Naheshi, how long have I known you?"

"All your life, my lady. I was your mother's secretary when you were born. I had just come to Amurru." *You are all my life, too,* he thought. *Before you, I was dead. You are my life. Oh, what have I done, dear gods, dear gods? What have I done?*

A desperate, visceral need to confess his betrayal overwhelmed him. Either she forgave him and lifted the curse from his soul—or she hated him, and that would be the capital punishment he deserved. This was the moment the gods had given him. This was the hour of his judgment. He might never have another.

He took his tiny store of courage in both hands. "My lady, I... I have something terrible to admit to you..." he began in a tremulous voice.

"I know, Naheshi. Everybody knows. They all laugh about it."

His heart stopped. *Dear gods!*

The queen chuckled a little, almost apologetically. "You're in love with me, aren't you?"

Naheshi was taken aback and found his courage evaporating. He could not tell her now what he'd meant to say: *It was I who spied on you and turned you in. It is I who have brought you to this.* He began to shake with suppressed sobs. He couldn't tell her. She trusted him. She knew he loved her. Better to be a laughingstock than the object of her hatred. How could he tell her that, out of fear for his worthless hide, he'd sold her out again and again? He was far, far worse than his father.

"Oh, my dearest lady..." he managed to say, gnawing his lip.

She squeezed his hand. "I haven't been very nice to you sometimes, poor old Naheshi. You've always done your best for me. I know Mama thought you'd keep me out of trouble. If only they had married me to somebody else but Ammi. It was just so boring. He never really loved me. Can you imagine that? A man has a beautiful young wife, and he prefers an old fat cow. How's a girl supposed to put up with that? He just wanted children. It was all about him. Of course I fell in love with Abishu. What did they expect?"

Naheshi was scarcely listening, his heart pulverized under the weight of his own cowardice.

"Naheshi, could you write a letter to the Great King for me? No one has told him my side; he's only heard what Ammi has said."

He could hear that bright determination in her voice that he knew so well. She still refused to believe this was the end. "Of... of course, my lady," he choked. *It won't go anywhere, though. They won't let you send a letter. You'll be dead by the time it reaches the Great King anyway.*

"Ah, but there's no light. What do we do then, do you think? We need a plan."

"My lady, I... I have something to tell you..." He tried again to confess, propelled by a pain as inexorable as death. "I... I... it was I who... that is, all this is..." He was shaking so hard with weeping that he could hardly speak. And he was afraid to speak, because it could mean the end of everything for him. If she hated him...

"Out with it, Naheshi. You always do this. Do you have a plan? Spit it out."

"I... I have a friend who did something terrible, my lady. He... he betrayed someone he loved. He—"

"Oh, Naheshi, for the love of the Lady Shaushga. Is this the moment?" Her voice rose in irritation. "We need to get out of here, and here you are talking about some friend's woes. Think of a way to escape, will you? For a person who's so overeducated, you're not very smart sometimes." She threw down his hand and drew away from him a little, leaving him weeping silently, festering in his unconfessed guilt.

Soon, Naheshi heard a small hiccupping sound, and the queen's hand groped along his arm again. He turned to her, although he could see nothing, and folded the hand in his.

"My lady?"

"I can't think of anything," she whimpered. "Maybe this *is* the end. Maybe Abishu won't come. Maybe I'll... I'll die after all."

She clung to him, weeping quietly, and Naheshi, his heart bursting, wrapped his other arm about her heaving shoulders. He held her to his chest, hardly breathing, letting the tears trickle down his neck unwiped.

"I don't want to die, Naheshi," she whispered after a while, her voice that of a small, frightened girl. "People shouldn't have to die this young."

"No, my lady."

"What is death like, do you think?"

He felt that if his dying life had been a rehearsal, death itself had to be unspeakably awful—loss after loss. Aloud, he repeated the comforting verities he had learned as a child. "They say that for kings and royalty, it is a pleasant meadow with all their ancestors around. Your father will be there waiting, my lady. It will be a joyful reunion." *For the rest of mankind, though, the prospect is dreary,* he thought dully. *We won't even know who we are.* That was not such a displeasing proposition in his own case.

"I'll see Papa again?"

"Yes, my lady, and you can go hunting together, and...

and he can dress up like a lion to scare you—" Naheshi felt his voice break and slide.

"But Mama is still alive…"

"Someday, she'll join you, and the dead have no sense of time, so it will be as if in a moment, as if she had stepped into another room and returned. And my lady's brother and sisters, and her children."

"My children," she murmured sadly. "And Abishu?"

"Of course, my lady. He is a prince."

"Will you be there with me, dear Naheshi, as you have always been?"

"Probably not, my lady. Although who knows?"

But she wanted him; she wanted him. The tears came out of him in a kind of howl, but it was not wholly sorrow. It struck him that in a cursed life like his, such a moment might rank among his happiest.

Naheshi could not have said whether the queen had slept at all that night, only that dawn seemed to arrive on the swift wings of the falcon. He could hardly stand up when the guards came to get Taddu. He'd sat unmoving for all those hours while she'd clung to him, perhaps awake, perhaps asleep. He himself had never closed his eyes. His thoughts were both sweet and dark. He prayed with all his might that he had received his longed-for absolution from her, oblique though it was. How could he know? Without her forgiveness, his life was as surely over as her own.

The prince's rescue had not taken place, of course. This turn of events hardly surprised Naheshi, but he was sorrowful on behalf of his mistress. There was no crueler torment than hopes raised and then dashed. How well he knew that. Taddu met the day puffy eyed and bedraggled. He tried to comb her hair a little with his fingers and arrange her clothing. The seriousness of her plight was sinking in. By the light of the soldiers' torches, he could see that the queen's calm was very fragile. Her breaths were shallow, her glance uneasy.

He encouraged her in a faltering whisper. "My lady comes from a long line of warriors. Be brave. Think of your father."

She clung to him with round eyes for a moment, fear dancing across her features, then turned to face the guards. In a silent gesture that was almost priestly, one of them extended a rope to bind her wrists. She held them out hesitantly then suddenly changed her mind, slapped down his hands, and made a desperate dash for the door.

The room erupted into chaos. Two of the guards blocked her, grabbing for her arms. She shrieked, "No! No! I don't want to die! It isn't fair!" Two others converged on her, twisting her elbows back and dragging her off her feet while they tied the rope. She howled and kicked backward at their shins until they too were yelling and cursing. The torches guttered and jigged as their bearers tried to keep their balance in the fray. Someone knocked a table off the stack in the corner, and it fell top downward on the tiles with a heavy clatter. There were grunts and curses.

"Naheshi, help me! Don't let them take me!" the queen screamed. Naheshi shrank away, his hands over his mouth, too horrified to speak, her cries echoing inside the emptiness of his heart. But then he reached out toward her as if his ineffectual gesture might save her. He felt as if he were a ghost whose touch could not be felt by the living, as if he were watching her through a curtain. He felt as if his limbs could scarcely move, as if every action were weighted, as if he were underwater... as if he were extending his hand to her from another world.

By that time, the soldiers had carried her beyond his reach. Naheshi continued to huddle there with one hand out, struck to stone in his helplessness. Taddu was writhing so violently that they dropped her facedown on the floor. She cried out in pain but scrambled to her feet and lurched through the door, her cap and veil falling off, her braids lashing back and forth as she dodged. The guards converged on her and tripped her up, and she fell to the floor, but with her hands behind her back, she clutched at the doorframe, kicking out at anyone who approached her.

They pried her fingers loose and bound her ankles then picked her up and carried her into the corridor by her shoulders and feet as if she were a carpet. Their captain settled his helmet back on his head with a surly expression on his face. "Walk if you want to, my lady. Otherwise, we'll just carry you. But you will come with us, see."

"Take your hands off me, you savages." Then she screamed, "I'm a king's daughter, damn it! I've been tricked! This isn't fair! I've been tricked! Unhand me! Naheshi, help! Help me!"

She was writhing like an eel as they wrestled her down the empty corridor, sending maniacal shadows flittering around the torchlit walls. Her tearful screams echoed from the high-beamed ceiling: "Please! No! No! Please! Nooo!"

Naheshi, his heart pounding, snatched up her fallen veil and pressed it to his lips, as much to stifle his sobs as anything. He was in turmoil, his stomach as painfully knotted as the ropes around his mistress's wrists. She did not forgive him. She was not reconciled to her fate. She didn't want to die. She was rebuking him, accusing him, hating him, even without knowing it. Yes, she had been tricked... by him. She was cursing him. He inhaled the perfume of her hair from the veil with a shuddering breath and begged the gods to let him drop dead on the spot. The self-loathing was more than he could bear.

"You can come if you want," the torch-bearing captain called out behind him. "The whole royal household will be there, and the council."

Naheshi trailed after the undignified little procession, unsteady on his feet, lightheaded and ill from sleeplessness and lack of food, too weak to support the grief that clawed at his heart. If he tried to save her, they would beat him to porridge at the first movement. But she kept calling his name as if he could do something. He *had* done something—he'd betrayed her.

The accusation pounded in his temples like a pulse. *She doesn't forgive me. It is I she is cursing.*

Every shriek was a blade in his flesh.

At the bottom of the stairs, while the soldiers made a second effort to secure their raging prisoner, Naheshi stumbled into the court of the royal dead. It was already filled with people. The ruling family, at least all but the smaller children, sat along the porch at the right. The slaves and employees of the household stood at the opposite end of the courtyard, while the *maryannuma* lords and the council were ranged along the side walls. In the center, a wooden platform had been constructed with a tree stump perhaps a cubit tall set up in the middle of it. Naheshi joined the ranks of the servants, where he propped his back against the wall, the veil balled in his trembling hands. Standing tall above the crowd were the eunuchs of the chancery and old Agipsharri, who looked somber and sneerless for once. Somewhere in the chancery ranks, Ili-milku would be standing, but he was too short to make out in the half-light of dawn. It was darker than normal because of the clouds, although no rain was falling. Lit torches flared along the walls.

Up on the porch, between its columns, sat the king in his white high-priestly robes and tall tasseled cap—not the cuckolded husband but lord of life and death, the voice of the gods on earth. The queen mother sat at his right, a shriveled little mummy of a woman stooping under the weight of her great Egyptian wig. She stared straight ahead. Pizidku was seated at the king's left, her veil drawn across her mouth and her eyes closed. Next to her stood her son Prince Ibi-ranu, young and proud, his gaze cutting back and forth like a hawk's.

Which of you bears the guilt for this? Which of you finally spoke those words: "Let her die"? Does it torture you as it tortures me, or is it just one more atrocity in the name of the security of the kingdom? To his surprise, he didn't see Ini-tesshub or his Hittite officials around.

Pipes and drums sounded. Naheshi pulled himself out of his reverie. He heard a disturbance approaching from within the palace. The four soldiers and their officer appeared in a block, Taddu—on her feet now—hurried along willy-nilly within the fortress of their armored bodies. Her shoulders were heaving with exhaustion, her eyes were wild, her clothing disarranged. A trickle of blood leaked from her nose.

A gigantic soldier, tall and thick, had stepped up onto the platform, holding in his massive hands a sword as long as a half-grown boy. The crowd, which had been sober and quiet, grew absolutely still. The king pronounced a prayer to Shapshu and Tsaduk, god of justice.

Two of the guards hustled the queen up onto the platform, where she swayed for a moment between them, facing the royal family. Her hands were bound before her, her eyes crazed with terror, the kohl running in sooty smears down her cheeks. She sobbed and pleaded, fingers clasped, straining forward in her bonds. "Help me, Auntie! Please, please; I'm your brother's child! Pizidku, help me! Ammi, you can't do this to me! I'm your wife! I'm the mother of your children! Tell them to stop, please, please!" The royal party returned her stare expressionlessly, except for Queen Pizidku, who never raised her gaze.

Naheshi hung upon his mistress with his eyes, begging her to cry out, "I forgive everyone who did this." But instead, King Ammishtamru gestured to one of the soldiers, and the man bound a gag around the queen's mouth, struggling to tie it as she tossed her head to and fro. Silenced, she seemed to grow tiny in the presence of those bronze-clad men, like a little trapped bird. She looked around jerkily, seeking someone. Was it Prince Abdi-sharrumma—or was it her Naheshi?

I am here, my lady. Oh forgive me, won't you? Please, please forgive me...

The soldiers pushed her down on her knees in front of the stump, drawing her hands out before her, compelling her to embrace the block. She bucked and twisted, trying to resist, her muffled screams resounding, until someone pulled her braids over her shoulders and nailed the ends of them to the platform above her head, forcing her facedown upon the stump. Naheshi remembered the fine curling hairs that made a point at the back of her neck and the warm, sweet perfume that rose up from her body.

The king stood again and made a little speech about how all those, bar none, who sought to harm the sovereign and the kingdom would be struck down by the justice of the gods. A listener who knew no more than what Ammishtamru himself had told him would never have realized that this woman had betrayed her husband with his brother.

And then, just before the headsman did his work, a second prisoner came up to the door, surrounded by soldiers, his face bruised and hopeless, his dull gaze watching the slow rise of the sword. *Prince Abdi-sharrumma.*

But Naheshi had eyes only for Taddu. She hadn't seen her prince. Beneath the gag, her high-pitched voice rose in terror and outrage. Her shoulders hunched and jerked convulsively. In desperation, her brow beat against the wooden stump, but her hair held her fast. The sword reached its apogee and started down. Time seemed to slow. The blade fell at the pace of a sunset. Naheshi's eyes were frozen to the sight in spite of himself. He struggled to breathe.

The sword struck. With a sound like that of a splitting melon, the queen's head dropped from her shoulders, her cries abruptly silenced. Her body fell to the boards, flailing about in a gruesome parody of joyous dance, the blood spurting rhythmically from her neck.

There were gasps from the crowd. Somewhere, a woman gave a wail, and then it was stifled. A few servants pressed their hands to their mouths to muffle their cries, but in general, an uneasy hush reigned. It was not every day a queen was put to death. The *maryannuma* whose family members had participated in the rebellion had to be thinking long thoughts.

Naheshi watched the red blood spouting and the headless body going slack and sagging awkwardly sideways with arms still caught around the stump. The blood gradually slowed. Mercifully, the queen's head was facing the other direction, pinned to the platform by its braids, but the bloody neck was visible, with its concentric rings of muscle and bone. Pizidku hid her face in the crook of her arm. Naheshi's stomach contorted, and he retched, but nothing came out. He was shaking, making strange sounds. He managed to raise his trembling hands to his face as if he could press the hideous vision back into his eyes and make it never to have happened.

Forgive me, my lady; oh, forgive me, forgive me.

At the other end of the court, Abdi-sharrumma was being led to the steps of the platform, but Naheshi was barely conscious of what was going on around him. He was frozen in that hellish moment when the sword had descended upon the fragile neck of his mistress, the sight reliving itself endlessly behind his eyelids. He felt himself getting light-headed and leaned over, still clutching his face. Pain racked his whole body, and anguish twisted his heart. She was dead. The gods had taken her from him. She would go to her royal paradise, and he would never see her again, neither here nor hereafter. Her perfect little body would be thrown to the dogs. She was dead—unforgiving—and he had killed her.

He fell to his knees. No one looked at him; their eyes were fixed on the execution of the prince. They did not notice that someone else was dying before their eyes, that a slave had crumpled to the ground, clutching a piece of embroidered gauze, sobbing. Although he might get to his feet in a few minutes, his soul was already dead.

CHAPTER 23

NAHESHI WAS SWEPT FROM THE court at the end of the ceremony along with the rest of the servants, who trooped out in a somber cortege once the royal family and the *maryannuma* had departed. He wanted to be alone. He needed a place to spend the night, a place to sit and think—to plan, indeed, because he had plans to formulate. Yet he realized that he could no longer call the palace *home*. He could try to find Ili-milku—but no, it wasn't fair to burden that good man with the weight of Naheshi's filthy soul. Agipsharri? No. The chamberlain was on his own. Death had cut him out of the herd.

He wandered up the steps with the others out of sheer force of habit. Scribes were entering the chancery; the business of the palace needed to go on as usual. He lingered for a moment, hoping Ili-milku would happen along, but that was only self-indulgence.

He continued walking, staggering, clutching in his hands his mistress's veil. He was awkward at the best of times, but now he could hardly keep his long body upright. The walls seemed to tilt and the floor to rise up, beckoning him to lie down. He felt he was walking sideways like a fly. He passed the queen's apartments. Pizidku would be inside. She was kind; he didn't hold her responsible for any of this. In fact, he was tempted to knock on her door and collapse at her feet, hoping she would take him in. But he kept on. A few other servants were heading for their lodgings. He saw the door of his apartment ajar, as the soldiers had left it. On an impulse, he slid out the exterior bar and took it inside, and only then did he bolt the door behind him from within.

It was a mistake. This was no longer his cozy little nest but the bleak cell where he had passed the queen's last night on earth with her. It was light outside; still, the blocked windows to the balcony made it impossible to see much. He stumbled over the fallen table, and it rekindled his memories of the morning's struggle. He unshuttered the little window in the kitchen room so it wouldn't be pitch-black and pulled himself up the stairs, but the roof-terrace door was nailed shut, and he couldn't manage to wrench out the nails with his bandaged hand. Naheshi tried to unpile some of the furniture so he could sit down, but he only succeeded in dropping a stool on his foot, and he felt so weak that he could hardly drag the piece across the room.

After a few minutes, he was gasping for breath, and he ended up sitting on the floor on the pallet he'd spread for the queen the night before—only hours earlier. It felt like another age. He slumped to the ground, his back against the wall, and raised the veil to his face, breathing in the last fleeting breaths of her perfume ever to grace his life—his miserable, guilty, accursed life.

He tried to picture her as he had known her: full of

spirit with flashing eyes, quick movements, and swinging braids. He pictured her hands, no bigger than a child's, always in motion—touching his arm, pulling him down on the bed beside her, entwined in his hair. He tried to recall her high-pitched voice, which could be so seductive, cunning, and cajoling—outraged, even—and was always very much alive. But her hideous last moment wanted to come between his mind's eye and these sweet visions— the desperate struggle at the block, the falling head, the fountain of blood, the unnatural slump of the headless body. Suddenly, his stomach turned inside out, and he heaved up bile. He had no food inside to relinquish, but his belly hurt as if he'd been kicked. Why couldn't it have been he on the platform, his head rolling? What had he done? *Oh, sweet gods...*

⁂

A whole watch of the morning had passed. Naheshi had some serious planning to do, but he felt so unspeakably weary that he could scarcely keep his mind focused. Fear had left him. His life was over, and he had no good thing left to lose—and, therefore, nothing left to fear. He aimed at nothing less than redeeming his worthless life with a single honorable action. He would finally play the man—another pretense, to be sure, but dishonesty seemed to define him. He would exact revenge on whoever had tricked the queen into going to her death. Or was that himself? Perhaps he should be put to death. That would happen soon enough. But first, justice had to be done. He would never have betrayed Taddu by himself. Who had made him spy on the queen? Who could be said to be at the root of her death? King Ammishtamru? The Old Dragon?

Surely not the Great King; he was too far away.

Not Shaushga-muwa or the Great Lady. They'd played their parts but only out of helplessness, because they had no choice. He felt nothing but pity for them. He put them into his own category: that of the weak. The real instigator, he felt sure, was Ahat-milki. She'd always hated her niece, never missing a chance to cut and humiliate her. Ammishtamru had been content to divorce his wife, but someone had made him change his mind, and who could that have been but his mother?

Naheshi tried to picture himself driving a knife into the dried-up little body of the queen mother and realized he couldn't do it. She was too much like his Taddu in appearance, despite the forty years' difference in age. The fact that she was a woman was probably enough to make him helpless to harm her, at least directly. Women were too small. He wasn't strong, but he was so much bigger that it seemed heinous to attack a woman. Besides, most women had been relatively nice to him. Well, not the queen mother, but the Great Lady. And his own mother had loved him, he felt sure. How could he hurt the dowager without laying hands on her, though? Poison?

Then it occurred to him that he could complete the punishment the gods themselves had wreaked on her: deprive her of her last son. He would kill the king.

✦

Naheshi chided himself for being such a poor excuse for a plotter. He kept falling asleep right there on the floor of his old apartment, when he had such important plans to lay. Several more watches of the day had passed. He was mortally hungry on top of everything. No doubt, that could explain his sense of weakness, but there was nothing he could do about it. He was no longer an employee of the palace, so he could scarcely just wander down to the kitchen and ask for a meal. His clothes were disgustingly dirty. More than ever in his life, he was an outsider, and that was saying a lot. To whom did he even belong? His mistress was dead. Was he the Great Lady's property again? The king had been paying his wages. Was he the king's slave now?

That gave him an idea: he would seek an audience with the king to determine just that. He could request a job at the chancery. No one would think it was anything but perfectly normal. And then... what? He would spring at the king with a bared blade. Ammishtamru would be guarded, of course. Or not. Naheshi realized he had no idea. Even without guards, the king was a strong, muscular man, accustomed to wielding arms. How hard would it be for him to wrest a knife out of the would-be assassin's hand? The only thing Naheshi had ever done with a knife was to sharpen his stylus. He would be quite satisfied if the king killed him in a scuffle, but he didn't want to fail in his assassination. He supposed he needed to start by writing a letter to Lord Takhulinu, asking for an audience.

Naheshi pulled himself to his feet and tottered down the hall to the chancery. He knew a few of the scribes at work there. They looked up, nodded, but did not ask what he was doing among them. He sat down at the long table and pulled a damp tablet toward him. It took an extraordinary amount of effort to compose a simple letter; his head felt as if it were underwater. His handwriting was as lopsided as a drunk's, but at least it was legible. He decided he should take it in person to the vizier's office, and he had just pushed back his stool and headed for the door when Lord Urtenu entered. They almost collided.

"My lord! Forgive me." Naheshi bowed unsteadily.

"Oh, it's you, Nahish-shulmanu. I was just wondering how I might get in contact with you. Step outside a moment, won't you?"

He followed the queen mother's secretary into the corridor.

"See here, Nahish-shulmanu, the dowager queen wants to reward you for all you've done for the king lately, but nobody knew exactly where you were and if you were going back to Amurru or not."

Naheshi held out a shaky fist with his tablet. "Actually, my lord, I have right here in my hand a letter to Lord Takhulinu asking for an audience with the king. I thought perhaps there might be a place for me in the chancery. I speak and write three languages."

"A very reasonable request. I'm sure we can do something." He eyed Naheshi. "Are you sick? You're as white as whey."

"It… it was a difficult morning, my lord." Naheshi heard his voice crack and slide upward in spite of himself. He averted his eyes in the automatic reaction of shame. *Be brave. They can't hurt you now.*

The secretary blew out wearily through his lips, like a horse. "Yes, it was, wasn't it? I understand your attachment to the young queen must have made it very hard. And yet you did what was right. The kingdom is grateful to you,

Nahish-shulmanu. Well, give me that letter if you want to. I certainly have the king's ear. I'll see what I can do for you about a position."

"Thank you, my lord."

"Think nothing of it. Where can we find you?"

"I, uh, took the liberty of reoccupying my old apartment, which seemed to be empty. I could move out, find something in the city if you prefer—"

Lord Urtenu patted the air reassuringly. "No, no, you're fine. Are your things still there?"

"No, my lord. I don't know who got them."

"Well, let me look around. They're probably stuck in storage somewhere." Urtenu took the tablet.

"Thank you, my lord." Naheshi bowed, and the queen's secretary moved off on his way.

Could I drive a knife into his flesh? Naheshi tried to picture Urtenu writhing, crying out, and bleeding. *I don't think I could do it to anyone—probably not even to Agipsharri, at least not anymore.*

And yet justice had to be done. The gods would lend him a strength greater than his own. He had an unaccustomed sense of solidity, he realized, as if he could no longer so easily be uprooted or blown over. Even with an empty stomach, even exhausted, trembling, and dull eyed, he felt real, for once. He felt adult.

And his request was on its way to the king's ear.

⚜

That evening, darkness had fallen early as wet clouds rolled back in. Naheshi broke down and approached the kitchen for something to eat, and he stuffed down a quail with shaking hands, letting the juices and fat seep into his mouth. *Oh gods, the caramelized onions.* His jaws hurt at the smell of his fingers afterward. He felt he could start all over again if he dared go back for another. He reproached himself for his ravenous appetite when he had witnessed such horror that very morning, but it helped strengthen him. He'd become so weak that he'd been afraid for his mission. With his belly full, he felt sharper. He would do this. He would not fail.

He was cramming stuffed prunes into his mouth in the dark when someone knocked at the door.

"Who's there?" he called, swallowing with a gulp.

"A message from the king."

Naheshi unbolted the door and wiped his fingers on the hip of his tunic. A page stood outside, an envelope in his hand. Naheshi took it and tipped him. The clay was still damp. He broke open the end with his penknife and pulled out the tablet.

"To the eunuch Nahish-shulmanu, sometime chamberlain of the late queen. The king Ammishtamru son of Niqmepa requires your presence tomorrow morning at the second watch. Meet him at the dowager queen's palace." It was signed, "Takhulinu son of Sharri-haddu."

Thank you, all you gods! The first step of his redemption had been accomplished.

Sometime around midmorning Naheshi folded the queen's veil and slipped it inside his tunic, against his heart. He went and stood in the porch of the palace to observe the changing of the guard. He gazed sadly at the beautiful winged cherubim with their smooth eunuch faces.

They're monsters, yet they're messengers of the gods, as I will be, bringing divine justice. He could not reverse what had been done to his body, but he'd be a man despite all that. He would not fail. He would avenge his lady and redeem himself. He would no longer be the cringing dog life had made of him—he would be a man.

He crossed the royal plaza, passing the sewer entrance. What memories: that hellish underground tunnel, the white squares of moonlight, little Taddu, so brave and adventurous, whispering, "Quiet! There are guards up there!" He felt tears tingling under his lids and pressed himself forward.

Forgive me; forgive me, my dearest lady.

He drew up to the gate that separated the royal enclosure from the city. The guards on duty had never seen him, but he had the late queen's seals at his belt. They passed him through without actually examining his credentials and pointed him left up the narrow street toward the square that fronted the dowager's mansion. He wished he were cleaner and more respectably dressed. His apartment was so dark he could scarcely be sure his hair was properly combed, and he hadn't had a bath since he'd left Amurru. He was starting to smell like pee.

There was a guard at the door of the queen mother's residence, which otherwise had the appearance of any large noble house. He showed his letter and was ushered into the vestibule, where her female servant received him. As odd as it seemed, someone had once told him that the queen mother employed no eunuchs. Other soldiers stood about, a clear sign that the king was present.

"One moment, sir. I'll see if the king is ready to receive

you." She ran off up the stairs and a minute later returned. "Please follow me."

He hauled himself up the stairs in her wake. The staircase opened into the large and pleasant salon with its windows only along one side. The other side, he realized, abutted the city walls. The floor was strewn with carpets; the long table the old queen used as her desk was pushed against the wall between two windows. King Ammishtamru, splendid in a heavily embroidered tunic and a shawl of costly purple, was seated in a fine chair perpendicular to the windows, his mother in another. She seemed to have dwindled since the previous morning. Her back was straight, but the weight of her sorrows had begun to bow her thin neck. Her clothes hung nearly hollow. She barely looked at him as he entered, her painted eyes pits of darkness. Naheshi tried to hate her and found that he could not—quite the contrary; he felt sorry for her—but he still had to do what he had to do.

However, Lord Urtenu was present as well, and that was a complication indeed. Let them kill him if they would, but he could not afford to have anyone so able-bodied come between him and the king. Urtenu was oldish and rather small, but he looked quite hale, and he certainly had training in arms, like any *maryannu*.

I must not fail.

Naheshi bowed deeply, trying to overcome the hammering of his heart. He felt suddenly ill prepared and vulnerable. But he had nothing to lose. He would not fail.

The king spoke first, as was fitting. "Here, what's your name?"

"Nahish-shulmanu, my lord king."

"Nahish-shulmanu. My mother has told me of the role

you played in unraveling the conspiracy against my life and my kingdom over the last few months, sometimes at considerable risk to yourself, as I understand. That was very brave. We thank you." Ammishtamru leaned back in his chair, looking comfortable and satisfied with himself. His throne was secure.

"Thank you, my lord."

"You're an Assyrian, I understand?"

"Yes, my lord." The pounding of Naheshi's heart increased.

The king threw back his head and gave a rich, growly laugh. "Ha ha! What a black eye for Tukulti-ninurta! His plot foiled by one of his own! I guess you know your king is probably engaged in battle with Tudhaliya at this very moment?"

"No, my lord. I didn't. And *you* are my king, my lord."

Ammishtamru turned to the dowager queen triumphantly. "You see, Mother? These people are as loyal as dogs. I don't know why you have such a prejudice against them."

He seemed in rather high spirits, but his mother barely opened her lips to murmur in her deep, throaty voice, "To each his own."

"So what shall we do for you, Anen-shulmanu?"

Naheshi flinched at the botching of his name, but it meant nothing to him any longer.

"What kind of reward would you like? Gold? Land? I'm afraid I can't give you your balls back." The king chuckled at his joke.

No, but I can, Naheshi thought, letting the humiliation

wash over him. *I can be a man again... and you're making it easier.*

Lord Urtenu interposed in his quiet, reasonable way, "The late queen's chamberlain has expressed an interest in a position in the chancery, my lord." He turned to Naheshi. "I believe you said you were multilingual, Nahish-shulmanu?"

"Yes, my lord. I read, write, and speak Akkadian and Ugaritic, of course, but also Hurrian."

"It sounds as if he would be a welcome addition to our staff, my lord. If Lord Takhulinu agrees, naturally."

"And if not, you can make use of him in my lady mother's chancery." The king grinned at the old queen out of the corner of his eye, but her expression never changed.

There was a moment of awkward silence, then the dowager turned to Ammishtamru and said, still expressionless, "If you will excuse me, my son, it has been a difficult few days. Unless you have some particular need for my presence, I would ask your leave to return to my chambers."

"Of course, of course." The king watched her depart, his eyebrows furrowed a little in what might have been concern or annoyance.

Naheshi felt his hatred crumble completely away. He knew pain when he saw it. Yet he had to achieve his vindication. He had to. He could not die unforgiven. He realized his audience was probably drawing to an end, and he had not acted.

"If I could make one more request of my lord king..." he began meekly.

"Of course. If you'd like gold or something, too, just speak up."

"Simply to have my old apartment in the staff quarters back, my lord. At the moment, I have no place to live, and I took the liberty of spending the night there, but of course, someone else may have claimed it."

"Deal with it, Urtenu," instructed the king.

Ammishtamru rose from his chair and drifted over to the window, gazing out at the sky beyond the royal chapel, his arms folded across his chest as he leaned against the frame. The audience was clearly over. Naheshi was starting to breathe in a painful staccato; his throat was constricting. The moment was upon him. He bowed low, gently beginning to draw his penknife from its case at his waist, but his belly overhung it in that position. He rose and continued to move it silently upward, trying to think of something to say to keep the king talking. Meanwhile, no doubt assuming Naheshi was on his way out of the room, Urtenu had turned his back and moved between him and the king. *Damnation!*

The secretary was leaning against the table to the left of the window, looking at a gold jewel case there. His hand drifted quietly toward something on the tabletop. "My lord, do you see the smoke over there in the lower town? That couldn't be an attack, could it? Surely the conspirators have not regrouped so quickly?" Urtenu pointed toward the window.

The king craned his neck to see. Naheshi pulled his knife free and began to totter toward him, when all at once, to his astonishment, he saw Lord Urtenu, still at the table, raise a long dagger, the pommel of its golden hilt protruding from his fist. What was he doing?

Dear gods! Naheshi thought, panicked. *My very worst nightmare. He is going to stop me before I can reach the king.*

But Urtenu was facing the king.

The old man's head swiveled to look at Naheshi, who had hesitated. They locked eyes for an instant of mutual shock, and Naheshi quailed, the penknife dropping silently from his fingers onto the carpet. But then the secretary's expression of fear became one of comprehension. Urtenu made a little gesture of invitation toward the king's back. He laid the dagger softly down on the table, pushing it a bit toward Naheshi.

Ammishtamru, still looking back and forth through the window, growled, "Where, Urtenu? I don't see anything." He glanced briefly behind him at the queen's secretary, but neither Urtenu nor Naheshi held a weapon anymore. He turned again to the window, unperturbed.

The secretary backed away from Naheshi, keeping his eyes fixed on his, and made his little gesture again—a kind of sweep of his fingers, as if to say "after you"—and crossed behind the king to the next window. Still following the eunuch from the corner of his eye, he pointed toward the horizon, murmuring, "There, my lord. Perhaps it's more visible from this angle."

Naheshi realized Urtenu was trying to stay out of range in case the unexpected assassin was after him as well. This bizarre pantomime had to be just as unnerving for the secretary as it was for him. He felt increasingly off-balance. Was Urtenu going to intercept him or not?

But the king glanced over his shoulder again and saw Naheshi still hanging about. "That's all, eunuch; you can go now," he ordered, his voice gruff with irritation, and turning away once more, he strode after Urtenu toward the farther window. Naheshi heard him grumbling under his breath, "That damned woman. Is there no end to the trouble she's caused? I should have known better than to marry her. Her father was half-crazy, and so was she."

An icy flame ignited in Naheshi's breast; anger clashed like cymbals in his heart. No one could talk that way about his beloved lady—his perfect, beautiful lady. How dared Ammishtamru speak harshly of her? He had never loved her. He had never deserved her.

My sweet lady, I will avenge you. Only forgive me, I beg of you...

Naheshi's heart thundered in his ears so that he felt his pulse throughout his whole body: *boom-boom-boom-boom.* His fingers crept around the golden hilt of the dagger. It was solid, heavy, and already warm from Urtenu's hand. Its polished blade caught the light from the windows in a complicit wink. The knife was like a living thing within his fist. The *karubuma* carved upon it were the agents of the gods' will. He was just the messenger of their messengers, bringing divine justice. He could not fail.

Naheshi's eyes were fixed on the broad back of king, who was nearing the second window, where Urtenu stood. There was nothing else in the world but Naheshi's target. He lurched forward a few quick steps, the dagger raised. Suddenly, Ammishtamru turned. He saw the eunuch but did not yet register the knife, and his brows contracted with annoyance. He opened his mouth to say something, and Naheshi threw himself upon him, looming over him.

The king raised his hands, his eyes growing wide, but it was too late; he was taken completely off guard. From the height of his long arm, Naheshi brought the dagger down with all his considerable weight behind it. Urtenu watched from behind the king. He shrank back and made no move to intervene. A shock ran through Naheshi's fingers as the knife struck bone, slid, and plunged its long blade into the thick muscle of the king's chest, just to the left of the breastbone. Ammishtamru heaved a gasp, and his ringed hands clutched at Naheshi's arm, but already, his strength was waning. Naheshi staggered against the king, pressed momentarily to his bloody chest. He struggled not to fall on top of him as the latter lost his balance.

Naheshi let go of the dagger hilt and tore himself away, jumping back with a cry of terror and triumph. He could sense his hair standing on end, and felt he must be surrounded by a nimbus of light, like an image of the gods.

The king uttered a strangled grunt and sagged backward while Urtenu jumped forward to break his fall. Ammishtamru's eyes were wide with shock and outrage, his mouth open but unable to utter a word. Incredulous, he reached up to touch the blood soaking the breast of his tunic. Then his arm dropped. He stiffened a moment and grew limp, his head dropping forward. He was dead.

Urtenu lurched a little under the weight of his king, who was larger and heavier than himself. The secretary slowly lowered Ammishtamru's shoulders to the floor and straightened up, rearranging his shawl.

Silence enveloped the room for a long, awful space.

Naheshi stood panting, his teeth bared in a savage grin, tears prickling behind his lids. He was seized with a kind of exaltation. He'd done it! He'd done it!

Oh, my lady, he prayed, *I have avenged you. Now you will forgive me.*

He looked up to see Urtenu facing him, motionless, his eyes wide beneath their bushy brows, the slightest smile breaking the impassivity of his face. The golden hilt of the dagger was standing up from the king's chest, a dark stain spreading around it, dying the purple shawl with a yet more precious hue. Naheshi knelt, his vision blurred with tears, and pulled the blade out. The king did not move. There was no sign of the rising and falling of his ribs that would have proclaimed him alive. His mouth was still agape in the midst of his pointed red beard, his eyes still wide with surprise. The faithful dog had bitten his master, and no one had expected that.

You are a murderer, Naheshi told himself, as if even he were unable to believe it. *You have stabbed a man to death, a consecrated king, your master. But a life for a life: isn't that what the laws of gods and men demand? She is avenged. The queen mother is punished. I am redeemed.*

And part of him thought in shivering exhilaration, *I didn't fail.* And part of him looked up to gape through his tears at Urtenu, uncomprehending. The secretary was breathing a little hard, but he seemed quite calm. Their eyes met again.

"We must do what we have to, isn't it so?" Urtenu murmured in his melodious voice as if to excuse the future rather than to explain the past. Then he called loudly, "Guards! Guards! To me! Someone has murdered the king!"

Armed men came pouring into the room, the old queen behind them, her garments flying, like a goddess of vengeance.

Naheshi felt as if he were outside his own body and could picture exactly what they would see: the Lord Urtenu standing upright and, at his feet, the late queen's Assyrian eunuch chamberlain, crouched over the prone body of the king. A gold-hilted Alashiyite dagger in the eunuch's hand. Blood smearing his sleeve and the front of his clothing. His linen-white face streaked with tears but a grin stretching from dimple to dimple. A great continent of dark blood staining the king's broad chest. A gold jewel case, fallen to the floor, and another small knife lying a few cubits away.

"Seize him!" cried the dowager in a voice like a carrion bird. She fell to her knees beside the king, her last son, and strained to lift his shoulders. Urtenu squatted to assist her.

The guards grabbed Naheshi by the elbows and dragged him bodily to his feet, tearing the knife from his unresisting grasp. He felt dazed, trying to make sense of Urtenu's actions but still more overcome by the shock of his own success. They lashed his arms behind his back and stripped off his belt in case he carried any more weapons. The queen's veil slid to the floor.

"I did it so she—" he began, but one of the soldiers clouted him backhanded across the mouth. The pain and the metallic taste of blood on his tongue brought him back to his senses. He didn't even want to try to explain or to excuse himself. No. The justice of the gods had been done. He had avenged his beloved lady. Let them do with him as he deserved.

"You ungrateful piece of dog shit," spat the old queen, rising to her feet. She stood before him, not much taller than his waist, her voice the growl of a she-wolf ready to spring. "Have you creatures no human feelings? Why?

Why? He just expressed his willingness to give you nearly anything you wanted."

Naheshi smiled at her, almost apologetically, and said nothing. Urtenu's strange complicity confused him, but above all, he felt relief. *Relief!* It washed through him in a warm torrent, and all the muscles that had been clenched in anticipation finally relaxed, leaving him limp and tottering. He'd done it. The tears ran down his face in a cleansing flood, releasing him within and without from a lifetime of failure. He'd finally freed himself from shackles worse than servitude.

The queen was saying, "Did you see what happened, Urtenu?"

"I did, my lady."

She jerked her gaze, poisonous, back to Naheshi. "What have you to say for yourself, you disgusting capon?"

"I did it."

She turned away from him and knelt at her son's side again. Suddenly, she broke into a wail and began to rock back and forth over his chest. Urtenu gazed curiously at Naheshi as the soldiers dragged him, stumbling, away. And the old queen finally got her moment to mourn her children. Her keening followed Naheshi all the way to the door and out into the street.

CHAPTER 24

THE SOLDIERS LOCKED NAHESHI UP in a room in the guard post that overlooked the main entrance to the palace. Just a few tens of cubits away lay the royal chapel and the ritual banquet hall where the late king's family had celebrated their *marz'ikhu* in honor of the dead dynasts, among whom Ammishtamru now found himself. A tiny, high-placed window to the north let in such light and air as the room provided. Immediately next to the guard post was the double gate that separated the royal plaza from the city at large and, on the other side of that, the public entrance to the palace. He might as well have been on the far side of the Great Inland Desert.

They'd thrown him into the room without ceremony, not caring that he stumbled to the stone floor. His wrists weren't bound, so he supposed no one thought him very dangerous. His belt had been taken away, though, and his rings and his shoes. He sat on the floor in a strange state of calm. At last, the awful ordeal of his life was nearing an end. The room was cool and dark, but although he might have followed the passage of the hours by the movement of the sun across his north window, time seemed to have stood still. The stone walls devoured all sound, or maybe no one was about. An occasional faint voice or clatter of arms came from the guard post next door; once in a while, someone would yell something from across the plaza, but it seemed curiously dull and distant. *Perhaps it is I who am so far away. Perhaps I'm passing to the land of the dead already.*

In the afternoon, the obsequies for the deceased king were held in haste. Naheshi heard the traditional local melodies for the first time: the sweet, sad strains of men's voices, as deep as the throat of Motu. It had to be Ibi-ranu presiding, although he would not be consecrated formally until that evening. Naheshi claimed the prayers for himself. Even though he couldn't make out the words, their rich tones comforted him like a cut of fat, roasted meat. He felt both exhausted and lightened, like one who had wept so hard that he had no more tears to shed.

He'd done it. He had punished the dowager queen for her role in Taddu's death. He had avenged his mistress. Soon he, too, would be put to death, and justice would be accomplished all round. Calm satisfaction filled him. Men might not understand why he'd had to do this deed, but the gods would know. Shamash, lord of justice, would know. Scores were settled, and he, Nahish-shulmanu, had no more reason to live. He hardly even cared anymore why Urtenu had turned on his master; that was between Urtenu and the gods. Naheshi was the minister of their justice—that was all. Naheshi's life would be over in hours, and none of his failures would matter anymore.

At some point, a soldier unlocked the door and set a plate of congealing porridge and a mug of water inside.

He seemed neither angry nor vengeful. Did he not care that this prisoner had murdered his king? Naheshi didn't even crawl over to get it. He sat with his back against the wall, watching the square of sunlight travel slowly along the opposite side of the room. There was scarcely a thought in his head, just relief that it was all over. His responsibilities were about to cease. He hadn't felt this tranquil since childhood—or perhaps ever. No one expected anything of him, for once. He'd accomplished the one deed he was meant to achieve, so he could no longer fail.

The sun had passed out of sight, yet a little light still lingered when someone unlocked the door again, and a man entered. At first, Naheshi couldn't see who it was, but the voice made it clear, as did the brief glimmer of torchlight on a bald head before the door creaked shut.

"Nahish-shulmanu," Urtenu said in his matter-of-fact tone. From his shawl, he drew the queen's crumpled veil and tossed it to Naheshi. "I suppose all this is about the queen's death, isn't it?"

Urtenu paused, his back against the door as if to reassure himself that his life was not in danger. But Naheshi sat silently without moving, the veil on his lap, his untied hands limp at his sides, so the secretary came closer, looking around to assure himself that the guard had left.

"You seem remarkably calm for someone who will be disemboweled tomorrow, after having his nose and ears cut off."

"I did it," said Naheshi.

Urtenu made no response to this. Instead, he advanced and laid at the prisoner's feet a tiny stoppered bottle. "Your deed is advantageous for me, whatever your personal motive, and I wouldn't have you think I am ungrateful. This is a painless and quick-acting poison. I suggest you spare yourself the horrors of a state execution and die on your own terms."

Naheshi eyed the little vessel then smiled at his visitor. "Funny, no one's ever offered to let me *live* on my own terms."

"No, I suppose not. Well, use it or don't. Do you know what happened? Are you at all curious why I... took the action I did?" The secretary's eyes were piercing under their bushy brows.

Naheshi sat unmoving against the wall with his legs stretched out. He said nothing. What was there to say?

Lord Urtenu shrugged. "No? I see you're already beyond earthly curiosity. But I'll tell you anyway. Let's say it is my gesture of respect for you who are at the threshold of the gods.

"My family has lived in this city for a thousand years, Nahish-shulmanu. Our overlords have come and gone—Hatti now; before that, Mizri; before that, Mitanni—but our loyalty has always been with the welfare of Ugarit. I have children and grandchildren and, very soon, even great-grandchildren. This gives me a profound interest in seeing that what is right for Ugarit's future is done—not for Hatti's future, not for anyone else's, but for our own. So yes, I am relieved that our new young king Ibi-ranu will turn to the Assyrians for more advantageous treaty terms, something that Ammishtamru would never have done. Perhaps you can't understand that, but men with families need to think of the future."

He moved closer to Naheshi. "Would Heshmi-sharrumma have taken the same steps if his coup had succeeded? I don't know, so I never allowed myself to become involved with his machinations, although we all knew he was plotting even before you described the details of the plot. I did consider withholding your full revelation from the queen mother, by the way. The welfare of the kingdom clearly required the removal of Taduhepa, but I still wasn't sure about Prince Heshmi-sharrumma." Urtenu spread his hands with a shrug as if acknowledging that Naheshi might disagree with him.

"However, it was increasingly my opinion that he was a bitter man whose agenda was more about vindicating himself than about doing what was right for Ugarit. Perhaps you would know about that; I know you pretended to be part of his group for a while. That took courage, by the way. The kingdom is grateful."

He must have seen the thin, ironic smile that twitched across Naheshi's face, because he added quickly, "Yes, we are grateful. But the brave soldier's best gift to a grateful country is frequently his life, is that not so?"

"I didn't do it for the kingdom," said Naheshi, surprised to find himself answering a *maryannu* lord in this way yet pleased at his own boldness.

Urtenu eyed the eunuch, digesting his words, but he continued implacably as if this explanation were something he needed to complete for his own sake. "I don't know if you were present when the late king's younger brother was executed. That was a windfall from the gods. We sent the false note about a rescue mission to the young queen, as perhaps you have figured out by now, to assure that neither you nor her brother might try to free her before her extradition, and then someone suggested that the same sort of bait might draw out Prince Abdi-sharrumma. As it happened, he was still around, hoping ineffectually that Taduhepa might be saved. We found out where, thanks to another of your... colleagues in the Lady Pizidku's household, who seems to have been somehow involved in the plot but who betrayed his fellow conspirators in exchange for his pardon. The queen's call for rescue was more than the prince could resist. He was trapped and brought to justice. That knife on the queen mother's table, by the way, was his. So in a sense, his revolution succeeded."

Naheshi listened without moving as Urtenu heaved a sigh. *It was not the prince who killed the king,* the eunuch thought with satisfaction. *It was I, Nahish-shulmanu, whom everyone considered a spineless dog.*

"No doubt, I would never have resorted to violence on a personal level—after all, I am an old man—but the opportunity was too good to miss. And then when I turned and saw what you were prepared to do, it was a gift from the gods. I felt suddenly that we were collaborators, you and I, whatever your motive. You had already demonstrated your devotion to Ugarit, and although many people would not have seen it that way, this was simply the final act. I salute you for your courage, Nahish-shulmanu."

Naheshi could see the shine of Urtenu's eyes in the half darkness. *Courage? Nahish-shulmanu?* He had never thought to hear those words in the same breath. It was enough to have redressed one death with another, bravely done or not. That was all the laws of men and gods demanded. Taddu was avenged. She would forgive him now, surely. He had atoned for the crimes of his cowardice. He pictured her in the paradise of her royal family, raining absolution down upon him like a gentle dew. In the darkness, the corners of his mouth curled up.

"Well, I won't burden you with any more talk of this world, Nahish-shulmanu," Urtenu said. "I highly recommend the contents of the bottle. You are a slave and a foreigner, and the executioner will do his worst with you, you know. It won't be a clean beheading like our royal plotters received. Goodbye. May Motu accept you peacefully."

He retreated to the door and knocked on it, still keeping Naheshi in his view, and when the guard unbarred it, Urtenu passed out of sight into the darkness.

Naheshi drew the little bottle toward him and set it at his side. He took up the veil from his knees and pressed it to his cheek. Some time passed. Naheshi savored in his heart the words "I salute you for your courage."

Do you hear that, my lady?

Yes, he had finally acted like a man. He felt clean, newly made, as if some larval skin had sloughed off and the real Naheshi had emerged, all shiny and brave. He was basking in that thought when he heard voices outside the door. It screeched open again, and two figures, lit by the glow of an oil lamp, passed inside.

"Master!" cried Anani. He swooped upon the prisoner, falling on his knees, grasping and kissing Naheshi's hands, weeping brokenheartedly all over his master's fingers. His shoulders shook with the violence of his emotion.

Naheshi patted his head, touched. "Anani, you wonderful man. What are you doing here?"

"I brought him. He wanted to say goodbye, and so did

I," said the man with the lamp, and Naheshi saw that it was Ili-milku, his eyes red with tears. "He says he has something to confess to you."

"Ili-milku. Maybe it's better not to be seen as my friend. Someone might think you were in on my plot." Naheshi smiled.

But the scribe sank to the floor beside him and embraced the prisoner as best he could with Anani clinging to Naheshi's arm. "Speak, Anani," Ili-milku urged the servant. "Your master won't be mad at you now."

The little slave raised his tear-ravaged face, his mouth trembling with grief. "Oh, master, I've done somethin' awful. And at one point, you seemed to know about it, and that scared me bad. I just gotta get it off my chest before... before... well, before, so you won't think bad about me when... anymore."

So I was right: he was selling me out, thought Naheshi with a sinking of the stomach. The thought dealt him more pain than he realized he was still capable of feeling.

But Anani bawled, "Oh, master, I betrayed my former master. I stole a jar of olive oil from him. He'd sold a bunch of 'em to the temple of Ba'al, and then he didn't give 'em the full number, and I just couldn't stand the idea of cheatin' the gods, so I snuck one away from his stall and slipped it to the priests on the sly. He woulda beat the shit out of me if he'd known. And then you asked me who we owes our loyalty to, and I was way scared you knew what I'd did. If you thought I wasn't honest, maybe you'd sell me, and you was the best master ever. I wouldn't never have cheated *you*, my good master. I... I... I love you." His words dissolved into incoherent sobs.

Naheshi tousled the servant's shaggy head. *The dear boy. So that was it. All that suspicion for nothing. How like me.* "It's all right, Anani," Naheshi assured the slave, his own eyes prickling. "It would never have crossed my mind that you were disloyal."

Ili-milku rocked back on his heels and cast a glance around the darkness of the cell. "I just can't believe this is happening. You didn't really do... what they say, did you?"

"This seems to be a day for confessions." Naheshi indulged a bittersweet little smile. "I did it, Ili-milku."

The scribe eyed him for an instant but then shook his head. "No, my old friend. I can't believe it. You, the most scrupulously loyal person in the whole damn palace? It's unimaginable. I just don't know what to think. Listen, as I've told you, I have some knowledge of the law. If you want, I can try to find a loophole or beg for a mitigated sentence or—"

"Ili-milku, I appreciate your offer, but don't soil your reputation. You need to think of your children. It's cut-and-dried. There was a witness. I did it. That's all. And I'm more than happy to go. I really have nothing else to live for, do I?"

Because she *is gone. The vivid little sun of my dark world is gone.*

"Of course you do! You're still young, you're skilled, and we... we care about you. I was going to invite you to my house for dinner; I was—" Ili-milku's voice broke, and he bit his lip, his face crumpling.

Naheshi hung his head, suddenly fearing that emotion would master him as well. He clapped the scribe on the shoulder and clung there a moment, silent, then he murmured, "Once, I would have given my right hand to be able to talk to you, Ili-milku—to tell you how confused I was, to beg you to help me know what was the right thing to do. But I never did. My mistakes are all my own—and that silence was one of them. How many times I've chosen badly, my friend. And now there are no more choices to be made. I'm glad. I'm really relieved. You can't imagine. All I have to do now is let the gods rid the world of me."

"Naheshi, just for me, can't you tell me why you… the king… I just don't understand," Ili-milku pleaded brokenly.

"It had to be done… for justice's sake, Ili-milku. I was just the messenger of the gods, like… like a *karubu*." Naheshi laughed a little, for once unembarrassed by the high pitch of his voice. "I doubt if that makes any sense. I've talked so much to myself that I don't know if what I say out loud makes any sense anymore."

"I wish I understood, my friend, but I can't hate you for it. Whatever you were thinking, you must have felt you had a good reason. Were you… part of the plot?"

"No, no. Politics mean nothing to me. It just… needed to be done, and there I was. It was the least of my crimes; believe me. You're all better off without me." He envisioned Taddu's perfect little face beaming at him in surprise and pride. *"Naheshi, look at you! You did it! Who guessed you were so brave! But everybody knows what warriors the Assyrians are."*

"No, I don't accept that for a minute—"

"My friend." Naheshi fumbled for Ili-milku's hand and clutched it briefly then let it go. "That word has meant more to me than you can know. But I'm at peace now. Don't waste your tears on me. The future is something people like me have no stake in, as everyone keeps reminding me, and the present is just about over. It's all in the hands of the gods. Go, my... my friend."

Ili-milku got to his feet. He gently lifted Anani, who was sobbing openly, and helped him move away from his former master. The two men made their way to the door in a wobbly globe of yellow light.

"You need a *zaluzi*," Naheshi called.

Ili-milku stopped. "What's that, my friend?"

"You need the kind of melody called a *zaluzi* for your poem. It will be magnificent. People will never forget it."

Ili-milku mouthed, "Thank you," and his face dissolved.

He knocked for the guard, the door opened, and he and Anani slipped through.

Naheshi was alone in the darkness now. At daybreak, his life on this earth would end with slow brutality, surrendering one body part after another in an agonizing spectacle that would fulfill the city's need for vengeance. He did understand that need, yes. He thought one last time of his mistress, imagined her sweetly forgiving visage. He kissed her veil. *Farewell, my dearest lady.* He felt beside him for the little bottle, unstoppered it, lifted it to his lips, and drank.

The darkness grew light little by little, until a luminous golden twilight filled the cell. The walls melted into brightness, and Naheshi found himself standing out of doors, in freedom, high upon the platform of a temple, the type he had known in his childhood—a *ziggurat*, a man-made mountain. He was neither surprised nor fearful. This was as it should be. Below him were the royal plaza, the palace, the city walls, and the blue bar of the sea, all very distant. He heard the pure, clear voice of a child lifted in a hymn. It was the liturgy of coronation of the new king rising from the chapel, but the child's voice was not far away outside as it should have been. It was welling up from his own heart. Over his head arched the sky, the cloudless rosy gold of dawn, and the gods were listening above. He could see himself from the outside—a tall, thirty-eight-year-old being of angelic beauty—and yet he was within himself as well. Something was swelling within that self—a note, a sunrise, a life that was more than his own, the song of the gods themselves, the song that created the heavens and the earth—and then the moment came, and he opened his mouth, and the music poured out like that made by the stars as they passed: a celestial, throbbing, melancholy arc of song that was at the same time supremely joyous. He could feel his lungs and his throat pulse with the physicality of the music, but the sound seemed to be not his own; it descended from above and wrapped around him like an embrace. It was not a mere human voice; it held within it all the sorrow of conquered peoples, fallen cities, and abandoned altars, and nonetheless, it was a song of joy. Tears starred his lashes, yet his heart was bursting with unbearable ecstasy.

THE END

Enjoy this book? Don't miss the next free-standing story in the Empire at Twilight series. Here is a taste of *The Sun at Twilight*:

I T WAS DAWN. THE MAN stood with his back to the
rocks in the vain hope of blocking the wind and snow
from his eyes. They were bleary and watering, but not
from the snow or sleeplessness, although he hadn't slept.
Before him, the court cut into the bedrock was full of ash,
hissing and steaming as the snowflakes died in the cooling
remnants of the bone fire that had burned all night. The
Old Women had not yet come with their tongs to pick
out the calcined bones of the man's father, wash them with
wine, and soak them in oil.

The man was alone. No one had dared to stay with
him, watching all night as the pyre blazed against the winter
darkness. They must have seen in his eyes that he wanted
to keep vigil by himself. Even his mother had discreetly left
him to his solitude. She knew as well as anyone that he had
need of reflection, this son with his inclination to silence.

He needed to invoke the guidance of the gods, and yet
he could not find any words.

The man was now the *labarna*, emperor of all the lands
that called Hatti their master. He feared he no longer knew

who he was or who he should be. Until three days ago, he had been Prince Tashmi-sharrumma—an imperfect, uncomfortable identity he had inhabited for thirty-five years. But since three days ago, things had changed. The old king had become a god. Tashmi-sharrumma had been consecrated in his place. He was now Tudhaliya, Great King, the fourth of that name. Now he alone must shepherd the people of the Storm God; he alone bore responsibility for injustices and wrongdoing. From within his fur-lined cloak, Tashmi-sharrumma drew a deep, unsteady breath. His new name and his new responsibility perched upon him awkwardly, a little too big, a little too heavy.

Within the young king's chest, fear hunkered like an unquiet animal. His father had been a great king, but his sins were many. And now they were Tashmi-sharrumma's own. Suddenly "alone" was a frightening word, even for a man who valued solitude.

"Storm God of Hatti, forgive my father's wrongs. Don't bring his guilt down upon my head and the heads of your people," Tashmi-sharrumma murmured, his breath hanging in a cloud before his face. Cloud and words dispersed into the air. He watched the snowflakes' manic descent. The ash was still too hot for the snow to begin piling up, but the air was thick with it, veiling the brutal gray wall of rock that rose at his back, softening the gray rock of the buildings across the court. Rock was alive, divine... but not kindly. Tashmi-sharrumma shivered.

He stared up into the falling snow now. The very air was seething with it; flakes struck him in the eyes and melted upon his face, mingling with his tears. The funeral party would be lucky not to be trapped up here in the mountain *hekur*, the Stone House, mortuary temple of the late king Hattushili son of Murshili, near though it was to the city walls. The rites would go on for a fortnight, and then everyone would return to the capital if the roads were not impassable. Tashmi-sharrumma almost hoped the return would be delayed.

He was not a coward, he told himself. He had fought on the field of battle since he'd been twelve years old. He had served as the chief of his father's bodyguard from his eighteenth year. He had been a priest of the Storm God of Nerik almost since he was old enough to read, facing the hostile onslaughts of darkness armored only in the power of ritual words. He had learned to set aside his own preferences and pleasures for the needs of the kingdom, a campaign that took perhaps even more courage. But he couldn't repress the sense of dread that sat like a suffocating weight upon his chest.

He was the son of a usurper. He would be punished.

Now the black-wrapped Old Women—the priestesses of Lelwani, Queen of the Underworld—were approaching, their tongs in hand. Tashmi-sharrumma watched them as they began their duties, scattering the ash, quenching the coals with wine, completing the work the Storm God himself had begun. Steam rose in angry clouds from the extinguished ashes so that the priestesses seemed to be pouring out smoke from their beakers. Their mantles whipped in the wind; the wind moaned through the rock; the rock stood watch in leaden silence. Far from keeping the young king warmer, its presence at his back radiated cold like a piece of bronze left out in the winter. He turned away from the priestesses. Although they were the only human figures in a world of stone and ice, the women's proximity did not comfort him. They were like the black ravens that violate the bodies of the dead on the battlefield.

Tashmi-sharrumma suspected he was almost invisible where he stood, his gray wolf-fur cloak one with the gray of the stone. The women did not seem to see him. Their voices, half blown away on the wind, rose in broken pieces of melody as they chanted. They stooped from time to time, lifting an unburnt fragment of bone with their tongs and dropping it into a silver urn. This very night, the late king's mortal remains would be cushioned in purple wool and laid upon his chair, and he would preside for one last time at the banquet his family shared with him.

ACKNOWLEDGMENTS

The author gratefully acknowledges all those who have helped her in the production of this book. To the wonderful women of my writers' group, for their critique and encouragement, my thanks. To Lynn McNamee and her editorial team at Red Adept—Jessica, Sarah, and Susie—profound gratitude (and Lynn, for so many other forms of help). To the flexible and talented gang at Streetlight Graphics for the cover and map. To my cousin and her husband, my technology guru: thanks, guys. To Enid, who urged me forward by her support, I can't thank you sufficiently. And most of all, to my husband, Ippokratis, who put up with the months of fixation it takes to write a novel, many, many thanks.

ABOUT THE AUTHOR

N.L. Holmes is the pen name of a professional archaeologist who received her doctorate from Bryn Mawr College. She has excavated in Greece and in Israel, and taught ancient history and humanities at the university level for many years. She has always had a passion for books, and in childhood, she and her cousin (also a writer today) used to write stories for fun.

Today, since their son is grown, she lives with her husband and three cats. They split their time between Florida and northern France, where she gardens, weaves, plays the violin, dances, and occasionally drives a jog-cart. And reads, of course.

Made in the USA
Middletown, DE
15 July 2021